between mothers
and daughters

THE WOMEN'S STORIES PROJECT
Susan Koppelman, editor

Between Mothers and Daughters:
Stories Across a Generation

The Strange History of Suzanne LaFleshe
and Other Stories of Women and Fatness

The Other Woman:
Stories of Two Women and a Man

Women in the Trees:
U.S. Women's Short Stories About Battering and Resistance,
1839–2000

Between Mothers and Daughters

Stories Across a Generation

Edited and with an Introduction
by Susan Koppelman

Foreword by Alix Kates Shulman

THE FEMINIST PRESS
AT THE CITY UNIVERSITY OF NEW YORK
New York

Published by the Feminist Press at the City University of New York
The Graduate Center
365 Fifth Avenue
New York, NY 10016
www.feministpress.org

First Feminist Press edition, 2004

Originally published in 1985 by The Feminist Press

Library of Congress Cataloging-in-Publication Data
Between mothers and daughters : stories across a generation / edited and with an intro-
duction by Susan Koppelman ; foreword by Alix Kates Shulman.— 1st Feminist Press
ed.
    p. cm.
  Originally published: Between mothers & daughters. New York, N.Y. : Feminist Press,
1985.
  ISBN 1-55861-459-1 (pbk. : alk. paper)
  1. Mothers and daughters—Fiction. 2. Short stories, American—Women authors. 3.
Women—United States—Fiction. 4. Domestic fiction, American. I. Koppelman,
Susan. II. Title: Between mothers & daughters.

PS648.M59B48 2004
813'.010835252—dc22

                        2004019064

Text and cover design by Dayna Navaro
Cover art: "Maia and Leila Do Their Hair" by Anita Klein. Reproduced courtesy of
Boundary Gallery, London.
Printed in the USA on acid-free paper by McNaughton and Gunn, Inc.

09 08 07 06 05 04   5 4 3 2 1

◇

This book is dedicated to

Frances Bollotin Koppelman

my mother and friend

sine qua non

◇

Song of Purification

Our Mother who created us
from a single drop of blood
from her holy womb,
Our mother, who gave us this design
of body,
these protected parts,
this internal architecture,
Our mother who enabled us
to cunningly feed and nourish,
to be the cavern of life,
Oh mother, who has protected us
with hair, with lashes, in the pits
of the arm and womb,
Our mother, who made us as womankind,
we act with your strength
and in your dignity,
We are protected and unprotected,
like you and unlike you,
each of us different in her faith,
her coloring, the shape of her body,
each of us alike in our structure.
Oh, mother, rejoice with us
in this meeting of your daughters!

E.M. Broner

CONTENTS

KOPPELMAN'S TREASURE

ALIX KATES SHULMAN

It is a well established fact of literary history that women writers pioneered the English novel, women playwrights were among the most popular on London's Restoration stage, women fiction writers participated in the creation of the American short story and brought it to new heights of popularity. But no matter how original, popular, or appreciated they may have been in their own time, women writers have usually faded into oblivion soon after death. Peruse any recent roster of writers past—from course syllabi to publishers' backlists—and even after decades of active feminism you will see a depressing gender imbalance. With a few iconic exceptions, women's works are soon forgotten, robbing us of insight and pleasure, and skewing our understanding of the past—until a feminist resurgence produces the hunger and scholarship that lead to their rediscovery and return to print.

The Second Wave of U.S. feminism was profoundly lucky to have in Susan Koppelman just such a hungry, committed, and very independent scholar to lead this work of recovery. Even before there were university women's studies departments, she began her feminist scholarship, editing what is probably the first collection of Second Wave criticism, *Images of Women in Fiction: Feminist Perspectives*, published in 1972. At about the same time, she launched her ambitious life-project: to pan the archives for forgotten (and undervalued) nuggets of women's literature. A passionate reader and devotee of the short story, Koppelman gradually became one of the country's leading authorities on U.S. short fiction by women.

Her persistent search has yielded up a treasure of thousands of women's stories, many of which might otherwise have remained lost in the stacks. She maintains a personal archive of more than 3,500 and estimates that she has read more than 25,000. The earliest come from early nineteenth-century gift books and annuals; the most recent from contemporary "literary" and genre (science fiction, mystery, and romance) magazines and anthologies; and some come from feminist publications of both the women's suffrage and women's liberation movements. At least half of the treasure Koppelman uncovered in long-defunct nineteenth- and early twentieth-century popular illustrated magazines—in their time often the only, and usually the most remunerative, outlet for publication of even the finest literature by women.

So far, she has published seven thematic anthologies of women's stories, on subjects of crucial concern to women, with more on the way. And although these books include but a small portion of the total treasure in Koppelman's collection, her anthologies have provided the reading public with invaluable views of life in this country, past and present, as seen through women's eyes. By organizing her anthologies thematically, placing smack in the middle of her books' titles the devalued subject matter and concerns that have historically marked women's lives and literature, Koppelman has defied that devaluation. With such titles as *Old Maids, Between Mothers and Daughters, The Other Woman,* and *Women's Friendships,* and collections on the themes of nineteenth-century lesbians (*Two Friends*), battering and resistance (*Women in the Trees*), and women and fatness (*The Strange History of Suzanne LaFleshe*), these anthologies lead the reader deep into the complexities that underlie the tragedies and triumphs, the sufferings and joys of more than one and a half centuries of diverse and varied women's lives. By de-fragmenting a single complex theme before our eyes through a carefully selected range of stories of different eras, different angles, and different styles, Koppelman invites us to compare and contrast—and thereby to begin to comprehend. Out of a handful of disparate yarns she magically knits a multicolored garment of enduring substance.

Many unexpected aesthetic delights await Koppelman's readers.

Here are stories alternately, and sometimes simultaneously, gripping, poignant, sly, funny, disturbing, surprising, brave, and always illuminating. As an early advocate of the importance of popular culture (a field still unnamed while she was earning her doctorate in literature), Koppelman has smartly side-stepped the issue of "quality" by which the literary establishment has traditionally devalued the writings and interests of women as trivial, transitory, or dull. Like the largely female audience who always valued stories by women no matter what their origin or what the critics said, without apology Koppelman takes women's work seriously, finding it every bit as important as men's contributions to the ongoing project of consciousness that is literature. Through a process of distillation, she has selected from thousands of possibilities; artfully balanced collections that span time, region, faith, class, race, ethnicity, sexuality, dis/ability, generation, age, and experience. The stories in these anthologies range from the first short story ever published in the United States by an African American (the 1859 "The Two Offers" by Frances Ellen Watkins Harper), through ethnic fiction by early twentieth-century Jewish writer Martha Wolfenstein and Hispanic writer Maria Cristina Mena, to once best-selling novelists like Susan Glaspell, Kate Chopin, and Dorothy Canfield, to fiction by such recently acknowledged masters of the form as Zora Neale Hurston, Sandra Cisneros, and Joanna Russ. Each of the anthologies can shock us out of complacency; taken together they help to correct a biased history. And many of the individual stories can deepen our understanding of ourselves—such is the power of literature.

This tireless work of search-and-preserve—a lifelong labor of love—is Koppelman's gift to us. To ensure that her gift endures (for such are the vicissitudes of publishing and gender politics that already some of Koppelman's anthologies are hard to come by), the Feminist Press has launched an exciting and ambitious program, the Women's Stories Project, which will appropriately begin with the publication of several Koppelman anthologies, including a new collection as well as important reprint volumes. The project also plans to establish an online catalogue of hundreds more stories by U.S. women writers, selected under Koppelman's expert supervision. In this way, a new generation of creative artists, feminist seekers, specialized scholars, teachers, and ordinary readers alike will have easy access to a nineteenth- and twentieth-

ACKNOWLEDGMENTS

Literary scholars with special knowledge about the writers of these stories have generously enriched this volume by sharing information and sources with me. I would like to thank the following: Gary Sue Goodman for Caroline Healey Dall; Carol Farley Kessler for Elizabeth Stuart Phelps; Josephine Donovan, Emily Toth, Helen Eisen, Susan Allen Toth, and Nancy Walker for Alice Brown and Mary E. Wilkins Freeman; Jeanne O'Grady Ryan, Barbara Grier, Amy Baldwin, and Judith Schwarz for Helen Hull; Beverly Seaton for Helen Reimensnyder Martin; Janet Sharistanian and Emily Toth for Tess Slesinger; Timothy Murray and Beryl H. Manne of the Washington University Library's Special Collections and Deborah G. Lambert for Fannie Hurst; Elizabeth Schultz for Hisaye Yamamoto; and Joanna Russ for James Tiptree, Jr.

Additionally, a group of mothers and daughters of various ages, backgrounds, and perspectives, working sometimes as teams and sometimes individually, read between thirty and sixty mother-daughter stories each, to help decide which would be best in this collection. They discussed the stories with each other and with me in person, in letters, and during long-distance telephone calls. I want to thank Judith Arcana, author of *Our Mothers' Daughters* (Berkeley: Shameless Hussy Press, 1979), Gail Mills and Lisa Mills Merkle, Edith and Marilyn Probe, Hilary and Nikki Salk, Gail Robbins, Jamie-Lynn Richardson, Naomi and Eve Kane, Joanna Russ, Dorothy Ann Chase, and Nancy Hinkebein for sharing their ideas and feelings about the stories and the relationships between mothers and daughters.

Many of the authors of these stories have been active in helping shape the volume. They have been extraordinarily openhearted and I want to thank them for making the work on this volume such a rich experience. Joanna Russ, Ann Allen Shockley, and Tillie Olsen, all old friends, have been, as always, supportive of my work and generous in their participation. New friendships with Alice Sheldon,

Hisaye Yamamoto DeSoto, Guadalupe Valdes, and Arny Christine Straayer make this project already the most rewarding of my work life.

Finally I want to express my gratitude to those who form my personal support network, who have, in all the most practical ways, expressed their belief in the value of this work and their benevolence toward me: Emily Toth, Joanna Russ, Cathy Davidson, and David Elliott. Further, I am indebted to Lois Neville; Allison King; Tom, Tim, and Matt Douglas; Jack Finn; and Mr. and Mrs. Catz for generous help when it was most needed. My husband, Dennis Mills, and my son, Edward Nathan Koppelman Cornillon, have made sacrifices of their convenience, their time, and their justified expectations over and over again. Words desert me when I try to express my continuing amazement and joy and Dennis's consistent support of my work and loving participation in the partnership that is our marriage. It is often said that family members can't teach each other things; disproving that is the most fun part of our family life. Nathan helped me conquer my technology anxiety and taught me to use his word processor. It has transformed my work life, and I am forever grateful. Now that I've made a book for Grandma, I agree with him that it's time he and I made a book for each other about mothers and sons.

I would like to extend my thanks and appreciation to the wonderful and gifted authors I have included in this expanded edition: Jane Bradley, Beth Brant, Merrill Joan Gerber, Preety Kalra, Nicholasa Mohr, Andrea Benton Rushing, and Alma Luz Villanueva. I am grateful to Drs. Julia Penelope, Kathie Carlson, and Paula Caplan for the generosity in consulting with me about the new introducion. Thank you for your cooperation in working with me on this project.

Jean Casella, Director and Publisher, The Feminist Press, imagined the Women's Stories Project and has done the daunting work to bring it into being. I salute her, cherish her, and find working with her heart-warming and inspiring.

Stacy Malyil, Associate Editor, The Feminist Press shepherded *Between Mothers and Daughters* into production, managed the search for cover art, and oversaw getting permissions to reprint the original material and to include the new material.

Dayna Navaro, Production and Design Manager, did layout and design.

Elizabeth Afton and Michelle Rodriguez, interns in the editorial department assisted in obtaining permissions, searching for cover art, and proofreading the manuscript.

My husband, Dennis Mills, my mother, Frances Koppelman, my son and daughter-in-law Edward Nathan Koppelman and Ellen Cornillon, my beloved friend Emily Toth, all continue to enrich my life and work. Riff-Raff at the age of eighteen continues to impose his feline values on our life. And we have been blessed with the great gift of grandparenthood, welcoming Jasmine Grace Cornillon and Sarah Jade Cornillon into our family in 1998 and 2001 respectively with joy beyond what we could ever have anticipated. In October 2003 we were thrilled to welcome Malcolm Hinkebein, the son of Patrick and Michelle, into our family. Life is good.

Introduction

Women who write fiction write stories about mothers and daughters. Often, a woman writer's first published story is about the relationship between a mother and a daughter. Nor do women writers abandon this subject as they grow in their craft and their lives. They return to the literary contemplation and portrayal of mothers and daughters again and again throughout their careers. Women of every race, ethnicity, religion, region, and historical period write stories about mothers and daughters, and the similarities among the stories are greater than the differences because what we share as women, at least in terms of this primary relationship, is more than whatever else divides us. Stories about mothers and daughters seem like different facets of one great universal story that includes not only all the stories we have, but all those still lost and all those yet to be written.

When story makers and story audiences explore a particular subject repeatedly over a long period of time, that subject gains what contemporary theologians describe as the "sacred dimension."[1] Sacred dimensions provide perspectives on reality and help shape and give focus to life. Reading important stories about a subject that is important in our own lives and discovering how important that subject has been in the lives of other women helps us identify our connections with the women who have lived before us and the women with whom we share the present.

The eighteen stories in this collection were chosen from almost one hundred written by women living in the United States between 1830 and 1980.[2] The sacred relationship between mothers and daughters is clear not only from the multitude of stories on the subject, but from the passion, intensity, and the ritualized interactions that characterize them. The stories in this collection share that passion and intensity, they capture those rituals, and they represent a wide variety of approaches to this sacred subject.

Mothers and Daughters Up Against the Patriarchy

The most common mother-daughter story describes the patriarchal harvest of the nubile daughter with or without her mother's protest or resistance. Whether through the force of law, the promise of luxury, or the simple guarantee of survival, this reaping of the daughters is always accompanied by overtones of economic exchange. And always the intent of the proposed exchange is clear: sex for protection, sex for food, sex for survival. The male sense of entitlement turns on the contemporary vestiges of the *droit du seigneur,* the legal right of the feudal lord to rape the female serfs on his estate. Hebrew, Greek, and Roman slave owners enjoyed the legal sexual plunder of female slaves, as did white southern United States slave owners, as in "Annie Gray: A Tale," the first story in this collection. The *droit du seigneur* has metamorphosed into sexual harassment at work and at school. At home, it is most blatant in the incestuous rape of daughters by their fathers or by men who stand in the place of fathers.

Such a threat leads to tragedy in "Old Woman Magoun." In that story, the grandmother, who has been conditioned to act not only as nurturer and care-provider, but as guardian of her grand-daughter's chastity, is forced to realize that she cannot protect the girl any longer. Indeed, she cannot protect herself. At the command of the patriarchy, the mother figure is expected to change from guardian of chastity to panderer and pimp. She is expected to seduce her charge to the will of their mutual master, to "turn her out." Refusal of the father's demand to make the girl available invites retribution and punishment, from something as active as the invocation of the law to compel compliance, as in "Old Woman Magoun," to something as passive as the withdrawal of proffered financial help, as in "Recuerdo."

What are the mother's feelings? What are her choices? How

will the daughters respond? These questions are raised repeatedly in the stories in this collection, sometimes with grimness
and despair, as in "Old Woman Magoun," "Oats for the Woman,"
and "Recuerdo," sometimes with subtle conspiratorial humor,
as in "The Women Men Don't See," and sometimes with the
passion of the mother's compelling desire to ensure her daughter's freedom, as in "Seventeen Syllables."

In some stories, the mothers see no hope of escaping or even
of surviving if they defy the patriarchy; therefore, they seek the
least painful accommodation to reality for their daughters,
themselves, and the community of women with whom they
identify their interests. Many mothers and mother-surrogates
advise manipulative compliance as in "A Marriage of Persuasion"
and "The Lawd Don't Like Ugly." In the matriarchal world in
which loyalty between mother and daughter comes first, as in
"The Women Men Don't See," the daughter who betrays their
mutual best interests because of personal preferences or illusions
about romantic love would be no heroine, but simply squeamish,
self-indulgent, and selfish, as she is seen by her mother in "A
Marriage of Persuasion."

Where there is no true freedom, there can be no true love.
Mothers know that, especially mothers who are the victims of
multiple oppressions. Daughters, feeling the first stirrings of the
flesh in their early adolescence, and befuddled by the myth of
romantic love, often do not. Because the choice between loyalty
to oneself and loyalty to a beloved is not one a free person
should have to make, and because the daughters do not yet
understand that in the patriarchy women are not free persons,
they often resent their mothers for whatever choices are urged
on them (as in "A Marriage of Persuasion," "Seventeen Syllables,"
and "Recuerdo").

The young women don't yet understand that their mothers
aren't the ones forcing them to choose between love and
autonomy, between self-possession and economic survival. Heterosexual girls don't want to believe their mother's warnings
about men and women's lot in the patriarchy. They want to be
able to trust those whom they find sexually attractive. They are
unwilling to adopt an attitude or accede to knowledge that would
make it impossible to trust the object(s) of their desire. They

instinctively understand that sexual interaction with an untrustworthy, dangerous, and/or exploitive partner inhibits healthy sexual functioning. It is natural for them to wish to protect their sexuality.[3] Although this sexual motif runs through many of the stories, it is clearest in "Seventeen Syllables."

When the daughters become women and learn to understand more of the world, mothers and daughters tend to become co-conspirators, as in "The Women Men Don't See," rather than adversaries, as in "A Marriage of Persuasion." In "Seventeen Syllables," the narrator moves from rejecting her mother's vision to understanding and accepting it, but only after the passage of many years and her mother's death. In "Mother to Dinner," the conflict between a daughter's loyalty to her mother and her desire for her husband is still a raw wound.

How can a mother teach her daughter to survive? Sacrifice of the self may be the price of survival for a woman in the patriarchy. Mothers are supposed to teach their girl babies, as they have learned from their own mothers, to sell themselves ("A Marriage of Persuasion," "The Lawd Don't Like Ugly"), to submit ("Old Woman Magoun"), to bargain with their bodies for subsistence ("Recuerdo"), to embrace the men who have exploited their mothers ("Oats for the Woman"), and to service and serve their masters ("Annie Gray: A Tale"). Daughters often hate their mothers for bearing them female into a world that will not tolerate a woman's survival intact—and for collaborating or seeming to collaborate in breaking their daughters to the will of the patriarchy. But when women become mothers themselves, they understand the fear and the love, the ignorance and the hope that drive mothers to bind their daughters' feet, to submit them to clitoridectomies, to encourage addiction to diet pills, or to advocate intellectual self-castration. They also understand better the ways in which their mothers did protest and try to warn and protect them. And they learn something about the cost to a mother of even trying to protect her daughters, as in "Oats for the Woman."

The major factor determining the nature and extent of the conflict between mother and daughter, and between them and the patriarchy, is the age at which the daughter begins to be beset by patriarchal demands for sexual performance. "Old

Woman Magoun," "Oats for the Woman," "Recuerdo," and "The Lawd Don't Like Ugly" are variations on this subject.

"Old Woman Magoun" tells of life in white New England when child custody law blatantly favored the father and when a man's ownership of his children was undisguised. Fifty-seven years later, "Recuerdo" describes a world in which nothing has changed for women, though it deals with Mexican-American culture, a different natural environment, a different religious tradition, and a different cultural patina—but the "Recuerdo" tale is very familiar: Can a female custodian of a female child protect the girl from the depredations of those who own them both? Can the mothers overcome their powerlessness, interrupt the short-circuiting of their love, and stop the rape of those they have nurtured?

Both "Oats for the Woman" and "Recuerdo" have strong implications of incest. The mother is forced to confront the sacrifice of her daughter to the same man who sexually abused her. Only in "The Lawd Don't Like Ugly" does the mother figure attempt to give her surrogate daughter psychological tools to protect her from the impact of the sacrifice—as inescapable for the black girl as it is for the white girl, the Jewish girl, and the Mexican-American girl. The black mother in "The Lawd Don't Like Ugly," recognizing the apparent inevitability of the harvest of the daughters by the masters of the world, tries to help her surrogate daughter choose the least offensive of the predators, the one likely to inflict the least damage, to offer the most protection, and to prove the least divisive of the relationship between the mother and the daughter. But the choices are limited to those who offer themselves or can be enticed, and the choices can never be made with any certainty.

The Quest for Identity

Stories about women's quests for identity are usually written from the perspective of daughters (a perspective every woman retains, even after she has become a mother herself). The daughter wants to define either her own identity or that of the woman she has known only as "mother." In some stories, such as "I Stand Here Ironing," a mother assesses her own sense of identity.

Stories about daughters who search for and joyfully find their identity in community with their mothers and the world of women to which their mothers belong have been ignored by literary historians and critics until recently. However, daughters often discover or create their identities through union and identification with their mothers and the world of women, as in "The Way of Peace." In that story, Lucy Ann achieves union with the world, the ways, and the place in the order of things of her mother by assuming her mother's identity while simultaneously asserting her own. As she does so, she faces down the power of "brotherly love," or benevolent patriarchy. Lucy Ann doesn't wish a place for herself in their world, especially not the place reserved for her: the visiting old maid aunt. She doesn't wish to be identified in terms of secondary biological roles. If she must accept a biologically determined label, it will be the most primary in her life: the daughter of her mother.

The daughter may also discover or create her own identity by separating from her mother in one of three ways. In modern times, a daughter most often leaves home when she marries a man of her choice, as Anna wishes to do in "A Marriage of Persuasion." This story espouses the romantic idea that identity is achieved through separation from the mother and the identification of personal romantic/sexual preferences, the choosing of a father for her children. Such an understanding of how to achieve identity not only forces a woman into biological roles, but it almost forces separation from the community of women. The daughter is propelled by marriage into isolation from the private language and priorities of the women's culture she has lived in until marriage. Such is the experience of the narrator of "Mother to Dinner."

The romantic illusion that a woman can "find herself" in isolation from her community has been dangerous for women. It tricks a young woman into abandoning the world that has nurtured her. Identity and the community of women have been transformed into competitive ideas in "A Marriage of Persuasion." Anna believes that she will be injured in her search for identity if she cannot live in accord with her personal romantic/ sexual preferences. Because Anna's point of view dominates the story, the world of the mothers is drawn without sympathy or love. Nevertheless, Anna gives in to the needs of that world. Does she have any other choice?

The daughter may also separate from her mother by leaving home to pursue a goal that she and her mother have agreed is right for her, as in "Mrs. Gladfelter's Revolt." Mrs. Gladfelter loves her daughter "with a passionate devotion" and perceives her as the repository of "the poetry and romance of her life." This maternal passion for the daughter represents yet another aspect of the search for identity: a mother transfers to her daughter those elements of her own self that she most treasures. What she hadn't the opportunity to cherish or the foresight to protect in herself, she finds the courage to defend in and for her beloved daughter. This represents a transfer of the portion of women's identity that is communal and historical. In that transfer, the mother has a renewed sense of self. The mother becomes an active participant in history and the daughter becomes an active recipient of a matriarchal tradition.

The third way that a daughter may separate from her mother is by apprenticing herself to an adult other than her mother as a model for the kind of adult woman she wishes to become, as in "The Fire."[4] Cynthia has embraced a vision of adult womanhood lived in accordance with values and goals different from her mother's. The daughter who separates herself from her mother in this way is rejecting either her mother, her mother's way of life, or both.

Dee has also separated from her mother by apprenticing herself in another world. "Everyday Use" is unusual, not only because the mother tells the story, but because the two daughters, sisters, search for their identity in different ways. One daughter's sense of identity is rooted in the maternal past; the other daughter's sense of identity hinges on her strong self-esteem. Dee thinks she has found her "roots" by leaving home, but her roots and even the name she has rejected come from the women's community she has dismissed. Dee's mother seems to consider Dee's search for identity outside the circle of the women's community to have been a farce and a failure—but, ironically, entirely in keeping with Dee's character, or identity. Mama's analysis and assessment of Dee's search has enabled her to understand and value more acutely her other daughter's search for identity in family history and women's community. Her newly found and expressed regard for Maggie sparks Maggie's self-esteem.

Thamré's revelation in "Old Mother Goose" is that she can reject her mother's way of life while accepting and loving her mother. She can include in her expanded and enriched sense of identity a sense of herself as the loving daughter of a loving mother.

If the search for identity is undertaken in the direction of the daughter's roots in the world of women, then the relationship between the mother and the daughter is portrayed as "comic," i.e., as tending towards the preservation and enhancement of their relationship and/or the community of women to which they both belong. If the direction of the quest takes the daughter away from the mother, their relationship is portrayed as "tragic," i.e., as suffering from chronic failed intentions, failed communications, alienation, and separation.

Another kind of quest story tells of the daughter's search for understanding of the nature and identity of the woman who is her mother. The daughter wants to know who her mother is, instead of how she functions as a mother. Most of these quest stories take place soon after the death of the mother. The setting for these stories is sometimes the time of preparation preceding the burial. But more often the stories are set after the formal mourning period has ended and the daughter must go through her mother's personal effects. In the process of sorting, the daughter begins to think about her mother as a woman apart from her role as "mother." She seeks evidence of continuity in the life of the dead woman who was once a little girl, a daughter, herself. It is often the little things the daughter finds that her mother has stored and treasured that reflect continuity and reveal cherished memories. Another setting for such stories is the death watch that the daughter keeps for her mother. Often the mother wanders in and out of consciousness, in and out of the present. And for the first time, the daughter hears bits and pieces of her mother's life that have nothing to do with her mothering life, as in "Annie Gray: A Tale."

Only after the mother approaches death or after she has died does the daughter feel safe wondering about this woman who has given life to her. Now she can consider her mother's dreams, ambitions, sexuality, disappointments, and vices without fear of consequences to herself or to their relationship. If she discovers, for instance, that her own birth had been unwelcome and inconvenient, perhaps even destructive in her mother's life, she needn't worry about how to continue a relationship with a woman to whom her very life has been a threat or a disappointment. "Autobiography of My Mother" is unique in this sense: A daughter examines these aspects of her mother's life as a woman, including the impact of her own birth on her mother's life, while her mother is still alive.

Occasional Stories

Some of the stories about relationships between mothers and daughters were written for special holiday issues of magazines, most often women's magazines, where they would have been read in a context of recipes for festive foods and patterns for gala clothes. Many literary artists have scorned such occasional literature because it calls upon writers to respond to stimuli for literary production other than their own imaginations and creative impulses. Poet laureates, whose job requires them to compose poetry commemorating special state occasions, such as military victories, bicentennials, and coronations, have often been ridiculed as literary hacks. And yet some of the most stunning and lasting poems have been elegies and odes, just as some of the most stirring music in the world's repertoire has been composed for specific military, religious, and patriotic occasions.

As functional art, occasional literature is often assumed to be trite and sentimental. But when an entire literary genre is dismissed by the arbiters of literary taste, something other than literary judgment is responsible. Many genres (historical romances, Gothics, and occasional stories) have been dismissed as trivial: these are all genres in which women have been the primary creators and audiences.[5] Although men have also written occasional stories, women writers have been primarily responsible for this genre's evolution as an art form.

Many occasional stories written by women commemorate holidays connected to events in nature, such as harvest, the winter solstice, and the vernal equinox. Overtly connected to the contemporary holidays that modern religions have assigned to those ancient natural celebrations, these stories are rich with covert allusions to the ancient meanings of the natural events.

Two stories in this collection are occasional stories. "Old Mother Goose" appeared first as a Christmas story; "The Way of Peace" is a Thanksgiving story. The seamless connection between private life and public event makes these two stories among the finest examples of this form of literature. However, because of the custom of reprinting stories without complete information about their original publication, readers have generally been denied the information necessary to make clear the occasional nature of many stories.

The transition from contemporary religious occasion to ancient woman-oriented occasion is clear in "Old Mother Goose." The story represents an appropriation of Christian myth. The disgraceful mother, Old Nell, who has conceived and given birth to her daughter out of wedlock, first looks to a male deity for justification and forgiveness when she says, "If God be for me, my girl won't be against me!" By the end of the story, once their reunion has been accomplished and their relationship transformed, Old Nell, dying, asks, "If my girl was for me . . . could He be against me . . . ?" She feels her salvation has been accomplished. She has been, as it were, born again—through the love and sacrifice of her daughter.

Life-Cycle Events

Besides the public occasions discussed above, there are private occasions in all lives about which there is also a rich occasional literature.

The impulse to create rituals is a basic component of human psychology and spirituality. Those ritual traditions most rich, varied, and deeply affecting celebrate occasions in the lives of individuals, such as birth, death, mating, and the assumption of adult responsibility in a community. In most societies, the rituals for these life-cycle events are different for males and females.

Rituals celebrating or commemorating the special life-cyle events of women have survived from pre-literate societies, although almost entirely in vestigial forms.[6] These rituals are tied to biological events, such as menarche and child-birth, and are connected to fertility, reproduction, and the presumption of heterosexuality.[7]

The rituals that have grown up to honor special events in women's lives are preserved in women's short stories. The ritual occasions in a relationship between mother and daughter are regularly captured for all time in these stories, and women's ritual celebrations and commemorations share common elements and patterns.

Among several life-cycle events frequently memorialized in mother-daughter stories, menarche is especially important. This physical event is accompanied by the growth of the daughter's own sexuality. Mothers in these stories respond to their daughters' physical development with an often desperate attempt to make them understand what it means to be a woman in a man's world. The mother may try to warn her daughter about what life is like for women by revealing her own life history. The mothers' stories in "Annie Gray: A Tale" and "Seventeen Syllables" are intended as cautionary tales.

The occasion of the onset of puberty has been most thoroughly explored by minority women writers. These stories tend to be resolved with the daughter accepting her mother or mother-surrogate's advice and vision, as in "The Lawd Don't Like Ugly." The mystification and mythology that cloud the understanding of life for majority-culture women often lead to resolutions in which the daughter and the mother or mother-surrogate become alienated in life, as in "A Marriage of Persuasion," or separated by death, as in "Old Woman Magoun."

Other biological events commemorated in life-cycle stories are deaths of mothers, as in "Annie Gray: A Tale," and "The Way of Peace," and birthdays, as in "A Birthday Remembered."

Biological milestones are not the only life-cycle events portrayed in these stories. Among the journeys and choices celebrated and commemorated in the life-cycle stories are the separations and reunions of mothers and daughters. "Mrs. Gladfelter's Revolt" takes its shape from the preparations for and eventual separation of a mother and daughter, while "Old Mother Goose" and "High Heels" are structured around reunions and the healing of a rift between mother and daughter. When the reunion is coupled with the restoration of the relationship, the air of ceremony is heavy, portentous. When the reunion does not accomplish reunification but merely underlines the distance between the women, as in "Everyday Use," the ceremony is observed in the breech.

Every turning point in the life of a mother or daughter precipitates a crisis in their relationship, and mothers and daughters engage in a pattern of interaction and communication on these occasions that is shared across time, space, and cultural heritage with other mothers and daughters. Because this pattern is so familiar to women readers, the writer has great latitude for using the most subtle forms of artistic literary innuendo and ellipsis. But for these suggestive art forms to be available to an artist who wishes to communicate seriously with an audience, the artist must know that she shares a culture with all its nuances and idioms and perspectives with an audience. She must be able to write to her own community, not to foreigners, who would require explanations, analogies, and simplifications. Women writing for an audience of women are inferential and notational— and we can piece together women's shared culture from the ceremonies we decipher in these short stories.

The Pause

A women's holiday may be celebratory, (such as the celebration of a happy reunion or a birthday) or a holiday may be commemorative (such as a *yahrzeit*—a Jewish anniversary of a death— or a funeral). Whether celebratory or commemorative, these holidays have much in common: neither the mother nor the daughter accomplishes any domestic maintenance or administration. They pause in the business of life and concentrate their attention only on each other.

These pauses in the dailiness of life have a special character of their own. A ritual has evolved and the performance of that ritual provides the structural framework for many mother-daughter stories that focus on life-cycle events. The ritual has three phases.

The first phase of the ritual calls for a recitation of the relationship between the mother and the daughter. In these first brief exchanges they remind each other of what has taken place in their collective past. For instance, Tobie reminds Aunt El in "A Birthday Remembered" that "I never forget your birthday" and "You *know* what I like!" And in "High Heels," the rapprochement between the mother and daughter, each filled with fear and guilt about the other, begins with the daughter, who blurts out, "Hey, remember the candy kisses you gave me? . . . Remember the matching red blouses?" These remarks are allusive and elliptical, but for readers for whom this type of communication is a cultural given, such remarks resonate with meaning. This shared recounting of herstory acknowledges and reinforces the bond between mother and daughter.[8]

The second stage in the ritual is the assessment of the relationship. The women ask themselves how or why something happened that didn't work, that put distance between them, that alienated them from one another. It is during these sometimes silent ruminations that the reader learns all she needs to know to follow the action into the future. This phase ends with the rendering of a judgment on the past.

The third and final phase of the ritual is the projection into the future of the relationship. In the act of making this projection about the future course of the relationship—and the projection grows out of the judgment made on their past—commitment to the continuation of the relationship is implicit. The commitment may be indicated in various ways: subtly, as in the statement, "Next time we get together, the strawberries will be in season," or in as complex and definitive a manner as Thamré's final short speech to her audience, "If you will *excuse* me, I will leave you now, and take my mother home."

The Disgraceful Mother

"Disgraceful mother" stories portray unconventional mothers and their daughters' struggles to resolve their feelings about their mothers and about themselves as the daughters of such women. Aspects of their character and behavior that violate narrow partriarchal rules for women cause mothers to be labelled "disgraceful." The daughters do not write stories about their mothers' failures to fulfill themselves as artists or intellectuals or athletes or spiritual or political leaders. They write about their mothers' failures to be sexually conventional and circumspect,[9] about their mothers' depressive withdrawals from "normal" functioning, about the drunkenness or drug addiction that renders their mothers slovenly, unpredictable, or "unladylike," and about the poverty and hard physical labor that have left their mothers frazzled, bedraggled, and impatient. Daughters are shamed by these mothers who don't conform to social ideals. In fact, some stories tell of daughters' resentment of their mothers' failures to fulfill conventional female roles, while disregarding the mothers' successes as artists or professionals.

If the daughter learns to separate herself from her mother's "sins," to reject whatever guilt she has assumed or has had to live with in a society that has inflicted guilt upon her, she may turn her back on her mother and make a separate life for herself. Or she may try to understand her mother on her mother's own terms. She may realize she can love an imperfect woman simply because that woman is her mother.[10]

Mid-nineteenth-century temperance tracts include drunken mother stories, although many more describe drunken fathers. From the 1890s until Prohibition, drug-addicted mother stories reflect that period in women's history when doctors routinely prescribed opium-based elixers for women's menstrual cramps, depressions, and general restiveness—and turned thousands of healthy women into addicts. During Prohibition, drunken mothers began to appear in stories about middle- and upper-middle-class women. The daughters appear more passive and victimized in these stories than they did in the temperance stories, which usually portrayed families from the lower socio-economic levels with daughters taking heroic action on behalf of the disabled parent.

During the first thirty years of the twentieth century, stories began to appear about mothers who were sexually suspect—who led sexually unconventional lives. And starting in the 1960s, we begin to find stories about mothers who are mad, insane—mothers whose emotional functioning has gone "wrong." Today, "disgraceful" mothers in short stories may be addicts or alcoholics, mentally ill or sexual outlaws; all are presented as "problems" to be solved by overburdened and ambivalent daughters.

"Old Mother Goose" is the grandmother of all the "disgraceful mother" stories. It provides the pattern for all the rest. "Old Mother Goose" portrays the most disgraceful of all mothers: drunk, drug-addicted, and not only promiscuous, but a one-time prostitute. She is ugly, dirty, unkempt, and stupid—as low as a woman can sink. And her daughter has become all the best that a woman can be: pure, disciplined, beautiful, well-groomed, tastefully dressed, and brilliantly talented (as a performer of male composers' creations—the only ladylike kind of brilliance permissible). "Old Mother Goose" is about a lady and a tramp, about a beautiful princess and an ugly witch. When there is a contradiction between the ideal of motherhood projected by the society and the daughter's perception of her own mother, the daughter must find some way to explain and live with the discrepancy between the ideal and the real. At stake is not only love and respect for her mother, but love and respect for herself. Thamré has rejected the woman who is her mother and embraced an ideal, mourning its absence in her childhood and projecting that image as a goal for herself. In the course of the story, she comes to embrace the woman who is her mother, freeing herself to create a life that is authentic instead of imitative. Quite often, the passage from rejection to acceptance of her mother is for the daughter the passage from emotionally dependent childhood to autonomous adulthood.

Women have written many stories about disgraceful mothers, about mothers whose every breath, every action, embarrasses their daughters and represents a violation of the ideal mother image—whether that image is of the woman whose price is far above the rubies of Biblical tradition, the image of the pure virgin/madonna from Christian tradition, or the floor-scrubbing, dirty collar-ring defeating, loving-from-the-oven mother of secular commercial tradition. Most of these stories end with a reconciliation between mother and daughter, if not in life, at least in the daughter's heart. The daughters grow to understand that, for their own psychological health and spiritual wholeness, they must acknowledge their mothers' separateness and their own innocence of guilt by association with her "disgrace." In "Old Mother Goose," guilt by association is replaced with respect by association. This fairy-tale-like resolution presents yet another pattern for the transformation of mother-daughter relationships.

Surrogate Mothers

In some stories women other than biological mothers are central. These women come to mothering in various ways and for various reasons, but the element of choice in their accession to the responsibility for the care of daughters is always clear, as it often is not in stories about biologically related mothers and daughters. That these women—grandmothers, stepmothers, older friends—choose to act as mothers and that we recognize their behavior as mothering behavior raises important questions about the nature and meaning of motherhood. Is the *mother* the biological parent of the child, or the woman who brings her up? That question, which has been an element around which conflict whirls in many television dramas, doesn't seem to engage the imagination of women who write short stories for women readers. None of the surrogate mothers represented in this collection wonders for a moment whether she is more the "real" mother than the biological mother. She simply relates to the younger female in ways that we immediately recognize as "mothering." Is the mother the one who shapes the girl to the demands of the repressive patriarchal culture, as does the mother in "The Fire," or is she the one who helps the girl see ways to remain self-possessed, to achieve independence, and to find a way to name herself, as does the surrogate mother in that story? Is the mother the one who nourishes the body or the one who feeds the soul? Does the mother teach the arts of deception or the art of self-expression? Which is Queenie learning in "The Lawd Don't Like Ugly?" And which art is the art of survival?

There are three more stories that deal with the relationship between girls and mother-substitutes, or surrogate mothers: "Old Woman Magoun," about a grandmother, and "Oats for the Woman" and "A Birthday Remembered," about step-mothers.

As Meridel Le Sueur has suggested in her short story, "Biography of My Daughter,"[11] we are all mothers of all women younger than ourselves.[12] Hers is a political utopian suggestion, arising out of a socialist perspective and strong solidarity with working-class women across the generations. Her suggestion is echoed in many utopian works by women, such as Joanna Russ's novel, *The Female Man* and Marge Piercy's *Woman on the Edge of Time*,[13] in which society has been organized so no two human beings are ever forced into each other's company or into economic or psychological dependence on another human being for any reason, including the biological relationship of parent and child. In these utopian blueprints for a better future, the relationships between mothers and daughters are casual, less intense because less stressed, and affectionate, but not passionate, as they are in so many of the mother-daughter stories in this collection. The biological link, divorced from economic considerations, is never romanticized.

But in the patriarchy, none of the conditions of the utopian worlds prevail. People are forced into parental relationships; relationships are tense, and the biological links are often romanticized. So why do the step-mothers in "Oats for the Woman" and "A Birthday Remembered" willingly choose to be mothers to girls they haven't given birth to? The two women enter into mothering for different reasons. In the Hurst story, it is the promise of financial security, kindness, and safety that puts Hattie in a position to mother Effie; in "A Birthday Remembered," love draws Ellen into Tobie's life. But it is important to realize that these two women embrace their mothering roles.

Motherhood is the socio-political condition of all adult females mandated by the patriarchy, and it seems that when a woman enters a marriage in which there are already children—at least in the stories I have found—they embrace them. They know how to be mothers; they know about nurturance and intelligent caring. Margaret Mead has described a Melanesian culture in which each member is responsible, in a caring, parental way, for each younger member of the community.[14] No one is without a nurturer, and none is without the responsibility to nurture. Meridel Le Sueur suggests that the social structuring of human responsibility in this way is a tactic for the oppressed to achieve a revolution. Her radical vision has been shared by women writing about nurturant relationships between women, and that vision is reflected in the surrogate-mother stories in this collection.

Multiple Oppressions

Women who are the victims of multiple oppressions have fewer illusions about love, romance, and the benevolence of male culture than women who are only the victims of sexism. The higher the class of a woman and the more privilege she has inherited by virtue of her skin color or group membership, the more likely she is to be sentimental about the potential for emotionally honest and mutually rewarding relationships between women and men. However, women who are the victims of multiple oppressions are much less naive. The more powerless the woman, the less attempt men make to disguise the nature of their expectations and demands. In "A Marriage of Persuasion," Anna is under the illusion of the myth of romantic love, the myth that there is a possible right man to whom she will desire to submit herself as an act of love. And she does not question that compliance, yielding, deference, and submission are appropriate postures for a woman toward a man. Anna believes that love means assuming that posture willingly. Her mother knows better, but has only been forced to that knowledge by recent poverty. And she hasn't brought up her daughters to know that.

In contrast, the mother in "Recuerdo" has known since her own girlhood that there isn't much difference for a woman between what is expected from her by a man she loves and is loved by, and from a man who wants to buy sexual and domestic services from her. She does know, however, that the financial benefits may differ from one arrangement, one man, to another. And, like the surrogate mother in "The Lawd Don't Like Ugly," she supports her daughter's entrance into a liaison with a man most likely to provide her with material security and safety, if not happiness. In both stories, as well as in "Oats for the Woman," the men being compared with each other, potential lovers with potential buyers, belong to the same oppressed groups to which the women belong.

"Annie Gray: A Tale" offers a contrast between a noble man of the oppressed enslaved people and a careless white man. But the story, a deathbed confession, serves more as an indictment of slavery than it does of the patriarchy. In most stories by minority women, the writers are at pains to present minority men as superior to men of the oppressor group. If the minority men aren't all good, they are at least better, less oppressive, less victimizing, less dehumanizing of the minority women than are the men who belong to the oppressor group. But the stories by minority women that portray mothers and daughters confronting the patriarchy make no real distinctions between men of the oppressor and oppressed groups. All men have access to more power and wealth than do minority women.

The largest number of mother-daughter stories have been written by Jewish women—a great many of them testaments of love and witnesses to a culture that the daughters were nurtured by, but are leaving behind. Jewish women writers have also provided the greatest number of "disgraceful mother" stories, stories about drug addicted and alcoholic mothers, stories about manic-depressive and schizophrenic mothers, stories about daughter-exploiters. Black women have begun to write these stories, too, and, most recently, Chicana and Puerto Ricana writers have published some "disgraceful mother" stories. All of these stories portray not only daughters coping with their mothers' "sins," their mothers' failures to conform, but also upwardly mobile daughters exploring the guilt they feel for rejecting the cultures their mothers have spent their lives sustaining and maintaining.

Black women's culture is particularly characterized by mother love. The book dedications of black female critics and editors, the short stories by black women writers, and the lyrics sung by the "girl" groups on the Motown label attest to a combination of love and gratitude to the women credited with teaching their daughters about life and helping them dream and achieve lives inaccessible to their mothers.[15] If communication seems more honest between minority mothers and daughters, the threats to their survival are great, and there isn't much room for inefficient hypocrisy and euphemism.[16] Growing up with a clear vision of the way things are may be traumatic when reality is terrible, but no one has been able to determine whether that trauma is more or less damaging than the trauma of growing up in ignorance and suffering brutal disillusionment. Whose psyche will survive with fewer disabling scars and more self-love: Queenie of "The Lawd Don't Like Ugly" or Anna of "A Marriage of Persuasion?"

Conclusion

The nature of motherhood is complex and as often obscured by sentimentality as by bitterness and pain. Mothers and daughters are often alienated from each other. Daughters feel anger for many reasons: because they see their mothers pressuring them to conform to society's expectations of girls and women, or because they find their mothers paying too little attention to those expectations and offering scant emotional support to daughters attempting to conform. Mothers grow angry at daughters either because daughters don't fulfill their expectations or because their daughters expect too much of them. Such anger and its resulting alienation grow not primarily from clashes between unique personalities and temperaments but rather from the external and internalized social pressures to relate and accept responsibilities to and for each other in terms of the culturally defined roles of mother and daughter. Indeed, the relationship between mothers and daughters, formalized further by such other factors as class, religion, race, and ethnicity, may conceal and inhibit those unique selves. However, most mothers and daughters try to make the best of things; they pitch in with a good will to take care of what must be cared for in the best way they know. Usually that has meant reproducing in the daughters' lives an experience very much like the mothers'.

In the last decade, because of the most recent wave of the women's liberation movement, the relationship between mothers and daughters had come under increasing, frequent, intense, and passionate examination.[17] Women are reclaiming women's lives and women's flesh. Not only are women saying, "Keep your hands and your laws off my body," and "My body, my self—I have the right to feel pleasure and to know strength," but also "I lay claim to the bond of flesh—and all that means—between myself and the woman who was first in my life, and the women in whose lives I have been first." Mothers and daughters are reclaiming each other, not by embracing the roles they have been so long girdled by, but by embracing the unique person each finds the other. Thus, we now have a great surge of books and panels, study groups and therapy groups, lectures and classes on the subject of the mother-daughter relationship.

But long before this recent activity began, women had been writing short stories about this special relationship. While not denying or ignoring the differences among us, we read these stories to find what we share, what binds us together, and how other women have learned to transcend the rules and the roles, to learn that mothers and daughters can be sisters. There are literally hundreds of mother-daughter stories. These eighteen were chosen from nearly a hundred of the very best.

NOTES

1. In *Diving Deep and Surfacing: Women Writers on Spiritual Quest* (Boston: Beacon Press, 1980), Carol P. Christ has defined the sacred dimension as that "which orient(s) a person to the ... great powers that establish the reality of their world. These powers ... are the boundaries against which life is played out, the forces against which a person must contend, or the currents in whose rhythms she must learn to swim. They sometimes provide revelation when the self is at a loss. ... They may provide a (potent) sense of meaning and value. ... They may ground a person in powers of being that enable her to challenge conventional values or expected roles" (p. 3).

2. An extremely useful international bibliography, listing more stories about mothers and daughters, as well as treatments of this relationship by social scientists, literary critics, and others appears in *The Lost Tradition: Mothers and Daughters in Literature*, ed. Cathy N. Davidson and E.M. Broner (New York: Frederick Ungar Pub. Co., 1980). The bibliographers, Ann M. Moore, Gail M. Rudenstein, and Carol Farley Kessler, refer to their 500+item compilation as a "Preliminary Bibliography."

3. A mother's support of a daughter's lesbian sexuality may encourage healthy sexual functioning for her daughter and allow her daughter to pay attention to her mother's experience in and knowledge about the patriarchy.

4. Quest stories, or searches for identity, are common in traditional male literature. In these stories, a boy about to become a man explores how that transition can be accomplished, what act he must perform, what name he is to be known by, who he will be as a man separate from all other men. Often an older man will accompany him on his quest, serving as a kind, wise teacher, making suggestions, pointing out directions, and warning of dangers. But the boy must commit an important act or achieve an important goal on his own. By that act (e.g., killing a bear or a dragon or an alien invader, losing his virginity, stealing another man's emblem of power) or that achievement (earning the title of Dr., or Green Beret, or All American, or Knight of the Round Table), he comes to be, generally, a man, and, specifically, his own man.

Occasionally, women write stories in which women quest after identity in these traditional male ways, as if it were something to wrest from life, rather than something to grow into, to learn to know, and to tend and nurture. Such stories often center on a girl with a sense of vocation which, if followed, will take her far from the women's world in which she has been raised and where she has been expected to spend her life.

5. A longer discussion of the ways in which women's genres, women writers, and the tastes of predominantly female audiences have been discounted appears in *How to Suppress Women's Writing*, by Joanna Russ (Austin: University of Texas Press, 1983).

6. These survivals are usually at the level of superstitious behavior. Superstitions represent the rote remnants of systems of belief whose substance has been lost through repressions or dispersal of the members of the culture who shared that system of thought. For a discussion of the process of the development of superstitious behavior as the result of repression, see *The Secret Jews*, by Joachim Prinz (New York: Random House, 1973). For a discussion of vestigial menarche rituals, see *The*

Curse: A Cultural History of Menstruation, by Janice Delaney, Mary Jane Lupton, and Emily Toth (New York: E.P. Dutton and Co., 1976).

7. Women in the contemporary feminist spirituality movement are recreating and creating rituals for contemporary women's lives. The attention they have brought · to this basic ritual-making, occasion-marking component of women's psychology and spirituality has inspired a new vision through which to filter our understanding of women's creative artifacts. The ritual elements of women's work and lives are now more visible whether we look at women's quilts, women's cooking, women's conversation, or women's writing.

8. The first part of the pause ritual is like the first part of a consciousness-raising group meeting, during which women tell each other parts of the stories of their lives, providing the data for the analysis of the patriarchy upon which the theory for feminist revolution is built.

9. The meaning of sexual non-conformity varies greatly over time. At the beginning of this century, it often meant simply that the mother was divorced. In later decades it often referred to an extra-marital liaison, condemned no matter how dreadful the marriage nor how abusive, irresponsible, or absent the husband. In some stories written since the 1960s, mothers have been prostitutes. I have found no stories in which a mother is perceived as disgraceful by her daughter because the mother is a lesbian. There are, however, several stories in which, as in "A Birthday Remembered," a lesbian mother or mother-surrogate worries that her daughter might think she is disgraceful. The worry is always unfounded.

In nineteenth-century "disgraceful mother" stories, sexual non-conformity never appears as the single "sin." Non-compliance with expected sexual behavior is always part of a general portrayal of disgrace, and among the other "sins" there is always at least one form of substance abuse.

10. Christian versions of this story have strong parallels with the myth of redemption; Jewish women writers' stories rely on the perspectives of the social sciences, turning variously to psychology, sociology, history, and political science to understand a world that includes drunken, promiscuous mothers and broken-hearted, humiliated daughters.

11. Originally published in *American Mercury,* January 1935; reprinted in *Salute to Spring* (New York: International Publishers, 1940, 1977, 1980).

12. Many of my friends and colleagues (most of us are in our thirties, forties, and fifties) complain that many younger women want mothers,

rather than friends or lovers or colleagues. We are offended by the
endless demand for nurturing. And yet we want nurturing, too. But
we want relationships in which nurturance is reciprocal. In our friendships, we reciprocate—carefully—and negotiate nurturance, as well as
jokes, gossip, and household hints as we share in the search and the
struggle for peace and social justice.

In our experience, the fantasy most common among women about
surrogate mothers is not the wicked, threatening, jealous stepmother.
The real fantasy is the fairy godmother who can and will make all your
dreams come true. I think we are always vulnerable to the attractions
of a woman who will mother us, and we often make demands for
mothering on women in positions of apparent authority. One of the
real problems that women who teach in higher education have to deal
with is the expectation by their students, male and female, that they
will be "motherly." Such expectations are not harbored about male
professors who, therefore, have more time for research and other
"professional" activities, and whose evaluations by students don't reflect
those disappointed expectations. This need and demand for mothering
behavior, or nurturance, from older women by younger women has
been documented in numerous studies by various social scientists.

I am no less guilty of wanting endless mothering. This emotional
neediness is not only a burden put on older women by younger women,
but it represents a kind of ageist, stereotypical thinking. My mother
once said to me, with justified exasperation, "Susan, now that you are
working so hard to liberate women from oppression, will you please
liberate me from your need for my approval!" I'm trying, Mommy.

13. A Bantam Book, New York, 1975, and a Fawcett Crest Book,
New York, 1976.

14. I know that there is now a vast Mead revisionism underway, but
whether or not her descriptions were less or more accurate than those
of other anthropologists in the field, the cultural constructs she reported
on are important and have entered our culture at the deepest levels.
They are part of our intellectual history and, in some cases, they have
fueled our utopian dreams.

15. In an interview for *Something About the Author*, Alice Walker tells
about three important gifts her mother gave her, each one delivering
a message about her mother's hopes for her and her support of Walker's
dreams for herself. "The second gift was a suitcase, a high school
graduation gift, as nice as anyone in Eatonton had ever had. That
suitcase gave me permission to travel and part of the joy in going very
far from home was the message of that suitcase. Just a year later I was
in Russia and Eastern Europe."

16. Candelaria Silva commented on this straight talk between mothers and daughters who are women of color. In her review of *This Bridge Called My Back: Writings by Radical Women of Color* (Boston: Persephone Press, 1981; reissued by Kitchen Table Press, New York, 1984), in the *New Women's Times Feminist Review* 22, July/August, 1982, she writes: "Some of our common colored stuff is that: most of us have seen more death than white feminist/females ever encounter—just growing up. Many of us had mommas, grandmommas, aunts and other women tell us directly and not-so-directly, that our 'pussy was a commodity.' Most of us grew up knowing we would *have* to work."

17. The article that has most influenced my thinking about the mother-daughter relationship is "The Impact of the Nazi Occupation of Poland on the Jewish Mother-Child Relationship," by Renee Fodor, *YIVO Annual of Jewish Social Science*, 1956–1957, vol. 11. This article was brought to my attention by my friend, Barry Mehler, about seven years ago. I am grateful to him for the article and for many fine discussions.

I have read the article repeatedly and it haunts me. I am overwhelmed by analogies between the situation of those Jewish mothers of sons and daughters, and the situation of mothers and daughters in the patriarchy, but after much thought and many discussions with friends, I decided not to draw those analogies in this essay because of the danger of seeming to trivialize the experience of those who suffered through the attempted genocide of world Jewry.

INTRODUCTION

1. A Glance at Mother/Daughter Work Since 1976 in Literature and Popular Culture

The subject of mothers and daughters and the relationships between them provokes intense responses from most women. During long late-night telephone and IM conversations, via snail mail or email, or sitting across a table from our friends, we talk about our mothers, our daughters, or both. We brag, complain, blame, speculate, remember, celebrate, confess—and we tell stories. And just like the rest of us, women who write do the same, providing us with more stories about this endlessly different and eternally similar relationship than any other relationship.

Two books by white, ethnically undifferentiated American women from the last quarter of the twentieth century have fueled passionate and furious conversation[1]: Adrienne Rich's 1976 *Of Woman Born: Motherhood as Experience and Institution* (W.W. Norton) and Nancy Friday's *My Mother, My Self: The Daughter's Search for Identity* the following year (Delacorte Press). These now classic books have expanded and publicized our private and intimate talks about this primal relationship. These two books made public and national (and even international, to some extent) what has long constituted a private and intimate talk between and among women. Lyn Lifshin's 1978 anthology *Tangled Vines: A Collection of Mother and Daughter Poems* has continued to build an audience. But the conversation about mothers and daughters, their love for each other, the grief of the mother when she is separated from her daughter, the abduction or seduction of the daughter by the patriarchy was already an old story when Homer first told it. The story/myth of Demeter and Persephone, summarized below by Jungian therapist and scholar Kathie Carlson, continues to play an important role today in mother/daughter analysis whether by psychologists, literary scholars, religious scholars, or historians.

Kore, beloved daughter of the grain goddess Demeter, was picking flowers in a field when suddenly the earth cracked open. Out of the chasm leapt Hades, Lord of the Underworld. Snatching Kore, he carried her away to his kingdom beneath the earth. "A rape! a rape!" screamed the girl. When Demeter learned of her daughter's fate, she searched relentlessly, grieving and appealing to Zeus, the 'father of the gods,' to ensure her daughter's return. But Zeus had allowed this abduction. In rage, Demeter withdrew her gift of grain. People were starving and the gods received no harvest offerings. Zeus relented and sent for Kore but, because she had eaten some pomegranate seeds below, she had to spend part of the year as Hades' wife. Now known as Persephone, Queen of the Dead, she moved between her mother's and husband's worlds, marking the seasons of spring and winter.[2]

Since the publication of the original version of *Between Mothers and Daughters: Stories Across a Generation* in 1985, interest in mothers and daughters as an area of study within many of the traditional intellectual disciplines has flourished. Scholarly single-authored monographs have been published in psychology, literature, cultural studies, popular culture, religious studies, sociology, anthropology, and, of course, women's studies. One of the most influential and controversial of these studies is Sara Ruddick's *Maternal Thinking: Toward a Politics of Peace*, constantly in print since its 1989 publication by Houghton Mifflin. An equally important book published that same year is Paula Caplan's *Don't Blame Mother* in which this thoughtful feminist clinical and research psychologist outlines ten dangerous myths that encourage animosity rather than alliances between generations of women.

Multi-disciplinary, multi-generic anthologies of mother/daughter writings have been published with increasingly specific population foci, such as *Double Stitch: Black Women Write about Mothers & Daughters with Poems, Stories, and Essays* and *Her Face in the Mirror: Jewish Women on Mothers and Daughters*. Collections of personal essays about mother/daughter relationships have gained wide readership, such as Louise Rifkin's 1987 book *Different Daughters: A Book by Mothers of Lesbians*, now in its third edition.[3] The Association for Research on Mothering, a scholarly organization, has two thematically focused conferences each year and produces a journal.[4] Essay collections focus on particular aspects of the mother/daughter relationship such as Hope Edelman's best-selling 1995 book, *Motherless Daughters: The Legacy of Loss* which introduced into public consciousness the subject of women who lose their mothers early in their lives to death or separation. *Transformative Motherhood: On Giving and Getting in a Consumer Culture* looks at motherhood from the perspective of women whose "reproductive encounters do not match up to cultural standards," bringing into the conversation mothers who are not or cannot mother (although they *are* mothers) because of child loss or relinquishment and mothers who become mothers by surrogacy, adoption, or fostering. *The Conversation Begins: Mothers and Daughters Talk About Living Feminism* is a fascinating set of essays by feminist mothers and daughters attempting to provide a snapshot of the effect of feminism on their mother/daughter relationships in a particular historical moment.

The partitioning of the topic "mothers and daughters" into increasingly more focused sub-topics further stimulates both private and public considerations. Since feminist literary scholars have won the struggle to legitimize the authority of diaries and letters as literary genres, more and more diaries written by women, especially from the nineteenth century, are being published. An alternative source for the history of family relationships, gender roles, and the politics of the American nation as it struggled to survive and thrive is now available. Often isolated, lonely, depressed by the conditions of their lives, subject to dangers both inside and outside their homes, and exhausted by their endless labor, pioneer women imagined their daughters growing up, finding their mothers' diaries, and proving themselves sympathetic readers. These women wrote diaries to leave as legacies to their daughters, assuming their readers would come to their words only after their own deaths.[5] The diaries functioned, in a sense, as letters sent into the future. However, actual letters between mothers and daughters, filled with details of daily life, reports of books being read, social activities, worries, joys, and advice, were regularly exchanged in the present, whenever that was. Karen Payne's 1983 collection *Between Ourselves: Letters Between Mothers and Daughters, 1850-1982*, published by Houghton Mifflin, provides a memorable sampling of these exchanges written in English.[6]

Explorations of the mother/daughter relationship, portrayals of the bonds, the intimacy, and the conflicts, flourish in all forms of popular culture as never before. Mother/daughter movies are certainly not new to the medium, on both the large and small screen. Two classic stories about mothers and daughters have been filmed more than once: *Imitation of Life*, based loosely and then a second time even more loosely, on Fannie Hurst's novel by that title, was made in 1934 and 1958; Olive Higgins Prouty's novel *Stella Dallas* has been filmed three times (1925, 1937, and 1990). More recently, from the 1983 *Terms of Endearment* to the 2003 *Freaky Friday* (which is the third remake of the story), mother/daughter films continue to hit the big screen and bring in droves of women to laugh and cry with their mothers, daughters, and friends at what they recognize up on the screen.[7]

As women have become more prominent in music as independent performers, writing more of the songs they sing and exercising increased power over the contents of their albums and concerts, celebrations of mothers and grandmothers have become part of their repertoire. Female singers and musicians such as Jeannie C. Riley, Dolly Parton, Jessica Andrews, Tori Amos, and Madonna have sung about their complex maternal relationships, such as their identities as granddaughters, leaving the "nest," and losing a mother in childhood.[8]

There seems to be no end to how we can look at this relationship. In fact, typing "Mothers" and "Daughters" into the amazon.com book search engine brings up 84,556 hits (as of May 29, 2004). The same search at google.com results in 886,000 hits. All kinds of ideas, perspectives, stereotypes, and agendas bump against each other, each jostling for the right to be considered the truest or the best, the most horrible or the most unusual, portrayal of what is or should be the mother-daughter relationship. The experience of maternal abuse described in Christina Crawford's book about her life with her mother Joan, and in the film based on it, *Mommie Dearest,* seems to have broken the silence that has surrounded physical and sexual abuse of daughters by their mothers.[9] And, as our population ages and the pressures on the "sandwich generation" intensify, we have also seen a breaking of the silence that has surrounded elder abuse.

The same shift in convention that made it possible to talk for the first time openly about abusive mothers and daughters also made it possible to write about the abuse of mothers by fathers, step-fathers, and boyfriends, and the response of daughters to that abuse. Both the stories by Jane Bradley ("Noises") and Preety Kalra ("Home") portray some of the consequences for daughters of the abuse of their mothers by their fathers. Although the two stories arise from very different cultures and belong to entirely different structural and stylistic sub-genres, the most important sub-genre they represent is The Cautionary Tale: when a mother is abused, so, too, is her daughter; a blow to the body of one is a blow to the heart and soul of the other.[10]

Between Mothers and Daughters: Stories Across a Generation remains the only multi-racial, multi-ethnic, multi-faith-community, multi-generational, multi-regional, multi-class, multi-sexualities, multi-dis/ability historical collection of mother/daughter stories by U.S. women writers, expanded now to include more recent stories. The collection of mother/daughter stories in my files has topped four hundred written between the 1820s and 2004. I'm sure I have found only a portion of those written in English by U.S. women. I am pleased to have been given the opportunity to expand the original collection with the addition of seven more stories and this additional commentary.

2. Ethnicity, Language, and Mother/Daughter Relationships

In recent years, stories written in the United States by women immigrants, women from First Nations, and women from non-English speaking U.S. communities are being recovered and translated. For instance, *Found Treasures: Stories by Yiddish Women Writers,* edited by Forman et al. (University of Toronto Press, 1994) makes available to English-language readers stories originally written in Yiddish in

America. Equally exciting is the appearance of stories written in the dialects of the ethnic and racial cultures from which their authors emerge and which, with increasing insistence, they choose to use in their literary work. Some writers append glossaries to their fiction so readers can understand (not necessarily the formal dictionary meaning of) the words they use which are rooted in other languages than standard received English. Other writers don't bother to provide glossaries or footnotes: if you can't figure out the meaning from the context, get a dictionary or take a course or go to a grocery store in a different part of town and beg someone to explain. Other writers switch languages in the middle of a story or even in the middle of a collection of stories with no explanation, no warning, and no apologies. For instance, in "Dichos", in Patricia Preciado Martin's *El Milagro and Other Stories* (University of Arizona Press, 1996), a girl who is sent to spend every Saturday with her great-grandmother, Mamanina, absorbs barrio culture effortlessly and carries on bi-lingual conversations:

> "I have to talk to her in Spanish because she has never learned English, only a few words like "enough is too many." Besides, she says, "What for? No one in this old barrio speaks English anyway, and I'm going back to my ranchito in Mexico someday." Sometimes I can't think of a word, or I pronounce something funny or use the wrong verb, and she corrects me but never criticizes.
>
> "Oh, Mamanina," I sigh, "esta tortilla esta tan sabrosa."
>
> She smiles. "Cuando hay hambre, no hay mal pan," she says all humble-like. And all the time she's pat-pat-patting and rolling out tortillas, she's keeping her eye on the simmering pot and stirring with a big wooden spoon or adding a pinch of this or that.
>
> I am taking big bites out of the tortilla and gulping it down, and the butter is running down my arm, but she doesn't scold.
>
> "To tell you the truth, Mamanina," I confide in my halting Spanish, "I didn't have a very good week."
>
> "De la olla a la boca a todos se le cae ta sopa," she consoles.
> (p.14)

In Alicia Gaspar de Alba's collection *The Mystery of Survival and*

Other Stories (Bilingual Press/Editorial Bilingüe, 1993) the author includes two stories out of the eleven entirely in Spanish. And in *Babaylan: An Anthology of Filipina and Filipina American Writers* edited by Nick Carbo and Eileen Tabios, we encounter stories and poems written in several languages, most translated into English, but not all. Although mother/daughter(s) relationships and the grandmother/mother/daughter(s) subject matter is Merrill Joan Gerber's "vein of truth," one aspect of her personal truth almost entirely missing from all but her most recent stories is her ethnicity. Ashkenazi Jewish ethnicity is missing from her stories because had they been clearly Jewish, filled with references to Jewish foods and folkways, punctuated with Yiddish words, word reversals, intonations, and sayings, she would not have found ready publication opportunities for her stories. Gerber commented on this absence: "I was writing for a Middle American magazine in the sixties and seventies—for *Redbook*. They had me take out all ethnic references. . . ."[11]

These remarks are one of the few instances in American literary history where we have documented evidence of the influence of and interference by publishers on the ethnic content in U.S. literature. This valuable revelation prompts a rethinking of the history and development of our literature and of the roles played by publishers who held the economic power, and ethnic writers who wanted to tell their stories and also needed to earn a living. How much literary "assimilation" was voluntary and how much seduced or coerced?

The same absence of manifest reference to Jewish ethnicity is true of the stories of another writer whose explorations of the mother/daughter relationship are numerous, rich, and varied: Fannie Hurst—although readers who are members of or familiar with the culture recognize that characters in many of Hurst's stories were Ashkenazi Jews as is the case in "Oats for the Woman." The struggle between the generations of immigrant women and their American-born daughters about food, eating, flesh, and fatness has been one of the primary arenas in which the conflict between Old World and New, traditional cultural loyalty to family and American individualism, and custom and assimilation has been waged, and class mobility has been gained or lost. This conflict about "proper embodiment" between immigrant and American-born generations of mothers and daughters is one of the conflicts to which we gain access when we open ourselves to the stories of the Borderlands.[12] Another is the question of how adult life partnerships are to be entered into. Arranged marriages? Exogamous or endogamous marriages?[13] Honoring the mother's way of life by recreating it or honoring the American ideal of individualism, individual choice and leaving behind the mother's traditions? Does the Jewish American daughter keep a kosher kitchen or does she drive through the fast food burrito place? Does the Chicana daughter make her own hominy and grind it in the *metate* she inherited from her grandmother—or does she stop at the deli for a pound of hot lean corned beef and a nice *tzitzel* rye? Does the Italian American daughter spend her day stirring a pot of sauce or does she open a bottle and pour the contents into a microwave safe dish—or does she order Chinese take-out?[14]

What would U.S. literature be like had there not been such a determined de-ethnicization of our polyglot literary population? Would the stories have been different or would just the language in which they were told be different? If the language is different, can the story be the same? Are the mother/daughter stories told in the special tongues of ethnic communities different from the stories told in standard received English?

Writers who use what Gloria Anzaldua calls "border language" and various dialects now assert that their language and their writing is Literature of the most venerable, noble, and mainstream kind. Their work is as much "American Literature" as poetry by Emily Dickinson or a novel by Edith Wharton, Kate Chopin, or Joyce Carol Oates. The emergence of an unapologetically bilingual Latina/Chicana literary culture, such as that represented by the women whose work is included in *Infinite Divisions: An Anthology of Chicana Literature* (see Alma Luz Villanueva's story "Her Choice," reprinted from that anthology, in this collection) and the definition of the language of the Borderlands by Gloria Anzaldua in her now classic 1987 book *Borderlands/La Frontera: The New Mestiza* gives us an idea of what might have been, what is becoming, and what might yet be:

> The switching of 'codes'. . . from English to Castilian Spanish
> to the North Mexican dialect to Tex-Mex to a sprinkling of

Nahuatl to a mixture of all of these, reflects my language, a
new language—the language of the Borderlands. There, at
the juncture of cultures, languages cross-pollinate and are
revitalized; they die and are born. Presently this infant language, this bastard language, Chicano Spanish, is not
approved by any society. But we Chicanos no longer feel that
we need to beg entrance, that we need always to make the
first overture—to translate to Anglos, Mexicans and Latinos,
apology blurting out of our mouths with every step. Today we
ask to be met halfway.

In "A Candle in a Gale Wind," African–American author Alice
Childress spoke to this issue of "right" language with eloquence:

The political atmosphere of a country shapes the intellect of
the majority of its citizens—toward conformity. Even when a
writer seeks to evade and omit all that is political, because it
is politic to do so, that then becomes political. In the USA we
profess and proclaim freedom of thought and expression. . . .
Consider Black English and the furor it causes. "Zis and zat"
when uttered by the French is considered charming, but "dis
and dat" as an Africanism is ridiculed as gross and ugly. The
echo of European accents and linguistic spillovers into
American 'English' fall easily upon our ear. Africanisms cause
a shudder. Many Blacks now say hail and farewell with the
Italian ciao. So what? Maybe I shoulda stood in bed and not
sperl ya day awready. Okay? Like enough with the jabber and
the bla, bla, bla. Got it? See what I mean?[15]

Many similarities exist between this current movement from the
borders into the center of literature by the many versions of American
English alongside the one once considered the only literary language—
standard received English—and the nineteenth-century literary regionalism movement and the early twentieth-century immigrant literary
movement.[16] The stories in this book by Elizabeth Stuart Phelps, Mary
E. Wilkins Freeman, Alice Brown, and Helen Reimensnyder Martin
are examples of literary regionalism at its best. Fannie Hurst, although
she was second-generation American-born, and first-generation

American-born Hisaye Yamamoto, stand as representatives of the immigrant literary movement.

The language of the Borderlands begins to be represented in this collection of stories about mothers and daughters with Guadalupe Valdes' 1973 story "Recuerdo." Sherley Anne Williams and Nicholasa Mohr represent the continued creation of the Borderlands literary movement in the 1970s. But the use of Borderlands language represents a choice a writer makes and not an inevitable corollary of membership in a particular ethnic or racial group. The choice to use one or another of the dialects of American English, one of the Borderland dialects, or the standard dialect is not a choice available to all writers; some are limited to the standard dialect because it is the only one they know. Others, as we learn from the comments Gerber made about editorial intervention, choose the standard dialect because it is the only way they know to get their work published. Ben Franklin is credited as the first to say "Freedom of the Press belongs to those who own the Presses," but the saying has long been a rallying cry for social change movements as new periodicals and publishing houses have been created to publish the words, the thoughts, the literary and cartoon art of social justice advocates and minority cultural preservationists.

How fortunate that more and more of the Borderland language communities have begun to support literary publications, such as *El Grito del Sol, Revista Chicano Riqueña, Comadre, De Colores: Journal of Chicano Expression and Thought, El Fuego de Aztlan* and *Maize: Xicano Art and Literature Notebooks*, that provide a home for stories written in those dialects.[17] Equal recognition must be given to feminist and lesbian periodicals that have opened their pages to the literature written by women in the Borderland dialect of womanspeak.[18] Unfortunately, none of those publications have been well-supported enough to survive let alone pay their writers enough money so that they can "quit their day jobs," i.e., make the proverbial leap to full-time writer who lives on her literary earnings. Typically these publications do not have lengthy life spans—nor are they widely available in bookstores or frequently archived in libraries. Borderland dialect stories are the ones most likely to get, and most quickly getting, lost. Their preservation is as much literary recovery as is the rediscovery and preservation of the short stories by women from the nineteenth century. The foreign language newspapers and magazines from the nineteenth- and twentieth-century that did publish women's fiction have only begun to be searched. The work of retrieval remaining in this area is as great as all that has already been accomplished in retrieving Anglo-American and African-American women writers of the nineteenth century.

What about contemporary white heterosexual women writers? These are the women most traditionally included in literary anthologies—at least while they are alive and young and conventionally attractive—and, most important of all, connected by marriage or otherwise to important literary men.[19] Are they being ignored? Are they being left out of the anthologies in favor of those minority women who are being embraced—this year? Are brilliant contemporary heterosexual white women practitioners of the short story being lost almost as soon as they have been found? Why don't we find (to mention just a few) Lorrie Moore, Amy Bloom, Alice Dark, Lynne Sharon Schwartz, Moira Crone, Amy Hempl, Mary Gaitskill, Sheila Schwartz, Kit Reed, Mae Briskin, Catherine Brady, Pam Durbin, Mary Clearman Blew, Joanne Greenberg, Hortense Calisher, Jill McCorkle, Meg Files, Antonya Nelson, Mary Gordon, Molly Giles and any number of other contemporary women writers in anthologies? Are they being ignored because it isn't "the time for their kind" just now?

These writers are not *just* heterosexual white women; each represents a unique voice, a region, a history, an ethnicity, a social class, a faith community, a generation. . . . Irish-American, Southern, Southwestern, Western, New Englander, Midwestern, Polish-American,[20] Mid-South, French-American, German-American, Italian-American Catholic. . . . It is perhaps the non-Anglo white ethnic writers who are being the most assiduously ignored by the World of Official Literature in these last few decades—although those ethnic communities have, by now, raised up a second, third, or fourth generation of hyphenated-Americans who have begun to take their places in the intellectual professions and have begun to "lobby" through the creation of societies, organizations, and publications for the recognition of the creative work of "their" people.[21]

What is and remains clear is the sad reality that more writers—artists of all kinds—will always be excluded from the official history, the canon, the syllabus, the anthology, than included; they will be left out and forgotten rather than integrated into the body of what is to be remembered. And what special obligations devolve onto us—whoever we are with this knowledge—as a consequence of this sad reality? I think we must always remember that we have read less of what is worthy of being read than exists, that whoever are our favorites, there are others just as good whom we haven't yet encountered, that what we know or think we know is less than what we don't know and haven't even imagined.

3. Mothers, Daughters, Good and Bad Bodies, and Good and Bad Behaviors

Earlier I wrote, "This conflict about 'proper embodiment' between immigrant and American born generations of mothers and daughters is one of the conflicts that we gain access to when we open ourselves to the stories of the Borderlands." But I do not mean to suggest for a millisecond that tales of the conflict *and conspiracy* between mothers and daughters about "proper embodiment" and "righteous behavior" are encountered only in the Borderland stories. In this collection the conflict either boils overtly or simmers covertly, either as the central theme or a leitmotif, in at least seven of the stories (perhaps you will notice it in more!).

Mothers are held responsible by the patriarchy for the daughter-product they "turn out." Perhaps the most egregious, tragic, and thoroughly discredited examples of this mother-blaming in the twentieth-century were the creation and application of the terms "schizophrenogenic mother"[22] and "refrigerator mother."[23] These labels were appalling; they imposed terrifying burdens on mothers and caused irreparable damage on many fronts, destroying individuals and relationships.

But the most obvious and widespread criteria by which a daughter is judged to be a successful or unsuccessful "product" are her physical conformity to a conventionally expected appearance and her behavioral conformity with her expected role. Both of these criteria are expressions of control—the patriarchy controls the standards of judgment, the mothers control their daughters learning of the standards and oversee the practicing of conformity to the patriarchal standards, and the daughters, once adult, demonstrate self-control if they continue to manifest conformity to the established standards. Is the daughter's body in bounds or out of bounds? Is she a body outlaw? Is there too much of her?[24] Too much of some parts and not enough of other parts? Does she have good hair or bad hair?[25] What about that nose? Too long? Too wide? Is she depilated enough? Femme enough? And the teeth! Are they straight enough? White enough? All there? Does she cover enough of her body? Too much? Is her taste in clothes, shoes, and jewelry classy or trashy? Did she "come into her womanhood" too early? Too late?

Whatever isn't right, isn't exactly right, is Mother's fault. Isn't it? So what is a mother to do? Patrol her daughter's body, police the nurturing and suppressing of her appetites, protest her deviations, plead for compliance, promise rewards for submission, present her own perfect performance of propriety as a goal to match?[26] Dr. Paula Caplan looks at the consequences of mothers' attempts to impose physical conformity on their daughters with compassion for both: "Often daughters develop eating problems in response to their mothers' efforts to starve them, ridicule and humiliate them, etc. It has been shown that it is in large measure mothers' own experiences of knowing how it is to be humiliated and rejected for being "overweight" that impels them— understandably feeling helpless to transform society's fear of women's weight in time to protect her daughter from rejection and mockery, should she gain weight—to try desperately to help their daughters fit the mold because they want to SPARE them that pain."[27] On the other hand, Dr. Kathie Carlson comments on the current situation vis à vis mothers and their daughters' bodies as one in which mothers' power has diminished considerably: ". . . in recent years, at least by the time her daughter is a teen . . . as a therapist and feminist and mother, I am overwhelmed by how much *worse* things have gotten with regard to young women and their relationships to their bodies: five year olds going on diets, grade school kids hating their bodies, size 0 being seen as the desired ideal by teens and college students. My experience and observation is that the greatest influences on young girls and women is the peer group and the media and the girl celebrities, singers, actresses, models, etc."[28]

However, the judging of bodies and behavior is not a one-way street. Daughters look at their mothers and assess what they see. What if the mother's body or behavior breaches the limits? How does the daughter deal with that? How does she feel about that? What is the impact on her life if her mother is "different?"[29] What kinds of relationships are possible between an out of the ordinary mother and her daughter? Do they collaborate in deviation? Does the daughter disown her mother, or at least distance herself from her? If the family—or the mother-daughter pair—lives on a borderland, or is the object of multiple oppressions, is deviance in one world deviance in the other(s)? In "Tell the Truth..." Nicholasa Mohr explores some of the dynamics of this conundrum.

And, on the third hand, assuming that the mother accepts that the choices about how her children shall be present in the world physically and behaviorally are hers, how is she to choose? Based on traditional values or contemporary fashions? What criteria does she use to make these choices? Andrea Benton Rushing's "Hair–Raising" pursues these questions.

Finally, if the daughter does not deviate in her behavior and does not have a "bad" body, as in, for instance, "A Marriage of Persuasion," does that mean these are moot issues? Or does compliance at that level simply pave the way for additional demands?

4. Genres, Sub-genres, Classifications, and Pecking Orders of Literature

In the dominant cultural mythologies, naming begins with Genesis. Some people think that naming is where our troubles begin. But perhaps it isn't actually naming that causes trouble but rather the way we *use* names to classify and create pecking orders. We use names to distinguish among phenomena, but we also use them to compare, to endow with or withhold value, to commemorate and to maim, to honor and to degrade. We learn the names given to others by third parties to rationalize prejudice, to compel fear, to trigger scorn, to justify oppression.

In the literary world, naming types of literature serves all of these same functions. Naming is practiced by the experts, the gatekeepers. Literary works that share common characteristics are given names that allow us to classify the works, to compare and contrast them, and to pass judgments about which are better or worse (if we think we can make that judgment for others) or, more simply, which we like more or less, within their type and between and among types.

The word used to classify kinds of literature is "genre." It means "category" or "type" or "kind." Early in the school years, children are taught genres of literature: plays, poems, novels, short stories, and, perhaps, nonfiction. Or they may first be taught that there are two genres of literature: imaginative or "made-up" and "real"; poems, plays, short stories, and novels are imaginative literature. "Real" literature includes biographies, autobiographies, memoirs, essays, histories—and perhaps journalism.

When I first learned about literary genres in elementary school, I was taught the names of genres as if they were permanent and unquestionable categories. In high school I learned about sub-genres of the genres; for instance, about poetry, Miss Edith B. Malin taught the terms lyric and epic, ballads and elegies, sonnets Shakespearean and otherwise; she taught us to value both imagist and narrative poetry.[30] Allegories and idylls, parodies, satires, and epitaphs, metaphysical and pastoral were all part of her syllabus. I did not learn about doggerel or greeting card verse, limericks, ditties, popular music lyrics, nonsense poetry, or concrete poetry. All the categories I learned about were called sub-genres of poetry.

As I made my way through college and graduate school I continued to encounter new sets of categories collected under the headings of "genre" and "sub-genre." What was meant by genre and sub-genre began to seem conditional, provisional, more a placeholder for the idea of category than a category.

I learned about novels of ideas, political novels, impressionistic novels, experimental novels, naturalist novels, stream of consciousness novels, and so forth. But these were all sub-genres of only one kind of novel, the only kind of novel ever considered in the higher education at the Good Schools I attended—and those were "literary novels."

Periodically, in the halls of Barnard or between the stacks in the Case Western Reserve Library or among the counters of books being remaindered in storied, independently owned bookstores, I would hear a snooty sniff followed by a dismissive tone of voice muttering the term "genre novel." Those were the novels that were somehow *not* novels, not worthy of being called "novels," not to be read (or have the reading admitted to) by serious, intellectually worthy, educated people.

But I knew that "genre novels" were the novels read by most novel-readers. "Genre novels" were the novels that writers might become rich by writing. Genre novel writers didn't win serious literary awards or receive prestigious grants; academics never admitted to reading them (unless they were recounting a period of serious illness); theses and dissertations were not written about them in departments of literature; academic libraries never bought them; and public libraries threw them out or sold them after their moment in the sun had passed.[31]

My years as part of the then brand-new community of Popular Culture scholars at Bowling Green State University brought me into contact with a group of people who embraced Genre literature and treated it with the same seriousness and respect as was demonstrated by those producing monographs on *Moby Dick* or *Finnegan's Wake*.[32] The members of the young association of intellectuals who banded together under the leadership of Ray B. Browne to create the Popular Culture Association produced their own serious and respectful—but also extraordinarily joyful—monographs on the sub-genres of genre novels: mystery, private eye, crime, ghost, fantasy, science fiction, adventure, westerns, historical, bodice rippers, horror, romance, occult, young adult, and something called variously "women's," "family saga," or "tear jerker."

I began my work in 1972 to discover, collect, and make available to readers the short stories written by U.S. women writers since the beginning of the short story in this country. Since the second weekend in November 1972, I have maintained a schedule of reading an average of three short stories by U.S. women writers every day, seven days a week, fifty-two weeks a year. I *believed* and *remembered* and *knew* of the existence of many stories that were never found in anthologies representing either the history of the short story genre or the best examples of the short story genre or the short stories of a particular period or region that had been written by women. I was greeted with raised eyebrows, disbelieving smirks, and dismissive remarks. The general tone and content was this: "Well, certainly they can't be any good or we would know about them. What are they? Genre stories?"

As I continued to read women's short stories, I began to unname the genres and the sub-genres. I couldn't explain, even to myself, why I was doing that. I only knew that those terms stood between me and

the stories, between me and my most authentic responses to the stories. It wasn't until my friend Joanna Russ, the great science fiction
novelist, short story writer, and critic, sent me a copy of Ursula Le
Guin's short story "She Unnames Them" that I began to understand
why I had begun to unname the literary genres and sub-genres: "They
seemed far closer than when their names had stood between myself
and them. . . ."[33]

Once I understand that my own prejudices were triggered by the
terms of literary classification, I came to a Janus-like decision: in my
reading and choosing of stories I would make no distinctions based on
sub-genres of short stories. At the same time, I would, in my anthologies, do my best to include as broad a spectrum of sub-genres as possible.

So in this collection of mother/daughter stories, the following sub-
genres appear: cautionary tale, coming of age story, flash fiction, short-
short story, literary story, young adult fiction, literary regionalism,
experimental fiction, science fiction, fantasy, realism, naturalism, working class stories, commemorative stories, various ethnicity stories, lesbian stories, disability stories, Occasional stories, political stories,
stream of consciousness stories, domestic violence stories, and so forth.
Note that the categories of sub-genres overlap; one story may represent
four or five. Just as multiple voices and points of views enrich us, so do
multiple genres, approached without preconceptions about the value
inherent in the sub-genres, deepen us.

5. Loss: The Lost, The Missing, The Stolen, The Dead

"The loss of the daughter to the mother, the mother to the
daughter, is the essential female tragedy."
—Adrienne Rich, *Of Woman Born.*

The devastation of daughter-loss is memorialized and mythologized for
all times in the passionate and grief-stricken story of Demeter and
Persephone. This story has survived from ancient times to enter the
realm of myth, archetypal theory, psychoanalytic theory, and literary
symbolism.[34] In our contemporary culture the myth has been used to
explore all kinds of maternal loss, from the pain of miscarriage, still-

birth, or infant death to, as in Beth Brant's 1985 "A Long Story," the abduction of Native American children from their birth families and communities by a government determined to destroy Native culture and solidarity, to the loss of custody by lesbian mothers, also in "The Long Story," to the abduction of fat children by a size-ist medical establishment, to the class-based abduction of children by protective services, to the loss via the transformation of the dependent girl into an independence-seeking, sexualized adolescent young woman, to the translation of the daughter into the wife or partner of a peer, to the always unnatural seeming death of the daughter before the mother because of illness, accident, criminal assault, war, or suicide.[35] Every one of these kinds of losses has been memorialized, grieved, recorded in a short story by a woman. Beth Brant's "A Long Story" is eloquent in its exploration of this painful loss; her story has the resonance of myth.

However, stories of daughter-loss are more historically recent than stories of mother-loss.[36] The most reasonable explanation for that has to do with the circumstances of life for mothers before birth control developments made it possible for a woman to control her fertility, before chores such as cloth making, clothes making, laundry, and food preservation were mechanized and commercialized, and before childbed fever was eradicated. Mothers rarely outlived their daughters to record their painful losses—except for the case of infant loss.

In the nineteenth century, infant mortality was so rampant that women created a new religion, a new concept of deity, to comfort them for the multiple maternal losses. Despite the extreme grief of infant and toddler deaths, those losses weren't mourned in significantly gendered ways. It is true, today, too, that the short stories that concern the illnesses and deaths of very young children are not stories in which the gender of the sick baby is most salient.[37] But once a child enters school, gender becomes significant and the stories of mother and child become, specifically, stories of mothers and daughters or mothers and sons.

A crucial aspect of the Demeter-Persephone story is that Demeter gets her daughter back from hell, from the underworld of the dead, for at least part of the year. A reading of "Noises" by Jane Bradley is particularly enriched by familiarity with this myth.

Reciprocally, the loss of mothers has often been commemorated in women's writing. Alice Brown's and Merrill Joan Gerber's stories in this collection, "The Way of Peace" and "Anna's Archive," are both memorial stories. A powerful story in the sub-genre of daughters processing their mothers' deaths is "Up a Tree" by Jessamyn West, from her collection *Crimson Ramblers of the World, Farewell* (Harcourt Brace Jovanovich, 1970). As is true with the representation of any particular subject, theme, or group of writers, the creation and publication of anthologies about mothers and daughters have both increased in number and became more specialized in terms of focus and genre. Collections of writing about the loss of mothers range from the 1992 collection of personal essays, *Loss of the Ground-Note: Women Writing About the Loss of Their Mothers* edited by Helen Vozenilek to Sinclair Browning's 2002 *Feathers Brush My Heart: True Stories of Mothers Touching Their Daughters' Lives After Death.*[38]

It would be possible to assemble an entire collection of daughters' stories about mothers' deaths from my files and still face the difficult decisions about which to include and which to leave out—until another time.

6. Transitions: Losses and Gains, Time and History

There is no permanence. There is only transition. And yet many people talk of transition as if it were some sort of passage between periods of stability. We are no longer even certain when the transition from life to death occurs. From the moment we are born, we are transitioning to death, but what actually constitutes the instant when life ceases is more in question than it has ever been. So what is meant when we talk about life-transitions in literature? Certain periods are generally defined as being more "about" change than others. For instance, adolescence is generally viewed as a critical transition period in the life of a person and in the relationships they have with those around them. Alma Luz Villanueva's story "Her Choice" is, in many ways, an archetypal story of the transformation of a mother's daughter into a sister-woman, of an adolescent girl into an independent woman. The relationship between mother and daughter is transfigured by the change.

In a way quite similar to the Villanueva story, Nicholasa Mohr's story "Tell the Truth…" is also about an important shift in the mother/daughter relationship. When Vickie lies for her mother, she is not just "obeying" her mother; she is making a crucial choice to align herself with the matriarchy instead of the patriarchy. This story might also have been called "Her Choice."[39]

As the grandmother of two little girls, Jasmine Grace, six years old, and Sarah Jade, three years old, I am seeing transitions every bit as dramatic and relationship-transforming as the adolescent to adult. I watch first one and then the next child evolve from that period of life when all of safety, security, and happiness is represented by the joyful, monkey-like clinging to Mommy to the period when a child blithely waves good-bye and heads off for a weekend with Grandma and Grandpa. The mother loses her gratifying incarnation as the Holy of Holies and becomes Mom-the-Rock-of-Ages-who-picks-us-up, prepares food for us, puts bandages on the ouchies, pats our backs till we fall asleep, and meets all our little animal needs. Her little ones wave good-bye and don't look back while the mother's responsibilities and workload aren't reduced. As far as I know, this transition has seldom been rendered in literature.

It is interesting to speculate about the relative absence of attention to this earlier transition. Could it be that the toddler transition comes at a time in a woman's life when her workload is so enormous that she doesn't have time or energy to write about it and so the stories that might be told get lost?

The adolescent departures have been thoroughly documented time and again. And could the frequent publication of literary renderings about the female adolescent transition to self-determining young woman have something to do with the perception of the young woman as now sexually available or attractive or vulnerable to men?

7. Conclusion

What has been told, what remains to be told, what is told in these stories and the stories in my files, the stories as yet unrecovered, the stories that are told in poetry and song, in personal confessional essays and in scholarly articles, in the eighty-four thousand plus books listed on amazon.com, are each only part of the whole story which, taken all together, will never finish being told. The whole story can only be known by someone who can hear or read all of them simultaneously without giving precedence to any one of them, giving equal value to all of them. It is in the chorus of voices rather than in any individual voice that the whole story resides.

NOTES

1. I refer to Rich here as white and ethnically undifferentiated although a number of years after the publication of this book she claimed a Jewish identity. Published in 1986, *Your Native Land, Your Life: Poems* includes her essay "Split at the Root: An essay on Jewish identity," first published in 1982.

2. Summary sent to me by Dr. Carlson via email on July 17, 2004 after a lengthy instant messenger conversation discussing the contemporary uses of this myth. Dr. Carlson's book, cited below, explores these issues in great depth.

3. The third edition was published by Cleis Press in 2001. Barbara Grier, writing under the pseudonym "Gene Damon," began writing book reviews for the second (known) lesbian periodical in the U.S. in 1956. She later went on to found, (with her partner), Naiad Press, the first lesbian publishing company. Grier's mother, Mrs. Doris Lyles, published "My Daughter is a Lesbian" in 1958 in *The Ladder*. She wrote that though she did not understand her daughter's "association" with her "mate," she thought "there are no two more normal persons alive than my daughter and her charming associate." The tone of Grier's mother's essay is very similar to the tone of most of the essays in Rifkin's collection. Later issues of *The Ladder* documented a lesbian mothers' discussion group. This information is condensed from "Every Magazine is New Until You've Read It" by Linda Rosewood Hooper, March 1990. *http://people.ucsc.edu/~rosewood/writing/essays/the%20ladder complete.htm#What_Was_The_Ladder.*

4. The Association for Research on Mothering can be reached at *http://www.yorku.ca/crm*. The brochure reads, in part, as follows:

> The Association for Research on Mothering (ARM) is the first feminist international organization devoted specifically to the topic of mothering-motherhood. ARM was officially launched in September 1998...Members include: scholars, writers, activists, social workers, midwives, nurses, therapists, lawyers, teachers, politicians, parents, students, and artists. They come from more than 20 countries, as well as numerous local and international agencies, governmental and social, and community groups that work for, and on behalf of mothers.

5. For an exploration of these issues, see "Mothers, Daughters, Diaries: Literacy, Relationship, and Cultural Context" by Judy Nolte Temple and Suzanne L. Bunkers, pp.197-216, in *Nineteenth-Century Women Learn to Write*, edited with an introduction by Catherine Hobbs, University Press of Virginia, 1995.

6. For those who read French, or who studied French beyond the first year, the

famous letters of Madame de Sevigny to her daughter will be familiar. In Provence, there is still an annual summer festival in which the letters are read and celebrated.

7. The first version of *Freaky Friday* was a Disney production in 1976, the second was a made-for-television movie in 1995.

8. Musical grieving for lost mothers is neither new nor gender limited. In 1925, Jack Yellen (lyrics) and Lew Pollack (music) wrote "My Yiddishe Mama" for Sophie Tucker (1884-1966); she recorded the song in English on one side, Yiddish on the reverse. It was a huge hit in 1928 and continued to be part of the repertoire of many singers from Billie Holiday to Connie Francis to Neil Sedaka to Mandy Patinkin. The song is a lament about the loss of Yellen's mother.

9. The book was published by HarperCollins in 1978 and it has been in print ever since. The film came out in 1981 and, after its initial failure at the box office, it became a cult classic.

10. See the expanded version of my *Women in the Trees: U.S. Women's Short Stories about Battering and Resistance, 1839-2000*, The Feminist Press, 2004, for more stories that portray and explore these issues.

11. In an interview with Mario Materassi, "On the Edge of the Action," which took place in Florence, Italy in the fall of 1996.

12. "…the Borderlands are physically present wherever two or more cultures edge each other, where people of different races occupy the same territory, where under, lower, middle and upper classes touch, where the space between two individuals shrinks with intimacy." From "Preface" to *Borderlands/La Frontera: The New Mestiza*, by Gloria Anzaldua, San Francisco: Aunt Lute Books, 1987.

13. Traditionally these terms have referred to the custom of marrying someone outside of (ex-) or inside of (end-) your tribe, clan, religious community, kinship group, etc. The concern has been, primarily, with the way the children will be reared. Which culture will be preserved for another generation while the other is allowed to languish? Over time, however, the issue has been complicated by the recognition of multiple identities. Consider, for instance, the 2002 case of Sharon Duchesneau and her lesbian partner, Candace McCullough, selecting their sperm donor on the basis of his family history of deafness in order, as McCullough explained, "to increase our chances of having a baby who is deaf." Their choice to deliberately engineer a child who would be deaf, as they are, aroused bitter controversy. Is deafness a culture or a disability? The argument raged. But there was no talk of engineering either a daughter or homosexual child. So the "very deaf" son born to them shares only one aspect of their shared cultures/identities. As deaf lesbians, are they an endogamous or an exogamous couple? Do they share religious or ethnic identities? See *http://www.jewishworldreview.com/0402/mcelroy041202.asp*

14. Some of the poems, stories, and personal essays (creative nonfiction) in *The Milk of Almonds: Italian American Women Writers on Food and Culture* edited by Louise DeSalvo and Edvidge Giunta, The Feminist Press, 2002.

15. From "A Candle in a Gale Wind" by Alice Childress in *Black Women Writers*

(1950-1980): A Critical Evaluation by Mari Evans, Anchor Books, 1984, pp.113-114.

16. For a discussion of literary regionalism and immigrant literature in the late nineteenth- and early twentieth-century in the United States and how those literary movements were particularly important in their connections to women's literature of embodiment, see my Afterword in *The Strange History of Suzanne LaFleshe and Other Stories of Women and Fatness*. The Feminist Press, 2003, pp.237-240.

17. There have been ethnic community publications as long as sufficiently large ethnic communities to support such enterprises have existed in the United States. Often these papers can only be found via the ethnic shops in the ethnic enclaves or in their religious institutions. But Finnish, Italian, Ukranian, Polish, Russian, Serbian, Yiddish, German, Arabic, etc. newspapers were subscribed to regularly by the public libraries in cities with major ethnic communities as long as the libraries and the publications have been in existence. *Rafu Shimpo*, the largest Japanese-American publication, was established in 1903. Poems have usually found a place in these newspapers because—especially when they are very short—they can handily fill out a column of print. *Rafu Shimpo* has provided a home for some of Hisaye Yamamoto's finest work, began publishing the lovely stories by Wakako Yamauchi in the 1960s, included work by performance artist Denise Uyehara and multigeneric writer Patricia Wakida. *Al Jadid* magazine, launched in 1995, is an Arab-American publication edited by Elie Chalala, an adjunct professor of political science at Santa Monica College where he teaches politics and history of the Middle East. *Al Jadid* includes fiction by Arab-American women such as Diana Abu-Jaber.

18. Dr. Julia Penelope, linguist, early lesbian feminist separatist, one of the founders of the fields of women's studies and lesbian studies, and, currently an independent scholar and freelance editor, in an email on July 16, 2004, reminds me specifically "of lesbian journals such as *The Ladder* (launched in October 1956), *Sinister Wisdom* (launched in 1976 and still publishing), *Common Lives, Lesbian Lives* (begun in 1977), *Lesbian News* (LA), *Chrysalis*, and *Conditions*. For years, *Sinister Wisdom, Common Lives, Lesbian Lives*, and *Conditions* published cutting-edge lesbian political theory, much of it still taught in college and university courses. They also published a lot of fiction." In 1975, Arno Press (now defunct) published a complete, bound photo-reprint of *The Ladder*.

19. E.g., for instance, Mary McCarthy's anthology history during and after her marriage to critic and literary historian Edmund Wilson; Caroline Gordon during and after her marriage to critic and anthologist Alan Tate; Shirley Jackson while married to literary theorist Edgar Stanley Hyman and after her death; Katharine Fullerton Gerould, longtime fiancée of Morton Fullerton, Edith Wharton's famous lover. These wonderful writers are examples of women who "got their due", i.e. literary recognition appropriate to their writing, only while they were married to or otherwise romantically involved with men with significant power in the literary

world. All of them have since disappeared from the anthologies. And we feminists, bent on the job of recovering those who have been lost, who have never had their due, let these women fall further by the wayside. What is to be done?

20. A paradigmatic example of what I am talking about is found in the opening lines of John Merchant's January 1998 essay, "Recent Polish-American Fiction" from *The Sarmatian Review* (Vol. 18, No. 1): "There has always been a Polish-American voice in American literature, though it has not always been an *English* one and it has not been one generally heard beyond the Polish-American community." *The Sarmatian Review* is a triannual publication of the Polish Institute of Houston. The journal "deals with Polish, Central, and Eastern European affairs, and it explores their implications for the United States." It can found online at *http://www.ruf.rice.edu/%7Esarmatia/404/242mast.html.*

21. Writing in the same 1998 issue of *The Sarmatian Review*, the uncredited editor makes this point well: "In order to be noticed in American Society, a common-interest group (we prefer this designation to the ideologized 'minority') has to be described in a language that incorporates the idiom of the day and remains comprehensible to the group in question."

22. "Influenced by the psychoanalytic theory of Freud and others, many researchers of the mid-20th century focused on the relationship between family dynamics and the onset of schizophrenia. Specifically, researchers emphasized the poor quality of the mother-child relationship as crucial to the development of schizophrenia. The type of parent thought to induce schizophrenia was termed a *schizophrenogenic mother.*" *http://www.ns.purhcase.edu/psych/Psychobio_of_Schizophrenia/history/history.htm.*

23. "From the 1950s through the 1970s, children with autism were widely thought to be victims of inadequate parenting. Influenced by Psychologist Bruno Bettelheim, mental health and medical professionals claimed that autism was the product of mothers who were cold, distant, rejecting—unable to 'bond properly.' They were labeled 'refrigerator mothers.' Though this disastrous theory began to be seriously challenged in the mid-1960s, its effects lingered for decades. For an exploration of this form of mother-blaming, see the film *Refrigerator Mothers* by David Simpson, J.J. Hanley, and Gordon Quinn, Kartemquin Films." *http://www.fanlight.com/catalog/films/*

24. See my collection *The Strange History of Suzanne LaFleshe and Other Stories of Women and Fatness*, The Feminist Press, 2003, for stories that portray various and very different maternal strategies for dealing with daughters who have "too much" body, especially "The Food Farm" by Kit Reed and "This Was Meant to Be" by Alberta Hughes Wahl.

25. We certainly see the good hair/bad hair issue at play in "The Lawd Don't Like Ugly!" The mother-figure who can "handle" that deviation becomes the mother-figure whose authority the daughter-figure accepts.

26. Date: Thu, 01 Jul 2004 18:58:47 –0000
Source: Private online listserv dealing with size acceptance
Re: Dieting Makes Little Girls Fatter, Study Finds
Over at bigfatblog.com recently a lot of the women were responding to that study that said that many/most fat women began dieting as girls, and I was shocked at how many posters said they had developed disordered eating patterns in response to their parents' (usually mothers') efforts to feed them starvation diets, ridicule and humiliate them, etc. Clearly that's an ideal way to ensure your child will have problems with weight and body image.

27. From an email from Dr. Caplan to Susan Koppelman, Monday, July 19, 2004.

28. From an email from Dr. Carlson to Susan Koppelman, Monday, July 19, 2004.

29. See the discussion of "The Disgraceful Mother" and the story "Old Mother Goose" in the original introduction to the collection, pp. xxviii-xxx. See also the story "Forty-Five" by Fannie Hurst in my collection, *The Stories of Fannie Hurst*, The Feminist Press, 2004. In this story, a daughter in the full bloom of a young woman on the hunt for a husband nags her mother into a complete remake of her face and body with entirely unexpected results.

30. Miss Malin was my English teacher for two years at Cleveland Heights High School, Cleveland Heights, Ohio. We remained in touch until she died at the age of 104.

31. I was one of those who didn't talk about my "private" reading. But you can be certain that I, like most lit majors, read well beyond the syllabi! The secrecy associated with reading pornography is minor compared to the secrecy associated with reading pulp romances! I am delighted that The Feminist Press is reprinting the classic pulps from the 1930s, '40s, and '50s.

32. *Moby Dick* is an 1851 American novel by Herman Melville that has achieved iconic status among certain scholars but seldom bought or read unless assigned. However, from among those once upon a time assigned to read the novel, a fan community has evolved. *Finnegan's Wake* is a 1939 novel by James Joyce, an Irish author from Dublin who has also achieved iconic status and a community of fans who participate in activities related to James Joyce that remind me very much of the *Star Trek* community.

33. From LeGuin, U.K. (1987). *Buffalo Gals and Other Animal Presences*. Markham, Ontario: Penguin, pp. 194-196.

"LeGuin tells the tale of a woman who asks Adam to take back the name he had given her just as he had given names to all the animals that the Creator had brought before him. She had already persuaded the animals and the birds and the insects and the fishes to accept namelessness. They had agreed and decided to give back their names. For most of them the act of unnaming had been very easy since the names given to them had left them utterly indifferent. She must have suspected that for humans the effect of unnaming might be quite dramatic. The effect she had been after, of becoming more attached to the world, was even more powerful than she had anticipated. After the unnaming she had discovered with surprise how close she felt to the creatures around her.

They seemed far closer than when their names had stood between myself and them like a clear barrier: so close that my fear of them and their fear of me became one and the same fear. (p.195)

When things get unnamed we can no longer ignore the hidden contours of the phenomena that words tend to hide like blankets of snow. For Adam language was only a tool to gain dominion over the earth and its inhabitants." Max Van Manen, "The Pathic Nature of Inquiry and Nursing," in *Nursing and the Experience of Illness: Phenomenology in Practice*, edited by Irena Madjar and Jo Walton. London: Routledge, pp.17-35.

34. I recommend in particular *Life's Daughter/Death's Bride: Inner Transformations Through the Goddess Demeter/Persephone* by Kathie Carlson, (Shambhala Publications, 1997) for an examination of the role of this myth in contemporary life.

35. See Cheri Erdman's *Nothing to Lose: A Guide to Sane Living in a Larger Body*, HarperSanFrancisco, 1995, pp.3-4, for her narrative of being sent, as a five-year old, to a residential treatment facility for children for one year because of her weight.

36. A moving story of daughter-loss is another of Alma Luz Villanueva's stories, "The Burden" about a mother who boxes up the belongings of her thirteen-year-old daughter who was kidnapped and murdered. In *Weeping Women: La Llornona anf Other Stories* (Bilingual Press/Editorial Bilingüe). Pamela Sargent's story "The Shrine" also speaks to daughter-loss. It is a story of the perfect daughter who ruined everything by having a breakdown—depression—after her first year at Wellesley, returning home to find her mother had maintained her bedroom as a shrine to the perfect girl she once was. Sargent's story first appeared in Rod Serling's *The Twilight Zone Magazine* in December 1982 and was included in *The Best of Pamela Sargent*, edited by Martin H. Greenberg, Academy Chicago Publishers, 1987.

37. See particularly in this regard "People Like That Are The Only People Here" by Lorrie Moore which originally appeared in *The New Yorker*, and was reprinted in *BASS 1998* and *The O.Henry Prize Awards 1998*. It is written by a mother who discovers her baby son has cancer.

38. There are online sites dedicated to mutual support for motherless daughters, such as *http://www.geocities/motherlessdaughtersonline.html*, and local and regional groups that meet to share grief and consolation, stories, strategies, brunches and those occasions when being motherless is most painful.

39. See "Mothers and Daughters Up Against the Patriarchy, pp. xvi–xix in this book for an exploration of this idea. Nicholasa Mohr's story "Tell the Truth . . ." should be read in this context.

WORKS CITED/RECOMMENDED READING

Baker, Christina L. & Christina Baker Kline (Eds). (1996). *The Conversation Begins: Mothers and Daughters Talk About Living Feminism.* New York: Bantam Books.

Braziel, Jana Evans & Kathleen LeBesco (Eds). (2001). *Bodies Out of Bounds: Fatness and Transgression.* University of California Press.

Caplan, Paula. (1989). *Don't Blame Mother.* New York: HarperCollins. An expanded and updated introduction was published in 2000 and the book remains in print.

Carbo, Nick & Eileen Tabios (Eds). (2000). *Babaylan: An Anthology of Filipina and Filipina American Writers.* San Francisco: Aunt Lute Books.

Edut, Ophira (Ed). (2004). *Body Outlaws: Rewriting the Rules of Beauty & Body Image,* 3rd Edition. With a Foreword by Rebecca Walker. Seattle: Seal Press. Originally published as *Adios, Barbie* in 1998.

Friday, Nancy (1977). *My Mother, My Self: The Daughter's Search for Identity.* New York: Delacorte Press. Tenth anniversary edition published by Bantam Dell in 1987. Twentieth anniversary edition published by Delta Books in 1997.

Koppelman, Susan (Ed). (2004). *Women in the Trees: U.S. Women's Short Stories About Battering and Resistance, 1839-2000.* New York: The Feminist Press. First edition published by Beacon Press, 1996.

Koppelman, Susan (Ed). (2003). *The Strange History of Suzanne LaFleshe and Other Stories of Women and Fatness.* New York: The Feminist Press.

Koppelman, Susan (Ed). (1985). *Between Mothers and Daughters: Stories Across a Generation.* New York: The Feminist Press.

Koppelman, Susan (Ed). (1984). *The Other Woman: Stories of Two Women and a Man.* New York: The Feminist Press.

Layne, Linda L. (Ed). (1999). *Transformative Motherhood: On Giving and Getting in a Consumer Culture.* New York University Press. This collection of U.S. ethnographic studies is a useful adjunct for courses in anthropology, family studies, women's studies, and disability studies.

Lifshin, Lyn L. (Ed). (1978). *Tangled Vines: A Collection of Mother and Daughter Poems.* Boston: Beacon Press. Revised edition published by Harcourt Brace & Co., 1992.

Moskowitz, Faye (Ed). (1994). *Her Face in the Mirror: Jewish Women on Mothers and Daughters.* Boston: Beacon Press. Useful in both Jewish Studies and Women's Studies.

Parker, Gail (Ed). (1972). *The Oven Birds: American Women on Womanhood, 1820-1920.* New York: Doubleday. A discussion of the grief of a mother over the loss of their babies.

Rebolledo, Tey Diana and Eliana S. Rivero (Eds). (1993). *Infinite Divisions: An*

Anthology of Chicana Literature. Tucson, AZ: University of Arizona Press.

Scott-Bell, Patricia, Sheftall-Guy, Beverly, Royster, Jones, Jacqueline, Wood-Sims, Janet, Willis-Decosta, Miriam and Lucie Fultz (Eds). (1991). *Double Stitch: Black Women Write About Mothers and Daughters with Poems, Stories, and Essays.* Boston: Beacon Press.

Caroline W. Healey Dall

Annie Gray: A Tale
1848

"Annie Gray: A Tale" was written by Caroline W. Healey Dall (1822–1912) as a contribution to the 1848 volume of The Liberty Bell, *the first abolitionist literary annual, published by the Massachusetts Anti-Slavery Society from 1839 to 1853 in order to raise funds for the fight against slavery. Attributed to "The Friends of Freedom,"* The Liberty Bell *was actually edited by Maria Weston Chapman and included work by such important anti-slavery activists as Frederick Douglass and Lydia Maria Child.*

This story is similar in structure and style to many published between 1825 and 1865 in the popular gift books and annuals that dominated the literary marketplace. These stories exhibit features of such personal genres as diaries, letters, and memoirs, and such formal genres as essays and sermons. Additionally, these early stories by women echo the oral tradition, as do the early stories of other minority or oppressed cultural groups when their members begin to practice the literary arts as they have been defined by the dominant culture. This rootedness in oral tradition accounts for the recurrent use of the framing device of a story within a story.

Caroline Healey Dall, whose contributions have been overlooked until recently, was a significant figure in her own time. Her biographer, Gary Sue Goodman, feminist historian and literary critic, summarizes her achievements:

> Dall was internationally known during her lifetime as an abolitionist, social reformer, feminist leader, and prolific author. She published over thirty books and hundreds of articles in which she analyzed diverse topics, from Egyptian history to contemporary scientific controversies. A pioneer in the organized Woman's Rights

Movement, Dall co-edited the first feminist newspaper in
America, *The Una,* and wrote scholarly studies of women's
history, literature, education, legal rights, and work. She
also founded or sustained numerous progressive organizations, including an early daycare school for working
women's infants, vocational schools for women, and the
American Social Science Association, a primary catalyst of
social reform after the Civil War.

*Dall left an immense collection of manuscripts, including daily journals
written from her adolescence until her death. This remarkably detailed and frank
record allows us to reconstruct aspects of women's experience that time and
reticence have generally buried. She included many facts, explanations, and
emotional reactions that required euphemism, fictionalization, or silence in her
public writing. From adolescence, Dall confronted patriarchal myths about
woman's nature and women's roles with naked truths about real women's lives.
She exposed common abuses fostered by women's economic dependence and
political powerlessness. But her father's tyranny, her mother's madness, and the
failure of her own marriage remained family secrets.*

*Dall's vocational choice is often attributed to her father's teaching. Mark
Healey, a wealthy Boston merchant and Unitarian liberal, taught her to read,
sent her to private schools, hired governesses and tutors, and bought her expensive
lyceum lecture tickets. He taught her that she had a responsibility to develop her
talents, to test all conventions by reason and conscience, and to discard the
superstitious dogmas that hindered the social march toward perfection. Noting
her facility for impromptu storytelling, her father even encouraged her to become
"a literary woman." "To his patience, prudence, and daily teaching," Dall
recalled, "I owe most of what I am, especially the self-control which has prevented
me from becoming the victim of ill-health."*

*Yet Dall's manuscripts reveal more complex causes for her feminism and her
powerful drive for self-expression through writing. It seems that her father's
unusually active role in her education was not chosen for feminist reasons, but
to compensate for her mother's invalidism. After almost dying during her
daughter's birth, Caroline Foster Healey endured nine more pregnancies during
the next sixteen years. Her temperament became erratic: she was often reclusive,
depressed, suspicious, hostile, and brooding. Dall later understood her mother's
eccentricity as "melancholia" and forgave her that she was "never a mother to
me" during her childbearing years. But as a child she felt abandoned, unloved,
and deprived of the perfect nurturing sympathy of the ideal mother depicted by
her contemporaries.*

*Although liberal, Mark Healey still expected his first-born child to cultivate
the feminine qualities prescribed by society—the "true womanhood" that historian
Barbara Welter has identified as "purity, piety, submissiveness, and domesticity."*

Mr. Healey demanded that Caroline assume her mother's household responsibilities while simultaneously continuing to study and to write; yet he removed her from school prematurely for failing to improve her opportunities. He judged her by perfectionist standards, criticized her harshly, and praised her rarely. He had no empathy for her struggles with heavy, often conflicting duties. He also prevented her from seeking other sympathy or guidance by forbidding her to speak of her mother's symptoms to anyone.

Annie Gray's death-bed confession has an element of fantasy for Dall, whose mother never confided the reasons for her depression and insanity. "Annie Gray: A Tale" not only illustrates the injustice of slavery, but also depicts women's sexual vulnerability, shame, and enforced secrecy. Rape, forced marriages, and unwanted pregnancies were taboo topics; even for an outspoken feminist, it was far easier to portray a woman as a victim of slavery or a "victim of ill-health," than as a victim of male lust and tyranny within the patriarchal family.

"His rest, his labor, pastime, strength and health,
Were only portions of his master's wealth;—
His love—O name not love—while men can doom
The fruit of love, to Slavery from the womb."—MONTGOMERY.

"And what man seeing this,
And having human feelings, does not blush,
And hang his head to think himself a man?"—COWPER.

On the finely macadamized road which leads from La Prairie to Montreal, a number of low stone cottages attract, by the quaintness of their aspect, the attention of the traveller. They seem to link America to the Old World, and prove that some few of her sons, at least, retained a love for its elder cities. As one saunters along this road at night-fall, while the red sun still lingers in the west, many things conspire to remind him that he has passed the "line of the States;" first of all, the broad, low houses,—built of stone, and floored with clay,—with overhanging attics, without casements, protected only by large wooden shutters, until the season becomes severe; then, the crowds of foreign-looking inmates, the lazy and untidy thronging the doors in antique costume, or smoking under the stoop in bed-gowns of blue calico, quilted petticoats of white, stout shoes, and broad straw hats,—the men wearing closely fitting provincial caps, decorated with tassels of red or blue, according to the character of their ancestral blood. The active still lingered amid the harvest, even at the late autumn season in which our tale commences, fully bedecked with pipes and petticoats. But many a happy circle, in a more fortunate interior, glistens with true English tidiness. The white-washed walls betray a love of cleanliness; which the trim children, the baby with its wide cap-border of snowy lace, clustering about the frugal board,—so tempting in its niceness to the tired passer-by—only confirm. A little further on, one detects many peculiarities, significant of the mixed races which inhabit the land, and the absence of district schools. The baker has painted over his door a most unnatural sheaf of wheat, and two crusty looking loaves, while the ale-house rejoices in a rough board, which, swinging to and fro, tempts its poor victim to a freshly tapped barrel, and a foaming glass.

Glad to find himself on ground which, if not wholly free, is certainly released from the fetters which bind his own soil, the American hardly remarks the many signs of slavery to sloth, to drinking, and the pipe, which painfully surround him. The sunny landscape, enlivened by groups of gaily dressed women, in the field, a thing unseen at home, cheats him into pleasant thoughts.

About a mile from La Prairie, he passes, on the right, a huge stone farm-house, of the olden sort. The eaves run back to the ground; heavy casements and broad shutters protect it from the winter winds. The enclosure seems neatly kept, and just above the ancient well-sweep, on which the large slow-growing lichens have kept a faithful tally of years, stands the stone crucifix. Beautiful symbol of a faith that he despises, it lifts itself up, with broad arms, to the height of twenty feet, enclosing in its bosom a time-worn shield—once a beautiful medallion—recording the sufferings of our Lord. It was a fair superstition, he thinks, which thus united the living spring and the Rock of Ages; and while he bows his head, and the now vanishing sun sends mellow gleams of light through oak and sumach and broad shadowy maples, suggesting pleasant dreams of the stained windows of those "prayers built into stone"—the once seen cathedrals of his father-land,—the vespers that his childhood whispered at his mother's knee, hallow afresh his heart and memory.

It was about four years ago that a traveller found himself aroused from such dreams by the coarse voice of a woman, who, as she closed the door of a small cottage on the other side of the dusty way, looked in at the window, saying, in French, "If your mother is'nt better by the midnight, Matty, you must come for me." We have always hated eaves-droppers, and have no desire to invest any such with the dignity of a hero. Our traveller was no philanthropist, but he was still young enough to be curious; and he crossed the road, to the cottage, towards which these words had been directed; and, sheltered by a wide shutter, the projecting hedge, and deepening twilight, he gazed directly in. A neater room than ordinary met his view; and there was something tasteful in the arrangement of the white muslin curtains, about a bed which stood near the window, that at once directed his attention to "Matty's mother." A female, whose light olive skin, rendered uncommonly transparent by illness, contrasted painfully with large voluptuous eyes, and glossy curls of extreme length, lay stretched upon the white pillow. As he gazed, a sweet but startling voice said to the girl who bent over it,— "Matty, open the shutters, that I may once more see the fading light." The girl approached him, and with a vehemence which brought the prominent Roman features of the stranger into some danger, threw back the shutter, and turned again to the bedside. Rapid as her movements were, the traveller read in features very unlike her mother's, (a plain but animated countenance and a somewhat awkward frame,) the history of a heart and head such as he had seldom met in one like her, indisputably of African blood.

What was it in the face of the girl, in the voice of the mother, that startled him with by-gone memories? But he came here to listen. "Matty," said the invalid, with a faltering voice, "I have always told you, that, at the last hour, you should know your mother's entire history. I have no longer the right to keep it back. It has been, alas! simply from the fear of agitating you with its horrors, that the communication has been so long delayed. Matty, your mother was a Slave!"

"I guessed it, mother," said the girl, "I guessed it, when I saw you rise from your sick bed, with kindling eyes, to shelter a poor fugitive."

"I would have laid down my life for her," said the invalid

earnestly; "but listen, for my breath is short. I was born on a
retired plantation in Westmoreland county, Virginia, within a
short distance of the spot where the great Washington first saw
the light. My mother I never knew. For the offence of giving
me birth, she was exiled from her home. My father, it was said,
was the favorite son of the old lady whom I remember as my
first mistress. Mrs. Elsie Gray was wealthy, generous, and aristocratic. Her property, at her death, which occurred when I was
about six years old, chiefly devolved upon my father; but for a
reason which I can easily guess, she did not choose to entrust
me to his care. I was bright, and, Matty,—I hope that there is
no harm in saying it now,—I was very beautiful. I had become
a favorite; and to her only other grand-child and namesake, a
girl about my own age, I was consigned, in an affectionate letter.
I saw that letter many years afterwards, and I cannot forget that
the old lady entreated her dear Elsie to shield me from what
she termed the *dangers* that had menaced my mother; and to
keep me, through life, carefully by her side. It was owing,
however, to the indolence of my new mistress, who resided in
the city of Georgetown, rather than to the old lady's recommen-
dation, that I received an excellent education. I was expected to
amuse and occupy my young mistress; and when she was too
wilful to study, I learned her tasks and taught them to her by
various devices. I slept on a trundle-bed at her side—she could
never bear me out of her sight—and as we grew older I read
aloud to her, while she was seated at her embroidery, or pursued
the quiet occupations of her station. My father died soon after
Madam Gray, and the estate passed into the hands of Elsie's
parents. For a number of years, we passed our summers in
Westmoreland; and groups of gay friends often accompanied
us. These were our most precious years of unfolding womanhood; they were spent in reading, in light employments, and
the joyous relaxations suiting our age. Rapidly as Elsie had
unfolded in beauty, and many as were her admirers, there were
not wanting those among them who had dared to whisper that
I was the lovelier; and I knew that it was true. You cannot
conceive, dear Matty, all that I suffered at such hours. In the
city, I was always in attendance on my mistress, unless, indeed,
at the private festival,—but it was always with her hat or shawl

hanging on my arm, and in a position which betokened my dependence; but in lonely Westmoreland such distinctions were not possible. In our rural festivities all depended upon my wit, my taste, and above all, *my activity*. I was in constant requisition; and so cultivated was my mind, and so fair my face,—for one of African blood,—that twice, dear Matty, I listened to words of affection from one who fancied himself my equal, and answered them with these few words,—'I am a Slave.' The first time, I can truly say, the words gave me no pain, save that which followed in the consciousness of my unprotected position,—of the impossibility of my ever marrying, in a manner that would satisfy at once myself and others. But painful as these thoughts were, they were soon banished by Elsie's affectionate care, and her childish promises, that her home should always be mine. I had been named for a great-aunt of Elsie's, and was familiarly known as Annie Gray.

"It is the custom of some Slaveholders to give their own surnames to their Slaves, and where we were known, this excited no surprise; but in Westmoreland it occasioned awkward mistakes. Among the summers that we passed there, the last two will ever remain impressed upon my mind. They were the last before my Elsie was married. There went with us, at these times, but two friends. One was a gay and dissipated man, named Meredith—my future master; the other, a distant connexion of Elsie's, from the North,—one who had been abroad, who had seen Wilberforce and Clarkson, who was the pupil of Channing. Until he came among us I knew little of Slavery,—but he expounded it; he set it before us in its true light; he pleaded against it; and in our hours of leisure he read to us from the books which he most valued. Under his influence my mind and heart expanded; a great change worked itself within me; I interested myself in the other Slaves; I tried to teach them; I talked to them of freedom, when now, for the first time, I understood it. My mistress liked to listen to him, for he was handsome and eloquent; and Meredith delighted to 'cut him up' for her amusement. He could not but feel my quiet sympathy; and though few were the words exchanged between us, we well understood each other. I never thought of loving *him*,—for I felt that I was not his mate; but he,—he met me at the table, at the fireside, and on the green sward. He little dreamt of what I knew.

"I have told you, that the first time I confessed my situation to one thus deceived, it gave me little pain; but the second,—I thank God that he did not require me to inflict all I then suffered, on myself!—the words came from Elsie's lips. It was at the close of our second summer, together,—a few weeks before Elsie's marriage. We were about returning to the city, and had gone in playful pilgrimage to the spot where Washington was born. Elsie gathered fig-leaves from a few venerable stumps, as we sat gazing at the lonely chimney which marks the site of his early home. Arthur rallied her on her inconsistency, spoke of the Slaves, and of the great beauty and distinguished ability of some. 'With all your chivalry,' exclaimed Elsie, 'I do not believe that you have ever guessed our Annie to be a Slave!'

"I sat at some distance, and my back was turned; but I could hear the husky voice, with which he asked, 'But she is surely your cousin, Elsie?'

" 'Ask Meredith,' was her only reply.

" 'No,' said Meredith, 'we do not believe that old story; she is only a Slave. To be sure Elsie's mother thinks that the old lady intended to free her, but she died before her letter was finished. So much the better for us. The said letter is the greatest gem in the old lady's casket.'

" 'But you,—surely *you* will emancipate her?' urged Arthur, turning to Elsie.

" 'That will be as Meredith says;' she answered, laughing.

"I heard their retreating footsteps, but I did not know all that I endured until some hours after, when I found Arthur bathing my forehead in spring-water, and read, in his pale face, his apprehensions for me. He staid but a moment after I was restored, and it was to utter, in a voice which he vainly strove to render steady, these few words,—'Find that letter, see if what they have told me is true,—then, fly with the rising sun. You know your route.' He pointed to the north, dropped a purse at my feet, and was gone.

"Often had I held within my hand, as I replaced Elsie's jewels, the precious letter of whose character I was so ignorant. This night, ere I retired, I did not hesitate to conceal it in my bosom.

I knew that Elsie had not looked at it for many years. I saw that the paper was rudely and *freshly* torn, but I was not prepared for the loving words I found within. I no longer doubted that freedom should have been mine, and I believed that Meredith stood between me and it. A Slave, then, I must ever be. I never saw Arthur again. In the morning Elsie learned that he had gone; and I pined in silence, for I knew too little of the world to follow his advice. I doubted not that the letter which had been so carelessly kept had contained either an express provision for my freedom, or a declaration of intentions equivalent to this. Why Meredith had destroyed it, I was too soon to know. Often I wandered alone over the beautiful heights, and under the warm sunshine gazed down upon the blue Potomac, the broad and fruitful vineyards of the Jesuits, and the rose-encircled dwellings of our friends; and, while my heart swelled, and my mind aspired, I asked of God—if I alone were created in vain!

"Elsie was married. Up to this time my duties had been nominal, but we now removed to a place of Meredith's, called Northwood, in South Carolina. Here I was entrusted with the duties of a housekeeper, and expected to confine myself to them. If I appeared at table, it was only to carve or to make tea; and when, a short time after, Meredith persecuted me with his dishonorable addresses, I no longer wondered that Elsie was dispirited, indifferent, and every way unlike her former self. Meredith threatened to be revenged upon me for my severity, and he kept his word. He knew that he was in my power; and soon after the birth of his first child, while Elsie was too feeble to dispute his will, he insisted on my marriage. God grant, dear Matty, that you may never know the agony I experienced at this prospect; I, whose heart was full of the absent Arthur,—who would rather have died than have brought a Slave into the world, and who could look for no union which would not bind me to ignorance, brutality, or irreligious coarseness! God had mercy upon me, however. I was united by Meredith's command, and the aid of a clergyman, (may Heaven have mercy on him also,) to one of the upper field-hands. With a malice well worthy of him, Meredith had, as he thought, selected one of the coarsest and least desirable men on the estate; but I soon learned to estimate a noble nature in my husband. He devoted himself to books, and in about a fortnight mastered the alphabet. I did not conceal from him the state of my own feelings, and I successfully strove to indoctrinate him into Arthur's sentiments. At the end of six weeks he disappeared, leaving me no clue as to his object, or the direction he had taken. But I did not misunderstand him. I knew that he was a free man, a hired hand, and that he was too proud of his wife to wish her to continue a Slave. The light in my eye filled Meredith with rage. For the first time I was whipped,—not severely,—for Elsie interceded for me with tears, and I could not tell what I did not know. I was then closely catechized as to the condition in which I had been left; and when I declared that I had no prospect of becoming a mother, I was told that if nothing was heard from my husband by the close of another six weeks, I must prepare myself again to be a wife. Distasteful as my marriage had been, my husband's nobleness toward me had entirely won my regard, and this declaration threw me into despair. Had I been a quarter Slave, I should have made my escape; but brought up in luxury with Elsie, I must have died ere I reached a free State. A few days of agony converted my despair into a fever on the brain. How long it lasted, I know not, but I was dragged from my bed to the altar; and, Matty, can you believe me—the same clergyman united me again to my master's steward! I felt all the profanation of the rite, but I was both too feeble and too bewildered to resist.

I would speak of this man with all respect, for he was your father, Matty; but he was both coarse in manner, and brutal in mind. He did not imitate the forbearance of my first husband; and in a few months, I became conscious of your existence. Since my marriage, Elsie had never dared to meet my eye; but she now sent me some delicate clothing for my unborn babe, by the woman who had charge of her own. I melted into tears; and to this, I believe, I owe the preservation of my reason. In the afternoon of this day a pedlar approached the plantation; and while he rested at the door of my cottage, the Slaves crowded about him. As they made their gay selections of trinkets and beads, he threw a significant glance at me, saying,—'Here is a box of soap, which you will like better.' Unwarned as I was, God alone could have inspired me with the presence of mind to conceal it, until his departure. It contained a message from my

absent husband, and filled me with conflicting emotions. It
enclosed five hundred dollars, which I was to leave in a farewell
letter to Elsie, as the price of my body, and then, if I chose, I
might fly with the still untouched sum which Arthur had left
me, or join him and his fortunes at a short distance from the
plantation. I could not love my second husband, but was it not
my duty to remain with him until I could give him his unborn
child? I debated, until I remembered that this child would be a
Slave,—perhaps a daughter,—and horror-struck at the thought,
I hurried my preparations for my departure. I left a letter full
of tenderness and reproaches for Elsie. I took with me her last
gift, and rejoined my preserver. Under sufferings and fatigues,
which accelerated your birth, we escaped to this place, where
we have lived ever since.

"In your infancy, dear Matty, you so resembled your father,
that I could not bear to look at you; and it was then, that I was
fully made to realize how far your adopted father's heart
exceeded mine in holiness. 'Annie,' he said, 'if this soul must be
born, you ought to be thankful that it was born to you, and not
to another,—born a free woman, and not a Slave.' And from
him, I learnt to love you, as you have always deserved."

The girl's breast heaved. Tears had been raining from her
eyes,—she clasped her hands, and lifting them toward heaven,
let loose her smothered ire in these words—"O God! let me
pursue them to their death!"

"Matty," said her mother, mournfully, "that is the prayer of
a Slave. I expect from you the prayer of one whom Christ has
made free."

At this moment a tall, sad-looking Negro, with a noble
expression, entered the room. He bent and kissed the wife's
forehead, and laid his hand on the head of the child. "Be what
he has been and is," said the wife in a clear and loving tone, as
she gazed into his face, "and I doubt not, Matty, we shall know
each other in heaven!"

In the darkness of the night the traveller walked away, but
the tears were fast rolling over his cheeks. By the light which
streamed from a neighboring window, he looked at and kissed
a dried flower, which he took from his pocket-book. "She is but

Susan Pettigru King Bowen

A Marriage of Persuasion
1857

Upon receiving and reading a copy of Busy Moments of an Idle Woman
*(1854), published under the pen name "An Idle Woman," James Louis Pettigru,
a South Carolina lawyer, wrote to his daughter, Susan Pettigru King (1824–
1875),*

> You have burst upon me as an author almost as surpris-
> ingly as Miss Burney did on her unsuspicious parent. . . .
> I have no doubt you will receive a great deal of praise, for
> the dialogue is witty and sparkling, and the descriptions
> circumstantial and striking. I dare say that if you were to
> take to study, you might, in time, attain to the deliniation
> of the passions and rise to the walk in which Miss Austen
> is admired.

*King Bowen followed this collection of five stories with her only novel, the
semi-autobiographical* Lily *(1855); a novella and two short stories published
in one volume under the title* Sylvia's World, *and* Crimes Which the Law
Does Not Reach *(1859); another novella,* Gerald Gray's Wife *(1864); and,
four years later, a single, uncollected story in* Harper's Magazine, *"My Debut."*

*Her work is remarkable for its realism in a period characterized by sentimen-
tality. In a 1903 essay surveying fiction in his home state of South Carolina,
Ludwig Lewisohn praises her as "a woman of clear and vigorous spirit, eagerly
ready amidst a somewhat narrow social life, to think for herself and not afraid
to put her thought on record . . . she deserves praise." She was described by
George Wauchope in his 1910 book,* The Writers of South Carolina *as "the*

most distinguished woman novelist of ante-bellum South Carolina." *In* Lily, *through the voice of her heroine, King Bowen expressed her own commitment to literary realism: "If we undertake to write novels . . . heroes and heroines of the present day must act like men and women of the present day, or else they are mere Marionettes.*" *Her distaste for literary sentimentalism was matched by her disdain for the ideal of white Southern womanhood; she found both vapid and dishonest.* Critic J.R. Scafidel *concludes her 1975 essay in* South Carolina Women Writers *with the assessment that "King as a psychological realist very clearly belongs to the group of writers that includes William Dean Howells and Henry James."*

Today, Susan Pettigru King Bowen has all but disappeared, with the exception of an occasional footnote in histories of the Reconstruction. Her work has been out of print for over a century. Her literary reputation seems to have been obscured by responses to her later activities that left her with no champions.

Although her father was opposed to secession, he commanded such respect from South Carolina's Confederate aristocracy that he was given the job of codifying the state laws during the war in order to keep him and his family out of financial trouble. Susan's husband, Henry King, son of her father's law partner and junior member of the firm, enlisted on the Confederate side and was killed in 1862. However, one writer reports that she had left the marriage before his death and gone to work in the Republican administration in Washington, D.C. It was perhaps there that she met her second husband, Christopher Columbus Bowen, who moved to Charleston after the war. He represented South Carolina in Congress from 1868 to 1871 and thereafter served as Sheriff for Charleston County, a position of considerable power. After his marriage to Susan, he stood trial for bigamy. One historian reports that he was acquitted; another that he was convicted and served time in prison. In all the varying descriptions of Bowen's political and legal machinations, it is clear that his wife supported him in every way. She even published a weekly newspaper in which she exposed whatever skeletons she knew about in the closets of her husband's political enemies, thereby making herself a figure wholly inimical to Charlestonian society. Historians of the Reconstruction period treat Christopher Columbus Bowen as a dishonest and murderous villain. Her association with him, which represented an alliance not only with a man repellent to the society of her early youth, but also with a cause seen as wholly antagonistic to the world that had nurtured her, contributed to her expulsion from history.

As a writer, King Bowen deserves more attention than she has received. Her work seems to be informed by the bitter irony of a Cassandra who sees but cannot avert pain and danger. Her female characters view with a pitiless clarity the inequities and inadequacies of their circumstances. They have the courage to speak of what and how they see, but they lack the ability to take the kind of action that might lead to change. Their understanding of their own reality leaves them with few and painful choices between being vulnerable (and inevitably victimized) or heartless (and dead inside); between stifling conformity or self-defeating and isolating rebellion. Critic Rose F. Kavo writes that "the vision of young, trusting girls destroyed or embittered through their experiences with men haunts her novels."

"A Marriage of Persuasion," from Crimes Which the Law Does Not Reach, *was first published under the pen name Anne Marion Green in 1857 in* Russell's Magazine, *the preeminent literary monthly in antebellum Charleston, one of the chief cultural centers of the South. John Russell (whose bookstore had long been the main gathering place for the intellectual elite of the era), William Gilmore Simms, Henry Timrod, and editor Paul Hamilton Hayne were all involved in the magazine's six-volume lifetime. Susan Pettigru King Bowen was its chief supplier of fiction.*

"And so you refused him?"

"Yes, mamma."

"Without one word of hope?"

"Not one."

"Harshly? rudely?"

"I trust not. Finally and positively, I certainly did."

"Anna! I can't forgive you."

"My dear mamma, what have I done?"

"What have you done? Refused an excellent man; one whom any mother would be proud to see as her daughter's husband. Sent from the house the best friend I have—deprived us of our mainstay and support—insulted him—and—destroyed the great hope of my life!" The tears streamed from Mrs. Mansfield's eyes. She drew away her hand from her daughter's clasp, and tried to leave the room. Anna detained her.

"Dearest mother! you cannot be more grieved than I am. Mr. Gordon is a very worthy man—he has been a kind friend to us in adversity—he is, I believe, truly sincere in his love for me, and I regret very deeply that it should have brought us to this pass. I have not wounded him further than I could help, I assure you. He will return to visit us in his usual way, after a while; indeed, I hope to see so little change in our intercourse, that I would have spared you the annoyance of knowing this, had he not expressly desired that I should tell you."

"Ah, he is a forgiving and generous creature; a true Christian. Such a man as that to be so treated!"

Anna was silent.

"Anna," resumed her mother, with sudden energy, after a moment's pause, "do you love any one else? have you formed some absurd attachment which interferes with Mr. Gordon's undeniable claim to your affections?"

Miss Mansfield's noble and expressive face was calmly lifted to her mother's heated and excited gaze.

"No, mamma," she simply answered.

"Then, *why* can't you marry Mr. Gordon, and make me happy?"

"Because," and Anna's voice was firm, decided and honest. "Because I do not love him, and to marry him would make me very unhappy."

"Selfish as ever!" ejaculated Mrs. Mansfield. "Will you tell me what you dislike in him?" she pursued.

"I did not say I disliked Mr. Gordon, mamma."

"What you don't like, then? Why you don't love him?"

Anna smiled faintly. "Dear mamma! is there not a great difference between liking and being in love?"

"You are trifling with me most disrespectfully. Is it not enough that I should suffer this disappointment at your hands, and can you not spare me this beating about the bush? I wish a plain answer to a plain question. Is there anything about Mr. Gordon especially disagreeable to you? If so, what is it?"

"Nothing especially disagreeable, as a friend—as a man whom one sees three or four times a week; but as a husband, several things."

"May I, as only your mother—of course a very insignificant creature to wish or have your confidence—ask these several things?"

"In the first place, then, his appearance is not attractive to me."

"Gracious heaven!" cried Mrs. Mansfield, starting up; "do I live to hear my daughter express such a sentiment! His appearance! Do you not know that to think of such an objection is—the—the—very reverse of modest? Where have you got such ideas? To a truly virtuous woman, what are a man's looks? I might expect such an objection from a girl of low mind and vicious ideas, but not from Anna Mansfield. So this is your reason for not marrying an excellent, kind"——

"Not my only one, mamma," Anna interrupted gently; "it is one of them, but not the greatest. I named it first because it is, I think, very important; and I cannot see the impropriety which strikes you." A slight blush rose to her cheek, as she continued, "I should not like to engage myself to pass my life with a man whose attentions would be repulsive to me, if he had the right to take my hand—or—excuse me, mamma, I don't like to say any more on this point;" and then as the color deepened, she added in a lower voice, "You saw Frederick yesterday put his arm around Maria's waist, as he lifted her from the saddle; and, not caring for the presence of you, his aunt, and us, his cousins, he—a bridegroom of three months—he kissed her pretty blooming cheek, and drew her close to him. She blushed, and said, 'don't, Fred,' but evidently was not displeased. Now, could I endure?—Oh, mamma, pray don't talk about it. It makes me ill. I have named one of the smallest, and at the same time one of the greatest objections. Why dwell upon a difference of opinion, in many essential cases—a total want of congeniality—sympathy—taste, when this trivial reason (provided he possessed the others) is in itself so strong? Dear mamma, don't be angry—don't be disappointed. You would not wish to make me truly miserable? Perhaps in a year or two, Sally may be Mr. Gordon's choice; and Sally may take him as her beau ideal. Why do you want to get rid of me so soon?"

"Ah, my dear," said Mrs. Mansfield, "you know how poor we are now. Here I am with you four girls, and an income not much larger than in your dear father's time I spent upon my own dress. Is it wonderful that I long to see you settled? Heaven knows that I am not one of those mercenary mothers who would give their children to any man with money. No, indeed. I would not be so wicked. But when a gentleman like Norman Gordon—an honorable, trustworthy, generous creature—wishes to become my son, do you wonder that I should desire it too? I knew his father before him—I knew his mother—all good people; it is good blood, my child—the best dependence in the world. You are nearly twenty years old, and there are three younger than you; how can I help being anxious? And I who know what 'love-

matches' are—how many a girl goes to her ruin by that foolish
idea; marrying some boy in haste, and repenting at leisure—
children—no money—bills to pay—oh! my dear Anna, where is
the love then?"

"Mamma, am I making or thinking of making any such match?"

"But you may do it. I want to save you from this. I have a
horror of these romantic 'love-matches.' "

"Did you not love my father, mamma?" Anna asked, in a low
voice.

"Of course I did. All women should love their husbands. All
proper, well-regulated women do love their husbands."

"And yet you wish me to marry without love!"

"Love comes after marriage—every woman with good principles loves her husband. She makes the best of her bargain.
Life is a lottery, and if you draw a prize or a blank, you must
accept it as it is and be satisfied. Then, when a woman has sworn,
in the face of God and man, 'to love, honor and obey' her
husband, how can she reconcile herself to not doing it?"

"But, if she should not? if she finds it impossible? Oh, think
of that, mamma. Think of vowing solemnly in the face of
heaven—and breaking one's oath! Swearing to love, where you
feel indifference—promising to honor, where you see little to
respect—and vowing to obey, where your reason tells you there
is no judgment to make obedience possible! Taking upon your
shoulders, *for life*, a burden you cannot bear, and which it is a
crime to struggle under, or to cast aside!"

"You know nothing about it, Anna," Mrs. Mansfield said
impatiently; "it is not proper for a young girl to think and speak
in this wild way. Your mother is here to guide and direct you.
No good ever comes of a child arguing and setting herself up
in this manner, to teach those older and wiser than herself. The
Bible says, 'Honor thy father and thy mother'—it don't say,
'dispute with them.' I tell you what I heard from *my* mother,
and what every right-minded person knows. 'Make a good choice
in life; marry, and love will come afterward.' Love comes with
the—never mind. I will not say any more now. I hope sincerely
you have been careful of poor Norman's feelings. But you are
not apt to do that. You have lacerated mine enough, Heaven
knows."

"Oh, mamma! when—how?"

"In this business. When it would be so easy for you to make us all happy, and you prefer your own notions, and willfully act up to them." A flush of transient anger and indignation swept gustily over Miss Mansfield's face; but she conquered the emotion, and playfully taking a volume from a book-stand near, said, with perfect good humor, and meaningly, "May I read 'Clarissa Harlowe,' mamma?"

"No, put it down, Anna, and don't bother me with any further nonsense."

The daughter obediently withdrew, glad to escape so painful and so disagreeable an interview.

But although this was the first, it was by no means the last of such conversations. Every day the subject was renewed, but gradually Mrs. Mansfield changed her tactics. She no longer scolded or insisted; her reproaches were silent looks of misery— pathetic appeals to heaven "to grant her patience under her afflictions." She was very affectionate to her daughter—heart-rendingly so. Anna was called upon constantly to notice what a tender parent she was distressing. Each necessary privation in their reduced household (the father's honorable failure and death had brought them from affluence to comparative poverty,) was prologued and epilogued by sighs and suggestions. "If only Anna could"—and then a sudden pause and deep respiration.

"My own dear child," Mrs. Mansfield would sometimes say; "how I wish you had a new dress. That brown silk is very shabby; but we cannot, with our limited means, buy another, and yet I saw Jane Berryman sneering at it, with her flounced skirts spreading a mile behind her."

"Indeed, mamma, I don't care for Jane Berryman's sneers. It is very good of you to be anxious about it, but I think the old brown very becoming."

The next day a rich plaid silk, glossy and fresh, lay upon Anna's bed. "I could not stand it, my dear," said Mrs. Mansfield. "I must do without a new cloak this winter. A mother would rather starve with cold than see her daughter less handsomely dressed than she ought to be. Nothing is a sacrifice to *me*, for *you*, Anna."

In vain poor Anna protested and tried to return the silk, and exchange it for the very necessary cloak, whose purchase was now impossible. Mrs. Mansfield positively forbade her, and the thin black shawl which covered the widow's last year's bombazine was worn with a prolonged shiver, whenever Anna was near enough to hear and see.

Mr. Gordon soon returned to pay his usual visits—to offer his usual attentions—to make his usual presents, at stated times, of things which could permissibly be tendered. The visits Mrs. Mansfield received with great delight—the attentions were allowed; but the first basket of winter produce which arrived from Mr. Gordon's farm, she requested decidedly should be the last.

Clara, the youngest girl, a child of seven, cried lustily because her mamma said "These will be the last potatoes we shall ever eat." From the solemnity of the tone, the little thing fancied that potatoes—a very important item in her daily consumption— were tabooed forever. She desisted when she found that it was only the potatoes from the Gordon farm that fell under the restriction.

Day by day, week after week, this persecution continued. It was the unceasing drop of water that "stayed not itself" for a single instant. In despair, Anna went to consult an aunt, whose opinion she highly valued—whose principles were undoubted— an exemplary wife and mother, and a kind friend always to her niece. Anna recited her woes. "What must I do to escape this torment, my dear Aunt Mary? I feel and know my duty to mamma, I trust; but this life is wearing me out."

Aunt Mary smiled.

"And you don't like Mr. Gordon, dear?"

"I now detest him."

"Oh, for shame! How can you say so? Indeed, my child, I cannot but agree with your mother. This is an excellent match; and it seems to me that if you have no positive objection against his character and standing, you ought to reconsider Mr. Gordon's proposal."

"But, don't you understand that I don't in the least care for the man, except as an ordinary acquaintance. He is well enough as he is; but, do you too advocate a marriage made on such a foundation?"

"Anna! a love-match makes no marriage of love."

"*Voilà une chanson dont je connais l'air!*" said Anna, smiling bitterly in her turn. "You will all force me to marry this man, actually to get rid of him."

"Well, you could not do a better thing, I think?"

Anna returned home disconsolately; returned to the same wearying, petty, incessant, pin pricks, unencouraged by a single word. With all her affection for her mother, she could not but see her weakness in most cases; but on her aunt's judgment she relied, and what had been the result of the interview?—a decided approval of Mrs. Mansfield's wishes.

Let those who blame Anna Mansfield for her next step, pray to be kept from the same pit-fall. This is a mere sketch; but an outline to which all who choose may fill up the hints given. Those who believe that *they* would have been steadfast to the end, will have my admiration, if, when their day of trial comes, they hold firmly to the right; but—as we look around, have we not cause to think that there are many Mrs. Mansfields, and, alas! many Annas?

There came an evening, at length, when on Miss Mansfield's finger shone a great diamond, which dazzled tiny Clara's eyes and made her uncognizant of the tears in her sister's, as she asked wonderingly, "Where did you get such a beau-ti-ful ring?"

Mrs. Mansfield triumphantly said, "That is a secret, Clara."

"No secret for you, my little darling," Anna answered very low and gravely. "Mr. Gordon gave it to me as a pledge that I am to marry him."

"Do you love him, Annie?" Clara said, swallowing her surprise, with great, open, childish eyes.

"Don't ask foolish questions, Clara," her mother cried angrily. But the tears now rolled down the elder sister's white cheek, and she held the little girl close to her bosom, as she whispered, "you shall come and live with me, my own, and when you marry, I will not need, if God helps me, to ask *you* that question."

The day came—hurried on—and Anna Mansfield was Mrs. Norman Gordon. She was the owner of houses and lands—gold and silver—a perjured conscience and a bleeding heart. Very fine possessions were they, truly, and very proud Mrs. Mansfield was and is, of the hand she had in this righteous barter.

I see Mrs. Gordon frequently; she is very pale and cold, and kind. She has no children—Clara does live with her. Mr. Gordon is not happy, evidently; he has nothing to complain of in his wife. She is scrupulously polite to him, but there is not an atom of sympathy between them. He is prejudiced, uncultivated; and now that he has her, is terribly afraid of being ruled by her. It is a joyless household, and a very rich one. I watch Mrs. Mansfield's greedy gaze lighten broader and broader as the blaze of plate—the measured footfall of a train of servants—the luxurious profusion of their constant service, are spread out before her. She treads the "velvet pile" of carpets with a happy step, and adores her daughter's noble brow, when she sees shimmering upon it—reflecting a thousand lights—the mass of brilliants that binds, in its costly clasp, the struggling thoughts of what was once Anna Mansfield.

So we leave them. What of the end of all this? Is this grand automaton really dead, or does a heart, young and still untouched, lurk—strong, free and dangerous—in that quiet, unmoved and stately figure?

Elizabeth Stuart Phelps

Old Mother Goose
1873

First published in The Independent *on January 2, 1873, "Old Mother Goose," one of the earliest "disgraceful mother" stories, is also an occasional story, written for the Christmas issue of a publication for which Elizabeth Stuart Phelps (1844–1911) had already written a series of essays on women's issues in 1871. The story was included six years later in one of Phelps's volumes of short stories,* Sealed Orders. *It was written when Phelps, at age twenty-nine, was already a famous and successful writer.* The Gates Ajar *(1868), her first novel, had become a best-seller on two continents—a success that changed her life.*

Elizabeth Stuart Phelps was the daughter of a writer. Her mother, Elizabeth Wooster Stuart Phelps (1815–1852), wrote six books in fewer years, three of which were published before her death at age thirty-seven. Her last three books, one a collection of short stories titled The Last Leaf from Sunny Side, *were published posthumously. She had been the daughter of a minister who taught sacred literature at Andover Theological Seminary and an invalid mother. A writer from an early age, she signed her work "H. Trusta," an anagram of her real name, a device used by her daughter in "Old Mother Goose." A Christian conversion experience at age nineteen led her to renounce nonreligious writing. She soon became profoundly ill with a number of painful physical symptoms and depression, all of which receded when she began again to write secular fiction. Nevertheless, for the rest of her brief life, she was the victim of periodic bouts of depression. At age twenty-seven she married Austin Phelps, a minister at a Boston church. She had already learned how much she enjoyed life in Boston when she left Andover for school.*

When, six years later, her husband began to teach at the divinity school in

Andover, she was unhappy to return to the life her mother had lived. At the time of the move from Boston, where her mother was happy, to Andover, Mary Gray Phelps, their first child, was four years old. When her mother died four years later, Mary, choosing to take her mother's name, became Elizabeth Stuart Phelps. Less than two years after his wife's death, Austin Phelps married his dead wife's tubercular sister, who died within eighteen months. A third wife added two more sons to the family.

Like her mother, Elizabeth Stuart Phelps became a writer. But unlike her mother and grandmother, she chose for many years to live an independent literary life. Then, at age forty-seven, having been ill since the publication of her brilliant novel, The Story of Avis *(1877), the story of a talented painter whose artistic life is destroyed by marriage, she married a young writer, a man seventeen years younger than she, the son of an old friend. The marriage was a failure and she died alone.*

When she wrote "Old Mother Goose," however, she was a single woman, still committed to an independent, self-directed, literary life, unimpeded by the demands of nineteenth-century wife- and motherhood.

Peg Mathers, Old Mother Goose, combines all the characteristics of the disgraceful mother: she is sexually promiscuous; uses drugs and alcohol; and is dirty, poor, and publically wretched. She is also, perhaps, mad. In the enormous number of "disgraceful mother" stories that have since been written, there are none guilty of so many kinds of disgrace. Her daughter has, on the other hand, all the graces. Her transformation from her mother's daughter to her pure, successful, adored self is as much a fairy tale as is Heathcliff's sudden acquisition of wealth and triumphant return to Wuthering Heights. Thamré has come to seek out her disgraceful mother, to come to some sort of terms with her past. She has volunteered to set up and fund a charity to offer impersonal succor to such wretched women as her own mother. Finally she is forced to confront her mother, face to face, in the only community that knows their shared history.

In most "disgraceful mother" stories, the mother remains unchanged throughout; the daughter, however, is radically transformed from hatred and shame of her mother and profound unease about her own independent female nature, to some expression of acceptance, understanding, and forgiveness. The daughter's transformation invests, and causes the community to invest, the unchanged mother with respectability. Surely it is no coincidence that this story of a mother reclaimed and redeemed by her daughter was written, published, and read in the Christmas season—the time of year when the occasional story is told about a sanctified child believed by many to have been his mother's—and all Christians'—savior.

When Thamrè consented to sing for the citizens of Havermash, last year, nobody was more surprised than the citizens of Havermash themselves.

It was characteristic of Havermash to have attempted it. Nothing is too good for Havermashers. Were St. Cecilia prima donna for a season, it would appear to them quite natural to seek her services. Have they not a brown-stone post-office and a senator, a street railway and a county jail, a local newspaper, an author (the public need scarcely be reminded of the "Havermash Hand-Organ: a Tale of Love and Poverty"), and a shoe and leather trade? Transcending all, is not their city charter two years old?

When the Happy Home Handel Association, headed by little Joe Havermash (grandson of the original shoe and leather man, whose wooden cobbler's shop occupied the site of the present post-office in 1793), took upon itself the performance of an "oratorio" last Christmas eve, "We will have Thamrè," said Joe, serenely.

Still, when Joe came home from Boston, breathless and radiant, one night early in the season, with Thamrè's tiny contract (she wrote it on a card, he said, with her glove on, just in going out, and the card was as sweet now—see!—as the glove, and the glove had just the smell of one English violet, no more) to sing in the stone post-office at eight o'clock on Christmas eve, on such and such conditions (simple enough), and for such and such remuneration,—*that* was the astonishing part of it,—even Havermash was off its guard enough to be surprised.

"She'll come," said Joe. "I supposed she would. I meant she should. But the terms are *astounding*. I was prepared to offer her twice that. I'd pay a big slice of it out of my own pocket to get her here. There's no trouble about terms. Did you see what Max offered her? Do you know what she's getting a night in New York? Do you know what she asked us? Five hundred dollars, sir! Only five hundred dollars. Think of it, sir! But the conditions are the most curious thing. She scorns to take so little, maybe. I don't know. All I know is, every dollar of it is to go to old women who haven't lived as they'd ought to in this town. 'For the relief of the aged women of Havermash, who, having in their youth led questionable lives, are left friendless, needy, and perhaps repentant in their declining years.' That's the wording of the agreement. I signed it myself in her little red morocco notebook. Most curious thing all round! It's my opinion, sir, it *takes* a woman to get up an uncommon piece of work like that."

Last Christmas eve fell in Havermash wild and windy. The gusts fought furiously with each other at corners, and under fences, and over the bleak spaces in which the new little city abounded, and through which it straggled painfully away into the open country. Where the snow lay, it lay in tints of dead, sharp blue, cold as steel beneath the chilly light; where it was blown away, the dust flew fine and hard like powder. Overhead, too, there hung only shades of steel. One long, low line of corrosive red, however, had eaten its way through against the western hill-country, and looked like rust or blood upon a mighty coat of mail.

So, at least, Miss Thamrè fancied, shivering a little in her folded furs, as she watched from the car window the swooping of the night upon the bleak, outlying lands and approaching twinkle of the town.

It was a cheerless night for the prima donna to be in Havermash. Joe had been saying so all day. She thought so, it would seem, when he handed her from the cars. She scarcely spoke to him, nodding only, looking hither and thither about her, through the shriek and smoke, with that keen, baffling glance of hers, which all the world so well remembers. Joe felt rather proud of this. *He* knew what the eccentricities of genius were; was glad of a chance to show himself at ease with them. Had she bidden him stand on his head while she found her trunk, or sit on a barrel in the draught and wait for her to compose an *aria,* he would have obeyed her sweetly, thinking all the while how it would sound, told to his grandchildren on winter nights.

Half Havermash was at the station. All Havermash remembers that. It was with difficulty that Joe could get her to her carriage quietly, as befitted, to his fancy, the conduct of a lady's welcome.

"I did not expect to see so *many* people," said Miss Thamrè, in her pretty, accented, appealing way. "What are they here for?"

"I'm sure I don't know," said Joe, with a puzzled air, "unless they're here to see me."

This amused the lady, and she laughed,—a little genial laugh, which bubbled over to the ears of the people pressing nearest to her in the crowd.

"She laughs as well as she sings," said a member of the Happy Home Handel Association.

"She has the eye of a gazelle and the smile of a Sphinx," said the Author, and took out his note-book to "do" her for a religious weekly.

"She travels alone," said a mother of four daughters. (She had, indeed, come to Havermash quite alone, with neither chaperone nor maid.)

"She can wear silver seal and not look green," said a brunette, in black and garnet.

"She sees everything within a mile of her," said Joe to himself, as he held the hem of her dress back reverently from the carriage-wheels.

It would seem that she saw far and distinctly, for half within her carriage door she paused and said abruptly:—

"What is that? Let me see what that is!"

An old woman was pushing her way through the reluctant crowd; a very miserable old woman, splashed with mud. She had a blanket shawl over her head, and her unhealthy yellow gray hair blew out from under it, over her face before the wind.

A crowd of villainous urchins followed, pelting her with slush and snow, and volleys of that shrill, coarse boys' cry (one of the most pitiful sounds on earth) by which the presence of a sacred mystery or a sorrowful sin is indicated, not alone in Havermash.

"Old Mother Goose! Old Mother Goose! Hi, yi! there! Mother Goosey's out buyin' Christmas stockins for her dar-ter! Old Mother Goo-oo-ose!"

Everybody knew how old Mother Goose hated the boys (and with good reason, poor soul!); but nobody had ever seen her offer them violence before that night.

In a minute she had grown suddenly livid and awful to see, rearing her lank figure to its full height against the steel and blood-colored background of the sky, where a sudden gap in the crowd had left her alone.

"You stop *that!*" she fiercely cried; and dealt with a few bad blows to right and left before she was interfered with.

Annoyed beyond measure, Joe entreated Miss Thamrè to let him take her from the scene. She hesitated, lingered, turned after a moment's thought, and sank upon the carriage seat.

"You did not tell me who it was," she said imperiously; "I asked you. I like to be answered when I ask a question. I never *saw* such a miserable old woman!"

"One of your prospective beneficiaries, madam," said Joe, humbly. "A wretched old creature. The boys call her Old Mother Goose. Do not distress yourself about her. It is no sight for you."

"You say the boys call her—I never *heard* such a poor, sad name! Has she no other name, Mr. Havermash? Oh! *there* she is again."

A sudden turn of the carriage had brought them sharply upon the miserable sight once more. Old Mother Goose was sitting stupidly in the slush beside the hack-stands. Her shawl was off, and her gray hair had fallen raggedly upon her shoulders; her teeth chattered with chill and rage; there were drops of blood about her on the snow; a few of the more undaunted spirits among the boys still hovered near her, avenging themselves for their recent defeat by furtive attempts to purloin her drabbled shawl; and a savage expression of his country's intention to preserve virtuous order, in the garb of the police, stood threatening poor Old Mother Goose with the terrors of the law.

It was a sorry sight. A sorry sight Miss Thamrè seemed to find it. She leaned forward to the window. Joe could not prevent her; she would see it all. The silver shine of her fur wrappings glittered through the dusk, as she moved; one tiny gloved and fur-bound hand hung over the window's edge; a faint sweetness, like the soul of an English violet, stirred as she stirred, and stole out upon the frosty air.

"There!" cried the old woman, mouthing a hideous oath, "there's the lady! I'll see her yet, in spite of ye!"

Old Mother Goose staggered up from the mud, staring dully; but the silver-gray picture framed in the carriage window flashed by her in an instant. For an instant only the two women looked each other in the eye.

Miss Thamrè turned white about the chin. Her hand rose to her eyes instinctively, covered them, and fell. It must have been

such a miserable contrasting of life's chances to her young and
happy fancy!

"I've seen enough," she said. "Never mind!"

"Her name," said Joe, thinking to divert her from the immediate disturbance of the sight, "is Peg, I believe,—Peg Mathers.
You see the boys got it Old Mathers, then Old Mother, so Old
Mother Goose, I suppose; and quite ingenious, too, I think,
poor creature!"

Miss Thamrè made no reply. Quite weary of the subject, she
wrapped herself back into the carriage corner, and, asking only
how long a ride it was, drew a little silver veil she wore across
her face and said no more. Quite weary still she seemed when
Joe gave her his arm at the hotel steps (she had refused to accept
his or any other private hospitality in the place); and very wearily
she gave him to understand that she preferred to be alone till
the hour of her appearance before the Havermash public should
arrive.

Joe stumbled upon Old Mother Goose again, in running
briskly down the hotel steps.

She was wandering in a maudlin, aimless way up and down
the sidewalk at the building's front. Her shawl was gone, and
her gray head was bare to the wind, which was now as sharp as
high.

"What! *you* again?" said Joe. "What are you doing here, Peg?
I was ashamed of you to-night, Peg! The people had come out
to see a famous lady, and you must get to fighting with the boys
and frighten her. You disgraced the town. Better go home, or
you'll be in more mischief. Come!"

"I'm out hunting for my shawl, Mr. Havermash," said the old
woman, after a moment's sly hesitation. "I've lost my shawl.
Them boys took it, curse on 'em! I'd go to see the famous lady,
if I had my shawl."

"Better go home; better go home!" repeated Joe. "*She* doesn't
want to see *you*, Peg."

"Don't she, Mr. Havermash?"

Old Mother Goose laughed (or did she cry? She was always
doing one or the other. What did it matter which?), nodding
upward at the windows of the prima donna's parlors, where

against the drawn shades a slight, tall shadow passed and repassed now and then, faintly, like a figure in a dream.

"Don't she? Well, I don't know as she does. How warm she looks! She must be warm in them fur tippets that she wears; don't you think she must? I like to see a famous lady well as other folks, when I have my shawl. Mr. Havermash!"

"Well, well, well!" Joe stopped impatiently in hurrying away. "Would you rather I'd go home and say my prayers than fight the boys? I hate the boys!"

"Prayers, Peg? *Do* you say your prayers? What prayers do you say, Peg? Come!"

Mr. Havermash lingered, entertained in his own despite— thinking he would tell Miss Thamrè this; it might amuse her.

"I say my prayers," said Old Mother Goose, beating her white hair back from her face at a blow, as if she could give it pain. "I've said 'em this many years. I say: 'When the Devil forgets the world, may God remind him of the boys!' I don't feel so about girls, Mr. Havermash. Maybe, if I hadn't had one once myself, I should. My girl ran away from me. She ran away on a Christmas eve, thirteen years ago. Did ye ever see my girl? Mr. Havermash!"

But Joe was gone. He looked back once in running up the street (he was late to supper now; his wife waited to know if Miss Thamrè would receive a call from her, and would scold a bit,—women will, it can't be helped),—he looked back across his shoulder, and saw that Old Mother Goose was still hunting for her shawl beneath the glittering, curtained windows, where a shadow passed and repassed, high above her head, like the shadow of a figure in a dream.

Thamrè took no supper. It was six o'clock when she entered into her parlors and shut her doors about her. It was five minutes before eight when Mr. Havermash called to conduct her to the concert hall in the second story of the brown-stone post-office. It is quite evident, I think, that, in all the passage of the somewhat remarkable drama into which her appearance in Havermash resolved itself, no act can have equaled in intensity that comprised within those two solitary hours. Yet positively all that is known of it, even at this distant day, is that Miss Thamrè took no supper. Every boarder in the hotel knew that in half an hour. Loiterers and lion-hunters beneath the windows where the nervous shadow passed, picked it up, as loiterers and lion-hunters will. Even Old Mother Goose knew it—coming in to ask the hotel clerk if he had seen her shawl, and being for her trouble roughly shown the door.

Miss Thamrè, curtained and locked in Havermash's grand suite of rooms (of which the town is not unjustly proud, it may be said; in which the senator is always accommodated on election days; in which a Harvard professor and a Boston alderman have been known to spend a night; in which the President himself once took a private lunch, in traveling to the mountains), spent, we say, two hours alone. In all her life, perhaps, the lady never spent two hours less alone. For a year the public fancy has been a self-invited guest at the threshold of those hours. It is with reluctance that one's most reverent imagination follows the general curiosity across their sacred edge; and yet it is with something of the same inner propulsion which forces a dreamer on the seashore to keep the eyes upon the struggles of a little gala-boat wrecked by a mortal leak in calm waters on a sunny day.

One sees, in spite of one's self, the lady's soft small hands close violently on the turning key; the silver furs shine under the chandeliers as they fall, tossed hither and hither, to the floor; the little veil torn from the fine, refined, sweet face; the setness of the features and that pallor of hers about the chin.

One knows that she will pace just so across the long, un-homelike splendor of the gaudy rooms; that she will fold her hands behind her, one into the other knotted fast; that she will lift them now and then, and rub them fiercely, as if she found them in a deathly chill; that her hair will fall, perhaps, in her sharp, regardless motions, and hang about her face; that her head is bent; and that her eyes will follow that great green tulip on the Brussels carpet, from pattern to pattern, patiently, seeing only that, as the shadow of her on the curtain passes and repasses, telling only what a shadow can.

One listens, as she listens to the voices of the people passing on the pavement far below; one wonders, as she wonders what they say; if they speak of her, if they would speak of her tomorrow; and what it would happen they would say, should to-morrow bring forth what to-morrow might.

One hears, for she must hear, a Christmas carol chanted flatly by some young people in the street; the bustle of a hundred Christmas seekers coming homeward, with laden arms and empty pockets, from the little shops; one notices that she draws the shade, to see if holly is hanging in the windows, as it used to hang in Havermash, all up and down the street, by five o'clock,— and if she remembers how many times she has stolen out away in her clean hood, with some care that no one else need follow, shaming her, to see the holly herself and hear the carols sung, like happier little girls—how can one but seem to remember too? And when the church-bells ring out for Christmas prayers, melting through the obdurate mail of the welded clouds, till they seem to melt a star through, as still and clear as God's voice melting through a wrung, defiant heart,—if her set face quivers a little, can one prevent one's own from quivering as well?

Perhaps the church-bells ring in a vision with them, to the barred and curtained glitter of Miss Thamrè's rooms. Perhaps, by sheer contrast, her fancy finds the wretched creature whom she saw to-day, seated with the mud and blood about her, shut in from all the world with her, they two alone together in the dreadful, shining place.

Perhaps she seems to herself to escape it, fleeing with her eyes to the dimmest corner of the room. Perhaps she forces herself to face it, turning sharply back, and lifting her head superbly, as Thamrè can (the shadow on the curtain lifts its head just so, as a passer in the street can see). Perhaps she reasons with it, hotly, on this wise, as she walks:—

"I did not think, in coming to Havermash, you would strike across my way like this!"

"Heaven knows what restless fancy forced me here, Would to Heaven I had never come!"

"For thirteen years I have wondered what it would be like to look upon your face again. How *could* I know it would be like what it is,—so miserable, so neglected, so alone!"

Perhaps she argues sternly, now and then:—

"I have never left you to suffer, at the worst. You can not starve. The first ten-dollar bill I ever earned I sent to you. If you are too imbecile to watch the post, am I to blame? If you will have opium or rum for it, am I to blame? I've done my duty by your shameful motherhood, if ever wretched daughter did! What would you have, what will you have besides?"

Perhaps she droops and pleads at moments like a little child:—
"I have fought so hard, mother, for my name and fame! You gave me such a load of shame and ignorance and squalor to shake off! It has been such a long and bitter work! Let me be for a *little* while now, mother, *do!* Sometime before you die I'll search you out; but not just yet—*just* yet!"

Perhaps she falls to sobbing, as women will. Perhaps she flings her beautiful arms out, and slides with her face upon the stifling scarlet cushions of a little sofa, where she tossed her veil. Perhaps, in kneeling there, the bleeding, gray-haired figure stalks her by, and the quieter companionship of a troop of passive and exhausted thoughts will occupy her place.

It may be that she will think about a certain Christmas eve, windy and wild like this, and with a sky of steel and red almost like this. She thought of it in seeing the sunset from the window of the cars, remembering how a streak of red light crept into the attic corner, to help her while she packed a little bundle of her ragged clothes, thirteen years ago to-night.

It may be that she remembers counting the holly wreaths to keep her wits together as she fled, guiltily and sobbing for terror at the thing that she was doing, through the happy little town; that she saw crosses of myrtle and tuberoses in Mr. Havermash's drawing-room windows as she went by, and how grand they looked; and that a butcher's wife she knew was hanging blue tissue-paper roses in her sitting-room as she climbed the depot steps. She can even recall the butcher's name,—Jack Hash,— Mrs. Jack Hash; as well as a hot and hungry wonder that filled the soul of the desolate child that night, whether she should ever live to be as safe and clean and respectable as Mrs. Jack Hash, and how she would garland her sitting-room with blue tissue-roses on Christmas, if she did!

It may be that her fancy, being wearied, dwells more minutely upon the half comical, wholly pathetic irrelevance of these things than upon the swift and feverish history of the crowded interval between their occurrence and the fact that Helène Thamrè is kneeling in the Havermash hotel parlor, to-night, fighting all the devils that can haunt a beautiful and gifted woman's soul for her poor, old, shameful mother's sake.

Her battles for bread in factories and workshops, when first she cast herself, a little girl of fifteen bitter winters, upon the perilous chances of the world; worse contests, such as the outcast child of old Peg Mathers might not escape, being unfriended and despairing as the child had been; her desperate taxation of her only power, at last,—the voice which Heaven gave her, pure and sweet as its own summer mornings; the songs which she sang at street-corners before the twilight fell; the windows of happy people under which she chanted mournfully; the first solo which they gave her at a mission school into which she chanced; the friends who heard it, and into whose hearts God put it to stretch down their hands and draw her straightway into Paradise; her studies and struggles since in foreign lands; the death of the master who had trained her, and the falling of his great mantle upon her bewildered name,—these details, perhaps, float but mistily before her mind.

Sharp, distinct, pursuing, cruel, a single question begins to imprison her tortured thoughts. It took shapes as vague as smoke, clouds, fogs, dreams, at first; it looms as clear-cut and gigantic as a pyramid before her now.

If all the world should know next year, next week, to-morrow, at once and forever, what she knows?

If Havermash should learn, suppose, to-night, that little Nell Mathers, the unfathered and forgotten child of the creature at whose gray hairs the boys hoot on the streets, is all there is of Helène Thamrè (the very letters of the shameful name transposed to make the beautiful, false image), what would Havermash, falling at her feet this instant, do the next?

Perhaps to the woman's inner sense neither Havermash nor the world may matter much, indeed. She has kept, through deadly peril, soul and body pure as light. Not a sheltered wife, singing "Greenville" to her babies, vacant of ambitions and innocent of noisier powers, can show a hand or heart or name more spotless than her own. And now to dye them deep in the old, old, hateful shame! One must have *been* little Nell Mathers and have become Thamrè, I fancy, to measure this recoil.

Perhaps it seems to her more monstrous and impossible as the thought grows more familiar to her. Perhaps a certain hardness begins to creep across the pallor of her face; or it may be only that she has wound her fallen hair back from it, and exposed the carved exactness and composure of her features. It may be that she will argue to herself again, forgetting that the gray-haired vision left her long ago:—

"I could never make you happy, if I did. It would always, always be a curse to both of us. What have you ever done for me, that you should demand a right so cruel? You have no right, I say; you have no right!"

"And, if you speak, indeed, why, who believes you? What can your ravings do against Thamrè's denial, poor old mother!"

Perhaps she muses, half aloud: "You need a shawl, I see. You shall have a bright, warm shawl on Christmas Day. It is better for you than a daughter. Oh! a thousand times!"

Perhaps she laughs—as Thamrè does not often laugh—most bitterly; and that Joe Havermash, knocking at her door, hears, or thinks he hears, the sound, before she flashes on him, tall, serene, resplendent, in full dress and full spirit for the evening.

The Happy Home Handel Association were satisfied with the reception given by Havermash to their rendering of the oratorio of the Messiah last Christmas eve. On settees, in the aisles, on the window-sills, in the corridors, on the stairs, Havermash overflowed the brown-stone post-office.

Since the incorporation of the city (which is the Christian era of Havermash, and from which everything dates accordingly) nothing approaching such an audience had been collected for the most popular of purposes. Even Signor Blitz could not have eaten swords or played base ball with uncracked eggs before a quarter of the spectators; and the New England philosopher, it is well known, reads his lectures in Havermash to three hundred people.

In this triumph the Happy Home Handel Association felt compelled to own that Thamrè had her share, which for the H. H. H. A. was owning a great deal. When little Joe bowed the prima donna upon the somewhat uncertain (green cambric) stage, the East Havermash "orchestra" led off in a burst of applause, which threatened to shake the post-office to its foundation stone, and which fired even the leader's dignity of Joe's rotund person to ill-concealed enthusiasm. Even Mrs. Joe, gorgeous upon the front settee, in the opera dress that (it was well known) she wore in Boston, despite the ache of a secret chagrin that Miss Thamrè had received no callers, reflected the general pride and pleasure to the very links of her great gold necklace and the tiniest wrinkle of her rose-colored gloves. Even Mrs. Jack Hash, on her camp-stool, by the second left, though disposed by nature and training to be critical of anything headed by a Havermash, applauded softly with the feathered tip of her silver-paper fan upon the frill of her brown poplin upper skirt. Never had there been anything like it known in Havermash.

Like a bird, like a snow-flake, like a moonbeam, like a fancy, like nothing that the brown-stone post-office was accustomed to, Thamrè stole upon the stage. She stood for an instant poised, fluttering, as if half her mind were made to fly, then fell into her unapproachable repose, and at her leisure looked the great audience over, shooting it here and there with her nervous glance.

The packed house drew and held its breath. Women thought swiftly: Silver-gray satin, up to the throat and down to the hands. No jewelry, and a live white lily on her wrist! Young men saw her through a mist, and half turned their eyes away, as if they had seen a Madonna folded in a morning cloud. Reporters pondered, twirling a moustache end, pencil held suspended: Such severity is the superbest affectation, my lady! but it tells, as straight as a carrier-dove. Before she had opened her lips, Thamrè had conquered Havermash.

Conscious of this in an instant's flash, Thamrè grew unconscious of it in another. For an instant every detail in her house was in her grasp, even to Mrs. Jack Hash on the camp-stool and the critical attitude of the silver-paper fan; even to old Mother Goose, half fading into the shadow of the distance, quarreling with a doorkeeper about her ticket. The next she cast her audience from her like a racer casting his cloak to the wind. Her face settled; her wonderful eyes dilated; the hand with the lily on it closed over the other like a seal; the soul of the music entered into her, incorporate. She grew as sacred as her theme.

"That little country house," said a critic present, who had heard her before her best houses in the great world, "was on the knees of its heart that night. She never sung like that before, nor ever will again; nor any other artist, it is my belief. She minded the jerks of that orchestra and the flats of the Havermash *prime donne* no more than she did the whistling of the wind about the post-office windows. She rendered the text like an angel sent from heaven for the purpose. When she lifted that hand with the flower on it (she did it only in the chorus, 'Surely, he hath borne our griefs,' and in the tenor, 'Behold, and see,' and at one other time) I could think of nothing but

> 'In the beauty of the lilies
> Christ was born across the sea.'

Couldn't get it out of my head. I meant she should have been *encored*, when it was all over, to give us that itself; but for what happened, you know."

Did I say she grew as sacred as her theme? It might almost be said that its holy Personality environed and enveloped her. Reverent souls that listened to her that well-remembered night felt as if the Man of Sorrows confided to her the burden of his heart, as if he stooped to acquaint her with his grief, as if the travail of his soul fell upon her, and that with his satisfaction she was satisfied.

The sacred drama was unfolding to its solemn close, the wildness of the wind without was hushed, the Christmas stars were out, when Thamrè glided into her last solo,—that palpitating, proud, triumphant thing, in which the soul of Divine Love avenges itself against the ingenuity of human despair:—

> "If God be for us, who can be against us?
> Who can be against us?
> Who shall lay anything to the charge
> Of God's elect?
> It is God that justifieth.
> Who is he that condemneth?
> It is Christ that died."

It was at this point that the interruption came.

Shrill and sharp into the thrill of the singer's liquid, clinging
notes a quick cry cut:—

"Let me see her! Let me touch her! I can't abear it any longer!
Let me see my girl!" and, forcing her way like a stream of lava
through the packed and startled aisles, hot, wild, pallid, and
horrible, Old Mother Goose leaped, before a hand could stay
her, on the stage.

"I can't stand it any longer, Nell! It seems to craze my head!
I knew you from the time I heard you laughing to the depot. I
didn't mean to shame ye before so many folks, and I tried to
find my shawl. They said you wouldn't want to see your poor
old mother, Nelly dear. But I can't abear to hear you sing. Nell,
why, Nell, you stand up like the Almighty Dead to do it!"

The shock of the shrill words and their cessation brought the
house to its feet. Then came the uproar.

"Shame!" "Police!" "Order!" "Take her out!" "Arrest the hag!"
"Protect the lady!" And after that the astonishment and the
silence of death.

High above the wavering, peering mass, clear to the apprehension of every eye in the house, appeared a lily-bound,
authoritative hand. It motioned once and dropped—as the snow
drops over a grave.

By those who sat nearest her it was said that the flower
trembled on the lady's wrist a little; for the rest, she stood
sculptured like a statue, towering about the piteous figure at
her feet. Her voice, when she spoke,—for she spoke in the
passing of a thought,—rang out to the remotest corner of the
galleries, slipping even then, however, into Thamrè's girlish,
uneven tones.

"If you *please*, do not disturb the woman at this moment. She
is a very *old* woman. Let us hear what she has to say. Her hair
is gray. Let us not be *rough* or *hasty* till we have *thought* of what
she says."

Old Mother Goose rose from the floor, where she had fallen,
half-abashed, perhaps half-dazed at that which she had done.

"I've got nothing more to say." She fumbled foolishly in the
air to wrap the shawl which she had lost about her lean and
tattered shoulders. "I've said as this famous lady is my daughter,
that was Nell Mathers, and remembered by many folks in

Havermash thirteen year ago. I wouldn't have shamed her quite so much if I'd only found my shawl. It's cold, too, without a shawl. I'll go out now, and you can sing your piece through, Nelly, without the plague of me. I wouldn't have told on you, I think, but for the music and the crazy feeling that I had. It's most too bad, Nelly, to spoil the piece. I'll go right out."

She turned, stepped off, and staggered feebly, turning her bleared eyes back to feast upon the silent, shining figure, on whose wrist the lily glittered cruelly, as only lilies can.

"What a pretty sating gown you've got, my dear!" she said.

Mr. Havermash could bear it no longer. He took Old Mother Goose by the sleeve, hurrying up, saying: "Come, come!"

"The woman is drunk, Miss Thamrè. She shall not be allowed to insult you any more like this. In the kindness of your heart, you make a mistake, I think, if you will pardon me. See! she is quite beside herself. Something is due to the audience. This disturbance should not continue. Come, Peg, come!"

But Thamrè shook her head. She had grown now deadly pale,—at least so Joe thought, letting go the woman's arm, his own face changing color sharply, the baton in his fat, white-gloved hand beginning to shake.

"If you please, Mr. Havermash, I should like to know—the people will *pardon* me a moment, I am sure—I should like to know if this poor old creature has anything *more* to say."

"Nothing more," said Old Mother Goose, shaking her gray head, "but this, maybe, Nelly dear. I says to myself, when I sits and hears you singing,—I says, when you sang them words: 'If God be for me, my girl won't be against me! My girl can't be against me!'—over and over with the music, Nelly, so I did! If God be for me, how *can* my girl be against me?"

It was said that, when Helène Thamrè stretched down her lily-guarded hand, and, lifting the lean, uncleanly fingers of Old Mother Goose, pressed them, after a moment's thought, gently and slowly to her heart, she heard the sudden break of sobs in the breathless house; and, pausing to listen to the sound, flushed fitfully like a child surprised, and smiled.

"Ladies and gentlemen,"—her great eyes stabbed the audience through and through; she lifted the old woman's hand, that all might see,—"I am *sorry* that your entertainment should be disturbed. If you will *excuse* me, I will leave you now, and take my mother home."

Home? What home was there for Old Mother Goose and her outcast child in Thamrè's hotel parlors, on that or any other night? What home was there for Thamrè in the God-forsaken cellar whence the woman of the town had crawled? Apparently, the lady had not thought of this. Joe found her standing serenely as an angel when he came into the stifling little green room. She was still smiling. She had buttoned her silver furs about the old woman's shrunken throat.

"This will be warmer than your shawl, mother, don't you see?" he heard her say. "The boys shall never bother you in this, poor old mother! There!"

Mrs. Havermash came with her husband. The Boston opera-cloak was in disorder; her rose-colored gloves were wet and spotted.

"Miss Thamrè," said Joe, "may I make you acquainted with my wife? We would not urge upon you again the acceptance of a hospitality which has been already so decidedly refused; but perhaps, considering the state of your mother's health, we can make you more comfortable now at our home than you can be elsewhere. If you will do Mrs. Havermash and myself the favor to return with us—and her—in our own carriage to-night"—

Joe's grandfather, as has been said, cobbled shoes in a wooden shop; and even Mrs. Joe to-day will drink with her spoon in her tea-cup, you will notice, if you chance to sit beside her at a supper. But show me bluer blood, if it please you, than shall flow in the veins of him and his, to preserve the existence of this most cultivated instinct and the memory of this most knightly deed.

All the world knows how Thamrè suddenly and mysteriously disappeared a year ago from public and professional life. All the world has mourned, wondered, gossiped, caught at the wings of rumors, lost them, and so mourned again at this event.

All the world does not know with what a curious development of pride in and loyalty to the personality of little Nell Mathers, Havermash has struggled, till struggle has become useless, to enforce a reticence upon the subject of Thamrè's movements and their motives.

To a few friends, familiar with her private history for the past year, its results have seemed to crown its cost, I think. At least, she herself, having proved them so, has contrived to radiate upon us the light of her own content.

"You do not know the life," she said, at the outset, shaking her beautiful, determined head, "if you would ask me to return to it while my mother lives. Even my name will not bear the scorch of hers. The world is so hard on women! Do not urge me. Let me take my way. Perhaps God and I together can make her poor old hand as white as yours or mine before she dies."

Perhaps they did. It is known that when Old Mother Goose lay dying in her daughter's quiet house in Havermash, one frosty night, not many weeks ago, and after she had fallen, as they thought, past speech or recognition, she raised herself upon her pillow, and, stretching her hands, said slowly:—

"Nell! why, Nell! It is Christ that died! If my girl was for me, Nell, *could* He be against me, do you think?"

And further it is only known that Thamrè will sing this season in the oratorio of the Messiah on Christmas eve.

Alice Brown

The Way of Peace
1898

Alice Brown (1856–1948), a New Englander who became one of the most acclaimed short story writers in the United States during the peak years of her literary career, has been lost to readers for many decades. Although her brilliant stories were identified as among the best of those labeled "local color," she wrote during the years of declining interest in literary regionalism. Despite inclusion in a few fine collections of "local color fiction," she has presented difficulties for literary historians. Although her best were written in the early twentieth century, her stories seem to belong to the nineteenth century because of their style and their focus on women of middle age and older who had lived the first half of their lives during the nineteenth century in rural settings that remained stable despite urban industrialization. For these women, life did not change significantly when the new century began.

Brown published 17 novels, 4 volumes of plays, 3 of poetry, and 4 miscellaneous volumes of criticism, personal essays, and works for children during her career, which began in the early 1890s and continued for close to half a century. But it is the 115 stories collected in 8 volumes that justify claims for her of literary greatness. She is the inheritor of the literary tradition of Catharine Maria Sedgwick, Lydia Maria Child, Harriet Beecher Stowe, and the "regionalists" who befriended her and welcomed her as their youngest colleague.

Many of Alice Brown's stories focus on women in community and in communication with each other, very often across the generations. She depicts young women in willing discipleship to their mothers, grandmothers, or other chosen mentors in those generations. It is a spiritual discipleship in peace, grace, and joy. The greatest love in the lives of these women, the most significant "other," is often a woman of an older generation. And, of course, the model couple in that scheme is that of mother and daughter. She wrote about a world in which women were free to love each other, uninhibited by the new Freudian theories that had begun to reach the consciousness of the educated and artistic. Alice Brown was familiar with these ideas; however, her mothers and daughters live with, delight in, and love each other despite them.

Alice Brown never married and left little information about her family or her girlhood on a farm in New Hampshire. She spent her professional literary life as a respected member of a community of creative women, including Annie Fields, Sarah Orne Jewett, Mary E. Wilkins Freeman, Elizabeth Stuart Phelps, Harriet Prescott Spofford, and Helen Hunt Jackson. The Irish Catholic poet, Louise Imogen Guiney, was a central figure in Alice Brown's life. After a first trip together to England in 1886, the two women founded the Women's Rest Tour Association "to encourage other women to take their vacations as they had, with pack and stick, in foreign lands." It was Guiney's influence that led Brown in her later years to enter into serious study of Catholicism, although she never converted.

"The Way of Peace" was published in the Thanksgiving issue of Outlook (November 19, 1898) under the pseudonym Martin Redfield (later to be used in Brown's 1912 novel, My Love and I, as the name of a character who, according to Brown's biographer, Dorothea Walker, "prostitutes his art in a conflict between idealism and materialism"). It lifts the occasional story far above the limitations and conventions of the genre. A story of love and death, devotion and transcendence, "The Way of Peace" was included in Brown's second collection of stories, Tiverton Tales (1899).

The story is one in which many of the mother-daughter categories converge. Not only is there the obvious commemoration of a major life cycle event—the death of Lucy Ann Cummings's mother—and Lucy Ann's subsequent quest for an identity adequate to her altered circumstances, but there is also the gentle, loving, but nevertheless firm and persistent confrontation with the patriarchy in the persons of her brothers Eliza and John, who "would be good to her . . . always had been . . . were men-folks, and doubtless . . . knew best."

Although Alice Brown was never affiliated with any segment of the women's movement, her commitment to personal integrity in her own life and in the lives of her fictional characters led to frequent depictions of females who grow from complacent acceptance to active control of their destinies. Additionally, Brown's work contains frequent celebrations of the natural world and of the life of the spirit, both of which have been identified as characteristics commonly found in women's writing. In "The Way of Peace," the affirmation of the connection between this world and the next—to which Lucy Ann's mother has departed— is the tonic chord on which this virtuoso piece ends.

All eight volumes of Brown's short stories have been reprinted in recent years. The other seven are: Meadow-Grass: Tales of New England Life (1895), High Noon (1904), The County Road (1906), Country Neighbors

(1910), Vanishing Points *(1913)*, The Flying Teuton *(1918)*, *and* Homespun and Gold *(1920)*.

It was two weeks after her mother's funeral when Lucy Ann Cummings sat down and considered. The web of a lifelong service and devotion still clung about her, but she was bereft of the creature for whom it had been spun. Now she was quite alone, save for her two brothers and the cousins who lived in other townships, and they all had homes of their own. Lucy Ann sat still, and thought about her life. Brother Ezra and brother John would be good to her. They always had been. Their solicitude redoubled with her need, and they had even insisted on leaving Annabel, John's daughter, to keep her company after the funeral. Lucy Ann thought longingly of the healing which lay in the very loneliness of her little house; but she yielded, with a patient sigh. John and Ezra were men-folks, and doubtless they knew best.

A little more than a week had gone when school "took up," rather earlier than had been intended, and Annabel went away in haste, to teach. Then Lucy Ann drew her first long breath. She had resisted many a kindly office from her niece, with the crafty innocence of the gentle who can only parry and never thrust. When Annabel wanted to help in packing away grandma's things, aunt Lucy agreed, half-heartedly, and then deferred the task from day to day. In reality, Lucy Ann never meant to pack them away at all. She could not imagine her home without them; but that, Annabel would not understand, and her aunt pushed aside the moment, reasoning that something is pretty sure to happen if you put things off long enough. And something did; Annabel went away. It was then that Lucy Ann took a brief draught of the cup of peace.

Long before her mother's death, when they both knew how inevitably it was coming, Lucy Ann had, one day, a little shock of surprise. She was standing before the glass, coiling her crisp gray hair, and thinking over and over the words the doctor had used, the night before, when he told her how near the end might be. Her delicate face fell into deeper lines. Her mouth dropped a little at the corners; her faded brown eyes were hot with tears, and stopping to wipe them, she caught sight of herself in the glass.

"Why," she said aloud, "I look jest like mother!"

And so she did, save that it was the mother of five years ago, before disease had corroded the dear face, and patience wrought its tracery there.

"Well," she continued, smiling a little at the poverty of her state, "I shall be a real comfort to me when mother's gone!"

Now that her moment of solitude had struck, grief came also. It glided in, and sat down by her, to go forth no more, save perhaps under its other guise of a patient hope. She rocked back and forth in her chair, and moaned a little to herself.

"Oh, I never can bear it!" she said pathetically, under her breath. "I never can bear it in the world!"

The tokens of illness were all put away. Her mother's bedroom lay cold in an unsmiling order. The ticking of the clock emphasized the inexorable silence of the house. Once Lucy Ann thought she heard a little rustle and stir. It seemed the most natural thing in the world, coming from the bedroom, where one movement of the clothes had always been enough to summon her with flying feet. She caught her breath, and held it, to listen. She was ready, undisturbed, for any sign. But a great fly buzzed drowsily on the pane, and the fire crackled with accentuated life. She was quite alone. She put her hand to her heart, in that gesture of grief which is so entirely natural when we feel the stab of destiny; and then she went wanly into the sitting-room, looking about her for some pretense of duty to solace her poor mind. There again she caught sight of herself in the glass.

"Oh, my!" breathed Lucy Ann. Low as they were, the words held a fullness of joy.

Her face had been aging through these days of grief; it had grown more and more like her mother's. She felt as if a hand had been stretched out to her, holding a gift, and at that moment something told her how to make the gift enduring. Running over to the little table where her mother's work-basket stood, as it had been, undisturbed, she took out a pair of scissors, and went back to the glass. There she let down her thick gray hair, parted it carefully on the sides, and cut off lock after lock about her face. She looked a caricature of her sober self. But she was well used to curling hair like this, drawing its crisp silver into shining rings; and she stood patiently before the glass and coaxed her own locks into just such fashion as had framed the older face. It was done, and Lucy Ann looked at herself with a smile all suffused by love and longing. She was not herself any more; she had gone back a generation, and chosen a warmer niche. She could have kissed her face in the glass, it was so like that other dearer one. She did finger the little curls, with a reminiscent passion, not daring to think of the darkness where the others had been shut; and, at that instant, she felt very rich. The change suggested a more faithful portraiture, and she went up into the spare room and looked through the closet where her mother's clothes had been hanging so long, untouched. Selecting a purple thibet, with a little white sprig, she slipped off her own dress, and stepped into it. She crossed a muslin kerchief on her breast, and pinned it with the cameo her mother had been used to wear. It was impossible to look at herself in the doing; but when the deed was over, she went again to the glass and stood there, held by a wonder beyond her will. She had resurrected the creature she loved; this was an enduring portrait, perpetuating, in her own life, another life as well.

"I'll pack away my own clo'es to-morrer," said Lucy Ann to herself. "Them are the ones to be put aside."

She went downstairs, hushed and tremulous, and seated herself again, her thin hands crossed upon her lap; and there she stayed, in a pleasant dream, not of the future, and not even of the past, but face to face with a recognition of wonderful possibilities. She had dreaded her loneliness with the ache that is despair; but she was not lonely any more. She had been allowed to set up a little model of the tabernacle where she had worshiped; and, having that, she ceased to be afraid. To sit there, clothed in such sweet familiarity of line and likeness, had tightened her grasp upon the things that are. She did not seem to herself altogether alive, nor was her mother dead. They had been fused, by some wonderful alchemy; and instead of being worlds apart, they were at one. So, John Cummings, her brother, stepping briskly in, after tying his horse at the gate, came upon her unawares, and started, with a hoarse, thick cry. It was in the

dusk of evening; and, seeing her outline against the window, he
stepped back against the wall and leaned there a moment,
grasping at the casing with one hand. "Good God!" he breathed,
at last, "I thought 't was mother!"

Lucy Ann rose, and went forward to meet him.

"Then it's true," said she. "I'm so pleased. Seems as if I could
git along, if I could look a little mite like her."

John stood staring at her, frowning in his bewilderment.

"What have you done to yourself?" he asked. "Put on her
clo'es?"

"Yes," said Lucy Ann, "but that ain't all. I guess I do resemble
mother, though we ain't any of us had much time to think about
it. Well, I *am* pleased. I took out that daguerreotype she had,
down Saltash way, though it don't favor her as she was at the
end. But if I can take a glimpse of myself in the glass, now and
then, mebbe I can git along."

They sat down together in the dark, and mused over old
memories. John had always understood Lucy Ann better than
the rest. When she gave up Simeon Bascom to stay at home
with her mother, he never pitied her much; he knew she had
chosen the path she loved. The other day, even, some one had
wondered that she could have heard the funeral service so
unmoved; but he, seeing how her face had seemed to fade and
wither at every word, guessed what pain was at her heart. So,
though his wife had sent him over to ask how Lucy Ann was
getting on, he really found out very little, and felt how painfully
dumb he must be when he got home. Lucy Ann was pretty well,
he thought he might say. She'd got to looking a good deal like
mother.

They took their "blindman's holiday," Lucy Ann once in a
while putting a stick on the leaping blaze, and, when John
questioned her, giving a low-toned reply. Even her voice had
changed. It might have come from that bedroom, in one of the
pauses between hours of pain, and neither would have been
surprised.

"What makes you burn beech?" asked John, when a shower
of sparks came crackling at them.

"I don't know," she answered. "Seems kind o' nat'ral. Some
of it got into the last cord we bought, an' one night it snapped
out, an' most burnt up mother's nightgown an' cap while I was

warmin' 'em. We had a real time of it. She scolded me, an' then she laughed, an' I laughed—an' so, when I see a stick or two o' beech to-day, I kind o' picked it out a-purpose."

John's horse stamped impatiently from the gate, and John, too, knew it was time to go. His errand was not done, and he balked at it.

"Lucy Ann," said he, with the bluntness of resolve, "what you goin' to do?"

Lucy Ann looked sweetly at him through the dark. She had expected that. She smoothed her mother's dress with one hand, and it gave her courage.

"Do?" said she; "why, I ain't goin' to do nothin'. I've got enough to pull through on."

"Yes, but where you goin' to live?"

"Here."

"Alone?"

"I don't feel so very much alone," said she, smiling to herself. At that moment she did not. All sorts of sweet possibilities had made themselves real. They comforted her, like the presence of love.

John felt himself a messenger. He was speaking for others that with which his soul did not accord.

"The fact is," said he, "they're all terrible set ag'inst it. They say you're gittin' along in years. So you be. So are we all. But they will have it, it ain't right for you to live on here alone. Mary says she should be scairt to death. She wants you should come an' make it your home with us."

"Yes, I dunno but Mary would be scairt," said Lucy Ann placidly. "But I ain't. She's real good to ask me; but I can't do it, no more'n she could leave you an' the children an' come over here to stay with me. Why, John, this is my home!"

Her voice sank upon a note of passion. It trembled with memories of dewy mornings and golden eves. She had not grown here, through all her youth and middle life, like moss upon a rock, without fitting into the hollows and softening the angles of her poor habitation. She had drunk the sunlight and the rains of one small spot, and she knew how both would fall. The place, its sky and clouds and breezes, belonged to her: but she belonged to it as well.

John stood between two wills, his own and that of those who had sent him. Left to himself, he would not have harassed her. To him, also, wedded to a hearth where he found warmth and peace, it would have been sweet to live there always, though alone, and die by the light of its dying fire. But Mary thought otherwise, and in matters of worldly judgment he could only yield.

"I don't want you should make a mistake," said he. "Mebbe you an' I don't look for'ard enough. They say you'll repent it if you stay, an' there'll be a hurrah-boys all round. What say to makin' us a visit? That'll kind o' stave it off, an' then we can see what's best to be done."

Lucy Ann put her hands to her delicate throat, where her mother's gold beads lay lightly, with a significant touch. She, like John, had an innate gentleness of disposition. She distrusted her own power to judge.

"Maybe I might," said she faintly. "Oh, John, do you think I've got to?"

"It needn't be for long," answered John briefly, though he felt his eyes moist with pity of her. "Mebbe you could stay a month?"

"Oh, I couldn't do that!" cried Lucy Ann, in wild denial. "I never could in the world. If you'll make it a fortnight, an' harness up yourself, an' bring me home, mebbe I might."

John gave his word, but when he took his leave of her, she leaned forward into the dark, where the impatient horse was fretting, and made her last condition.

"You'll let me turn the key on things here jest as they be? You won't ask me to break up nuthin'?"

"Break up!" repeated John, with the intensity of an oath. "I guess you needn't. If anybody puts that on you, you send 'em to me."

So Lucy Ann packed her mother's dresses into a little hair trunk that had stood in the attic unused for many years, and went away to make her visit. When she drove up to the house, sitting erect and slender in her mother's cashmere shawl and black bonnet, Mary, watching from the window, gave a little cry, as at the risen dead. John had told her about Lucy Ann's transformation, but she put it all aside as a crazy notion, not likely to last: now it seemed less a pathetic masquerade than a strange by-path taken by nature itself.

The children regarded it with awe, and half the time called Lucy Ann "grandma." That delighted her. Whenever they did it, she looked up to say, with her happiest smile,—

"There! that's complete. You'll remember grandma, won't you? We mustn't ever forget her."

Here, in this warm-hearted household, anxious to do her service in a way that was not her own, she had some happiness, of a tremulous kind; but it was all built up of her trust in a speedy escape. She knit mittens, and sewed long seams; and every day her desire to fill the time was irradiated by the certainty that twelve hours more were gone. A few more patient intervals, and she should be at home. Sometimes, as the end of her visit drew nearer, she woke early in the morning with a sensation of irresponsible joy, and wondered, for an instant, what had happened to her. Then it always came back, with an inward flooding she had scarcely felt even in her placid youth. At home there would be so many things to do, and, above all, such munificent leisure! For there she would feel no need of feverish action to pass the time. The hours would take care of themselves; they would fleet by, while she sat, her hands folded, communing with old memories.

The day came, and the end of her probation. She trembled a good deal, packing her trunk in secret, to escape Mary's remonstrances; but John stood by her, and she was allowed to go.

"You'll get sick of it," called Mary after them. "I guess you'll be glad enough to see the children again, an' they will you. Mind, you've got to come back an' spend the winter."

Lucy Ann nodded happily. She could agree to anything sufficiently remote; and the winter was not yet here.

The first day in the old house seemed to her like new birth in Paradise. She wandered about, touching chairs and tables and curtains, the manifest symbols of an undying past. There were loving duties to be done, but she could not do them yet. She had to look her pleasure in the face, and learn its lineaments.

Next morning came brother Ezra, and Lucy Ann hurried to meet him with an exaggerated welcome. Life was never very friendly to Ezra, and those who belonged to him had to be doubly kind. They could not change his luck, but they might sweeten it. They said the world had not gone well with him; though sometimes it was hinted that Ezra, being out of gear, could not go with the world. All the rivers ran away from him, and went to turn some other mill. He was ungrudging of John's prosperity, but still he looked at it in some disparagement, and shook his head. His cheeks were channeled long before youth was over; his feet were weary with honest serving, and his hands grown hard with toil. Yet he had not arrived, and John was at the goal before him.

"We heard you'd been stayin' with John's folks," said he to Lucy Ann. "Leastways, Abby did, an' she thinks mebbe you've got a little time for us now, though we ain't nothin' to offer compared to what you're used to over there."

"I'll come," said Lucy Ann promptly. "Yes, I'll come, an' be glad to."

It was part of her allegiance to the one who had gone.

"Ezra needs bracin'," she heard her mother say, in many a sick-room gossip. "He's got to be flattered up, an' have some grit put into him."

It was many weeks before Lucy Ann came home again. Cousin Rebecca, in Saltash, sent her a cordial letter of invitation for just as long as she felt like staying; and the moneyed cousin at the Ridge wrote in like manner, following her note by a telegram, intimating that she would not take no for an answer. Lucy Ann frowned in alarm when the first letter came, and studied it by daylight and in her musings at night, as if some comfort might lurk between the lines. She was tempted to throw it in the fire, not answered at all. Still, there was a reason for going. This cousin had a broken hip, she needed company, and the flavor of old times. The other had married a "drinkin' man," and might feel hurt at being refused. So, fortifying herself with some inner resolution she never confessed, Lucy Ann set her teeth and started out on a visiting campaign. John was amazed. He drove over to see her while she was spending a few days with an aunt in Sudleigh.

"When you been home last, Lucy Ann?" asked he.

A little flush came into her face, and she winked bravely.

"I ain't been home at all," said she, in a low tone. "Not sence August."

John groped vainly in mental depths for other experiences likely to illuminate this. He concluded that he had not quite understood Lucy Ann and her feeling about home; but that was neither here nor there.

"Well," he remarked, rising to go, "you're gittin' to be quite a visitor."

"I'm tryin' to learn how," said Lucy Ann, almost gayly. "I've been a-cousinin' so long, I sha'n't know how to do anything else."

But now the middle of November had come, and she was again in her own house. Cousin Titcomb had brought her there and driven away, concerned that he must leave her in a cold kitchen, and only deterred by a looming horse-trade from staying to build a fire. Lucy Ann bade him good-by, with a gratitude which was not for her visit, but all for getting home; and when he uttered that terrifying valedictory known as "coming again," she could meet it cheerfully. She even stood in the door, watching him away; and not until the rattle of his wheels had ceased on the frozen road, did she return to her kitchen and stretch her shawled arms pathetically upward.

"I thank my heavenly Father!" said Lucy Ann, with the fervency of a great experience.

She built her fire, and then unpacked her little trunk, and hung up the things in the bedroom where her mother's presence seemed still to cling.

"I'll sleep here now," she said to herself. "I won't go out of this no more."

Then all the little homely duties of the hour cried out upon her, like children long neglected; and, with the luxurious leisure of those who may prolong a pleasant task, she set her house in order. She laid out a programme to occupy her days. The attic should be cleaned to-morrow. In one day? Nay, why not three, to hold Time still, and make him wait her pleasure? Then there were the chambers, and the living-rooms below. She felt all the excited joy of youth; she was tasting anticipation at its best.

"It'll take me a week," said she. "That will be grand." She could hardly wait even for the morrow's sun; and that night she slept like those of whom much is to be required, and who must wake in season. Morning came, and mid-forenoon, and while she stepped about under the roof where dust had gathered and bitter herbs told tales of summers past, John drove into the yard. Lucy Ann threw up the attic window and leaned out.

"You put your horse up, an' I'll be through here in a second," she called. "The barn's open."

John was in a hurry.

"I've got to go over to Sudleigh, to meet the twelve o'clock," said he. "Harold's comin'. I only wanted to say I'll be over after you the night before Thanksgivin'. Mary wants you should be sure to be there to breakfast. You all right? Cephas said you seemed to have a proper good time with them."

John turned skillfully on the little green and drove away. Lucy Ann stayed at the window watching him, the breeze lifting her gray curls, and the sun smiling at her. She withdrew slowly into the attic, and sank down upon the floor, close by the window. She sat there and thought, and the wind still struck upon her unheeded. Was she always to be subject to the tyranny of those who had set up their hearth-stones in a more enduring form? Was her home not a home merely because there were no men and children in it? She drew her breath sharply, and confronted certain problems of the greater world, not knowing what they were. To Lucy Ann they did not seem problems at all. They were simply touches on the individual nerve, and she felt the pain. Her own inner self throbbed in revolt, but she never guessed that any other part of nature was throbbing with it. Then she went about her work, with the patience of habit. It was well that the attic should be cleaned, though the savor of the task was gone.

Next day, she walked to Sudleigh, with a basket on her arm. Often she sent her little errands by the neighbors; but to-day she was uneasy, and it seemed as if the walk might do her good. She wanted some soda and some needles and thread. She tried to think they were very important, though some sense of humor told her grimly that household goods are of slight use to one who goes a-cousining. Her day at John's would be prolonged to seven; nay, why not a month, when the winter itself was not too great a tax for them to lay upon her? In her deserted house, soda would lose its strength, and even cloves decay. Lucy Ann felt her will growing very weak within her; indeed, at that time, she was hardly conscious of having any will at all.

It was Saturday, and John and Ezra were almost sure to be in town. She thought of that, and how pleasant it would be to hear from the folks: so much pleasanter than to be always facing them on their own ground, and never on hers. At the grocery she came upon Ezra, mounted on a wagon-load of meal-bags, and just gathering up the reins.

"Hullo!" he called. "You didn't walk?"

"Oh, I jest clipped it over," returned Lucy Ann carelessly. "I'm goin' to git a ride home. I see Marden's wagon when I come by the post-office."

"Well, I hadn't any expectation o' your bein' here," said Ezra. "I meant to ride round to-morrer. We want you to spend Thanksgivin' Day with us. I'll come over arter you."

"Oh, Ezra!" said Lucy Ann, quite sincerely, with her concession to his lower fortunes, "why didn't you say so! John's asked me."

"The dogs!" said Ezra. It was his deepest oath. Then he drew a sigh. "Well," he concluded, "that's our luck. We al'ays come out the leetle end o' the horn. Abby'll be real put out. She 'lotted on it. Well, John's inside there. He's buyin' up 'bout everything there is. You'll git more'n you would with us."

He drove gloomily away, and Lucy Ann stepped into the store, musing. She was rather sorry not to go to Ezra's, if he cared. It almost seemed as if she might ask John to let her take the plainer way. John would understand. She saw him at once where he stood, prosperous and hale, in his great-coat, reading items from a long memorandum, while Jonathan Stevens weighed and measured. The store smelled of spice, and the clerk that minute spilled some cinnamon. Its fragrance struck upon Lucy Ann like a call from some far-off garden, to be entered if she willed. She laid a hand on her brother's arm, and her lips opened to words she had not chosen:—

"John, you shouldn't ha' drove away so quick, t'other day. You jest flung out your invitation an' run. You never give me no time to answer. Ezra's asked me to go there."

"Well, if that ain't smart!" returned John. "Put in ahead, did he? Well, I guess it's the fust time he ever got round. I'm terrible sorry, Lucy. The children won't think it's any kind of a Thanksgivin' without you. Somehow they've got it into their heads it's grandma comin'. They can't seem to understand the difference."

"Well, you tell 'em I guess grandma's kind o' pleased for me to plan it as I have," said Lucy Ann, almost gayly. Her face wore a strange, excited look. She breathed a little faster. She saw a pleasant way before her, and her feet seemed to be tending toward it without her own volition. "You give my love to 'em. I guess they'll have a proper nice time."

She lingered about the store until John had gone, and then went forward to the counter. The storekeeper looked at her respectfully. Everybody had a great liking for Lucy Ann. She had been a faithful daughter, and now that she seemed, in so mysterious a way, to be growing like her mother, even men of her own age regarded her with deference.

"Mr. Stevens," said she, "I didn't bring so much money with me as I might if I'd had my wits about me. Should you jest as soon trust me for some Thanksgivin' things?"

"Certain," replied Jonathan. "Clean out the store, if you want. Your credit's good." He, too, felt the beguilement of the time.

"I want some things," repeated Lucy Ann, with determination. "Some cinnamon an' some mace—there! I'll tell you, while you weigh."

It seemed to her that she was buying the spice islands of the world; and though the money lay at home in her drawer, honestly ready to pay, the recklessness of credit gave her an added joy. The store had its market, also, at Thanksgiving time, and she bargained for a turkey. It could be sent her, the day before, by some of the neighbors. When she left the counter, her arms and her little basket were filled with bundles. Joshua Marden was glad to take them.

"No, I won't ride," said Lucy Ann. "Much obliged to *you*. Jest leave the things inside the fence. I'd ruther walk. I don't git out any too often."

She took her way home along the brown road, stepping lightly and swiftly, and full of busy thoughts. Flocks of birds went whirring by over the yellowed fields. Lucy Ann could have called out to them, in joyous understanding, they looked so free. She, too, seemed to be flying on the wings of a fortunate wind.

All that week she scrubbed and regulated, and took a thousand capable steps as briskly as those who work for the home-coming of those they love. The neighbors dropped in, one after another,

to ask where she was going to spend Thanksgiving. Some of
them said, "Won't you pass the day with us?" but Lucy Ann
replied blithely:—

"Oh, John's invited me there!"

All that week, too, she answered letters, in her cramped and
careful hand; for cousins had bidden her to the feast. Over the
letters she had many a troubled pause, for one cousin lived near
Ezra, and had to be told that John had invited her; and to three
others, dangerously within hail of each, she made her excuse a
turncoat, to fit the time. Duplicity in black and white did hurt
her a good deal, and she sometimes stopped, in the midst of
her slow transcription, to look up piteously and say aloud:—

"I hope I shall be forgiven!" But by the time the stamp was
on, and the pencil ruling erased, her heart was light again. If
she had sinned, she was finding the path intoxicatingly pleasant.

Through all the days before the festival, no house exhaled a
sweeter savor than this little one on the green. Lucy Ann did
her miniature cooking with great seriousness and care. She
seemed to be dwelling in a sacred isolation, yet not altogether
alone, but with her mother and all their bygone years. Standing
at her table, mixing and tasting, she recalled stories her mother
had told her, until, at moments, it seemed as if she not only
lived her own life, but some previous one, through that being
whose blood ran with hers. She was realizing that ineffable sense
of possession born out of knowledge that the enduring part of
a personality is ours forever, and that love is an unquenched
fire, fed by memory as well as hope.

On Thanksgiving morning, Lucy Ann lay in bed a little later,
because that had been the family custom. Then she rose to her
exquisite house, and got breakfast ready, according to the
unswerving programme of the day. Fried chicken and mince
pie: she had had them as a child, and now they were scrupulously
prepared. After breakfast, she sat down in the sunshine, and
watched the people go by to service in Tiverton Church. Lucy
Ann would have liked going, too; but there would be inconvenient questioning, as there always must be when we meet our
kind. She would stay undisturbed in her seclusion, keeping her
festival alone. The morning was still young when she put her
turkey in the oven, and made the vegetables ready. Lucy Ann

was not very fond of vegetables, but there had to be just so
many—onions, turnips, and squash baked with molasses—for
her mother was a Cape woman, preserving the traditions of
dear Cape dishes. All that forenoon, the little house throbbed
with a curious sense of expectancy. Lucy Ann was preparing so
many things that it seemed as if somebody must surely keep her
company; but when dinner-time struck, and she was still alone,
there came no lull in her anticipation. Peace abode with her,
and wrought its own fair work. She ate her dinner slowly, with
meditation and a thankful heart. She did not need to hear the
minister's careful catalogue of mercies received. She was at
home; that was enough.

After dinner, when she had done up the work, and left the
kitchen without spot or stain, she went upstairs, and took out
her mother's beautiful silk poplin, the one saved for great
occasions, and only left behind because she had chosen to be
buried in her wedding gown. Lucy Ann put it on with careful
hands, and then laid about her neck the wrought collar she had
selected the day before. She looked at herself in the glass, and
arranged a gray curl with anxious scrutiny. No girl adorning for
her bridal could have examined every fold and line with a more
tender care. She stood there a long, long moment, and approved
herself.

"It's a wonder," she said reverently. "It's the greatest mercy
anybody ever had."

The afternoon waned, though not swiftly; for Time does not
always gallop when happiness pursues. Lucy Ann could almost
hear the gliding of his rhythmic feet. She did the things set aside
for festivals, or the days when we have company. She looked
over the photograph album, and turned the pages of the "Ladies'
Wreath." When she opened the case containing that old daguerreotype, she scanned it with a little distasteful smile, and
then glanced up at her own image in the glass, nodding her
head in thankful peace. She was the enduring portrait. In
herself, she might even see her mother grow very old. So the
hours slipped on into dusk, and she sat there with her dream,
knowing, though it was only a dream, how sane it was, and
good. When wheels came rattling into the yard, she awoke with
a start, and John's voice, calling to her in an inexplicable alarm,

did not disturb her. She had had her day. Not all the family fates could take it from her now. John kept calling, even while his wife and children were climbing down, unaided, from the great carryall. His voice proclaimed its own story, and Lucy Ann heard it with surprise.

"Lucy! Lucy Ann!" he cried. "You here? You show yourself, if you're all right."

Before they reached the front door, Lucy Ann had opened it and stood there, gently welcoming.

"Yes, here I be," said she. "Come right in, all of ye. Why, if that ain't Ezra, too, an' his folks, turnin' into the lane. When'd you plan it?"

"Plan it! we didn't plan it!" said Mary testily. She put her hand on Lucy Ann's shoulder, to give her a little shake; but, feeling mother's poplin, she forbore.

Lucy Ann retreated before them into the house, and they all trooped in after her. Ezra's family, too, were crowding in at the doorway; and the brothers, who had paused only to hitch the horses, filled up the way behind. Mary, by a just self-election, was always the one to speak.

"I declare, Lucy!" cried she, "if ever I could be tried with you, I should be now. Here we thought you was at Ezra's, an' Ezra's folks thought you was with us; an' if we hadn't harnessed up, an' drove over there in the afternoon, for a kind of surprise party, we should ha' gone to bed thinkin' you was somewhere, safe an' sound. An' here you've been, all day long, in this lonesome house!"

"You let me git a light," said Lucy Ann calmly. "You be takin' off your things, an' se' down." She began lighting the tall astral lamp on the table, and its prisms danced and swung. Lucy Ann's delicate hand did not tremble; and when the flame burned up through the shining chimney, more than one started, at seeing how exactly she resembled grandma, in the days when old Mrs. Cummings had ruled her own house. Perhaps it was the royalty of the poplin that enwrapped her; but Lucy Ann looked very capable of holding her own. She was facing them all, one hand resting on the table, and a little smile flickering over her face.

"I s'pose I was a poor miserable creatur' to git out of it that way," said she. "If I'd felt as I do now, I needn't ha' done it. I could ha' spoke up. But then it seemed as if there wa'n't no other way. I jest wanted my Thanksgivin' in my own home, an' so I throwed you off the track the best way I could. I dunno's I lied. I dunno whether I did or not; but I guess, anyway, I shall be forgiven for it."

Ezra spoke first: "Well, if you didn't want to come"—

"Want to come!" broke in John. "Of course she don't want to come! She wants to stay in her own home, an' call her soul her own—don't you, Lucy?"

Lucy Ann glanced at him with her quick, grateful smile.

"I'm goin' to, now," she said gently, and they knew she meant it.

But, looking about among them, Lucy Ann was conscious of a little hurt unhealed; she had thrown their kindness back.

"I guess I can't tell exactly how it is," she began hesitatingly; "but you see my home's my own, jest as yours is. You couldn't any of you go around cousinin', without feelin' you was tore up by the roots. You've all been real good to me, wantin' me to come, an' I s'pose I should make an awful towse if I never was asked; but now I've got all my visitin' done up, cousins an' all, an' I'm goin' to be to home a spell. An' I do admire to have company," added Lucy Ann, a bright smile breaking over her face. "Mother did, you know, an' I guess I take arter her. Now you lay off your things, an' I'll put the kettle on. I've got more pies 'n you could shake a stick at, an' there's a whole loaf o' fruit-cake, a year old."

Mary, taking off her shawl, wiped her eyes surreptitiously on a corner of it, and Abby whispered to her husband, "Dear creatur'!" John and Ezra turned, by one consent, to put the horses in the barn; and the children, conscious that some mysterious affair had been settled, threw themselves into the occasion with an irresponsible delight. The room became at once vocal and with talk and laughter, and Lucy Ann felt, with a swelling heart, what a happy universe it is where so many bridges lie between this world and that unknown state we call the next. But no moment of that evening was half so sweet to her as the one when little John, the youngest child of all, crept up to her and pulled at her poplin skirt, until she bent down to hear.

"Grandma," said he, "when 'd you get well?"

Mary E. Wilkins Freeman

Old Woman Magoun
1905

Mary E. Wilkins Freeman (1852–1930), after an adolescence unsettled by increasing financial hardship, moved with her family from their familiar Randolph, Massachusetts home to Brattleboro, Vermont. There, attempts to achieve security and stability ended with the successive deaths of her only sibling, her younger sister Nan, in 1876, her mother in 1880, and her father in 1883. She was left alone, needing to support herself in a time when the only careers open to a young woman of her class were teaching and literature. She returned to Randolph and moved in with the family of her life-long friend Mary Wales, where she stayed through the years of her literary apprenticeship, and the years of her greatest success, until her ill-fated marriage to Charles Freeman, a New Jersey physician, in 1902. Their marriage was soon disrupted by Dr. Freeman's increasing alcoholism and its associated illnesses.

Freeman lived most of her life in a world of women and, when she became restless, her literary success gave her the financial independence to travel. She was part of the network of literary women whose hub was Annie Fields, the wife of Henry Fields, publisher and editor of the Atlantic Monthly. *Among these women were Sarah Orne Jewett, who had been the young Mary Wilkins's literary inspiration and model, and Alice Brown.*

Her first literary success came with the acceptance in 1883 by Harper's Bazaar *of the story "Two Old Lovers." By 1887 enough stories had been published in that periodical and in* Harper's New Monthly Magazine *to compile her first collection:* A Humble Romance and Other Stories. *A second collection,* A New England Nun and Other Stories, *appeared in 1891.*

Although Freeman left little in the way of personal reminiscence about her mother, at some point in her career she changed her given middle name of Ella to Eleanor, which had been her mother's name. The characteristic pair in many of her stories is either a mother and daughter, two sisters (one almost old enough to be the other's mother), or two women who stand, as in "Old Woman Magoun," in the stead of mother and daughter to each other. Intense and supportive relationships between such pairs are often central to her stories.

Freeman's genius lay in her ability to penetrate and illuminate the conjunction between necessity and desire in a woman's life. She tells her truths in ways that pierce the reader's heart as if with a boning knife. Her stories often focus on that moment in a woman's life when she must act in the face of conflict between her personal values and the demands of the "real world," whether social or natural. Her heroines often must make choices in no-win situations.

"Old Woman Magoun," first published in Harper's *in October 1905, and later included in her 1909 collection,* The Winning Lady and Others, *reflects elements of the Demeter and Persephone myth explored in depth in recent years by feminist scholars. Freeman was an erudite woman, and the powerful myths of the early Hebrew, Greek, and Roman cultures as they were encoded in the Hebrew Bible and in classical Greek and Roman drama left strong imprints on her fiction.*

"Old Woman Magoun" is a transformation of a classical Greek tragedy: Euripedes' Medea. *The story of the mother who murders her children to protect them from their corrupt father and to punish him for his betrayal and desertion of their mother is brought forward in time more than two millennia. The major force energizing this retelling is wrought by the shift in focus from the vision of a male storyteller to a female storyteller.*

Additionally, the custom of Freeman's times called for the polite masking of barbarism, and so motivated certain changes in the figures through whom the story is told. The killing of the child becomes the passive act of a mother-surrogate rather than the act of a mother stabbing her children with a knife. The betrayed and deserted Medea, wife and mother, is divided into two characters—Old Woman Magoun and her long-dead daughter. And the figure of the father is split into two men: one who exercises his patriarchal right to demand sexual access to his daughter, and the other who will actually carry out the rape.

The story can be read as a study of the incest theme, couched in Victorian gentility. The threat of incest and the sexual exploitation of female children by men with the privilege, the opportunity, and the habit of self-indulgence is the most important threat to the mother-daughter couple. This story is a model for stories in the category of mother and daughter vis-à-vis the patriarchy.

Mary E. Wilkins Freeman received the Howells Medal of the American Academy of Arts and Letters and was elected to the National Institute of Arts and Letters in 1926. Although her writing has often been narrowly categorized and stereotypically misinterpreted, it has never been completely unavailable and she has always retained an audience.

Freeman's first two volumes of stories have remained in print almost continually since their publication. Ten more volumes of her short stories have been reprinted in recent years: Pot of Gold and Other Stories *(1892);* Young Lucretia and Other Stories *(1892);* People of Our Neighborhood *(1898);* Silence and Other Stories *(1898);* Love of Parson Lord and Other Stories *(1900);* Understudies *(1901);* Six Trees *(1903);* The Wind in the Rose Bush and Other Stories of the Supernatural *(1903);* The Givers *(1904); and* Copy-Cat and Other Stories *(1914). Several others are unavailable. Five of her novels are back in print.*

The hamlet of Barry's Ford is situated in a sort of high valley among the mountains. Below it the hills lie in moveless curves like a petrified ocean; above it they rise in green-cresting waves which never break. It is *Barry's* Ford because one time the Barry family was the most important in the place; and *Ford* because just at the beginning of the hamlet the little turbulent Barry River is fordable. There is, however, now a rude bridge across the river.

Old Woman Magoun was largely instrumental in bringing the bridge to pass. She haunted the miserable little grocery, wherein whisky and hands of tobacco were the most salient features of the stock in trade, and she talked much. She would elbow herself into the midst of a knot of idlers and talk.

"That bridge ought to be built this very summer," said Old Woman Magoun. She spread her strong arms like wings, and sent the loafers, half laughing, half angry, flying in every direction. "If I were a *man*," said she, "I'd go out this very minute and lay the fust log. If I were a passel of lazy men layin' round, I'd start up for once in my life, I would." The men cowered visibly—all except Nelson Barry; he swore under his breath and strode over to the counter.

Old Woman Magoun looked after him majestically. "You can cuss all you want to, Nelson Barry," said she; "I ain't afraid of you. I don't expect you to lay ary log of the bridge, but I'm goin' to have it built this very summer." She did. The weakness of the masculine element in Barry's Ford was laid low before such strenuous feminine assertion.

Old Woman Magoun and some other women planned a treat—

two sucking pigs, and pies, and sweet cake—for a reward after
the bridge should be finished. They even viewed leniently the
increased consumption of ardent spirits.

"It seems queer to me," Old Woman Magoun said to Sally
Jinks, "that men can't do nothin' without havin' to drink and
chew to keep their sperits up. Lord! I've worked all my life and
never done nuther."

"Men is different," said Sally Jinks.

"Yes, they be," assented Old Woman Magoun, with open
contempt.

The two women sat on a bench in front of Old Woman
Magoun's house, and little Lily Barry, her granddaughter, sat
holding her doll on a small mossy stone near by. From where
they sat they could see the men at work on the new bridge. It
was the last day of the work.

Lily clasped her doll—a poor old rag thing—close to her
childish bosom, like a little mother, and her face, round which
curled her long yellow hair, was fixed upon the men at work.
Little Lily had never been allowed to run with the other children
at Barry's Ford. Her grandmother had taught her everything
she knew—which was not much, but tending at least to a certain
measure of spiritual growth—for she, as it were, poured the
goodness of her own soul into this little receptive vase of another.
Lily was firmly grounded in her knowledge that it was wrong to
lie or steal or disobey her grandmother. She had also learned
that one should be very industrious. It was seldom that Lily sat
idly holding her doll baby, but this was a holiday because of the
bridge. She looked only a child, although she was nearly fourteen;
her mother had been married at sixteen. That is, Old Woman
Magoun said that her daughter, Lily's mother, had married at
sixteen; there had been rumors, but no one had dared openly
gainsay the old woman. She said that her daughter had married
Nelson Barry and he had deserted her. She had lived in her
mother's house, and Lily had been born there, and she had died
when the baby was only a week old.

Lily's father, Nelson Barry, was the fairly dangerous degenerate of a good old family. Nelson's father before him had been
bad. He was now the last of the family, with the exception of a
sister of feeble intellect, with whom he lived in the old Barry

house. He was a middle-aged man, still handsome. The shiftless population of Barry's Ford looked up to him as to an evil deity. They wondered how Old Woman Magoun dared brave him as she did. But Old Woman Magoun had within her a mighty sense of reliance upon herself as being on the right track in the midst of a maze of evil, which gave her courage. Nelson Barry had manifested no interest whatever in his daughter. Lily seldom saw her father. She did not often go to the store which was his favorite haunt. Her grandmother took care that she should not do so.

However, that afternoon she departed from her usual custom and sent Lily to the store.

She came in from the kitchen, whither she had been to baste the roasting pig. "There's no use talkin'," said she, "I've got to have some more salt. I've jest used the very last I had to dredge over that pig. I've got to go to the store."

Sally Jinks looked at Lily. "Why don't you send her?" she asked.

Old Woman Magoun gazed irresolutely at the girl. She was herself very tired. It did not seem to her that she could drag herself up the dusty hill to the store. She glanced with covert resentment at Sally Jinks. She thought that she might offer to go. But Sally Jinks said again, "Why don't you let her go?" and looked with a languid eye at Lily holding her doll on the stone.

Lily was watching the men at work on the bridge, with her childish delight in a spectacle of any kind, when her grandmother addressed her.

"Guess I'll let you go down to the store an' git some salt, Lily," said she.

The girl turned uncomprehending eyes upon her grandmother at the sound of her voice. She had been filled with one of the innocent reveries of childhood. Lily had in her the making of an artist or a poet. Her prolonged childhood went to prove it, and also her retrospective eyes, as clear and blue as blue light itself, which seemed to see past all that she looked upon. She had not come of the old Barry family for nothing. The best of the strain was in her, along with the splendid stanchness in humble lines which she had acquired from her grandmother.

"Put on your hat," said Old Woman Magoun; "the sun is hot

and you might git a headache." She called the girl to her, and put back the shower of fair curls under the rubber band which confined the hat. She gave Lily some money, and watched her knot it into a corner of her little cotton handkerchief. "Be careful you don't lose it," said she, "and don't stop to talk to anybody, for I am in a hurry for that salt. Of course, if anybody speaks to you answer them polite, and then come right along."

Lily started, her pocket handkerchief weighted with the small silver dangling from one hand, and her rag doll carried over her shoulder like a baby. The absurd travesty of a face peeped forth from Lily's yellow curls. Sally Jinks looked after her with a sniff.

"She ain't goin' to carry that rag doll to the store?" said she.

"She likes to," replied Old Woman Magoun, in a half-shamed yet defiantly extenuating voice.

"Some girls at her age is thinkin' about beaux instead of rag dolls," said Sally Jinks.

The grandmother bristled, "Lily ain't big nor old for her age," said she. "I ain't in any hurry to have her git married. She ain't none too strong."

"She's got a good color," said Sally Jinks. She was crocheting white cotton lace, making her thick fingers fly. She really knew how to do scarcely anything except to crochet that coarse lace; somehow her heavy brain or her fingers had mastered that.

"I know she's got a beautiful color," replied Old Woman Magoun, with an odd mixture of pride and anxiety, "but it comes an' goes."

"I've heard that was a bad sign," remarked Sally Jinks, loosening some thread from her spool.

"Yes, it is," said the grandmother. "She's nothin' but a baby, though she's quicker than most to learn."

Lily Barry went on her way to the store. She was clad in a scanty short frock of blue cotton; her hat was tipped back, forming an oval frame for her innocent face. She was very small, and walked like a child, with the clap-clap of little feet of babyhood. She might have been considered, from her looks, under ten.

Presently she heard footsteps behind her; she turned around a little timidly to see who was coming. When she saw a handsome well-dressed man, she felt reassured. The man came alongside and glanced down carelessly at first; then his look deepened. He smiled, and Lily saw he was very handsome indeed, and that his smile was not only reassuring but wonderfully sweet and compelling.

"Well, little one," said the man, "where are you bound, you and your dolly?"

"I am going to the store to buy some salt for grandma," replied Lily, in her sweet treble. She looked up in the man's face, and he fairly started at the revelation of its innocent beauty. He regulated his pace by hers, and the two went on together. The man did not speak again at once. Lily kept glancing timidly up at him, and every time that she did so the man smiled and her confidence increased. Presently when the man's hand grasped her little childish one hanging by her side, she felt a complete trust in him. Then she smiled up at him. She felt glad that this nice man had come along, for just here the road was lonely.

After a while the man spoke. "What is your name, little one?" he asked, caressingly.

"Lily Barry."

The man started. "What is your father's name?"

"Nelson Barry," replied Lily.

The man whistled. "Is your mother dead?"

"Yes, sir."

"How old are you, my dear?"

"Fourteen," replied Lily.

The man looked at her with surprise. "As old as that?"

Lily suddenly shrank from the man. She could not have told why. She pulled her little hand from his, and he let it go with no remonstrance. She clasped both her arms around her rag doll, in order that her hand should not be free for him to grasp again.

She walked a little farther away from the man, and he looked amused.

"You still play with your doll?" he said, in a soft voice.

"Yes, sir," replied Lily. She quickened her pace and reached the store.

When Lily entered the store, Hiram Gates, the owner, was behind the counter. The only man besides in the store was

Nelson Barry. He sat tipping his chair back against the wall; he was half asleep, and his handsome face was bristling with a beard of several days' growth and darkly flushed. He opened his eyes when Lily entered, the strange man following. He brought his chair down on all fours, and he looked at the man— not noticing Lily at all—with a look compounded of defiance and uneasiness.

"Hullo, Jim!" he said.

"Hullo, old man!" returned the stranger.

Lily went over to the counter and asked for the salt, in her pretty little voice. When she had paid for it and was crossing the store, Nelson Barry was on his feet.

"Well, how are you, Lily? It is Lily, isn't it?" he said.

"Yes, sir," replied Lily, faintly.

Her father bent down and, for the first time in her life, kissed her, and the whisky odor of his breath came into her face.

Lily involuntarily started, and shrank away from him. Then she rubbed her mouth violently with her little cotton handkerchief, which she held gathered up with the rag doll.

"Damn it all! I believe she is afraid of me," said Nelson Barry, in a thick voice.

"Looks a little like it," said the other man, laughing.

"It's that damned old woman," said Nelson Barry. Then he smiled again at Lily. "I didn't know what a pretty little daughter I was blessed with," said he, and he softly stroked Lily's pink cheek under her hat.

Now Lily did not shrink from him. Heredity instincts and nature itself were asserting themselves in the child's innocent, receptive breast.

Nelson Barry looked curiously at Lily. "How old are you, anyway, child?" he asked.

"I'll be fourteen in September," replied Lily.

"But you still play with your doll?" said Barry, laughing kindly down at her.

Lily hugged her doll more tightly, in spite of her father's kind voice. "Yes, sir," she replied.

Nelson glanced across at some glass jars filled with sticks of candy. "See here, little Lily, do you like candy?" said he.

"Yes, sir."

"Wait a minute."

Lily waited while her father went over to the counter. Soon he returned with a package of the candy.

"I don't see how you are going to carry so much," he said, smiling. "Suppose you throw away your doll?"

Lily gazed at her father and hugged the doll tightly, and there was all at once in the child's expression something mature. It became the reproach of a woman. Nelson's face sobered.

"Oh, it's all right, Lily," he said; "keep your doll. Here, I guess you can carry this candy under your arm."

Lily could not resist the candy. She obeyed Nelson's instructions for carrying it, and left the store laden. The two men also left, and walked in the opposite direction, talking busily.

When Lily reached home, her grandmother, who was watching for her, spied at once the package of candy.

"What's that?" she asked, sharply.

"My father gave it to me," answered Lily, in a faltering voice. Sally regarded her with something like alertness.

"Your father?"

"Yes, ma'am."

"Where did you see him?"

"In the store."

"He gave you this candy?"

"Yes, ma'am."

"What did he say?"

"He asked me how old I was, and—"

"And what?"

"I don't know," replied Lily; and it really seemed to her that she did not know, she was so frightened and bewildered by it all, and, more than anything else, by her grandmother's face as she questioned her.

Old Woman Magoun's face was that of one upon whom a long-anticipated blow had fallen. Sally Jinks gazed at her with a sort of stupid alarm.

Old Woman Magoun continued to gaze at her grandchild with that look of terrible solicitude, as if she saw the girl in the clutch of a tiger. "You can't remember what else he said?" she asked, fiercely, and the child began to whimper softly.

"No, ma'am," she sobbed. "I—don't know, and—"

"And what? Answer me."

"There was another man there. A real handsome man."

"Did he speak to you?" asked Old Woman Magoun.

"Yes, ma'am; he walked along with me a piece," confessed Lily, with a sob of terror and bewilderment.

"What did *he* say to you?" asked Old Woman Magoun, with a sort of despair.

Lily told, in her little, faltering, frightened voice, all of the conversation which she could recall. It sounded harmless enough, but the look of the realization of a long-expected blow never left her grandmother's face.

The sun was getting low and the bridge was nearing completion. Soon the workmen would be crowding into the cabin for their promised supper. There became visible in the distance, far up the road, the heavily plodding figure of another woman who had agreed to come and help. Old Woman Magoun turned again to Lily.

"You go right upstairs to your own chamber now," said she.

"Good land! ain't you goin' to let that poor child stay up and see the fun?" said Sally Jinks.

"You jest mind your own business," said Old Woman Magoun, forcibly, and Sally Jinks shrank. "You go right up there now, Lily," said the grandmother, in a softer tone, "and grandma will bring you up a nice plate of supper."

"When be you goin' to let that girl grow up?" asked Sally Jinks when Lily had disappeared.

"She'll grow up in the Lord's good time," replied Old Woman Magoun, and there was in her voice something both sad and threatening. Sally Jinks again shrank a little.

Soon the workmen came flocking noisily into the house. Old Woman Magoun and her two helpers served the bountiful supper. Most of the men had drunk as much as, and more than, was good for them, and Old Woman Magoun had stipulated that there was to be no drinking of anything except coffee during supper.

"I'll git you as good a meal as I know how," she said, "but if I see ary one of you drinkin' a drop, I'll run you all out. If you want anything to drink, you can go up to the store afterward. That's the place for you to go to, if you've got to make hogs of yourselves. I ain't goin' to have no hogs in my house."

Old Woman Magoun was implicitly obeyed. She had a curious authority over most people when she chose to exercise it. When the supper was in full swing, she quietly stole upstairs and carried some food to Lily. She found the girl, with the rag doll in her arms, crouching by the window in her little rocking-chair—a relic of her infancy, which she still used.

"What a noise they are makin', grandma!" she said, in a terrified whisper, as her grandmother placed the plate before her on a chair.

"They've 'most all of 'em been drinkin'. They air a passel of hogs," replied the old woman.

"Is the man that was with—with my father down there?" asked Lily, in a timid fashion. Then she fairly cowered before the look in her grandmother's eyes.

"No, he ain't, and what's more, he never will be down there if I can help it," said Old Woman Magoun, in a fierce whisper. "I know who he is. They can't cheat me. He's one of them Willises—that family the Barrys married into. They're worse than the Barrys, ef they *have* got money. Eat your supper, and put him out of your mind, child."

It was after Lily was asleep, when Old Woman Magoun was alone, clearing away her supper dishes, that Lily's father came. The door was closed, and he knocked, and the old woman knew at once who was there. The sound of that knock meant as much to her as the whir of a bomb to the defender of a fortress. She opened the door, and Nelson Barry stood there.

"Good evening, Mrs. Magoun," he said.

Old Woman Magoun stood before him, filling up the doorway with her firm bulk.

"Good evening, Mrs. Magoun," said Nelson Barry again.

"I ain't got no time to waste," replied the old woman, harshly. "I've got my supper dishes to clean up after them men."

She stood there and looked at him as she might have looked at a rebellious animal which she was trying to tame. The man laughed.

"It's no use," said he. "You know me of old. No human being can turn me from my way when I am once started in it. You may as well let me come in."

Old Woman Magoun entered the house, and Barry followed her.

Barry began without any preface. "Where is the child?" asked he.

"Upstairs. She has gone to bed."

"She goes to bed early."

"Children ought to," returned the old woman, polishing a plate.

Barry laughed. "You are keeping her a child a long while," he remarked, in a soft voice which had a sting in it.

"She *is* a child," returned the old woman, defiantly.

"Her mother was only three years older when Lily was born."

The old woman made a sudden motion toward the man which seemed fairly menacing. Then she turned again to her dish washing.

"I want her," said Barry.

"You can't have her," replied the old woman, in a still stern voice.

"I don't see how you can help yourself. You have always acknowledged that she was my child."

The old woman continued her task, but her strong back heaved. Barry regarded her with an entirely pitiless expression.

"I am going to have the girl, that is the long and short of it," he said, "and it is for her best good, too. You are a fool, or you would see it."

"Her best good?" muttered the old woman.

"Yes, her best good. What are you going to do with her, anyway? The girl is a beauty, and almost a woman grown, although you try to make out that she is a baby. You can't live forever."

"The Lord will take care of her," replied the old woman, and again she turned and faced him, and her expression was that of a prophetess.

"Very well, let Him," said Barry, easily. "All the same I'm going to have her, and I tell you it is for her best good. Jim Willis saw her this afternoon, and—"

Old Woman Magoun looked at him. "Jim Willis!" she fairly shrieked.

"Well, what of it?"

"One of them Willises!" repeated the old woman, and this time her voice was thick. It seemed almost as if she were stricken with paralysis. She did not enunciate clearly.

The man shrank a little. "Now what is the need of your making such a fuss?" he said. "I will take her, and Isabel will look out for her."

"Your half-witted sister?" said Old Woman Magoun.

"Yes, my half-witted sister. She knows more than you think."

"More wickedness."

"Perhaps. Well, a knowledge of evil is a useful thing. How are you going to avoid evil if you don't know what it is like? My sister and I will take care of my daughter."

The old woman continued to look at the man, but his eyes never fell. Suddenly her gaze grew inconceivably keen. It was as if she saw through all externals.

"I know what it is!" she cried. "You have been playing cards and you lost, and this is the way you will pay him."

Then the man's face reddened, and he swore under his breath.

"Oh, my God!" said the old woman; and she really spoke with her eyes aloft as if addressing something outside of them both. Then she turned again to her dish washing.

The man cast a dogged look at her back. "Well, there is no use talking. I have made up my mind," said he, "and you know me and what that means. I am going to have the girl."

"When?" said the old woman, without turning around.

"Well, I am willing to give you a week. Put her clothes in good order before she comes."

The old woman made no reply. She continued washing dishes. She even handled them so carefully they did not rattle.

"You understand," said Barry. "Have her ready a week from today."

"Yes," said Old Woman Magoun, "I understand."

Nelson Barry, going up the mountain road, reflected that Old Woman Magoun had a strong character, that she understood much better than her sex in general the futility of withstanding the inevitable.

"Well," he said to Jim Willis when he reached home, "the old woman did not make such a fuss as I expected."

"Are you going to have the girl?"

"Yes; a week from today. Look here, Jim; you've got to stick to your promise."

"All right," said Willis. "Go you one better."

The two were playing at cards in the old parlor, once mag-

nificent, now squalid, of the Barry house. Isabel, the half-witted
sister, entered, bringing some glasses on a tray. She had learned
with her feeble intellect some tricks, like a dog. One of them
was the mixing of sundry drinks. She set the tray on a little
stand near the two men, and watched them with her silly simper.

"Clear out now and go to bed," her brother said to her, and
she obeyed.

Early the next morning Old Woman Magoun went up to Lily's
little sleeping chamber, and watched her a second as she lay
asleep, with her yellow locks spread over the pillow. Then she
spoke. "Lily," said she—"Lily, wake up. I am going to Greenham
across the new bridge, and you can go with me."

Lily immediately sat up in bed and smiled at her grandmother.
Her eyes were still misty, but the light of awakening was in
them.

"Get right up," said the old woman. "You can wear your new
dress if you want to."

Lily gurgled with pleasure like a baby. "And my new hat?"
said she.

"I don't care."

Old Woman Magoun and Lily started for Greenham before
Barry's Ford, which kept late hours, was fairly awake. It was
three miles to Greenham. The old woman said that, since the
horse was a little lame, they would walk. It was a beautiful
morning, with a diamond radiance of dew over everything. Her
grandmother had curled Lily's hair more punctiliously than
usual. The little face peeped like a rose out of two rows of
golden spirals. Lily wore her new muslin dress with a pink sash,
and her best hat of a fine white straw trimmed with a wreath of
rosebuds; also the neatest black openwork stockings and pretty
shoes. She even had white cotton gloves. When they set out, the
old, heavily stepping woman, in her black gown and cape and
bonnet, looked down at the little pink fluttering figure. Her face
was full of the tenderest love and admiration, and yet there was
something terrible about it. They crossed the new bridge—a
primitive structure built of logs in a slovenly fashion. Old Woman
Magoun pointed to a gap.

"Jest see that," said she. "That's the way men work."

"Men ain't very nice, be they?" said Lily, in her sweet little
voice.

"No, they ain't, take them all together," replied her grandmother.

"That man that walked to the store with me was nicer than some, I guess," Lily said, in a wishful fashion. Her grandmother reached down and took the child's hand in its small cotton glove. "You hurt me, holding my hand so tight," Lily said presently, in a deprecatory little voice.

The old woman loosened her grasp. "Grandma didn't know how tight she was holding your hand," said she. "She wouldn't hurt you for nothin', except it was to save your life, or somethin' like that." She spoke with an undertone of tremendous meaning which the girl was too childish to grasp. They walked along the country road. Just before they reached Greenham they passed a stone wall overgrown with blackberry vines, and, an unusual thing in that vicinity, a lusty spread of deadly nightshade full of berries.

"Those berries look good to eat, grandma," Lily said.

At that instant the old woman's face became something terrible to see. "You can't have any now," she said, and hurried Lily along.

"They look real nice," said Lily.

When they reached Greenham, Old Woman Magoun took her way straight to the most pretentious house there, the residence of the lawyer, whose name was Mason. Old Woman Magoun bade Lily wait in the yard for a few moments, and Lily ventured to seat herself on a bench beneath an oak tree; then she watched with some wonder her grandmother enter the lawyer's office door at the right of the house. Presently the lawyer's wife came out and spoke to Lily under the tree. She had in her hand a little tray containing a plate of cake, a glass of milk, and an early apple. She spoke very kindly to Lily; she even kissed her, and offered her the tray of refreshments, which Lily accepted gratefully. She sat eating, with Mrs. Mason watching her, when Old Woman Magoun came out of the lawyer's office with a ghastly face.

"What are you eatin'?" she asked Lily, sharply. "Is that a sour apple?"

"I thought she might be hungry," said the lawyer's wife, with loving, melancholy eyes upon the girl.

Lily had almost finished the apple. "It's real sour, but I like it; it's real nice, grandma," she said.

"You ain't been drinkin' milk with a sour apple?"

"It was real nice milk, grandma."

"You ought never to have drunk milk and eat a sour apple," said her grandmother. "Your stomach was all out of order this mornin', an' sour apples and milk is always apt to hurt anybody."

"I don't know but they are," Mrs. Mason said, apologetically, as she stood on the green lawn with her lavender muslin sweeping around her. "I am real sorry, Mrs. Magoun. I ought to have thought. Let me get some soda for her."

"Soda never agrees with her," replied the old woman, in a harsh voice. "Come," she said to Lily, "it's time we were goin' home."

After Lily and her grandmother had disappeared down the road, Lawyer Mason came out of his office and joined his wife, who had seated herself on the bench beneath the tree. She was idle, and her face wore the expression of those who review joys forever past. She had lost a little girl, her only child, years ago, and her husband always knew when she was thinking about her. Lawyer Mason looked older than his wife; he had a dry, shrewd, slightly one-sided face.

"What do you think, Maria?" he said. "That old woman came to me with the most pressing entreaty to adopt that little girl."

"She is a beautiful little girl," said Mrs. Mason, in a slightly husky voice.

"Yes, she is a pretty child," assented the lawyer, looking pityingly at his wife; "but it is out of the question, my dear. Adopting a child is a serious measure, and in this case a child who comes from Barry's Ford!"

"But the grandmother seems a very good woman," said Mrs. Mason.

"I rather think she is. I never heard a word against her. But the father! No, Maria, we cannot take a child with Barry blood in her veins. The stock has run out; it is vitiated physically and morally. It won't do, my dear."

"Her grandmother had her dressed up as pretty as a little girl could be," said Mrs. Mason, and this time the tears welled into her faithful, wistful eyes.

"Well, we can't help that," said the lawyer, as he went back to his office.

Old Woman Magoun and Lily returned, going slowly along the road to Barry's Ford. When they came to the stone wall where the blackberry vines and the deadly nightshade grew, Lily said she was tired, and asked if she could not sit down for a few minutes. The strange look on her grandmother's face had deepened. Now and then Lily glanced at her and had a feeling as if she were looking at a stranger.

"Yes, you can set down if you want to," said Old Woman Magoun, deeply and harshly.

Lily started and looked at her, as if to make sure that it was her grandmother who spoke. Then she sat down on a stone which was comparatively free of the vines.

"Ain't you goin' to set down, grandma?" Lily asked, timidly.

"No; I don't want to get into that mess," replied her grandmother. "I ain't tired. I'll stand here."

Lily sat still; her delicate little face was flushed with heat. She extended her tiny feet in her best shoes and gazed at them. "My shoes are all over dust," said she.

"It will brush off," said her grandmother, still in that strange voice.

Lily looked around. An elm tree in the field behind her cast a spray of branches over her head; a little cool puff of wind came on her face. She gazed at the low mountains on the horizon, in the midst of which she lived, and she sighed, for no reason that she knew. She began idly picking at the blackberry vines; there were no berries on them; then she put her little fingers on the berries of the deadly nightshade. "These look like nice berries," she said.

Old Woman Magoun, standing stiff and straight in the road, said nothing.

"They look good to eat," said Lily.

Old Woman Magoun still said nothing, but she looked up into the ineffable blue of the sky, over which spread at intervals great white clouds shaped like wings.

Lily picked some of the deadly nightshade berries and ate them. "Why, they are real sweet," said she. "They are nice." She picked some more and ate them.

Presently her grandmother spoke. "Come," she said, "it is time we were going. I guess you have set long enough."

Lily was still eating the berries when she slipped down from the wall and followed her grandmother obediently up the road.

Before they reached home, Lily complained of being very thirsty. She stopped and made a little cup of a leaf and drank long at a mountain brook. "I am dreadful dry, but it hurts me to swallow," she said to her grandmother when she stopped drinking and joined the old woman waiting for her in the road. Her grandmother's face seemed strangely dim to her. She took hold of Lily's hand as they went on. "My stomach burns," said Lily, presently. "I want some more water."

"There is another brook a little farther on," said Old Woman Magoun, in a dull voice.

When they reached that brook, Lily stopped and drank again, but she whimpered a little over her difficulty in swallowing. "My stomach burns, too," she said, walking on, "and my throat is so dry, grandma." Old Woman Magoun held Lily's hand more tightly. "You hurt me, holding my hand so tight, grandma," said Lily, looking up at her grandmother, whose face she seemed to see through a mist, and the old woman loosened her grasp.

When at last they reached home, Lily was very ill. Old Woman Magoun put her on her own bed in the little bedroom out of the kitchen. Lily lay there and moaned, and Sally Jinks came in.

"Why, what ails her?" she asked. "She looks feverish."

Lily unexpectedly answered for herself. "I ate some sour apples and drank some milk," she moaned.

"Sour apples and milk are dreadful apt to hurt anybody," said Sally Jinks. She told several people on her way home that Old Woman Magoun was dreadful careless to let Lily eat such things.

Meanwhile Lily grew worse. She suffered cruelly from the burning in her stomach, the vertigo, and the deadly nausea. "I am so sick, I am so sick, grandma," she kept moaning. She could no longer see her grandmother as she bent over her, but she could hear her talk.

Old Woman Magoun talked as Lily had never heard her talk before, as nobody had ever heard her talk before. She spoke from the depths of her soul; her voice was as tender as the coo of a dove, and it was grand and exalted. "You'll feel better very soon, little Lily," said she.

"I am so sick, grandma."

"You will feel better very soon, and then—"

"I am sick."

"You shall go to a beautiful place."

Lily moaned.

"You shall go to a beautiful place," the old woman went on.

"Where?" asked Lily, groping feebly with her cold little hands.
Then she moaned again.

"A beautiful place, where the flowers grow tall."

"What color? Oh, grandma, I am so sick."

"A blue color," replied the old woman. Blue was Lily's favorite
color. "A beautiful blue color, and as tall as your knees, and the
flowers always stay there, and they never fade."

"Not if you pick them, Grandma? Oh!"

"No, not if you pick them; they never fade, and they are so
sweet you can smell them a mile off; and there are birds that
sing, and all the roads have gold stones in them, and the stone
walls are made of gold."

"Like the ring grandpa gave you? I am so sick, grandma."

"Yes, gold like that. And all the houses are built of silver and
gold, and the people all have wings, so when they get tired
walking they can fly, and—"

"I am so sick, grandma."

"And all the dolls are alive," said Old Woman Magoun. "Dolls
like yours can run, and talk, and love you back again."

Lily had her poor old rag doll in bed with her, clasped close
to her agonized little heart. She tried very hard with her eyes,
whose pupils were so dilated that they looked black, to see her
grandmother's face when she said that, but she could not. "It is
dark," she moaned, feebly.

"There where you are going it is always light," said the
grandmother, "and the commonest things shine like that breast-
pin Mrs. Lawyer Mason had on today."

Lily moaned pitifully, and said something incoherent. Delirium
was commencing. Presently she sat straight up in bed and raved;
but even then her grandmother's wonderful compelling voice
had an influence over her.

"You will come to a gate with all the colors of the rainbow,"
said her grandmother; "and it will open, and you will go right
in and walk up the gold street, and cross the field where the

blue flowers come up to your knees, until you find your mother, and she will take you home where you are going to live. She has a little white room all ready for you, white curtains at the windows, and a little white looking-glass, and when you look in it you will see—"

"What will I see? I am so sick, grandma."

"You will see a face like yours, only it's an angel's; and there will be a little white bed, and you can lay down an' rest."

"Won't I be sick, grandma?" asked Lily. Then she moaned and babbled wildly, although she seemed to understand through it all what her grandmother said.

"No, you will never be sick any more. Talkin' about sickness won't mean anything to you."

It continued. Lily talked on wildly, and her grandmother's great voice of soothing never ceased, until the child fell into a deep sleep, or what resembled sleep; but she lay stiffly in that sleep, and a candle flashed before her eyes made no impression on them.

Then it was that Nelson Barry came. Jim Willis waited outside the door. When Nelson entered he found Old Woman Magoun on her knees beside the bed, weeping with dry eyes and a might of agony which fairly shook Nelson Barry, the degenerate of a fine old race.

"Is she sick?" he asked, in a hushed voice.

Old Woman Magoun gave another terrible sob, which sounded like the gasp of one dying.

"Sally Jinks said that Lily was sick from eating milk and sour apples," said Barry, in a tremulous voice. "I remember that her mother was very sick once from eating them."

Lily lay still, and her grandmother on her knees shook with her terrible sobs.

Suddenly Nelson Barry started. "I guess I had better go to Greenham for a doctor if she's as bad as that," he said. He went close to the bed and looked at the sick child. He gave a great start. Then he felt of her hands and reached down under the bedclothes for her little feet. "Her hands and feet are like ice," he cried out. "Good God! why didn't you send for some one— for me—before? Why, she's dying; she's almost gone!"

Barry rushed out and spoke to Jim Willis, who turned pale and came in and stood by the bedside.

"She's almost gone," he said, in a hushed whisper.

"There's no use going for the doctor; she'd be dead before he got here," said Nelson, and he stood regarding the passing child with a strange, sad face—unutterably sad, because of his incapability of the truest sadness.

"Poor little thing, she's past suffering, anyhow," said the other man, and his own face also was sad with a puzzled, mystified sadness.

Lily died that night. There was quite a commotion in Barry's Ford until after the funeral, it was all so sudden, and then everything went on as usual. Old Woman Magoun continued to live as she had done before. She supported herself by the produce of her tiny farm; she was very industrious, but people said that she was a trifle touched, since every time she went over the log bridge with her eggs or her garden vegetables to sell in Greenham, she carried with her, as one might have carried an infant, Lily's old rag doll.

Fannie Hurst

Oats for the Woman
1917

Fannie Hurst (1889–1968) took as her subject matter what she called the "common people." In her 1958 autobiography, Anatomy of Me, *dedicated "To My Friend The Anonymous Public," she remembers looking out of the window in the Hotel Astor*

"... on the anonymous masses ... the people who were to make up my social register. The unhyphenated Smiths and Joneses. The people who, if killed in a plane crash, were designated as 'and others.' ... Those people down there ... were composed of persons. People were persons!"

When she left her parents and her St. Louis home to live in New York City, she immersed herself in the city's crowds—on the subways, in the lunchrooms, along the avenues. She was a writer researching her subject.

In this choice of subject matter, she recognized her predecessors and colleagues as the great European realists and naturalists: Tolstoy, Dostoyevsky, Gorki, Dumas, Balzac, de Maupassant, Ibsen, Strindberg, Wedekind, Lagerloff, Undset, Bennett; and the Americans: O. Henry, Edwin Markham, and Edgar Lee Masters. At the same time that Hurst identified these writers with whom she felt kinship, she also insisted on her literary independence: "I do not recall that I ever consciously became the disciple of any one author. . . . "

While on the one hand, she saw herself as a sui generis primitive, as a sort of "sport" or mutant, arising from a nurturant and loving but uncomprehending environment as artiste complete, on the other hand, she was widely read, well educated, and a diligent student of the history of her craft. Besides the typically demanding and intense curriculum of the urban American high school at the turn of the century, Hurst also had had a fine classical literary education at Washington University in St. Louis as an undergraduate and later as a graduate student. She completed two additional years of graduate work at Columbia University. She always read and studied with the eye of an apprentice. From her earliest years, she wrote ceaselessly.

The apparently contradictory images of Fannie Hurst as naive self-created artist and as sophisticated inheritor and practitioner of an old literary tradition result from contradictions in her own life. As an American educated in the tradition of the "the best" in Western cultural history, her access to this past was undisputed. However, as a second generation, American-born, German-Jewish descendant of peasants, she knew of no literary tradition that was really hers. The duality of her hyphenated identity explains the duality of her self-image. Because she was a woman, she was set apart from literary achievement by both the Jewish tradition and the Western Christian tradition that had, by her time, come to be identified as the American tradition. This accounts for her perception of herself as an artist without precedent. She did not know of a feminist, or even a female, immigrant Jewish literary tradition.

Critics have often dismissed Fannie Hurst's characters as sentimental stereotypes. The critics who labeled her "sob sister" (borrowing the title of one of her own early stories) tended to think of the working class and of immigrants and their American-born children as "milling crowds" and "huddling masses," as collections of types, rather than as the persons she insisted in her life and her work that they were. The critics never really impugned the accuracy of her portrayals; rather, they denigrated her subject matter. They have thus far been successful in ridiculing her into ill-deserved obscurity.

But the millions of readers who made her the most beloved and one of the wealthiest writers in history, who belonged to the groups of persons about which she wrote—the waitresses, the models, the department store clerks, the laborers, the small business owners, the struggling immigrant mothers and fathers—found her characters and their stories every bit as real, as compelling, as individualized, as their relatives, their friends, and their own selves. They often wrote to ask her if she had been eavesdropping on their lives. A social activist and feminist, Hurst was a colleague of Eleanor Roosevelt from an early shared struggle for better wages and working conditions for domestic workers. She fought against racism, anti-Semitism, sexism, and homophobia, striving to alleviate the suffering she witnessed and wrote about. She has been accused of including too many happy endings, of falsifying the lives of her characters and betraying the inevitability of their stories. But she also wrote about those who didn't triumph. The stories of personal defeat are almost always women's stories, in which a woman comes into conflict with the patriarchy, not stories in which an immigrant comes into conflict with America.

Fannie Hurst published a total of nine volumes of short stories, seventeen novels, three plays, many articles on a variety of subjects, and she collaborated on several of the many films made from her stories and novels. Her work has been translated into eleven languages. "Oats for the Woman" was first published in Cosmopolitan *in June 1917, and was included in* Humoresque *(1919), her fourth volume of short stories.*

The story is both a surrogate mother story and one of a mother and daughter being confronted by the patriarchy in such a way that the happiness and safety of one can only be preserved by the sacrifice of the other. As is often the case in surrogate mother stories, where the absence of biological connection between the mother and the daughter makes the subject more abstract and less evocative of prurience, the real subject of the story is the threat of incest and the mother's anguish in the face of it. As in "Old Woman Magoun" and "Recuerdo," where the implicit threat is the same, the adolescent daughter's childlike innocence and trust are emphasized along with the maternal figure's helplessness and the complicity of all male figures, who might be expected to intervene and protect the women.

That women who toil not neither do they spin might know the feel of fabrics so cunningly devised that they lay to the flesh like the inner petals of buds, three hundred and fifty men, women, and children contrived, between strikes, to make the show-rooms of the Kessler Costume Company, Incorporated, a sort of mauve and mirrored Delphi where buyers from twenty states came to invoke forecast of the mood of skirts, the caprice of sleeves, and the rumored flip to the train. Before these flips and moods, a gigantic industry held semi-annual pause, destinies of lace-factories trembling before a threatened season of strictly tailor-mades, velvet-looms slowing at the shush of taffeta. When woman would be sleazy, petticoat manufacturers went overnight into an oblivion from which there might or might not be returning. The willow plume waved its day, making and unmaking merchants.

Destiny loves thus to spring from acorn beginnings. Helen smiled, and Troy fell. Roast pork, and I doubt not then and there the apple sauce, became a national institution because a small boy burnt his fingers.

That is why, out from the frail love of women for the flesh and its humors, and because for the webby cling of chiffon too often no price is too high, the Kessler Costume Company employed, on the factory side of the door, the three hundred and fifty sewers and cutters, not one of whose monthly wage could half buy the real-lace fichu or the painted-chiffon frock of his own handiwork.

On the show-room side of the door, painted mauve within and not without, *mannequins,* so pink finger-tipped, so tilted of instep, and so bred in the thrust to the silhouette, trailed these sleazy products of thick fingers across mauve-colored carpet and before the appraising eyes of twenty states.

Often as not, smoke rose in that room from the black cigar of the Omaha Store, Omaha, or Ladies' Wear, Cleveland. In season, and particularly during the frenzied dog-days of August, when the fate of the new waist-line or his daring treatment of cloth of silver hung yet in the balance, and the spirit of Detroit must be browbeaten by the dictum of the sleeveless thing in evening frocks, Leon Kessler himself smoked a day-long chain of cigarettes, lighting one off the other.

In the model-room, a long, narrow slit, roaringly ventilated by a whirling machine, lined in frocks suspended from hangers, and just wide enough for two very perfect thirty-sixes to stand abreast, August fell heavily. So heavily that occasionally a cloak-model, her lot to show next December's conceit in theater wraps, fainted on the show-dais; or a cloth-of-gold evening gown, donned for the twentieth time that sweltering day, would suddenly, with its model, crumple, a glittering huddle, to the floor.

Upon Miss Hattie Becker, who within the narrow slit had endured eight of these Augusts with only two casual faints and a swoon or two nipped in the bud, this ninth August came in so furiously that, sliding out of her sixth showing of a cloth-of-silver and blue-fox opera wrap, a shivering that amounted practically to chill took hold of her.

"Br-r-r!" she said, full of all men's awe at the carbon-dioxide paradox. "I'm so hot I'm cold!"

Miss Clarice Delehanty slid out of a shower of tulle-of-gold dancing-frock and into an Avenue gown of rough serge. The tail of a very arched eyebrow threatened, and then ran down in a black rill.

"If Niagara Falls was claret lemonade,
You'd see me beat it to a watery grave.

"That'll be enough canary-talk out of you, Clare. Hand me my shirt-waist there off the hook."

"Didn't Kess say we had to show Keokuk the line before lunch?"

"If the King of England was buying ermine sport coats this morning, I wouldn't show 'em before I had a cold cut and a long drink in me. Hurry! Hand me my waist, Clare, before the girls come in from showing the bridesmaid line."

Miss Delehanty flung the garment down the narrow length of the room.

"Minneapolis don't know it, but after this showing he's going to blow me to the frappiest little lunch on the Waldorf roof."

Miss Becker buttoned her flimsy blouse with three pearl beads down its front, wiping constantly at a constantly dampening brow.

"You'd shove over the Goddess of Liberty if you thought she had her foot on a meal ticket."

"Yes; and if I busted her, you could build a new one on the lunch money you've saved in your time."

"Waldorf! You've got a fine chance with Minneapolis. You mean the Automat, and two spoons for the ice-cream."

Miss Delehanty adjusted a highly eccentric hat, a small green velvet, outrageously tilted off the rear of its *bandeau,* and a wide black streamer flowing down over one shoulder. It was the match to the explosive effect of the *trotteur* gown. She was Fashion's humoresque, except that Fashion has no sense of humor. Very presently Minneapolis would appraise her at two hundred and seventy-five as is. Miss Delehanty herself came cheaper.

"Say, Hattie, don't let being an old man's darling go to your head. The grandchildren may issue an injunction."

A flare of crimson rushed immediately over Miss Becker's face, spreading down into her neck.

"You let him alone! He's a darn sight better than anything I've seen you girls picking for yourselves. You never met a man in your life whose name wasn't Johnnie. You couldn't land a John in a million years."

Miss Delehanty raised her face from over a shoe-buckle. A stare began to set in, as obviously innocent as a small boy's between spitballs.

"Well, who said anything about old St. Louis, I'd like to know?"

"You did, and you leave him alone! What do you know about
a real man? You'd pass up a Ford ride to sit still in a pasteboard
limousine every time!"

"Well, of all things! Did I say anything?"

"Yes, you did!"

"Why, for my part, he can show you a good time eight nights
in the week and Sundays, too."

"He 'ain't got grandchildren—if you want to know it."

"Did I say he had?"

"Yes, you did!"

"Why, I don't blame any girl for showing grandpa a good
time."

"You could consider yourself darn lucky, Clarice Delehanty,
if one half as good ever—"

"Ask the girls if I don't always say old St. Louis is all to the
good. Three or four years ago, right after his wife died, I said
to Ada, I said—"

A head showed suddenly through the lining side of the mauve
portières, blue-eyed, blue-shaved, and with a triple ripple of
black hair trained backward.

"Hurry along there with fifty-seven, Delehanty! Heyman's got
to see the line and catch that six-two Chicago flier."

Miss Delehanty fell into pose, her profile turned back over
one shoulder.

"Tell him to chew a clove; it's good for breathless haste," she
said, disappearing through portières into the show-room.

Miss Becker thrust herself from a hastily-found-out aperture,
patting, with final touch, her belt into place.

"Have I been asking you for five years, Kess, to knock before
you poke your head in on us girls?"

Mr. Leon Kessler appeared then fully between the curtains,
letting them drape heavily behind him. Gotham garbs her poets
and her brokers, her employers and employees, in the national
pin-stripes and sack coat. Except for a few pins stuck upright in
his coat lapel, Mr. Kessler might have been his banker or his
salesman. Typical New-Yorker is the pseudo, half enviously
bestowed upon his kind by *hinter* America. It signifies a bi-weekly
manicure femininely administered; a hotel lobbyist who can
outstare a seatless guest; the sang-froid to add up a dinner

check; spats. When Mr. Kessler tipped, it did not clink; it rustled. In theater, at each interval between acts, he piled out over ladies' knees and returned chewing a mint. He journeyed twice a year to a famous Southern spa, and there won or lost his expenses. He regarded Miss Becker, peering at her around the fluff of a suspended frock of pink tulle.

"What's the idea, Becker? Keokuk wants to see you in the wrap line."

Miss Becker swallowed hard, jamming down and pinning into a small taffy-colored turban, her hair, the exact shade of it, escaping in scallops. Carefully powdered-out lines of her face seemed to emerge suddenly through the conserved creaminess of her skin. Thirty-four, in its unguarded moments, will out. Miss Becker had almost detained twenty's waistline and twenty-two's ardent thrust of face. It was only the indentures of time that had begun to tell slightly—indentures that powder could not putty out. There was a slight bagginess of throat where the years love to eat in first, and out from the eyes a spray of fine lines. It was these lines that came out now indubitably.

"If you want me to lay down on you, Kess, for sure, just ask me to show the line again before lunch. I'm about ready to keel. And you can't put me off again. I'm ready, and you got to come now."

He dug so deeply into his pockets that his sleeves crawled up.

"Say, look here. I've got my business to attend to, and, when my trade's in town, my trade comes first. See? Take off and show Keokuk a few numbers. I want him to see that chinchilla drape."

She reached out, closing her hand over his arm.

"I'll show him the whole line, Kess, when we're back from lunch. I got to talk to you, I tell you. You put me off yesterday and the day before, and this—this is the last."

"The last what?"

"Please, Kess, if you only run over to Rinehardt's with me. I got to tell you something. Something about me and—and—"

He regarded her in some perplexity. "Tell it to me here. Now!"

"I can't. The girls'll be swarming in any minute. I can't get you anywheres but lunch. It's the first thirty minutes of your

time I've asked in five years, Kess—is that little enough? Let
Cissie show Keokuk the blouses till we get back. It's something,
Kess, I can't put off. Kess, please!"

Her face was so close to him and so eager that he turned to
back out.

"Wait for me at the Thirty-first Street entrance," he said, "and
I'll shoot you across to Rinehardt's."

She caught up her small silk hand-bag and ran out toward
the elevators. Down in Thirty-first Street a wave of heat met,
almost overpowering her. New York, enervated from sleepless
nights on fire-escapes and in bedrooms opening on areaways,
moved through it at half-speed, hugging the narrow shade of
buildings. Infant mortality climbed with the thermometer. In
Fifth Avenue, cool, high bedrooms were boarded and empty.
In First Avenue, babies lay naked on the floor, snuffing out for
want of oxygen.

Across that man-made Grand Cañon men leap sometimes,
but seldom. Mothers whose babies lie naked on the floor look
out across it, damning.

Out into this flaying heat Miss Becker stepped gingerly, almost
immediately rejoined by Mr. Leon Kessler, crowningly touched
with the correct thing in straw sailors.

"Get a move on," he said, guiding her across the soft asphalt.

In Rinehardt's, one of a thousand such *Rathskeller* retreats
designed for a city that loves to dine in fifteen languages, the
noonday cortège of summer widowers had not yet arrived.
Waiters moved through the dim, pink-lit gloom, dressing their
tables temptingly cool and white, dipping ice out from silver
buckets into thin tumblers.

They seated themselves beneath a ceiling fan, Miss Becker's
taffy-colored scallops stirring in the scurry of air.

"Lordy!" she said, closing her eyes and pressing her finger-
tips against them, "I wish I could lease this spot for the summer!"

He pushed a menu-card toward her. "What'll you have?
There's plenty under the 'ready to serve.' "

She peeled out of her white-silk gloves.

"Some cold cuts and a long ice-tea."

He ordered after her and more at length, then lighted a
cigarette.

"Well?" he said, waving out a match.

She leaned forward, already designing with her fork on the table-cloth.

"Kess, can you guess?"

"Come on with it!"

"Have you—noticed anything?"

"Say, I'd have a sweet time keeping up with you girls!"

She looked at him now evenly between the eyes.

"You kept up with me pretty close for three years, didn't you?"

"Say, you knew what you were doing!"

"I—I'm not so sure of that by a long shot. I—I was fed up with the most devilish kind of promises there are. The kind you was too smart to put in words or—or in writing. You—you only looked 'em."

"I suppose you was kidnapped one dark and stormy night while the villain pursued you, eh? Is that it?"

"Oh, what's the use—rehashing! After that time at Atlantic City and—and then the—flat, it—it just seemed the way I felt about you then—that nothing you wanted could be wrong. I guess I knew what I was doing all right, or, if I didn't, I ought to have. I was rotten—or I couldn't have done it, I guess. Only, deep inside of me I was waiting and banking on you like—like poor little Cissie is now. And you knew it; you knew it all them three years."

"Say, did you get me over here to—"

"I only hope to God when you're done with Cissie you'll—"

"You let me take care of my own affairs. If it comes right down to it, there's a few things I could tell you, girl, that ain't so easy to listen to. Let's get off the subject while the going's good."

"Oh, anybody that plays as safe as you—"

He raised his voice, shoving back his chair. "Well, if you want me to clear out of this place quicker than you can bat your eye, you just—"

"No, no, Kess! 'Sh-h-h-h!"

"If there ever was a girl in my place had a square deal, that girl's been you."

" 'Square deal!' Because after I held on and—ate out my heart

for three years, you didn't—take away my job, too? Somebody
ought to pin a Carnegie medal on you!"

"You've held down a twenty-dollar-a-week job season in and
season out, when there've been times it didn't even pay for the
ink it took to write you on the pay-roll."

"There's nothing I ever got out of you I didn't earn three
times over."

"A younger figure than yours is getting to be wouldn't hurt
the line any, you know. It's because I make it a rule not to throw
off the old girls when their waist-lines begin to spread that makes
you so grateful, is it? There's not a firm in town keeps on a girl
after she begins to heavy up. If you got to know why I took you
off the dress line and put you in the wraps, it's because I seen
you widening into a thirty-eight, and a darn poor one at that. I
can sell two wraps off Cissie to one off you. You're getting
hippy, girl, and, since you started the subject, you can be darn
glad you know where your next week's salary's coming from."

She was reddening so furiously that even her earlobes, their
tips escaping beneath the turban, were tinged.

"Maybe I—I'm getting hippy, Kess; but it'll take more than
anything you can ever do for me to make up for—"

"Gad!" he said, flipping an ash in some disgust, "I wish I had
a ten-cent piece for every one since!"

"Oh," she cried, her throat jerking, "you eat what you just
said! You eat it, because you know it ain't so!"

"Now look here," he said, straightening up suddenly, "I don't
know what your game is, but if you're here to stir up the old
dust that's been laid for five years—"

"No, no, Kess! It's only that—what I got to tell you—I—it
makes a difference, I—"

"What?"

"There's nothing in these years since, I swear to God, or in
the years before, that I got to be ashamed of!"

"All right! All right!"

"If ever a girl came all of a sudden to her senses, it was me.
If ever a girl has lived a quiet life, picking herself up and
brushing the dust off, it's been me. Oh, I don't say I 'ain't been
entertained by the trade—I didn't dodge my job—but it's been
a straight kind of a time—straight!"

"I'm not asking for an alibi, Becker. What's the idea?"

"Kess," she said, leaning forward, with tears popping out in her eyes, "I. W. Goldstone has asked me to marry him."

He laid down his roll in the act of buttering it, gazing across at her with his knife upright in his hand.

"Huh?"

"Night before last, Kess, in the poppy-room at Shalif's."

"Are you crazy?"

"It's the God's truth, Kess. He's begging me for an answer by to-night, before he goes back home."

"I. W. Goldstone, of Goldstone & Auer, ladies' wear?"

She nodded, her hand to her throat.

"Well, I'll be strung up!"

"He—he says, Kess, it's been on his mind for a year and a half, ever since his spring trip a year ago. He wants to take me back with him, Kess, home."

"Whew!" said Mr. Kessler, wiping his brow and the back of his collar.

"You're no more surprised than me, Kess. I—I nearly fell off the Christmas tree."

"Good Lord! Why, his wife—he had her in the store it seems yesterday!"

"She's been dead four years and seven months, Kess."

"Old I. W. and you!"

"He's only fifty-two, Kess; I'm thirty-four."

"I. W. Goldstone!"

"I know it. I can't realize it, neither."

"Why, he's worth two hundred thousand, if he's worth a cent!"

"I know it, Kess."

"The old man's stringing you, girl. His kind stop, look, and listen."

"He's not stringing me! I tell you he's begging me to marry him and go back home with him. He's even told his—daughter about me."

"Good Lord—little Effie! I was out there once when she was a kid. Stopped off on my way to Hot Springs. They live in a kind of park—Forest Park Street or something or other. Why, I've done business with Goldstone & Auer for fifteen years, and my father before me! Good Lord!"

"What'll I do, Kess?"

"So that's the size of the fish you went out and landed!"

"I didn't! I didn't! He's been asking me out the last three trips, and post-cards in between, but I never thought nothing of it."

"Why, he can't get away with this!"

"Why?"

"They won't stand for it out in that Middle West town. He's the head of a big business. He's got a grown daughter."

"He's got her fixed, Kess—settled on her."

"Hattie Becker, Mrs. I. W. Goldstone! Gad! can you beat it? Can't you just see me, when I come out to St. Louis pretty soon, having dinner out at Mrs. I. W. Goldstone's house? Say, am I seeing things?"

"What'll I do, Kess? What'll I do?"

"I tell you that you can't get away with it, girl. The old man's getting childish; they'll have to have him restrained. Why, the woman he was married to for twenty years, Lenie Goldstone, never even seen a skirt-dance. I remember once he brought her to New York and then wouldn't let her see a cabaret show. He won't even buy sleeveless models for his French room."

"I tell you, Kess, he'll take me to Jersey to-morrow and marry me, if I give the word."

"Not a chance!"

"I tell you yes. That's why I got to see you. I got to tell him to-night, Kess. He—goes back to-morrow."

He regarded her slowly, watching her throat where it throbbed.

"Well, what are you going to do?"

"I—I don't know."

"Where do you stand with him? Sweet sixteen and never been kissed?"

"He—he don't ask questions, Kess. I—I'm his ideal, he says, of the—kind of—woman can take up for him where his wife left off. He says we're alike in everything but looks, and that a man who was happy in marriage like him can't be happy outside of it. He—he's sized up pretty well the way I live, and—and—he knows I don't expect too much out of life no more. Just a quiet kind of team-work, he puts it—pulling together fifty-fifty, and somebody's hand to hold on to when old fellow Time hits you a whack in the knees from behind. But he ain't old when he talks that way, Kess; he—he's beautiful to me."

"Does he wear a mask when he makes love?"

"He's got a fine face."

"So that's the way you're playing it, is it? Love-stuff?"

"Oh, I've had all the love-stuff knocked out of me. Three years of eating out my heart is about all the love-stuff I can handle for a while. He don't want that in a woman. I don't want it in him. He's just a plain, good man I never in my life could dream of having. A good home in a good town where life ain't like a red-eyed devil ready to hit in deep between the shoulder-blades. I know why he says he can see his wife in me. He knows I'm the kind was cut out for that kind of life—home and kitchen and my own parsley in my own back yard. He knows, if he marries me, carpet slippers seven nights in the week is my speed. I never want to see a 'roof,' or a music-show, or a cabaret again to the day I die. He knows I'll fit in home like a goldfish in its bowl. Life made a mistake with me, and it's going to square itself. It's fate, Kess; that's what it is—fate!"

She clapped her hands to her face, sobbing down into them.

He glanced about him in quick and nervous concern.

"Pull yourself together there, Becker; we're in a public place."

"If only I could go to him and tell him."

"Well, you can't."

"It's not you that keeps me. Only, I know that with his kind of man and at his age, a woman is—is one thing or another and that ends it. With a grown daughter, he wouldn't—couldn't—he's too set in his ways to know how it was with me—and—what'll I do, Kess?"

"Say, I'm not going to stand in your light, if that's what's eating you. If you can get away with it, I don't wish you nothing but well. Looks to me like all right, if you want to make the try. I'll even come and break bread with you when I go out to see my Middle West trade pretty soon. That's the kind of a hairpin I am."

"It's like I keep saying to myself, Kess. If—if he'd ask me anything, it—it would be different. He—he says he never felt so satisfied that a woman had the right stuff in her. And I have! There's nothing in the world can take that away from me. I can give him what he wants. I know I can. Why, the way I'll make up to that little girl out there and love her to death! I ask so little, Kess—just a decent life and rest—peace. I'm tired. I want

to let myself get fat. I'm built that way, to get fat. It was nothing
but diet gave me the anæmia last summer. He says he wants me
to plump out. Perfect thirty-six don't mean nothing in his life
except for the trade. No more rooming-houses with the kitch-
enette in the bath-room. A kitchen, he says, Kess, half the size
of the show-room, with a butler's pantry. He likes to play
pinochle at night, he says, next to the sitting-room fire. He tried
to learn me the rules of the game the other night in the poppy-
room. It's easy. His first wife was death on flowers. She used to
train roses over their back fence. He loved to see her there. He
wants me to like to grow them. He wants to take me back to a
home of my own and peace, where life can't look to a girl like
a devil with horns. He wants to take me home. What'll I do,
Kess? Please, please, what'll I do?"

He was rather inarticulate, but reached out to pat her arm.
"Go—to it—girl, and—God bless you!"

Forest Park Boulevard comes in sootily, smoke-stacks, gas-
tanks, and large areas of scarred vacant lots boding ill enough
for its destiny. But after a while, where Taylor Avenue bisects,
it begins to retrieve itself. Here it is parked down its center, a
narrow strip set out in shrubs, and on either side, traffic, thus
divided, flows evenly up and down a macadamized roadway. In
summer the shrubs thicken, half concealing one side of Forest
Park Boulevard from its other. Houses suddenly take on detached
and architectural importance, often as not a gravel driveway
dividing lawns, and out farther still, where the street eventually
flows into Forest Park, the Italian Renaissance invades, somebody's rococo money's worth.

I. W. Goldstone's home, so near the park that, in spring, the
smell of lilacs and gasolene hovers over it, pretends not to period
or dynasty. Well detached, and so far back from the sidewalk
that interlocking trees conceal its second-story windows, an alcove
was frankly a bulge on its red-brick exterior. Where the third-
floor bath-room, an afterthought, led off the hallway, it jutted
out, a shingled protuberance on the left end of the house. A
tower swelled out of its front end, and all year round geraniums
and boxed climbing vines bloomed in its three stories.

Across a generous ledge of veranda, more vines grew quite

furiously, reaching their height and then growing down upon themselves. Behind those vines, and so cunningly concealed by them that not even the white wrapper could flash through to the passerby, Mrs. I. W. Goldstone, in a chair that would rock rhythmically with her, loved to sit in the first dusk of evening, pleasantly idle. A hose twirling on the lawn spun up the smell of green, abetted by similar whirlings down the wide vista of adjoining lawns. Occasionally, a prideful and shirt-sleeved landed proprietor wielded his own hose, flushing the parched sidewalk or shooting spray against hot bricks that drank in thirstily.

As Mrs. Goldstone rocked she smiled, tilting herself backward off the balls of her feet. The years had cropped out in her suddenly, surprisingly, and with a great deal of geniality. The taffy cast to her hair had backslid to ashes of roses. Uncorseted and in the white wrapper, she was quite frankly widespread, her hips fitting in tight between the chair-arms, and her knees wide.

A screen door snapped sharply shut on its spring, Mr. I. W. Goldstone emerging. There was a great rotundity to his silhouette, the generous outward curve to his waist-line giving to his figure a swayback erectness, the legs receding rather short and thin from the bay of waistcoat.

"Hattie?"

"Here I am, I. W."

"I looped up the sweet-peas."

"Good!"

He sat down beside her, wide-kneed, too, the smooth top of his head and his shirt sleeves spots in the darkness.

"Get dressed a little, Hattie, and I'll get out the car and ride you out to Forest Park Highlands."

She slowed, but did not cease to rock.

"It's so grand at home this evening, I.W. I'm too comfortable to even dress myself."

He felt for her hand in the gloom; she put it out to him.

"You huck home too much, Hattie."

"I guess I do, honey; but it's like I can never get enough of it. The first year I was a home body, and the second and third year I'm two of 'em."

"That's something you'll never hear me complain of in a

woman. There's a world of good in the woman who loves her home."

"It's not that, I. W. It's because I—I never dreamed that there was anything like this coming to me. To live around in rooms, year in and year out, in the lonesomest town in the world, and then, all of a sudden, a home of your own and a hubby of your own and a daughter of your own, why—I dunno—sometimes when I think of them days it's like life was a big red devil with horns and a tail that I'd got away from. Why, if it was to get me again, I—I dunno, honey, I dunno—I—just—dunno."

"You're a good woman, Hattie, and you deserve all that's coming to you. I wish it was more."

"And you're a good man—they don't come no better."

"I'm satisfied with my bargain."

"And me with mine, honey, if—if you don't mind the talk."

"S-ay, this town would talk if you cut its tongue out."

"You're my nice old hubby!"

"If I ever was a little uneasy it was in the beginning, Hattie—the girl—those things don't always turn out."

"It's her as much as me, I. W. She's the sweetest little thing."

"Never seen the like the way you took hold, though. I'll bet there's not one woman in a hundred could have worked it out easier."

"That's right—kid me to death."

" 'Kid,' she says, the minute I tell her the truth."

"Put on your cap, I. W.; it's getting damp."

He felt under the chair-cushions, drawing out and adjusting a black skull-cap.

"Want to go to the picture-show awhile, Hattie?"

"No. When Lizzie's done the dishes, I want to set some dough."

"Let's walk, then, a little. I ate too much supper."

"Just in the side yard, I. W. It's a shame the way I don't dress evenings."

"S-ay, in your own home, shouldn't you have your own comfort? You can take it from me, Hattie, no matter what Effie tells you, you're twice the looking woman with some skin on your bones. I want my wife when she sits down to table she should not look blue-faced when the gravy is passed. Maybe it's not the style, but if it suits your old man, we should worry who else it suits."

"It's not right, I. W., but I love it—this feeling at home for— for good." She rose out of the low mound she had made in the chair, tucking up the white wrapper at both sides. "Come; let's walk in the side yard."

A narrow strip of asphalt ran across the house-frontage, turning in a generous elbow and then back the depth of the lot. They paced it quietly in the gloom, arm in arm, and their voices under darkness.

"Next month is my New York trip. All of a sudden Effie begs I should take her. We'll all go. What you say, Hattie? It'll do us good."

"You take the kid, I. W. Lizzie needs watching. Yesterday I had to make her do the whole butler's pantry over. She just naturally ain't clean."

"You got such luck with your roses, Hattie; it's wonderful!"

They were beneath a climbing bush of them that ran along, glorifying a wooden fence.

She pulled a fan of them to her face. "M-m-m-m!"

"I must spray for worms to-morrow," he said.

They resumed their soft walking in the gloom. "Where's Effie?"

"Telephoning."

"I ask you, is it a shame a child should hang on to the telephone an hour at a time? Fifty minutes since she was interrupted from supper she's been there."

"What's the harm in a young girl telephoning, I. W.? All young folks like to gad over the wire."

"What can a girl have to say over the telephone for fifty minutes? Altogether in my life I never talked that long into the telephone."

"Let the child alone, I. W."

"Who can she get to listen to her for fifty minutes?"

"Birdie Harberger usually calls up at this time."

"Always at supper-time! Never in my life has that child sat down at the table it don't ring in our faces. The next time what it happens you can take sides with her all you want, not one step does she move till she's finished with her supper."

"As easy with her as you are, I. W., just as unreasonable you can get."

"On the stairs-landing for an hour a child should giggle into the telephone! I'm ashamed for the operators. You take sides with her yet."

"I don't, I. W.; only—"

"You do!"

A patch of light from an upper window sprang then across their path.

"She's in her room now, I. W.!" cried Mrs. Goldstone. "She hasn't been telephoning all this time at all. Now, crosspatch!"

"You know much! Can't you see she just lit up? Effie!"

A voice came down to them, clear and with a quality to it like the ring of thin glass.

"Coming, pop!"

The light flashed out again, and in a length of time that could only have meant three steps at a bound she was around the elbow of the asphalt walk, a coat dangling off one arm, her summery skirts flying backward and her head ardently forward.

"You'll never guess!"

She flung herself between the two of them, linking into each of their elbows.

"By my watch, Effie, fifty minutes! If it happens again that you get rung up supper-time, I—"

"It was Leon Kessler, pop; he didn't leave on the six-two. Can you beat it? Down at the station he got to thinking of me and turned back. Oh, my golly! how the boys love me!"

She was jumping now on the tips of her toes, her black curls bouncing.

"You don't tell me!" said Mr. Goldstone. "To-day in the store he says he must be back in New York by Monday morning."

She thrust her face outward, its pink-and-white vividness very close to his.

"Is my daddy's daughter going out in a seventy horse-power to Delmar Garden? She is!"

"Them New York boys spend too much money on the girls when they come. They spoil them for the home young men."

"Can I help it if he couldn't tear himself away?"

"S-ay, don't fool yourself! I said to him to-day he should stay over Sunday. After the bill of goods I bought from him this morning, and the way he only comes out to see his trade once in five or six years, he should stay and mix with them a little longer. That fellow knows good business."

She turned her face with a fling of curls to the right of her, linking closer into the soft arm there.

"Listen to him, Mamma Hat! Let's shove a brick house over on him."

When Mrs. Goldstone finally spoke there was a depth to her voice that seemed to create sudden quiet.

"Effie, Effie, why didn't you let him go?"

"Let him? Did I tie any strings to him? I said good-by to him in the store this afternoon. Can I help it that the boys love me? Why didn't I let him go, she says!"

Her father pinched her slyly at that. "*Echta* fresh kid," he said.

To her right, the hand at her arm clung closer.

"Effie, you—you're so young, honey. Leon Kessler's an old-timer—"

"I hate kids. Give me a *man* every time. I like them when they've got enough sense to—"

"Why didn't you let him go, Effie? Ain't I right, I. W.? Ain't I right?"

"S-ay, what's the difference if he likes to show her a good time? If I was a young man, I wouldn't pass her up myself."

"But, I. W., she's—so young!"

"Who's young? I'm nineteen, going on—"

"You've been running with him all the three days he's been here, honey. What's the use getting yourself talked about?"

"Well, any girl in town would be glad to get herself talked about if Leon Kessler was rushing her."

"Effie, I won't let you—I won't—"

Miss Goldstone unhinged her arm, jerking it free in anger.

"Well, I like that!"

"Effie, I—"

"You ain't my boss!"

"Effie!"

"But, papa, she—"

There was a booming in Mr. Goldstone's voice and a suddenly projected vibrancy.

"You apologize to your mother—this minute! You talk to your mother the way you know she's to be talked to!"

"I. W., she didn't—"

"You hear me!"

"I. W.! Don't holler at her; she—"

"She ain't your boss? Well, she just is your boss! You take back them words and say you're sorry! You apologize to your mother!"

Immediate sobs were rumbling up through Miss Goldstone.

"Well, she— I—I didn't do anything. She's down on him. She—"

"Oh, Effie, would I say anything if it wasn't for your own good?"

"You—you were down on him from the start!"

"Effie darling, you must be mad! Would I say anything if it wasn't for our girl's good to—"

"I—oh, Mamma Hat, I'm sorry, darling! I never meant a word. I didn't! I didn't, darling!"

They embraced there in the shrouding darkness, the tears flowing.

"Oh, Effie—Effie!"

"I didn't mean one word I said, darling! I just get nasty like that before I know it. I didn't mean it!"

"My own Effie!"

"My darling Mamma Hat!"

In the shadow of a flowering shrub Mr. Goldstone stood by, mopping. Mrs. Goldstone took the small face between her hands, peering down into it.

"Effie, Effie, don't let—"

Just beyond the enclosing hedge, a motor-car drew up, honking, at the curb, two far-flung paths of light whitening the street and a disused iron negro-boy hitching-post. Miss Goldstone reared back.

"That's him!"

"Effie!"

"Let me go, dearie; let me go!"

"But, Effie—"

"Say, Hattie, I don't want to butt in, but it don't hurt the child should go riding a little while out by Delmar Garden—a man that can handle a car like Leon Kessler. Anyways, it don't pay to hurt the firm's feelings."

There was a constant honking now at the curb, and violent throbbing of engine.

"But, I. W.—"

"Popsie darling, I'll be back early. Mamma Hat, please!"

"Your mother says yes, baby. Tell Kess he should come for Sunday dinner to-morrow."

She was a white streak across the grass, her nervous feet flying. Almost instantly the honk of a horn came streaming back, faint, fainter.

Left standing there, Goldstone was instantly solicitous of his wife, feeling along her arm up under the loose sleeve.

"It don't pay, Hattie, to hurt Kessler's feelings, and, anyhow, what's the difference just so we know who she's running with? It's like this house was a honey-pot and the boys flies."

She turned to him now with her voice full of husk, and even in the dark her face bleached and shrunken from its plumpness.

"You oughtn't to let her! You—hadn't the right! She's too young and too—sweet for a man like him. You oughtn't to let her!"

He stepped out in front of her, taking her by the elbows and holding them close down against her sides.

"Why, Hattie, that child's own mother that loved her like an angel couldn't worry no more foolishly about her than you do. Gad! I think you wimmin love it! It was the same kind of worrying shortened her mother's life. Always about nothing, too. 'Lenie,' I used to say to her, just to quiet her, 'it was worry killed a Maltese cat; don't let it kill you.' That child is all right, Hattie. What if he does like her pretty well? Worse could happen."

"No, it couldn't! No!"

"Why not? He 'ain't seen her since a child, and all of a sudden he comes West and finds in front of him an eye-opener."

"He's twice her age—more!"

"The way girls demand things nowadays, a man has got to be twice her age before he can provide for her. Leon Kessler is big rich."

"He—he's fast."

"Show me the one that 'ain't sowed his wild oats. Them's the
kind that settle down quickest into good husbands."

"He—"

"S-ay, it 'ain't happened yet. I'm the last one to wish my girl
off my hands. I only say not a boy in this town could give it to
her so good. Fifteen years I've done business with that firm, and
with his father before him. A-1 house! S-ay, I should worry that
he ain't a Sunday-school boy. Show me the one that is. Your old
man in his young days wasn't such a low flier, neither, if anybody
should ask you." He made a whirring noise in his throat at that,
pinching her cold cheek. She was walking rapidly now toward
the house. "Well, since our daughter goes out riding in a six-
thousand-dollar car, to show that we're sports, lets her father
and mother take themselves out for a ride in their six-hundred-
dollar car. I drive you out as far as Yiddle's farm for some sweet
butter, eh?"

"No, no; I'm cold. It's getting damp."

"S-ay, you can't hurt my feelings. On a cool night like this, a
brand-new sleeping-porch ain't the worst spot in the world."

They were on the veranda, the hall light falling dimly out and
over them.

"She's so young—"

"Now, now, Hattie; worry killed a Maltese cat. Come to bed."

"You go. I want to wait up."

"Hattie, you want to make of yourself the laughingstock of
the neighborhood. A grown-up girl goes out riding with a man
like Leon Kessler, and you wants to wait up and catch your
death of cold. If we had more daughters, I wouldn't have no
more wife; I'd have a shadow from worry. Come!"

"I'll be up in a minute, I. W."

He regarded her in some concern.

"Why, Hattie, if there's anything in the world to worry about,
wouldn't I be the first? Ain't you well?"

"Yes."

"Then come. I'll get a pitcher of ice-water to take up-stairs."

"I'll be up in a minute."

"I don't want, Hattie, you should wait up for that child and
take your death of cold. Because I sleep like a log when I once
hit the bed, don't you play no tricks on me."

"I'll be up in a minute, I. W."

He moved into the house and, after a while, to the clinking of ice against glass, up the stairs.

"Come, Hattie; and be sure and leave the screen door unhooked for her."

"Yes, I. W."

An hour she sat in the shrouded darkness of the elbow of the veranda. Street noises died. The smell of damp came out. Occasionally a motor-car sped by, or a passer-by, each step clear on the asphalt. The song of crickets grated against the darkness. An infant in the right-side house raised a fretful voice once or twice, and then broke into a sustained and coughy fit of crying. Lights flashed up in the windows, silhouettes moving across drawn shades. Then silence again. The university clock, a mile out, chimed twelve, and finally a sonorous one. Mrs. Goldstone lay huddled in her chair, vibrant for sound. At two o'clock the long, high-power car drew up at the curb again, this time without honking. She sat forward, trembling.

There followed a half-hour of voices at the curb, a low voice of undeniable tensity, high laughter that shot up in joyous geysers. It was a fifteen-minute process from the curb to the first of the porch steps, and then Mrs. Goldstone leaned forward, her voice straining to keep its pitch.

"Effie!"

The young figure sprang around the porch pillar.

"Mamma Hat! Honey, you didn't wait up for me?"

Mr. Kessler came forward, goggles pushed up above his cap-visor.

"Well, I'm hanged! What did you think—that I was kidnapping the kid?"

"How—how dared you! It's after two, and—"

Miss Goldstone began then to jump again upon her toes, linking her arm in his.

"Tell her, Leon! Tell her! Oh, Mamma Hat! Mamma Hat!"

She was suddenly in Mrs. Goldstone's arms, her ardent face burning through the white wrapper.

Mr. Kessler removed his cap, flinging it upward again and catching it.

"Tell her, Leon!"

"Well, what would you say, Becker, what would you say if I was to come out here and swipe that little darling there?"

"Oh, Leon—kidder!"

"If—what?"

"I said it!"

"Tell her, Kess; tell it out! Oh, mommie, mommie!"

He leaned forward with his hand on the back of the turbulent head of curls.

"You little darling, I'm going to put you on my back and carry you off to New York."

"Oh, mommie," cried Miss Goldstone, flinging back her head so that her face shone up, "he asked me in Delmar Garden! We're going to live in New York, darling, and Rockaway in summer. He don't care a rap about the New York girls compared to me. We're going to Cuba on our honeymoon. I'm engaged, darling! I got engaged to-night!"

"That's the idea, Twinkle-pinkle. I'd carry you off to-night if I could!"

"Mommie Hat, ain't you glad?"

"Effie—Effie—"

"Mommie, what is it? What's the matter, darling? What?"

"I—it's just that I got cold, honey, sitting here waiting—the surprise and all. Run, honey, and get me a drink. Crack some ice, dearie, and then run up-stairs in the third floor back and see if there's some brandy up there. Be sure to look for—the brandy. I—I'll be all right."

"My poor, darling, cold mommie!"

She was off on the slim, quick feet, the screen door slamming and vibrating.

Then Mrs. Goldstone sprang up.

"You wouldn't dare! Such a baby—you wouldn't dare!"

"Dare what?"

"You can't have the child! You can't!"

"What do you mean?"

"What do I mean?"

He advanced a step, his voice and expression lifted in incredulity.

"Say, look here, Becker, are you stark, raving crazy? Is it

possible you don't know that, in your place, nobody but a crazy woman would open her mouth?"

"Maybe; but I don't care. Just leave her alone, Kess, please! That little baby can stand nothing but happiness."

"Why, woman, you're crazy with the heat. If you want to know it, I'm nuts over that little kid. Gad! never ran across anything so full of zip in my life! I'm going to make life one joy ride after another for that joy baby. That kid's the showpiece of the world. She's got me so hipped I'm crazy, and the worst of it is I like it. You don't need to worry. As the boys say, when I settle down, I'm going to settle hard."

"You ain't fit to have her!"

"Say, the kind of life I've lived I ain't ashamed to tell her own father. He's a man, and I'm a man, and life's life."

"You—"

"Now look here, Becker. That'll be about all. If you're in your right senses, you're going to ring the joy bells louder than any one around here. What you got on your chest you can just as well cut your throat as tell; so we'll both live happy every after. There's not one thing in my life that any jury wouldn't pass, and—"

"I've seen you drunk."

"Well, what of it? It took three of us to yank old I. W. out from under the table at my sister's wedding."

"You— What about you and Cissie and—"

The light run of feet, and almost instantly Miss Goldstone was pirouetting in between them.

"Here, dearie! There wasn't anything like brandy up in the third floor. I found some cordial in the pantry. Drink it down, dearie; it 'll warm you."

They hovered together, Miss Goldstone trembling between solicitude and her state of intensity.

"Kessie darling, you've got to go now. I want to get mommie up-stairs to bed. You got to go, darling, until to-morrow. Oh, why isn't it to-morrow? I want everybody to know. Don't let on, Mamma Hat. I'll pop it on popsie at breakfast while I'm opening his eggs for him. You come for breakfast, Leon. You're in the

family now." He lifted her bodily from her feet, pressing a
necklace of kisses round her throat.

"Good night, Twinkle-pinkle, till to-morrow."

"Good night, darling. I won't sleep a wink, waiting for you."

"Me, neither."

"One more, darling—a French one."

"Two for good measure."

"Sleep tight, beautiful! Good night!"

"Good night, beautifulest!"

She stood poised forward on the topmost step, watching him
between backward waves of the hand crank, throw his clutch,
and steer off. Then she turned inward, a sigh trembling between
her lips.

"Oh, Mamma Hat, I—"

But Mrs. Goldstone's chair was empty. Into it with a second
and more tremulous sigh sank Miss Goldstone, her lips lifted in
the smile that had been kissed.

When Mr. Goldstone slept, every alternate breath started with
a rumble somewhere down in the depths of him and, drawn up
like a chain from a well, petered out into a thin whistle before
the next descent. Beside him, now, on her knees, Mrs. Goldstone
shook at his shoulder.

"I. W.! I. W! Quick! Wake up!"

He let out a shuddering, abysmal breath.

"I. W.! Please!"

He moaned, turning his face from her.

She tugged him around again, now raising his face between
her hands from the pillow.

"I. W.! Try to wake up! For God's sake, I. W.!" He sprang up
in a terrified daze, sitting upright in bed.

"My God! Who? What's wrong? Effie! Hattie."

"No, no; don't get excited, I. W. It's me—Hattie!"

"What?"

"Nothing, I. W. Nothing to get excited about. Only I got to
tell you something."

"Where's Effie?"

"She's home."

"What time is it?"

"Three."

"Come back to bed, then; you got the nightmare."

"No, no!"

"You ain't well, Hattie? Let me light up."

"No, no; only, I got to tell you something! I 'ain't been to bed; I been waiting up, and—"

"And what?"

"She just came home—engaged!"

"My God! Effie?"

He blinked in the darkness, drawing up his knees to a hump under the sheet.

"Engaged—how?"

"I. W., don't you remember? Wake up, honey. To Kess, to Leon Kessler that she went automobiling with."

"Our Effie engaged—to Leon Kessler?"

"Yes, I. W.—our little Effie!"

A smile spread over his face slowly, and he clasped his hands in an embrace about his knees.

"You don't tell me!"

"Oh, I. W., please—"

"Our little girl. S-ay, how poor Lenie would have loved this happiness! Our little girl engaged to get married!"

"I. W., she—"

"We do the right thing by them—eh, Hattie? Furnish them up as many rooms as they want. But, s-ay, they don't need help from us. He's a lucky boy who gets her, I don't care who he is. Her papa's little Effie, a baby—old enough to get engaged!"

"I. W., she's too—young. Don't give him our little Effie; she's too young!"

"I married her mother, Hattie, when she wasn't yet eighteen."

"I know, I. W., but not to Leon Kessler. She's such a baby, I. W. He—didn't I work for him nine years, I. W.—don't I know what he is!"

"I'm surprised, Hattie, you should hold so against a man his wild oats."

"Then why ain't oats for the man oats for the woman? It's the men that sow the wild oats and the women—us women that's got to reap them!"

"S-ay, life is life. Do you want to put your head up against a brick wall?"

"A wall that men built!"

"It's always hard, Hattie, for good women like you and like poor Lenie was to understand. It's better you don't. You shouldn't even think about it."

"But, I. W.—"

"If I didn't know Leon Kessler was no worse than ninety-nine good husbands in a hundred, you think I would let him lay a finger on the apple of my eye? I don't understand, Hattie; all of a sudden this evening, you're so worked up. Instead of happiness, you come like with a funeral. Is that why you wake me up out of a sleep? To cry about it? Don't think, Hattie, that just as much as you I haven't got the good of my child at heart. Out of a sound sleep she wakes me to cry because a happiness has come to us. Leon Kessler can have any girl in this town he wants. Maybe he wasn't a Sunday-school boy in his day—but say, show me one that was."

She drew herself up, grasping him at the shoulders.

"I. W., don't let him have our little Effie!"

"Nonsense!" he said, in some distaste for her voice choked with tears. "Cut out this woman foolishness now and come to bed. Is this something new you're springing on me? I got no patience with women who indulge themselves with nervous breakdowns. I never thought, Hattie, you had nothing like that in you."

Her voice was rising now in hysteria, slipping up frequently beyond her control.

"If you do, I can't stand it! I can't stand it, I. W.!"

He peered at her in the starlight that came down through the screened-in top of the sleeping-porch.

"Why?" he said, suddenly awake, and shortly.

"I worked for him nine years, I. W. I—I know him."

"How?"

"I know him, I. W. She's too good for him."

"How do you know him?"

"I—the girls, I. W. One little girl now, Cissie—I—I hear it all from my friend Delehanty—sometimes she—she writes to me. I—the models and—the girls and—and the lady buyers—they—they used to gossip in the factory and—I—I used to hear about it. I. W., don't! Let go! You hurt!" His teeth and his hands were very tight, and he hung now over the side of the bed and toward her.

"He—I. W.—he—"

"He what? He what?"

"He—ain't good enough."

"I say he is!"

"But he—I. W.—she—she's such a baby and he—he— You hurt!"

"Then tell me, he what?"

"I. W., you're hurting me!"

"He what—do you hear?—he what?"

"Don't make me say it! Don't! It—it just happened—with him meaning one thing all the time and—me another. I was thrown with that kind of a crowd, I. W., all my life. All the girls, they— It don't make me worse than it makes him. With me it was once; with him it's—it's— I didn't know, I. W. My mother she died that year before, and—I needed the job, and I swear to God, I. W., I—kept hoping even if he never put it in words he'd fix it. Kill me, if you want to, I. W., but don't throw our Effie to him! Don't! Don't! Don't!"

She was pounding the floor with her bare palms, her face so distorted that the mouth drawn tight over the teeth was as wide and empty as a mask's, and sobs caught and hiccoughed in her throat.

"I didn't know, I. W.! Don't kill me for what I didn't know!"

She crouched back from his knotted face, and he sprang then out of bed, nightshirt flapping about his knees, and his fists and his bulging eyes raised to the quiet stars.

"God," he cried, "help me to keep hold of myself! Help me! You—you—"

His voice was so high and so tight in his throat that it stuck, leaving him in inarticulate invocation.

"I. W.!"

"My child engaged to—to her mother's—you—you—"

"I. W.! Do you see now? You wouldn't let him have her! You wouldn't, I. W.! Tell me you wouldn't!"

"I want him if he touches her to be struck dead! I want him to be struck dead!"

"Thank God!" said Mrs. Goldstone, weeping now tears that eased her breathing.

Suddenly he leaned toward her, his voice rather quieter, but his forefinger waggling out toward the open door.

"You go!" he said, and then in a gathering hurricane of fury, "go!"

"I. W., don't yell! Don't! Don't!"

"Go—while I'm quiet. Go—you hear?"

She edged around him where he stood, in fear of his white, crouched attitude.

"I. W.!"

He made a step toward her, and, at the sound in his throat, she ran out into the hallway and down the stairs to the porch. In the deep shade of the veranda's elbow a small figure lay deep in sleep in the wicker rocker, one bare arm up over her head and lips parted.

In a straight chair beside her Mrs. Goldstone sat down. She was shuddering with chill and repeating to herself, quite aloud and over and over again:

"What have I done? What have I done? What have I done?"

She was suddenly silent then, staring out ahead, her hands clutching the chair-arms.

To her inflamed fancy, it was as if, beyond the hedge, the old disused hitching-post had become incarnate and, in the form of her naive and horned conception, was coming toward her with the whites of his eyes bloodshot.

Helen Rose Hull

The Fire
1917

Helen Rose Hull (1888–1971) grew up in Albion, Michigan, the daughter of teachers and the granddaughter of a printer. Her grandfather printed one of her stories when she was eight years old, and, thereafter, she thought of herself as a writer. She attended Michigan State University and completed a degree in philosophy at the University of Chicago, where she later did graduate work. She taught English at Wellesley College for three years. After collecting enough rejection slips to paper a wall in her house, she published her first story in 1915; eventually, her work appeared in such periodicals as Harper's Magazine, Century, Colliers, Cosmopolitan, The Ladies' Home Journal, *and* The Saturday Evening Post. *In 1916 she moved to New York City to begin her long dual career, teaching at Columbia University for nine months of the year and writing during the summer at her home in Maine.*

*A lesbian, Hull shared a long and productive life with Mabel Louise Robinson, a member of the creative writing faculty at Columbia. Three of Hull's first four novels—*Quest *(1922);* Labyrinth *(1923); and* Islanders *(1927)—reflect her commitment to the feminist issues of her time. Two of them depict lesbian couples in secondary roles, providing a sane and stable backdrop against which all the other characters and relationships are contrasted. Dorothea Brande, in a review of* Labyrinth *in* The New Republic *(November 7, 1923), complained that the "most satisfactory human relationship . . . is one between two women characters. Marriage shows up beside it as something dingy and unalluring, a whining and exacting state."*

The house with detached writing studio where Hull and Robinson spent their summers had been carefully renovated and they cherished it until Mabel's death at eighty-eight, when Helen was in her early seventies. The two of them had collaborated on a book about writing, Creative Writing, the Story Form, *in 1932. Along with Roger Sherman Loomis they also co-edited* The Art of Writing Prose, *a collection of essays by various well-known writers on their craft, in 1936.*

Helen Hull also published two collections of her short stories: Uncommon People *(1936), and* Octave, A Book of Stories *(1947); a collection of novellas,* The Flying Yorkshireman *(1938); and a collection of four short novels (or long short stories),* Experiment *(1940). There were more than a dozen other novels as well. Her literary output was prolific.*

In her story "Second Fiddle," a character exclaims, "We feel too much respect for forms—marriage and families. Have to take the lid off and look inside." That probing of family dynamics was the consuming focus of all her fiction. She looked at the effect on the sensitive child of growing up with a "weak" father and a "strong" mother, and then reversed the construct, examining the impact on a similarly lonely, sensitive, and idealistic child of an overpowering father and a shrinking mother. She frequently explored the pain of conflicting loyalties, sometimes portraying a child torn between parents at war with each other, and sometimes portraying young adulthood, when children separate from their parents to enter into new alliances.

Such a story is told in "The Fire," originally published in Century, November *1917, and reprinted in the lesbian periodical* The Ladder *and later in* Lesbians Home Journal: Stories from the Ladder *in 1976. Barbara Grier, co-editor of* The Ladder *and publisher of The Naiad Press, an American lesbian publishing house, wrote in her note on this story, "It is a tribute to the universality of [Hull's] talent that this story still has relevance today in defining the puberty patterns of the Lesbian."*

"The Fire" is discussed further by Lillian Faderman in Surpassing the Love of Men *(New York: William Morrow, 1981). Faderman writes,*

> There does in fact seem to be an erotic element in [Miss Egert's and Cynthia's] relationship which is inextricably mixed with their roles as the mentor of beauty and courage and the devoted pupil. . . . Although Cynthia bows to her mother's pressure and gives up Miss Egert, it is made clear that she will not give up Miss Egert's influence, which is portrayed as entirely positive and constructive in contrast with the pathetically narrow ideals that Cynthia's parents try to impose on their daughter.

Cynthia blotted the entry in the old ledger and scowled across the empty office at the door. Mrs. Moriety had left it ajar when

she departed with her receipt for the weekly fifty cents on her
"lot." If you supplied the missing gilt letters, you could read the
sign on the glass of the upper half: "H. P. Bates. Real Estate.
Notary Public." Through the door at Cynthia's elbow came the
rumbling voice of old Fleming, the lawyer down the hall; he
had come in for his Saturday night game of chess with her
father.

Cynthia pushed the ledger away from her, and with her elbows
on the spotted, green felt of the desk, her fingers burrowing
into her cheeks, waited for two minutes by the nickel clock;
then, with a quick, awkward movement, she pushed back her
chair and plunged to the doorway, her young face twisted in a
sort of fluttering resolution.

"Father—"

Her father jerked his head toward her, his fingers poised over
a pawn. Old Fleming did not look up.

"Father, I don't think anybody else will be in."

"Well, go on home, then." Her father bent again over the
squares, the light shining strongly on the thin places about his
temples.

"Father, please,"—Cynthia spoke hurriedly,—"you aren't going
for a while? I want to go down to Miss Egert's for a minute."

"Eh? What's that?" He leaned back in his chair now, and Mr.
Fleming lifted his severe, black beard to look at this intruder.
"What for? You can't take any more painting lessons. Your
mother doesn't want you going there any more."

"I just want to get some things I left there. I can get back to
go home with you."

"But your mother said she didn't like your hanging around
down there in an empty house with an old maid. What did she
tell you about it?"

"Couldn't I just get my sketches, Father, and tell Miss Egert
I'm not coming any more? She would think it was awfully funny
if I didn't. I won't stay. But she—she's been good to me—"

"What set your mother against her, then? What you been
doing down there?"

Cynthia twisted her hands together, her eyes running from
Fleming's amused stare to her father's indecision. Only an

accumulated determination could have carried her on into speech.

"I've just gone down once a week for a lesson. I want to get my things. If I'm not going, I ought to tell her."

"Why didn't you tell her that last week?"

"I kept hoping I could go on."

"Um." Her father's glance wavered toward his game. "Isn't it too late?"

"Just eight, Father." She stepped near her father, color flooding her cheeks. "If you'll give me ten cents, I can take the car—"

"Well—" He dug into his pocket, nodding at Fleming's grunt, "The women always want cash, eh, Bates?"

Then Cynthia, the dime pressed into her palm, tiptoed across to the nail where her hat and sweater hung, seized them, and still on tiptoe, lest she disturb the game again, ran out to the head of the stairs.

She was trembling as she pulled on her sweater; as she ran down the dark steps to the street the tremble changed to a quiver of excitement. Suppose her father had known just what her mother *had* said! That she could not see Miss Egert again; could never go hurrying down to the cluttered room they called the studio for more of those strange hours of eagerness and pain when she bent over the drawing-board, struggling with the mysteries of color. That last sketch—the little, purpling mint-leaves from the garden—Miss Egert had liked that. And they thought she could leave those sketches there! Leave Miss Egert, too, wondering why she never came again! She hurried to the corner, past the bright store-windows. In thought she could see Miss Egert setting out the jar of brushes, the dishes of water, pushing back the litter of magazines and books to make room for the drawing-board, waiting for her to come. Oh, she had to go once more, black as her disobedience was!

The half-past-eight car was just swinging round the curve. She settled herself behind two German housewives, shawls over their heads, market-baskets beside them. They lived out at the end of the street; one of them sometimes came to the office with payments on her son's lot. Cynthia pressed against the dirty window, fearful lest she miss the corner. There it was, the new street light shining on the sedate old house! She ran to the platform, pushing against the arm the conductor extended.

"Wait a minute, there!" He released her as the car stopped, and she fled across the street.

In front of the house she could not see a light, up-stairs or down, except staring reflections in the windows from the white arc light. She walked past the dark line of box which led to the front door. At the side of the old square dwelling jutted a new, low wing; and there in two windows were soft slits of light along the curtain-edges. Cynthia walked along a little dirt path to a door at the side of the wing. Standing on the door-step, she felt in the shadow for the knocker. As she let it fall, from the garden behind her came a voice:

"I'm out here. Who is it?" There was a noise of feet hurrying through dead leaves, and as Cynthia turned to answer, out of the shadow moved a blur of face and white blouse.

"Cynthia! How nice!" The woman touched Cynthia's shoulder as she pushed open the door. "There, come in."

The candles on the table bent their flames in the draft; Cynthia followed Miss Egert into the room.

"You're busy?" Miss Egert had stood up by the door an old wooden-toothed rake. "I don't want to bother you." Cynthia's solemn, young eyes implored the woman and turned hastily away. The intensity of defiance which had brought her at such an hour left her confused.

"Bother? I was afraid I had to have my grand bonfire alone. Now we can have it a party. You'd like to?"

Miss Egert darted across to straighten one of the candles. The light caught in the folds of her crumpled blouse, in the soft, drab hair blown out around her face.

"I can't stay very long." Cynthia stared about the room, struggling to hide her turmoil under ordinary casualness. "You had the carpenter fix the bookshelves, didn't you?"

"Isn't it nice now! All white and gray and restful—just a spark of life in that mad rug. A good place to sit in and grow old."

Cynthia looked at the rug, a bit of scarlet Indian weaving. She wouldn't see it again! The thought poked a derisive finger into her heart.

"Shall we sit down just a minute and then go have the fire?"

Cynthia dropped into the wicker chair, wrenching her fingers through one another.

"My brother came in to-night, his last attempt to make me see reason," said Miss Egert.

Cynthia lifted her eyes. Miss Egert wasn't wondering why she had come; she could stay without trying to explain.

Miss Egert wound her arms about her knees as she went on talking. Her slight body was wrenched a little out of symmetry, as though from straining always for something uncaptured; there was the same lack of symmetry in her face, in her eyebrows, in the line of her mobile lips. But her eyes had nothing fugitive, nothing pursuing in their soft, gray depth. Their warm, steady eagerness shone out in her voice, too, in its swift inflections.

"I tried to show him it wasn't a bit disgraceful for me to live here in a wing of my own instead of being a sort of nurse-maid adjunct in his house." She laughed, a soft, throaty sound. "It's my house. It's all I have left to keep me a person, you see. I won't get out and be respectable in his eyes."

"He didn't mind your staying here and taking care of—them!" cried Cynthia.

"It's respectable, dear, for an old maid to care for her father and mother; but when they die she ought to be useful to some one else instead of renting her house and living on an edge of it."

"Oh,"—Cynthia leaned forward,—"I should think you'd hate him! I think families are—terrible!"

"Hate him?" Miss Egert smiled. "He's nice. He just doesn't agree with me. As long as he lets the children come over—I told him I meant to have a beautiful time with them, with my real friends—with you."

Cynthia shrank into her chair, her eyes tragic again.

"Come, let's have our bonfire!" Miss Egert, with a quick movement, stood in front of Cynthia, one hand extended.

Cynthia crouched away from the hand.

"Miss Egert,"—her voice came out in a desperate little gasp,—"I can't come down any more. I can't take any more painting lessons." She stopped. Miss Egert waited, her head tipped to one side. "Mother doesn't think I better. I came down—after my things."

"They're all in the workroom." Miss Egert spoke quietly. "Do you want them now?"

"Yes." Cynthia pressed her knuckles against her lips. Over her hand her eyes cried out. "Yes, I better get them," she said heavily.

Miss Egert, turning slowly, lifted a candle from the table. "We'll have to take this. The wiring isn't done." She crossed the room, her thin fingers, not quite steady, bending around the flame.

Cynthia followed through a narrow passage. Miss Egert pushed open a door, and the musty odor of the store-room floated out into a queer chord with the fresh plaster of the hall.

"Be careful of that box!" Miss Egert set the candle on a pile of trunks. "I've had to move all the truck from the attic and studio in here. Your sketches are in the portfolio, and that's— somewhere!"

Cynthia stood in the doorway, watching Miss Egert bend over a pile of canvases, throwing up a grotesque, rounded shadow on the wall. Round the girl's throat closed a ring of iron.

"Here they are, piled up—"

Cynthia edged between the boxes. Miss Egert was dragging the black portfolio from beneath a pile of books.

"And here's the book I wanted you to see." The pile slipped crashing to the floor as Miss Egert pulled out a magazine. "Never mind those. See here." She dropped into the chair from which she had knocked the books, the portfolio under one arm, the free hand running through the pages of an old art magazine. The chair swung slightly; Cynthia, peering down between the boxes, gave a startled "Oh!"

"What is it?" Miss Egert followed Cynthia's finger. "The chair?" She was silent a moment. "Do you think I keep my mother prisoner here in a wheel-chair now that she is free?" She ran her hand along the worn arm. "I tried to give it to an old ladies' home, but it was too used up. They wanted more style."

"But doesn't it remind you—" Cynthia hesitated.

"It isn't fair to remember the years she had to sit here waiting to die. You didn't know her. I've been going back to the real years—" Miss Egert smiled at Cynthia's bewildered eyes. "Here, let's look at these." She turned another page. "See, Cynthia. Aren't they swift and glad? That's what I was trying to tell you the other day. See that arm, and the drapery there! Just a line—"

The girl bent over the page, frowning at the details the quick
finger pointed out. "Don't they catch you along with them?" She
held the book out at arm's-length, squinting at the figures. "Take
it along. There are several more." She tucked the book into the
portfolio and rose. "Come on; we'll have our fire."

"But, Miss Egert,"—Cynthia's voice hardened as she was swept
back into her own misery,—"I can't take it. I can't come any
more."

"To return a book?" Miss Egert lowered her eyelids as if she
were again sizing up a composition. "You needn't come just for
lessons."

Cynthia shook her head.

"Mother thinks—" She fell into silence. She couldn't say what
her mother thought—dreadful things. If she could only swallow
the hot pressure in her throat!

"Oh. I hadn't understood." Miss Egert's fingers paused for a
swift touch on Cynthia's arm, and then reached for the candle.
"You can go on working by yourself."

"It isn't that—" Cynthia struggled an instant, and dropped
into silence again. She couldn't say out loud any of the things
she was feeling. There were too many walls between feeling and
speech: loyalty to her mother, embarrassment that feelings
should come so near words, a fear of hurting Miss Egert.

"Don't mind so much, Cynthia." Miss Egert led the way back
to the living-room. "You can stay for the bonfire? That will be
better than sitting here. Run into the kitchen and bring the
matches and marshmallows—in a dish in the cupboard."

Cynthia, in the doorway, stared at Miss Egert. Didn't she care
at all! Then the dumb ache in her throat stopped throbbing as
Miss Egert's gray eyes held her steadily a moment. She did care!
She did! She was just helping her. Cynthia took the candle and
went back through the passageway to the kitchen, down at the
very end.

She made a place on the table in the litter of dishes and milk-
bottles for the candle. The matches had been spilled on the shelf
of the stove and into the sink. Cynthia gathered a handful of
the driest. Shiftlessness was one of her mother's counts against
Miss Egert. Cynthia flushed as she recalled her stumbling
defense: Miss Egert had more important things to do; dishes

were kept in their proper place; and her mother's: "Important! Mooning about!"

"Find them, Cynthia?" The clear, low voice came down the hall, and Cynthia hurried back.

Out in the garden it was quite black. As they came to the far end, the old stone wall made a dark bank against the sky, with a sharp star over its edge. Miss Egert knelt; almost with the scratch of the match the garden leaped into yellow, with fantastic moving shadows from the trees and in the corner of the wall. She raked leaves over the blaze, pulled the great mound into firmer shape, and then drew Cynthia back under the wall to watch. The light ran over her face; the delighted gestures of her hands were like quick shadows.

"See the old apple-tree dance! He's too old to move fast."

Cynthia crouched by the wall, brushing away from her face the scratchy leaves of the dead hollyhocks. Excitement tingled through her; she felt the red and yellow flames seizing her, burning out the heavy rebellion, the choking weight. Miss Egert leaned back against the wall, her hands spread so that her thin fingers were fire-edged.

"See the smoke curl up through those branches! Isn't it lovely, Cynthia?" She darted around the pile to push more leaves into the flames.

Cynthia strained forward, hugging her arms to her body. Never had there been such a fire! It burned through her awkwardness, her self-consciousness. It ate into the thick, murky veils which hung always between her and the things she struggled to find out. She took a long breath, and the crisp scent of smoke from the dead leaves tingled down through her body.

Miss Egert was at her side again. Cynthia looked up; the slight, asymmetrical figure was like the apple-tree, still, yet dancing!

"Why don't you paint it?" demanded Cynthia, abruptly, and then was frightened as Miss Egert's body stiffened, lost its suggestion of motion.

"I can't." The woman dropped to the ground beside Cynthia, crumpling a handful of leaves. "It's too late." She looked straight at the fire. "I must be content to see it." She blew the pieces of leaves from the palm of her hand and smiled at Cynthia. "Perhaps some day you'll paint it—or write it."

"I can't paint." Cynthia's voice quivered. "I want to do something. I can't even see things except what you point out. And now—"

Miss Egert laid one hand over Cynthia's clenched fingers. The girl trembled at the cold touch.

"You must go on looking." The glow, as the flames died lower, flushed her face. "Cynthia, you're just beginning. You mustn't stop just because you aren't to come here any more. I don't know whether you can say things with your brush; but you must find them out. You mustn't shut your eyes again."

"It's hard alone."

"That doesn't matter."

Cynthia's fingers unclasped, and one hand closed desperately around Miss Egert's. Her heart fluttered in her temples, her throat, her breast. She clung to the fingers, pulling herself slowly up from an inarticulate abyss.

"Miss Egert,"—she stumbled into words,—"I can't bear it, not coming here! Nobody else cares except about sensible things. You do, beautiful, wonderful things."

"You'd have to find them for yourself, Cynthia." Miss Egert's fingers moved under the girl's grasp. Then she bent toward Cynthia, and kissed her with soft, pale lips that trembled against the girl's mouth. "Cynthia, don't let any one stop you! Keep searching!" She drew back, poised for a moment in the shadow before she rose. Through Cynthia ran the swift feet of white ecstasy. She was pledging herself to some tremendous mystery, which trembled all about her.

"Come, Cynthia, we're wasting our coals."

Miss Egert held out her hands. Cynthia, laying hers in them, was drawn to her feet. As she stood there, inarticulate, full of a strange, excited, shouting hope, behind them the path crunched. Miss Egert turned, and Cynthia shrank back.

Her mother stood in the path, making no response to Miss Egert's "Good evening, Mrs. Bates."

The fire had burned too low to lift the shadow from the mother's face. Cynthia could see the hem of her skirt swaying where it dipped up in front. Above that two rigid hands in gray cotton gloves; above that the suggestion of a white, strained face.

Cynthia took a little step toward her.

"I came to get my sketches," she implored her. Her throat was dry. What if her mother began to say cruel things—the things she had already said at home.

"I hope I haven't kept Cynthia too late," Miss Egert said. "We were going to toast marshmallows. Won't you have one, Mrs. Bates?" She pushed the glowing leaf-ashes together. The little spurt of flame showed Cynthia her mother's eyes, hard, angry, resting an instant on Miss Egert and then assailing her.

"Cynthia knows she should not be here. She is not permitted to run about the streets alone at night."

"Oh, I'm sorry." Miss Egert made a deprecating little gesture. "But no harm has come to her."

"She has disobeyed me."

At the tone of her mother's voice Cynthia felt something within her breast curl up like a leaf caught in flame.

"I'll get the things I came for." She started toward the house, running past her mother. She must hurry, before her mother said anything to hurt Miss Egert.

She stumbled on the door-step, and flung herself against the door. The portfolio was across the room, on the little, old piano. The candle beside it had guttered down over the cover. Cynthia pressed out the wobbly flame, and, hugging the portfolio, ran back across the room. On the threshold she turned for a last glimpse. The row of Botticelli details over the bookcases were blurred into gray in the light of the one remaining candle; the Indian rug had a wavering glow. Then she heard Miss Egert just outside.

"I'm sorry Cynthia isn't to come any more," she was saying.

Cynthia stepped forward. The two women stood in the dim light, her mother's thickened, settled body stiff and hostile, Miss Egert's slight figure swaying toward her gently.

"Cynthia has a good deal to do," her mother answered. "We can't afford to give her painting lessons, especially—" Cynthia moved down between the women—"especially," her mother continued, "as she doesn't seem to get much of anywhere. You'd think she'd have some pictures to show after so many lessons."

"Perhaps I'm not a good teacher. Of course she's just beginning."

"She'd better put her time on her studies."

"I'll miss her. We've had some pleasant times together."
Cynthia held out her hand toward Miss Egert, with a fearful
little glance at her mother.

"Good-by, Miss Egert."

Miss Egert's cold fingers pressed it an instant.

"Good night, Cynthia," she said slowly.

Then Cynthia followed her mother's silent figure along the
path; she turned her head as they reached the sidewalk. Back
in the garden winked the red eye of the fire.

They waited under the arc light for the car, Cynthia stealing
fleeting glances at her mother's averted face. On the car she
drooped against the window-edge, away from her mother's
heavy silence. She was frightened now, a panicky child caught
in disobedience. Once, as the car turned at the corner below her
father's office, she spoke:

"Father will expect me—"

"He knows I went after you," was her mother's grim answer.

Cynthia followed her mother into the house. Her small brother
was in the sitting-room, reading. He looked up from his book
with wide, knowing eyes. Rebellious humiliation washed over
Cynthia; setting her lips against their quivering, she pulled off
her sweater.

"Go on to bed, Robert," called her mother from the entry,
where she was hanging her coat. "You've sat up too late as it
is."

He yawned, and dragged his feet with provoking slowness
past Cynthia.

"Was she down there, Mama?" He stopped on the bottom
step to grin at his sister.

"Go on, Robert. Start your bath. Mother'll be up in a minute."

"Aw, it's too late for a bath." He leaned over the rail.

"It's Saturday. I couldn't get back sooner."

Cynthia swung away from the round, grinning face. Her
mother went past her into the dining-room. Robert shuffled
upstairs; she heard the water splashing into the tub.

Her mother was very angry with her. Presently she would
come back, would begin to speak. Cynthia shivered. The familiar
room seemed full of hostile, accusing silence, like that of her

mother. If only she had come straight home from the office, she would be sitting by the table in the old Morris chair, reading, with her mother across from her sewing, or glancing through the evening paper. She gazed about the room at the neat scrolls of the brown wall-paper, at a picture above the couch, cows by a stream. The dull, ordinary comfort of life there hung about her, a reproaching shadow, within which she felt the heavy, silent discomfort her transgression dragged after it. It would be much easier to go on just as she was expected to do. Easier. The girl straightened her drooping body. That things were hard didn't matter. Miss Egert had insisted upon that. She was forgetting the pledge she had given. The humiliation slipped away, and a cold exaltation trembled through her, a remote echo of the hope that had shouted within her back there in the garden. Here it was difficult to know what she had promised, to what she had pledged herself—something that the familiar, comfortable room had no part in.

She glanced toward the dining-room, and her breath quickened. Between the faded green portières stood her mother, watching her with hard, bright eyes. Cynthia's glance faltered; she looked desperately about the room as if hurrying her thoughts to some shelter. Beside her on the couch lay the portfolio. She took a little step toward it, stopping at her mother's voice.

"Well, Cynthia, have you anything to say?"

Cynthia lifted her eyes.

"Don't you think I have trouble enough with your brothers? You, a grown girl, defying me! I can't understand it."

"I went down for this." Cynthia touched the black case.

"Put that down! I don't want to see it!" The mother's voice rose, breaking down the terrifying silences. "You disobeyed me. I told you you weren't to go there again. And then I telephoned your father to ask you to do an errand for me, and find you there—with that woman!"

"I'm not going again." Cynthia twisted her hands together. "I had to go a last time. She was a friend. I could not tell her I wasn't coming—"

"A friend! A sentimental old maid, older than your mother! Is that a friend for a young girl? What were you doing when I

found you? Holding hands! Is that the right thing for you? She's
turned your head. You aren't the same Cynthia, running off to
her, complaining of your mother."

"Oh, no!" Cynthia flung out her hand. "We were just talking."
Her misery confused her.

"Talking? About what?"

"About—" The recollection rushed through Cynthia—"about
beauty." She winced, a flush sweeping up to the edge of her fair
hair, at her mother's laugh.

"Beauty! You disobey your mother, hurt her, to talk about
beauty at night with an old maid!"

There was a hot beating in Cynthia's throat; she drew back
against the couch.

"Pretending to be an artist," her mother drove on, "to get
young girls who are foolish enough to listen to her sentimen-
talizing."

"She was an artist," pleaded Cynthia. "She gave it up to take
care of her father and mother. I told you all about that—"

"Talking about beauty doesn't make artists."

Cynthia stared at her mother. She had stepped near the table,
and the light through the green shade of the reading-lamp made
queer pools of color about her eyes, in the waves of her dark
hair. She didn't look real. Cynthia threw one hand up against
her lips. She was sucked down and down in an eddy of despair.
Her mother's voice dragged her again to the surface.

"We let you go there because you wanted to paint, and you
maunder and say things you'd be ashamed to have your mother
hear. I've spent my life working for you, planning for you, and
you go running off—" Her voice broke into a new note, a
trembling, grieved tone. "I've always trusted you, depended on
you: now I can't even trust you."

"I won't go there again. I had to explain."

"I can't believe you. You don't care how you make me feel."
Cynthia was whirled again down the sides of the eddy.

"I can't believe you care anything for me, your own mother."
Cynthia plucked at the braid on her cuff.

"I didn't do it to make you sorry," she whispered. "I—it was—"
The eddy closed about her, and with a little gasp she

dropped down on the couch, burying her head in the sharp angle of her elbows.

The mother took another step toward the girl; her hand hovered above the bent head and then dropped.

"You know mother wants just what is best for you, don't you? I can't let you drift away from us, your head full of silly notions." Cynthia's shoulders jerked. From the head of the stairs came Robert's shout:

"Mama, tub's full!"

"Yes; I'm coming."

Cynthia looked up. She was not crying. About her eyes and nostrils strained the white intensity of hunger.

"You don't think—" She stopped, struggling with her habit of inarticulateness. "There might be things—not silly—you might not see what—"

"Cynthia!" The softness snapped out of the mother's voice.

Cynthia stumbled up to her feet; she was as tall as her mother. For an instant they faced each other, and then the mother turned away, her eyes tear-brightened. Cynthia put out an awkward hand.

"Mother," she said piteously, "I'd like to tell you—I'm sorry—"

"You'll have to show me you are by what you do." The woman started wearily up the stairs. "Go to bed. It's late."

Cynthia waited until the bath-room door closed upon Robert's splashings. She climbed the stairs slowly, and shut herself into her room. She laid the portfolio in the bottom drawer of her white bureau; then she stood by her window. Outside, the big elm-tree, in fine, leafless dignity, showed dimly against the sky, a few stars caught in the arch of its branches.

A swift, tearing current of rebellion swept away her unhappiness, her confused misery; they were bits of refuse in this new flood. She saw, with a fierce, young finality that she was pledged to a conflict as well as to a search. As she knelt by the window and pressed her cheek on the cool glass, she felt the house about her, with its pressure of useful, homely things, as a very prison. No more journeyings down to Miss Egert's for glimpses of escape. She must find her own ways. Keep searching! At the phrase, excitement again glowed within her; she saw the last red wink of the fire in the garden.

Helen Reimensnyder Martin

Mrs. Gladfelter's Revolt
1923

There is scant biographical information available about Helen Reimensnyder Martin (1868–1939). She was born in Lancaster, Pennsylvania, to Henrietta Thurman and the Reverend Cornelius Reimensnyder, an immigrant German Lutheran pastor. Educated as a special student in English at Swarthmore and Radcliffe, she taught at a fashionable private school in New York City where she came in contact with the wealthy. After her marriage to Frederic C. Martin, a music teacher, in 1899, they settled in Harrisburg, Pennsylvania, where Helen Martin began to write. She published a novel every year, eventually producing thirty-six novels and two volumes of short stories. The couple had one daughter and one son. She wrote for middle-class literate audiences, publishing stories in McClure's, Century, Cosmopolitan, *and other periodicals. Her husband died in 1936 and she died three years later, at the age of seventy, in her daughter's home.*

She had one subject—the oppression of women—which she explored in two settings: sophisticated white high society and rural Pennsylvania Dutch society. Her high-society novels were not well received until after she had achieved recognition and success with her ethnic material.

Her work was successfully translated to the stage and screen. Her most famous and frequently reprinted novel, Tillie: A Mennonite Maid *(1904), was filmed in 1922 and produced on stage in 1924. Her 1914 Mennonite novel,* Barnabetta, *was turned into a play at the request of Minnie Maddern Fiske (1865–1932), one of the greatest theatrical artists in United States history.*

After a two-year absence from the stage during which Fiske acted in the earliest cinematic versions of Thomas Hardy's Tess of the D'Urbervilles *(1913) and William Thackeray's* Vanity Fair *(1915), Fiske, who had introduced Henrik Ibsen to American audiences, returned to the stage in the starring role in "Erstwhile Susan" (1916), the theatrical version of* Barnabetta. *It was later made into a film. Finally, two of Martin's society novels became films:* The Parasite *(1913) in 1925, starring Owen Moore and Madge Bellamy, and* The Snob *(1924) in 1924, starring John Gilbert and Norma Shearer.*

Martin has been variously praised for the authenticity of her portrayals of the Pennsylvania German ethnic community and for the comic exaggerations of characteristics presumed to be typical of its members. She has also been castigated for those same exaggerations, which have been labeled extreme, unfair, and cruel caricatures. In a 1916 interview published in the New York Evening Post, *to defend herself from these attacks, she said,*

> . . . the Pennsylvania Dutchman is parsimonious with
> everything but the labor of his women. He'll buy modern
> plows, an automobile to take his products to market,
> modern harness to save his horse. Up-to-dateness in the
> barn means more money in his pocket. But he won't
> spend a cent to save his wife or daughter a bit of work.
> That is what they are for—to work for men folk in the
> kitchen or near it.

She campaigned actively for women's suffrage and for socialism. Seeing significant connections between capitalism and the organized church, she opposed both of them. Beverly Seaton, a modern critic, has written about Martin that her central message was "The absolute necessity for a person to be independent of others, educated, able to earn a living, free to choose a vocation," adding that, for a woman, "money of her own is the key to control of her own life."

"Mrs. Gladfelter's Revolt" was first published in The Nation *on October 10, 1923, and later collected in Martin's second volume of short stories,* Yoked With a Lamb and Other Stories, *1930, which, along with her 1907 collection,* The Betrothal of Elypholate and Other Tales of the Pennsylvania Dutch, *has recently been reprinted. Of her novels, only* Tillie *is now in print.*

Unlike Mary E. Wilkins Freeman's better-known story, "The Revolt of Mother," (in A New England Nun, *1891) with which many readers have compared this story, "Mrs. Gladfelter's Revolt" not only involves a confrontation with the husband/father who embodies patriarchal authority, but does so for the purpose of expanding opportunities for the daughter and initiating real changes in the lives of mother, daughter, and father. In addition, the undercurrent of sexual feeling between the parents makes the story more complex than most stories portraying the struggle of a mother with her husband for the sake of their daughter.*

Written only three years after passage of the Nineteenth Amendment and published less than one month before the 1923 general election, this story might also be read as encouragement to newly enfranchised women to exercise their right to vote and as discouragement to men from interfering with women's impetus to do so.

I

Although Jacob Gladfelter's four robust sons had come out from under the rule of his heavy hand as strong, self-reliant young men, his wife and his only daughter had become, year after year, more and more submissive and cowed. To be sure, Jacob had always been a little more tolerant of self-assertion on the part of the males of the household, seeing that they would, in the end, have to be their own masters; but as a woman must always, according to the Pennsylvania Dutch standard of what was "womanly," acquiesce in the dominance of a man, either her father or her "mister," there was not the same reason for relaxing one's sway over them as in the case of the boys.

It had never occurred to Meely, Jacob's wife, to question her man's right to rule his own household. She would have thought him less than a man and would not have respected him if he had not governed her and their children with a firm hand. From that night when, meeting her for the first time at a barn dance, he had boldly snatched her from her partner, carried her bodily to his own sleigh and driven away with her under the very eyes of her dumfounded and indignant escort, she had been his abject slave.

Her sons loved and petted their little mother and their comely young sister Weezy—and walked over them rough-shod. In this they only followed the example of their father. Although Jacob Gladfelter, prosperous proprietor of the only general store in Virginsville, had always been, according to his lights, a kind, indulgent husband and father, he was first and foremost a man of strict conscientious scruples and he would have considered himself just as sadly lacking in his duty if he had ever let his women folks get out of hand as if he had failed to be a "good-purvider" or had neglected to engage the best procurable midwife for his wife's many confinements, keeping her on the job for as much as two weeks—which in Virginsville was almost going to the ragged edge of sentimentality. Jacob's contempt for the few men of his acquaintance who were so weak as to "leave the women boss" was unutterable. Besides this, in spite of his reputedly amiable disposition, there was a streak of obstinacy in his character that, once he had taken a stand, would not let him yield.

So jealously did Jacob guard his prerogative to decide all household matters that for his wife and daughter to make a suggestion was only to invite a sure denial of what they wanted. If he indulged them it must be in his own way, at his own convenience, and in what *he* considered pleasant for them. Was a new carpet to be bought, Mr. Gladfelter selected it. He would see no point in consulting his wife's taste in the matter because if she did not share his decided preferences as to carpets her preference would, of course, have to be sacrificed; and if she did share them, no use to consult her. Did the kitchen range wear out, it was Jacob who said whether it should be replaced by a gas-cooking stove. And on such questions as the higher schooling of the children Jacob simply announced to her what he intended to do.

When suffrage was given to women the four Gladfelter boys were hilarious at the idea of "Mom's wotin'." Jacob, considering the Amendment unscriptural and subversive of a stable social order, laid down the law for his family: "I won't give you the dare to wote, Mom! As fur Weezy, till she's at the wotin' age, I guess she'll be married and it'll be fur her mister to say dare she wote or not."

"It wonders me how a man ever knows who *to* wote fur," said Mrs. Gladfelter. "The candidates all seems all right till they're *in* oncet—and then—"

"Yes, *and then!* You said it!" blustered her son Elmer. "And then it's hell! Ain't?"

"Yes, ain't!" responded all the men.

When Weezy reached the age for "sittin' up Sa'rdays and

keepin' comp'ny with a Steady-Regular," her father magnani-
mously told her one evening at supper that he would now get
a new suite of furniture for the parlor. He had expected this
news to be received with gratitude and pleasure by Weezy and
her mother, and he was surprised at the awkward silence that
answered him. The truth was Meely and Weezy had come to
dread Jacob's taste in household furnishings.

"Please, Pop," Weezy ventured, "don't get yellow!"

Mrs. Gladfelter looked anxiously across the supper table to
note the effect upon her husband of such boldness. Jacob, eating
sausage and fried potatoes, did not reply.

"Yellow kreistles me!" Weezy shuddered.

No reply from Jacob.

"I like red better or such dark blue."

Jacob noisily sipped his coffee.

"Sooner'n have yellow, I'd *let* the parlor."

"So would I!" Mrs. Gladfelter, unexpectedly though timidly,
spoke in. "It's going on twenty years that I lived with our parlor
furniture and I'm used to it a little. I'd sooner let it be than get
new."

"You always were so much for yellow, Pop!" pleaded Weezy.
"I wouldn't like to keep comp'ny with a fellow with yellow
furniture!"

"And it's Weezy would use the room, not us," Mrs. Gladfelter
reasoned, taking refuge in addressing her son Albert rather than
her husband. "If Weezy don't favor yellow, I think it's a pity to
get yel—"

"Be peaceable, Mom!" Jacob quietly ordered her, with that
look of deadly obstinacy on his face which she and Weezy knew
to be the stone wall to any further advancement of *their* side of
a question. But something in her daughter's wistful, worried
eyes made her, this evening, strangely persistent.

"Us we might as well get what Weezy would like and yellow
ain't just to say so tasty in parlor furniture—it's not so bad in
wallpaper or carpet, though I'd sooner purfer red or blue, like
Weezy says, but yellow furniture, yet—"

"Be peaceable, Mom!"

"But Weezy's gettin' full-growed now, and if she don't take to

yellow, it's her has to set in the parlor, *we* never do, and it's
her—"

"Mom! Be peaceable!"

And Mrs. Gladfelter, with a long sigh, subsided.

Mr. Gladfelter felt it to be his clear duty, in view of this
incipient insubordination of his wife and daughter, to establish
his rightful authority by getting a parlor suite of the yellowest
yellow plush he could find.

It was when her father announced, upon Weezy's having
finished the village school course, that she was now "done
school," and must henceforth stay at home and help with the
housework and the general store, that Mrs. Gladfelter, for the
first time in her married life, was jolted into a real protest.

"Weezy not go to Millersville Normal!" she almost gasped,
"like all our boys have went! But Pop! Me I always conceited
you'd leave Weezy have schoolage, too, like our boys!"

Jacob did not think it necessary to offer any explanation of
his decision.

"But Weezy she was always smarter'n any of our boys, Pop—
her teachers all sayed she was smart! And she's always *counted*
on goin' to Millersville Normal. She's planned all her life to be
a school teacher!"

Jacob paid less attention to her plaints than he would have
paid to a fly's buzzing.

"I always missed it so myself, not having no schoolage, Pop,
I did think now my dotter was to have it! Why, look, Pop, how
much better she could marry, too, if she got good educated!"

Weezy, during this monologue of her mother's, was silently
weeping over her untasted supper.

Jacob, rising from the table, took a clothes-brush from a shelf,
brushed first his clothes, then his hair with the same brush, and
then, still without replying, turned away and walked into his
store in the front of the house.

Mrs. Gladfelter regarded her weeping daughter in an agony
of sympathy. That Weezy, so very much "smarter at the books"
than her big brothers, should be denied an education for no
other reason than that she was not a boy—for the first time in
her life the bald unreasonableness and injustice of such a
philosophy cut deep into her soul. She loved this daughter, her

only girl, with a passionate devotion such as her rowdy, unmanageable boys had not called forth from her. Weezy, always so tender and thoughtful for her, was the poetry and romance of her life. It seemed to her that she could not calmly submit to this ruthless destruction of her child's dearest hopes. She suddenly rose, went to Weezy and put her arms about her. "Never you mind, Weezy, I've always counted on your gettin' a good education and you're *a-goin'* to get it! Don't cry! *You're not stoppin' your schoolage!*"

Weezy dried her eyes and looked at her mother incredulously. "But, Mom, what can we do if Pop says no? The more we coax, the more stubborn-headed he'll get!"

"I know that. We won't coax. But you're a-goin' to get your nice education all the same!"

"But how, Mom? How will you get round Pop?"

"You know I got my interest money?"

"But Pop never gives it to you."

"I've never ast it off of him. But it comes in sich little pieces of paper called cupons. Pop keeps 'em in the safe. They give six hundred dollars a year. They're mine. My Pop inherited 'em to me. That'll be enough to keep you at school."

"But, Mom, what would Pop *say* if you took them cupons?"

"I don't mind what he says compared to how I mind your not goin' to school. I got to just choose between them two things— Pop bein' cross at me or you losin' your schoolin'."

"I never saw Pop really cross at you, Mom!"

"I have never gave him no reason to be. He can't rightly have cross at me fur takin' what's my own. Your Pop's a awful honest man, Weezy. Why, here this morning, Sally Bergstresser come in our store to buy a spool of thread off Pop, and Pop he reminded her she owed him a cent on the last spool she got— her not having knew thread had went up a cent and having only five cents along that time. Pop tol' her, 'It ain't that I want that cent, Sally, but there's my income tax, you see. I got to be wery honest about that, you understand.' Sally she laughed till I thought she'd bust! She sayed, 'Now, Jake Gladfelter, if that ain't like you! Takin' the trouble to get your income tax right to the penny!—where *some* wouldn't bother none if they was off a dollar or more!' Yes, Weezy, your Pop is that pertikkler that folks laughs at him yet! So I can't see that he could get cross at me fur takin' my own."

"Does he think it *is* yours, Mom, when you're married to him?"

"Well, the law calls it mine."

"The law gives you dare to wote, too, and Pop won't leave you."

"It makes me nothing, Weezy, if Pop is cross, so long as I can get you a good education."

Weezy shook her head hopelessly. "I'm under age. Pop could fetch me home from Normal."

Her mother's eyes gleamed with an adventurous daring that made her look to Weezy like a stranger. "Could he? Then I'll put you to a school that he won't know where you're at!"

"Why, Mom, you don't sound like yourself!" Weezy softly exclaimed. almost alarmed.

"Where could I find out about another school, Weezy?"

"Uriah Bergstresser mebby could tell you, Mom."

"Yi Bergstresser! Him!" Her mother was skeptical. "Why, him he was that dumb at Millersville Normal that they shed him at the end of the term!"

"I know, but he's traveled 'round a good bit."

"Yes, that's so, too. I mind that time he was to New York over, with his Pop. You mind how he tol' us New York's so big they couldn't find the end of it!"

"You mind, Mom, how he told us about the nice things they're got in that Metropolitan *Mu*-zeem in New York? Sich mummies and all. Och, me, I'd like now to see that *Mu*-zeem! Ain't, Mom? You mind Yi said that as far as *he* could see, they didn't seem to use that great big handsome building for a thing 'ceptin' to store all them things!"

"If you think, Weezy, Yi *could* tell us the name of another school than Millersville Normal, I'll ast him right aways."

"All right, Mom."

II

One Sunday morning early in September, when Weezy and her mother started out as usual for church, the girl surprised her father by kissing him good-by. Demonstrations of family affection being rare among the Pennsylvania Dutch, kissing being scarcely ever indulged in even when parting for a long time, Jake was puzzled—and pleased. He was very fond of little Weezy.

"Ain't you some early startin'?" he asked.

"It gives such a nice day, we thought we'd walk a piece-ways," answered his wife.

When the mother and daughter reached the church, they did not go in, but walked on to the Square where you took the trolley to the near-by city of Lancaster. From Lancaster, Mrs. Gladfelter sent a telegram to her husband: "Taking Weezy to Normal School. Be home Wednesday."

They stopped in Lancaster with Mrs. Gladfelter's brother Sam, who had recently moved there from Columbia unknown to Jacob. On Monday Sam helped his sister procure money on her bond and Mrs. Sam went with her and Weezy to outfit the girl for school. For the first time in her life Weezy was permitted to choose her own clothes, never having presumed to object to wear whatever her father had seen fit to buy for her.

Not even to her brother and his wife would Mrs. Gladfelter trust her secret—the name of the Normal School to which she was taking her daughter. "Millersville Normal," the only one they had ever heard of, being just four miles from Lancaster, she knew that they (and her husband too) would assume that that was where Weezy was going.

"It wonders me, Meely, that Jake leaves *you* to tend to all this business for Weezy—the money and buyin' and all! It ain't like him! Is he sick or whatever, and how's your Monday washin' gettin' done?" asked her sister-in-law.

"Fur oncet I'm just lettin' the washin', Mame! I'm lettin' everything! Fur oncet I don't care! I feel that light-headed and indiff'runt, I don't har'ly know what's over me!"

"Mebby you better see a doctor—not? What does Jake say at your bein' so light-headed and indiff'runt?"

"It makes me nothing what he says!" laughed Meely.

"My souls, Meely, you *better* see a doctor—it must be some serious!"

But Meely only laughed.

She doubted not that Jacob, immediately upon receiving her

telegram on Sunday, had gone to "Millersville Normal" to force her and Weezy to come home. She marveled at her own unruffled calmness in contemplating his amazement at not finding them there.

"Do you think, Mom, you *can* keep it from Pop where I'm at?" Weezy wondered.

"Weezy, your Pop will *never get it out of me!*"

When the time came to part with her daughter and return home, Mrs. Gladfelter's high spirits suddenly dropped.

"Och, Mom, I hate for you to go back home and face Pop!" Weezy mourned.

"It ain't facin' your Pop, I mind. It's—the thought of what home will be without you, Weezy."

Weezy clasped her close. "Mom! I love you so!"

But on her homeward trip, Mrs. Gladfelter's sadness at leaving her daughter lifted somewhat and the unconquerable buoyancy that had possessed her ever since her flight was again in the ascendancy. This first and only adventure of her whole life, this first taste of freedom, had seemed to re-create her into a new being—she was almost a stranger to herself.

When at four o'clock on Wednesday afternoon she walked blithely through the general store where her husband and two of her sons were at the moment waiting on customers, she greeted them gayly as she passed on out to the sitting-room back of the store. "Well, Jake! Well, boys!"

The boys stared at her, too bewildered to reply. But her husband did not look up. Not until she called them all to supper did Jake deign to come near her, and even then he did not speak to her or even look at her as he sat down and at once began to help himself to fried "ponhaus" and "smear case." Meely suddenly realized that however strong she might be to meet reproaches, his holding himself silently and icily aloof from her would be more than she could live with! If *this* was to be the weapon with which he would try to wrest her secret from her and regain his dominance—

"I was talkin' to such a lady educator here the other day," she smilingly told them as she poured their coffee, "and she explained me the arguments how it's my dooty now to use the wote. So at the next election, Pop, I'm wotin'," she cheerfully stated.

Her husband made no sign. But the boys who, affected by their father's grim mood, had been discreetly silent, sent up a shout of laughter at the huge joke of their timid little mother's going to the polls to vote.

"Here's the new woman!"

"Have a cig-arette, Mom?"

"It wonders me you didn't have your hair so bobbed while you was to Lancaster over!"

After supper Jake at once went back into the store, still without speaking to her. She had expected him to demand, the moment she appeared at home, what she had done with Weezy; and she had been fully prepared to resist his insisting upon knowing. But when that night he went to sleep at her side without having spoken to her, she saw that until she voluntarily offered him the explanations and apologies he considered due him, he meant to hold himself thus aloof. She knew how stubbornly he could hold out in a course like this. She could not live with him in such alienation. It would kill her in a month! They had never quarreled before in all the twenty years of their married life.

The next morning she stopped him as he was about to go into the store. "Please, Pop, leave Al tend store till I speak somethin' to you."

Jake, directing Albert with a backward motion of his thumb to go into the store, stood still and waited for his wife to speak.

"I've made up my mind, Jake, fur our Weezy to have a nice education like you gev our boys—and, Jake, you better know right aways that if I have to die fur it, I'm a-goin' to see that she gets it!"

"Where's she at?"

"I'll tell you when you pass me your promise you won't go and fetch her home."

"Where's she at?" he repeated, bringing his knuckles down upon the table with a shock that rattled the dishes.

Meely's answer was to meet his cold eyes with such unflinching determination in her own that in his utter astonishment at its unfamiliarity, he relaxed, his jaw dropped, and he stared at her in confusion.

"Jake, I want fur my dotter to be somepin' more'n I always

was—a cabbage-head. Our Weezy's a-goin' to have her chanct to get more out of livin' than I ever had a'ready."

Jake stared at her stupidly, incredulously. "I don't favor females bein' book-learnt! It's agin Nature!"

"An awful lot of females is goin' agin Nature then, fur there's a thousand girls at that there Normal School Weezy's at. If I'd been a little book learnt myself, I guess I wouldn't o' waited *this* long till I took my own mind fur somepin' oncet!"

"Where is that Normal School where Weezy's at?"

"Do you pass your promise like I sayed?"

"Answer to me, Meely!"

"When you pass your promise!"

"Meely!" he exclaimed, utterly exasperated, "if I'd o' knowed you'd ever turn out like this here, I sure never woulda married you!"

"Why, Jake!" protested Meely, shocked, "when us we're got three growed children, it's har'ly maur'l to say such a thing as that!—that you wouldn't o' married me!"

"But I don't har'ly *know* you like this, Meely!—you seem like a stranger to me!"

"Well, but, Pop, that must seem a pleasant change to you. Me, I'd *like* it to have a little change. I'm awful used to you, Pop," she sighed. "A little change would do me good—"

"Meely! What fur talk is this?"

"Yes, well, I mean it, Jake. Sometimes I think I'm a little tired of you—that I do."

Again their eyes met and Jake, with a strange pang of fear in his heart, saw, in the straight, fearless gaze of the little woman whom, up to this hour, he had always regarded with a queer mingling of affection and contempt, that for once in his life he had encountered his match in obstinacy. Deep down in his soul he knew that he was beaten.

Tess Slesinger

Mother to Dinner
1935

Tess Slesinger's mother never forgave her for writing "Mother to Dinner," according to Janet Sharistanian, Slesinger's biographer.

Augusta Slesinger, daughter of a Russian-Jewish immigrant, had been the dominant presence in her daughter's childhood—and she was an extremely unconventional mother. She successfully directed a child guidance clinic, ran the Jewish Big Sister organization, and helped establish the New School for Social Research. Late in life, she became a dedicated psychoanalyst—while her husband, a Hungarian-Jewish immigrant who had studied to be a lawyer, plodded away in his father-in-law's business at a garment industry job he despised. On the day after their fiftieth wedding anniversary, Slesinger's parents separated and never saw one another again.

Tess Slesinger (1905–1945) observed her mother's competence, energy, and power—and absorbed her parents' liberal ideas about sexuality and self-expression. A neighbor reported her astonishment at the sight of Tess's brothers singing and dancing around a table in celebration of her first menstrual period.

As a child, Tess had declared that she would be a writer and nothing else. "I was born with the curse of intelligent parents, a happy childhood, and nothing valid to rebel against," she once said, "So I rebelled against telling the truth. I told whoppers at three, tall stories at four, a home-run at five: from six to sixteen I wrote them into a diary."

At Ethical Culture Society schools, Slesinger absorbed socialist ideals; at Swarthmore College she studied creative writing and Freud, and later claimed she had been dropped for flunking algebra and being caught smoking on campus. In 1927 she was graduated from the Columbia School of Journalism, where she studied fiction, and in 1928 she married Herbert Solow, the scholarly, intense assistant editor of the Menorah Journal, *a Jewish/Marxist magazine. The* Menorah Journal *crowd argued Marxism, pursued their ambitions as writers, and saw themselves as stars in the intellectual drama of the 1930s. In 1934 they picketed a publisher who, they felt, treated his staff unfairly—and Slesinger was one of eighteen writers arrested and jailed.*

Many of Slesinger's colleagues argued abstractly about "the workers" or "alienated labor" or "class politics," but Slesinger, a skeptic, took a down-to-earth personal view. In her short stories, many of her male characters declaim and act on high principles, but they miss the everyday details and emotional currents that women see. It was the friction between these emotional realities and the high principles that provided the conflict in many of the short stories she published in the Menorah Journal, The New Yorker, Scribner's, Vanity Fair, *and other prestigious magazines. In a late unfinished novel, Slesinger described a political organizer as "a brilliant imitation of a complex human being," but in her short stories she used pointed and poignant details to describe women, such as the daughter "sliding the bread into the shining modern breadbox" and feeling "a strong nostalgia for the worn-out tin that had stood for years on her mother's shelf."*

New York intellectual circles grew too narrow for Slesinger. Her marriage lasted only four years. She published The Unpossessed *(1934, reprinted 1984, The Feminist Press) and* Time: the Present *(her short story collection, 1935)— and headed west. She replaced an unfulfilling marriage with one combining love and work. With her second husband, Frank Davis, she wrote screenplays, gave birth to two children, and joined the bitter struggle to form the Screen Writers Guild.*

Slesinger's screen credits include "The Good Earth," based on Pearl Buck's novel about Chinese women's struggles for survival as wives and mothers and daughters. She also adapted A Tree Grows in Brooklyn, *Betty Smith's bittersweet novel about a girl's coming of age and learning to side with her mother in the battles between men and women.*

Slesinger rarely wrote short stories after she went to Hollywood and never finished her own second novel. She died of cancer in 1945 at the age of thirty-nine. Augusta Slesinger, who lived to be seventy-nine, outlived her daughter by seven years.

"Mother to Dinner" is about how daughters love, honor, fear, hide from, and long for their mothers—and how that mother-daughter knot is invisible to men. When Augusta Slesinger read "Mother to Dinner" as an insult from her daughter, she saw only the pain in it, and denied the longing.

Katherine Benjamin, who had been Katherine Jastrow for something less than a year, said Goodafternoon to the groceryman and, stooping to the counter, gathered two large and unwieldy packages close to her body, balancing one elbow on her hip so that the hand, crawling to the top, could hold sternly separate the bottle of milk from the package of Best Eggs. The thin, one-eyed errand boy who sprawled on an empty packing-box near the door leaped to his feet and opened it with a flourish and a "hot, isn't it?" And sliding past him, curving her body to make a nest for the projecting bundle, she heard the screen door swing lightly closed behind her, flutter against the wood frame in a series of gently diminishing taps.

Why did one say Goodafternoon instead of Goodbye to tradesmen and teachers, she wondered, following her packages as they bobbed evenly down the street before her, recalling (as she adjusted her gait to her burden) countless times when she had waited, in middies and broad sailor hats, for her mother's comforting "Good*morning*, Mr Schmidt," and Mr Schmidt's answering "*Good*morning, Mrs Benjamin, *good*morning I'm sure." And now Katherine, no longer in middies or accompanied by her mother but modestly wearing a ring on her left hand, heard herself kindly bidding Mr Papenmeyer Goodafternoon, and feeling, as she said it, very close to her mother, feeling almost, as she nodded firmly to him, that she was her mother. (Gerald predicted with scorn that it would not be long before Katherine would speak of Mr Papenmeyer as "my Mr Papenmeyer" and he suspected that she would even add, in time, "he never disappoints"; but she was not to suppose, he said, that he would glance benignly over his *Saturday Evening Post* as her father did, and listen.)

Katherine hugged her packages like babies; in them lay, wrapped in glossy wax paper, in brown paper bags, in patent boxes, the dinner to which Katherine's mother and father were coming as guests . . . The dinner over which Katherine would frown at Gerald politely insulting Mrs Benjamin; over which Mr Benjamin would cough and insist on the worst cuts of everything . . . She hoped nervously that Gerald would not be insolent and argumentative, that her mother would not be stupid. . . . She must protect them both . . . And she began to dread the strangeness which always oppressed her on beholding her mother in a house which was her home and not her mother's. . . .

Ridiculous, she said brightly, I'm not going to let *that* happen again . . .

The spire of the church on the corner raised itself in the form of a huge salt-shaker against the mild, colorless sky. The sun, a blurred yellow lamp, glimmered palely behind veils of soiled cloud; it might rain, for the air was sodden, the leaves on the tree before the church hovered on the air with a peculiar waiting indifference, like dead fish turned over on their backs and floating in still water.

And for years to come she, "Mrs Gerald Jastrow," would walk, heavily laden with her thoughts and her packages, in Fall, in Winter, and in Spring, from Mr Papenmeyer's meat-and-grocery store through these same streets, past the church with its salt-shaker spire, past the row of low brick houses, past the tall india-rubber apartment with the liveried doorman shuffling his feet under the awning, stretched like a hollow wrinkled caterpillar to the curb, to her own home, which she shared with Gerald, of whom she had never heard two years before . . .

Katherine's fingers, tapping the sagging bundles, reviewed their contents. Meat—Mr Papenmeyer's recommended cut for four—bread, milk, corn, tomatoes—without her asking, the clerk had passionately assured her they were firm—two large packages it amounted to, one small slippery one under her elbow, and her purse. By a minute flexing of her left hand she could feel the key tucked neatly in her glove to save her trouble when she reached her door. An absurd ritual, that, said Gerald; one which in the sum total could not save her much trouble. You've picked up all these damn habits, he said, from your mother: they're a waste of time, they take more time to remember than simply to leave out; be careful, Katherine, before you know it you will be keeping a platinum-framed market-list. But these little rituals made doing the things fun, Katherine argued; when she re-membered, at the grocer's before picking up her packages, to tuck the key in her glove, a horde of vague recollections, almost recollections of recollections, unravelled pleasantly in her mind. They gave meaning to what would otherwise be just marketing; they formed a link not only with yesterday and tomorrow, but with other women squinting at scales and selecting dinners for

strange men to whom they found themselves married; with, if
you like, her mother, who had been doing these things every
day for thirty years. You may say pooh Gerald, she said, but
there are many things which you, who are after all a man, cannot
be expected to know; why two years ago you didn't even know
me . . .

Were the flat faces she had left haggling over green peas and
punching cantaloupes aware of the waiting uncertainties, the
uprooting, the transplanting, the bleeding, involved in their
calmly leaving their homes to go to live with strangers? Strangers—
husbands—Gerald A. Jastrow—I met a boy named Gerald A.
Jastrow at a party, he asked to take me home—I am sorry, I am
seeing a boy named Gerald Jastrow, he has a cowlick which
trembles when he argues—but mother I am seeing Gerald
tonight—Gerald says, Gerald thinks—I am going to be married—
his name? (*whose* name?—oh, the Stranger's)—his name is Jastrow, Gerald Jastrow—I've been married for eleven months—
my husband's name is Gerald Jastrow, no I don't know him,
he's a Stranger to me, but I put away his male-smelling underwear. . . . Katherine reached the sidewalk just in time to avoid a
cab which sped down the street in front of her house.

She smiled brightly at the elevator man, an expert, busy,
kindly smile; she felt again like her mother. "Wouldn't be
surprised if a storm blew up," Albert said to her shrewdly,
resting his hand in a friendly way on the lever. (A storm, she
didn't want a storm, Katherine thought, suddenly frightened;
Gerald might say what he liked about the risk of motoring being
greater than that of flying, and the chance of being murdered
in sleep greater than that of being struck by lightning: she
wouldn't fly, and she cowered before thunder and lightning.)
"Oh do you think so?" said Mrs. Gerald Jastrow, and she looked
in awe at the elevator man, as if it was all in his hands whether
a storm came or not. "Oh I hope not," she pleaded. The elevator
stopped on a level with her floor, her door was before her,
familiar, with its arty streaks, its brass knob and keyhole, the
number 21 in black painted letters. Albert, slamming the door
of his cage, determined to go the whole hog. "Well I wouldn't
be surprised," he said, and dropped suddenly out of sight.

Katherine could not bear to drop a single one of her burdens,

now that she had come so far; she made a series of supreme
efforts, balancing, juggling, squirming, forcing her key out of
her glove with fractional, inch-worm motions, still carefully
separating the bottle of milk from the package of Best Eggs,
evoking a new muscle to keep the small package from slipping.

And then she was in, in her own house, with the door shut
behind her, and the yellow curtains dancing on the window
panes, the stove standing, homely and patient, in the small
kitchen, the chairs sitting in friendly fashion, as if themselves
guests at a tea-party, just as she had left them . . .

Suddenly she was overcome by a swift engulfing depression.
She stood at the door of the yellow room and was unable to put
down the packages in her arms. The air in the room stood hot
and heavy, waiting, like Albert, with melancholy assurance, for
storm; the curtains flapped treacherously.

What nonsense, she said crisply, amazingly comforted by a
slant of faint sunlight which quivered through the gloom. Look,
she said, it is my own house . . . Reassured, she dropped her
packages on the kitchen table. But someone should be there to
greet her, she felt, to rise from one of those friendly chairs and
say to her: What did you buy? How was Mr Papenmeyer the
butcher? Was the one-eyed errand boy there today? Come in,
take off your hat and gloves, I am glad you are home . . . A year
ago she would have stood at the door and shouted *Moth-er*,
where *are* you? And if Mrs Benjamin had not come in haste at
her call, a white-aproned German maid (Mrs Benjamin chap-
eroned their love-affairs so successfully that they generally stayed
with her for years, like obedient nuns) would have come and
said, Oh Miss Katy, your mother said to tell you she went over
to your Aunt Sarah, your uncle's not feeling just right.

But she would call *up* her mother, she thought gleefully,
running to the telephone: Hel*lo*, mother, what do you think I
bought for supper? The butcher said . . . Do you think there
will be a storm, mother? . . . As she lifted the receiver from its
hook she thought she heard faint steps behind her; Gerald, she
thought in a flash, and slid the receiver back to its place. Of
course it wasn't Gerald, at four o'clock in the afternoon, of
course it wasn't anybody; but suppose he had come upon her

telephoning her mother: she could hear him say, as he had said last Sunday, catching her at the telephone (and of course one thought of one's mother on a long Sunday), Oh for God's sake, Katherine, like a two-year-old baby you are always running home to mother . . . Cut off from her mother. Yet Gerald was right, she mustn't, she mustn't.

Loneliness surrounded Katherine like a high black fence. Then why not call up Gerald, why not rush to the telephone and call Gerald at his office (where she could never visualize him); if only she could call him up and say to him: I have just come home to our house. It is pleasant and cool, the curtains are still yellow. I shall take off my dress and read. Then I shall cook dinner, for you, for me, for my father and mother—you haven't forgotten they are coming? you'll come early?—*Gerald, what are you doing?* But she knew his firm "Jastrow speaking," and she could guess, if she dared to go beyond it, at his business-like: "What do you *want*, dear?" Well, what *did* she want, she wondered impatiently, and strained to discover whether that was thunder or furniture moving.

Probably Gerald was right, she thought wearily—for he was so often "right" in a logical, meaningless way—that thinking about every small thing, attaching significances to every moment, wishing to communicate every small thought, was, besides being sentimental, "an imbecilic waste of time." Gerald railed against sentimentality, and, charmingly, disarmingly, gave way to it at moments. When the moment passed Gerald shed it like a wet bathing suit, and emerged cool and casual, forgetful and un-touched. But with her mother, these moments grew into com-fortable hours, never forgotten, linking one with another, re-maining always, a steady undercurrent, ready to rise and fill them at the lightest touch.

And sliding the bread into the shining modern breadbox she felt a strong nostalgia for the worn-out tin that had stood for years on her mother's shelf. This cold affair of shelves and sliding doors, glittering knobs and antiseptic lettering suggested too much newness, too little use and familiarity; her mother's loomed in contrast, a symbol of security, almost a refuge from storm. And yet Mrs Benjamin, with the vision of that old, battered, loyal thing in the back of her mind, had come with

Katherine graciously, gayly even, to buy this tawdry substitute. (My little girl, she had said to the clerk, smiling ironically at him and drawing him into her sympathy, would like that Modern Breadbox. It was as if she had said, My little girl has tired of her old mother, she wants the latest thing in young men, one that can scientifically explain away the fear of lightning.) Feeling warmly bound to her mother, she caught herself opening and slamming the little door a second, unnecessary time, an old nervous habit of her mother's. For a moment she felt purified, intensely loyal, as if by this gesture she had renounced the new for the old. She walked from the kitchen with her mother's tired, elastic step, the step of a stout woman who has shopped all day, whose weary body will neither submit to rest nor ignore the stern orders of fashion. It was a step singularly unsuited to Katherine's slimness, but it was comfortable now, familiar; she slid gratefully into it, like one falling into a cushioned rocker which is too large for the body but provides, nevertheless, a warm and comfortable harbor. And so she bent her body back from the waist and became her mother, balancing her stout body, carrying the heaviest part bravely before her. (Your mother navigates like a boat, Gerald had said to her once. Katherine, ruefully succumbing to the justice of the description, had come starkly awake on the edge of falling asleep that night, and cried bitterly, not because Gerald, whom she hated for sleeping soundly beside her, had said it, but because she had laughed.)

Oh of course Gerald was "right," she told herself. And yet, this coming home eagerly, her arms aching with pleasant weights, delighting in facing those yellow curtains again, with no one to greet her, and unable to telephone because what she had to say to her husband was irrelevant—her mother wouldn't like it, she felt. But between two people who lived together, why should anything be irrelevant? nothing she could ever say, she knew, would be irrelevant to her mother: how eagerly Mrs Benjamin had awaited reports of adventures no more important than a shopping expedition, a subway jam, a lunch engagement. (Oh but that had been stupid, stupid—inadequate. You told your mother insignificant things because you knew she wouldn't understand the important ones. Gerald's words: but true, true.) But Gerald himself had so *little* concern for the small things she did all day that she refrained from telling him anecdotes which she passionately feared might bore him, but which, nevertheless, she collected like bouquets of precious flowers to lay before him if she dared. Looking about the empty room, Gerald's desk standing solidly in one corner reproved her; she became irritated that her mind flew so often to thoughts of her mother. . . .

Like a human shuttle she wove her way between these two, between Gerald and her mother, the two opposites who supported her web. (Why couldn't they both leave her alone?) When she was with her mother she could not rest, for she thought continually of the beacon of Gerald's intelligence, which must be protected from her mother's sullying incomprehension. And when she was with Gerald her heart ached for her deserted mother, she longed for her large enveloping sympathy in which to hide away from Gerald's too-clear gaze. From sheer hopelessness and irritation, tears filled her eyes. . . .

She was glad to escape from the kitchen, for she had begun to hate Mr Papenmeyer's excellent foods, which would merge artfully and serve as the camouflage of a family battle. As long as the dinner lasted, she knew the conversation could be kept meager and on a safely mediocre level. But Katherine, sitting between her mother and father, and eyeing her husband with apprehension, would know that around her own table, consuming food she herself had prepared, a victim would be fattened for slaughter, a victor strengthened for battle. And whoever won, Katherine lost . . . Oh come, she told herself, exasperated, this isn't the Last Supper . . .

But that wasn't furniture moving, she told herself grimly, crouching on the window-sill and regarding the street which was lying quietly in its place before her house—not twice, she said, that's Albert's thunder. It rumbled from a great distance, as though it were in hiding.

Certainly, she thought, her mind returning, like a dog worrying a bone, she lived with Gerald on a higher plane—if her misery was sometimes more acute, her pleasure, in proportion, was more poignant. While they had felt nothing deeply, Katherine and her mother, as they had built up, over tea-tables, simple patterns of thought, simplified ways of looking at things. What if Katherine had had to stoop her mind so that they might stay together? at least they could talk, at least they kept each other company. (Gerald said their talk was no more than gossip; he said that Katherine and her mother had shut themselves up in a hot-house, talking and comforting each other for griefs that could never come to them while they remained in their lethargic half-life.) But in a world like this, thought Katherine, where thunder-storms can creep on one ruthlessly, why shouldn't two people who love each other hide away and give one another comfort?

Thunder rumbled more constantly now. Katherine, suspicious of it, in spite of its distance, detected in its muffled rolling a growing concentration, as if it were slowly gathering its strength, as if it were winding itself up for a tremendous spring. Should she telephone Gerald?—*no.*

The thought of Gerald frightened her. He led such a curious existence apart from her every day from nine till six. Katherine and her mother had always known exactly what the other was doing, at almost every hour in the day. It was a comfort to stop suddenly, look at one's watch, and think "Mother's at the dentist's now" or "I should think mother would be on the way home now." But there were times when Gerald was in the room with her, sitting beside her, lying beside her in bed, when she didn't know exactly where he was. . . .

Gerald said—and with some justice, she admitted to herself—that she and her mother had lived like two spoiled wives in a harem kept by a simple old gentleman who demanded nothing of them beyond their presence and the privilege of supporting them. But because of his docility one could not take seriously a possible injustice to him. Beside his work downtown, Mr Benjamin mailed their letters, called for their purchases, or did any of the little errands which they had spent the day in pleasantly avoiding. If he entered the room where Katherine and her mother were talking, it had seemed quite natural for Mrs Benjamin to say, "Dear, we are talking"; it seemed natural because of the peaceful expression with which Mr Benjamin picked up his *Saturday Evening Post* on the way out of the room. All Katherine's uncles were disposed of in the same way by her aunts.

Gerald referred to the Benjamin men as "poor devils," as "emasculated boobs". You resent me, he said to Katherine, because you have a preconceived idea of the rôle to which all husbands are relegated by their wives; you'd like to laugh me out of any important existence. (Indeed, it was only at moments when he was away and when she was performing, in his absence, some intimate service for him, that she could look upon Gerald as her mother looked upon her father; with ease, with possession, with a maternal tolerance touched by affectionate irony. Here were things of which she could be certain: that he rolled his underwear into a ball and dropped it on the floor, that he left his shoes to lie where they fell, that he draped yesterday's tie around the back of a chair. But she could never achieve this intimacy in his presence: when Gerald was with her, when she *thought* about Gerald, it faded; there was more strangeness.) Gerald again! She was aware of a wish to sink Gerald into the bottom of her mind: she was too much aware of him; when she read, when she visited, when she noticed things, it was always with the desire to report back to Gerald: nothing was complete until Gerald had been told.

She and her mother had discussed and reported everything. But she could no longer be alone with her mother, for it seemed as though Gerald sat in taunting effigy between them, forcing Katherine for her mother's sake to deprecate him, for his sake to protect him, from obscurity, from misrepresentation, from neglect . . .

His presence, even now, while she was alone, sat heavily, reproachfully, in the empty rooms, forbidding her to call him up, forbidding her to recall comfortably past days she had spent with her mother. This was not living, Gerald said, to spend one's hours in introspective analysis, to brood over the past. Katherine's flights he called "a worthless luxury, like the visits of the rich to Palm Beach or Paris." But it was living, Katherine knew unhappily; she was living most acutely.

The room darkened suddenly. Something of the tension which would be upon her later, as it always was when her mother and Gerald were in the same room, came upon her now, as she sat straining for the sound of thunder, watching shades of gloom silently lay themselves in the hot room. Katherine held her breath waiting for thunder, for rain, anything. Voices of children floated reassuringly up from the street, and in a moment the sunlight reappeared, tentative, tempting one to believe in it for all its faintness. The thunder sounded like the chopping of wood in a far-off field. Katherine longed for her mother. She wished she were not so near the heart of the storm.

She hated herself for thinking of her mother. But not to think of her demanded a complete uprooting, demanded a final shoving off from a safe dock into unknown waters. Besides, she felt guilty toward her mother, she brooded over her as one does over a victim, pitying him, resenting him and utterly unable to forget him.

For against her mother Katherine felt that she had committed a crime. She had abandoned that elderly lady for a young man who, from her mother's point of view, had been merely one of several who had taken her to dances, to dinner, who had kissed her in the parlor, with whom finally, inexplicably, she had come to have more dates than with any other. She had abandoned her mother, left her sitting at home with no more evening gowns to "take in", no one to sit up for, no young men to laugh about in the bathroom at four o'clock in the morning when Katherine came home. She had left her to sit opposite an old man at dinner every evening, she had imposed upon her the tragedy of being a guest in her own daughter's house; she had reduced her to a stranger.

But a little bit her mother had the advantage. She had seen Gerald, after all, in the absurd rig of tuxedo and stiff shirt, calling upon her daughter with flowers, with books, leaping to his feet when she (Mrs Benjamin) entered the room. She had watched Gerald for a year politely talking parlor politics with Katherine's father, posturing ridiculously when he held Katherine's coat, becoming perforce friendly with the elevator boys in the Benjamin apartment, slinking shamefacedly before a doorman who had seen him too often. Nothing, Katherine reflected, could be more unreal, more unconvincing, than a young man in the act of courting. She could never forgive Gerald for having let her mother observe him in that rôle. (Equally she could never forgive her mother, blameless as she was, for having seen him.) Her mother could never take seriously, surely, a marriage which had grown from love-making in taxi-cabs which had been reported to her with amusement by Katherine, brushing her teeth in the bathroom. She had not shared with her mother the tortuous transition which had left her no longer an amused observer, but a helpless, suffering participant. All the indication Mrs Benjamin had had of Katherine's growing need of Gerald was a burst of hysteria and a state of nervous irritability which had succeeded the usual calm of Katherine's disposition—before suddenly one evening, preparing her charity report in a black lace dress, she was confronted by two embarrassed young people who declared their ridiculous intention to marry.

This, Katherine felt, she should have spared her mother. She should not have caused her, so heartbreakingly, to drop her charity report on the marble table and to look suddenly at her daughter with reproachful eyes, saying, half-humorously, What, daughter, tired of your old mother already?

She had left her parents for no reason, they had given her no cause to leave them, she had left them for no better reason than that when Gerald said to her that he would never again ask her to marry him, she had been seized with panic lest he meant it.

Gerald, who two years before had not existed. Whereas her father and mother had fed her porridge, given her blackboards, measured her growth against a door, for a long period of twenty years during which Gerald had never heard of her. She was unsafe, she cried internally. She was living with a stranger in a strange land where storms evolved closely about one. She was living with a stranger who had no knowledge of the first twenty years of her life, the major portion of her life. She was living in a strange land where her childhood had no existence. It was unreal, it was unsafe, it was terrifying. Gerald liked to hear her tell stories of her childhood; but it was as if, when she told him little things she remembered, she and he were together contemplating the childhood of a stranger. She held tightly to the arms of her chair, but the slippery wood was repelling. Suddenly everything was reduced to an absurdity. It was, to Gerald, as though she had not begun to exist until he had noticed her two years before, at a party, and asked to take her home; but suppose she had not come to the party—she had come only out of boredom; or suppose, to make it more ridiculous, she had not worn the particular blue dress which had caught Gerald's eye? and he hadn't asked to take her home? Their life together seemed no more than the result of a series of insignificant accidents. Could it be real? Could she share the rest of her life with a stranger whose eye had casually fallen on a blue dress? With someone who had known her for only two years out of her twenty-two?

Katherine felt herself to be struggling somewhere in the middle, between two harbors, unable to decide whether to swim backward or forward, tempted almost to close her eyes and quietly drown where she was. Shuttle, shuttle, she murmured to herself, miserably, exasperated at her weakness, her helplessness.

Smoking in the yellow room, she waited with unhappy certainty for Albert's storm which would surely come now. The air was oppressive, sullenly pregnant. It was as if an evil thing crouched in the room, waiting for birth. Dark was gathering in shades, permitting still a faint yellowish gloom. Wind was dead. Katherine, fearing and hating the coming storm, nevertheless feared and hated the moments of waiting even more. A clock on the mantel slowly ticked off the moments she would have to wait; it was in league with the coming storm. Her body was chill in the midst of heat.

She was weary already with the nervous effort she would make to bring Gerald and her mother close to each other, with her own struggle to remain equally close to both of them, simultaneous with her desperate attempt to conceal from each the affection she felt for the other. Gerald and her mother sitting and eating in this room, which now was the home of the storm, would be a cat and mouse, quietly stalking each other under cover. (Was this true? or did their struggle for supremacy take place merely in her own mind? Because she must know, she must know.) Katherine would twist herself this way and that to keep the evening characterless and blessedly dull, rather than immerse them all in the horror of an argument, in which their superficial sides would represent symbolically their eternal, fundamental resentment. Katherine must take no sides, Katherine must flit nervously from one side to the other, breaching gaps with hysterical giggles, throwing herself into outbursts of hysterical affection, making a clown of herself in order to distract these two who fought silently for her. She was loathsome to herself.

Her mind struggled with a remote memory. Something— perhaps the slumbering quality of the air which sheltered the coming storm so that its pent-up evil would suddenly roll forth and smother the world—reminded her of a thing which seemed to have happened when she was a child. Frowning, she gazed into herself to recall. And it came back to her. She had cried one day for her mother and they had told her that Mrs Benjamin had gone to Atlantic City for two days and that this young lady would take care of Katherine while her mother was away. Katherine kicked and screamed, but Miss Anna proved so entertaining—she showed her how to make a whole family of paper dolls live through a day's work and play—that she forgot her mother and was surprised to hear the next day that she would be home in an hour. Suddenly she hated Miss Anna, and when Mrs Benjamin came home she found her daughter crying angrily, Miss Anna bewildered, murmuring, But she seemed so happy, she seemed perfectly happy . . . I was not happy for a minute, Katherine screamed, I was waiting the whole time for my mother to come back.

Enraged with herself, she wondered whether she retained somewhere the idea that because her life had begun with her mother, it would end with her, whether some childish part of her could not accept their parting as final and looked upon her life with Gerald as no more than an interlude. Oh Gerald, Gerald, she sobbed, I am worse than unfaithful to you . . . I hate my mother, she is a venomous old woman who tries to keep me from you. . . . The injustice to her mother overwhelmed her. She hated herself. She felt like the child of divorced parents, driven from one to the other and unable with either to make a home.

I have been married during every month except June, she thought, lifting her head and quietly looking, as if to remember, about the room. She was comforted by Gerald's desk, which had been with her during eleven months. Thunder, blasting the earth in a distant place, filled the room. She had been married for eleven months and had never told her mother anything but housekeeping troubles. Why? A second roll of thunder sounded.

She was surrounded, she could not escape. She was suspended, she could take refuge with neither Gerald nor her mother, she was caught fairly by the thunder . . .

Deception had begun with her engagement. One had to keep one's eyes constantly glowing, however terrifiedly they looked at the approaching cliff, one's words constantly gay and effervescent, lest one's mother look searchingly at the prospective bride and say, But are you sure, Darling, absolutely *sure*? Of course one was not sure. One was suspended, even as now, with thunders rolling in from all sides. (I ought to start the dinner, I ought to start the dinner: I *can't*, I can't.)

During a wedding trip one was awakened to innumerable things, most of them delightful, all of them terrifying. A longing had filled Katherine intermittently to be back from this trip of surprises: she pictured herself talking to her mother all day for many days, sharing with her, not details, but the contemplation, of intimacies. It seemed to her the most delicious part of the trip, that she would return and talk about it to her mother. Gerald's jealous allusions to her mother she had accepted with a tolerant smile; his analyses—for it was then that he had violently expounded his harem theory—meant nothing to her, they seemed to have no connection with reality. "Dearest mother," she had written, "all the things I have to tell you! I can hardly wait to see you . . . So many things have happened. And of course, Gerald being a man . . ." (Was that lightning, or was it the mere lifting of the curtain by the wind? The dinner, the dinner was waiting to be cooked: I won't *touch* it.)

The awful farce at the station, where Mr and Mrs Benjamin had come to meet them, came to her vividly now. Mr Benjamin, having screwed his courage to the point of making Katherine remember his presence long enough to kiss him, retiring to help Gerald, competently wasting time with the luggage in the background, mother and daughter swaying in a series of embraces—Katherine was suddenly lost, locked, imprisoned, in the

body of a stout, fashionable stranger. Why doesn't she look at
me? she thought, all she wants is to hold me, to squeeze me, to
choke me to death, it never occurs to her to look in my face.
Sweeping her daughter to one side, Mrs Benjamin sprang forth
to smother Gerald. She had no right to, cried Katherine wildly
to herself, as she turned from her father's vague embrace, and
all the things which Gerald had said of her mother came back
to her and they seemed true. And at the same time she felt
passionately that Mrs Benjamin must not expose herself to
Gerald's unsympathetic eye; horrible embarrassment arose in
her, when, thank God, she saw that Mrs Benjamin in her
eagerness had missed her aim; her kiss floated on past Gerald's
clean indifferent cheek—he at least was unsullied, and at the
same time her mother was protected from nakedness. Mrs
Benjamin, discarding Gerald, threw her arms around Katherine
once more, with force and meaning, and kissed her in great wet
gulps. "Katherine, Katherine," she sobbed, rocking her great
body from side to side, "I've got you again, darling. Let's leave
all these men and go off together, darling." Katherine felt
fastidious, she drew her body back delicately from the impact
of her mother's.

Mrs Benjamin shook off the two men, she carried Katherine
off to a tea-room—their old favorite tea-room—for lunch, a
confidential lunch it was supposed to be, but Katherine had
grown to hate tea-rooms, a month with Gerald had taught her
to hate shrimp salad . . . Mrs Benjamin, suddenly squeezing her
hand under the candle-lit table, looked into her eyes, her own
eyes fatuous, confident, worried and questioning, "Katherine,
darling Katherine, now tell me the 'many things' you wrote
about." Katherine, looking into her mother's avid eyes, knew
that she could never tell her anything again.

How horribly she must have hurt her, thought Katherine,
gravely hurt herself at the recollection. In bed beside Gerald
that night she had lain, trying to make the night go faster, so
that she might see her mother and change what she had done.
She thought of her mother lying sleepless, even as she was,
beside a sleeping husband, thinking, bitterly thinking, of the
thing that had happened between them. But Katherine could
never undo the thing that was between them, for it was Gerald

who stood between her mother and herself, just as her mother
stood between herself and Gerald.

Well, *was* Albert's storm coming or wasn't it, she thought
impatiently, and beat out her cigarette on the window-sill,
dropped the dead stub and watched it hurtle past awnings and
window-boxes and land haphazardly in the gutter. (And what
about the dinner?)

A clap of thunder brought her trembling to her feet. It had
traveled with treacherous silence from a great distance to burst
like a shell in her ear. And now lightning quivered across the
pewter sky in a blinding streak. Katherine, trembling, holding
to the mantel, felt all the elements of storm gathering closely
about her. The intense heat and stillness in the room vibrated
with suppressed force. She had a sense of something evil,
something unhealthy, waiting beneath the table to be born. The
room was alive, awake, crouching before the storm, waiting in
every sense for its approach.

She laughed aloud, nervously, when the thunder sounded
next, meek and far-off; it rumbled for a few seconds, then it
rolled toward her with increasing force until something cut it
off sharply in the height of its passion. The storm was playing
with her; it was here, but it played at hiding, it retreated and
advanced so that she could never be sure of it.

What was she to do, what was she to do? Should she, could
she telephone?—*no.*

Thunder shook the house. Malicious streaks of lightning drew
themselves across the sky, lighting up the gloom until the day
shone for a second like steel. Suddenly night came. Winds came
alive and tore drunkenly down the street. Another long rever-
berating crash of thunder, incredibly near and ear-splitting.
There was a moment of suspension, while only the wind moved.
And then the sky retched and large cold drops of rain like stones
pelted the windowpanes . . .

Panic seized Katherine. She rushed to the window to escape.
She was afraid of the room. It rocked with unhappy speculation.
She stood at the window facing in, and saw how the storm was
fed from within her room. The lightning lit it like quick fire,
the thunder sounded in it long after it had died outside.

The thunder bounced about the room, striking at corners, rolling over furniture, shaking the walls, groveling derisively at her feet.

It seemed to her that before the next clap of thunder she must have reached a decision or she would die. But what decision, she cried, striking her fist against the window? What decision? about what? The problem was obscure. (She imagined her mother struck by lightning, her stout body collapsing with dignity under a tree, she heard herself telling Gerald with triumph as an overtone to her grief, My mother is dead, I have only you now.) And if the problem was obscure, how much more obscure the solution. (She imagined Gerald struck by lightning, a look of hurt surprise in his eyes as he fell beneath a tree, murmuring something about scientific chance, she heard herself telling her mother, strange relief mingling with her sorrow, Gerald is gone, mother, I shall have to come back to you.) And the next thunder rolled down a hill, louder and louder, faster and nearer, and fell to the bottom, bursting into cannon balls, exploding with insane crashes, and in a thousand voices splitting the earth in its center. Katherine burst into passionate tears.

Now everything was the storm. The storm, which had circled about the room, wished for closer nucleus, and entered her body. The lightning pierced her stomach, the thunder shook her limbs, and retreated, growling, to its home in her bowels. There was no escape for her; she was no longer imprisoned in the storm: the storm was imprisoned in her.

She stood in a shaking lethargy, she had no will, no feeling. She was frozen; she was a shell in which storm raged without her will. All the world had entered the room . . .

It came to her slowly that there was a new sound in the air, a sharp metallic ring that repeated itself at intervals. She had no idea how long she might have been hearing it in the back of her head before she took notice of it. Now it rang again, sharply, there seemed to be fright in it, or anger, she could not tell which. On stiff legs she ran down the hall toward the door, by reflex knowing that it was the doorbell which had sounded. But with her hand on the knob something held her back. She could not force herself to turn the knob, to move her hand, even to call out, Wait, wait . . .

Was it her mother, or was it Gerald? Which, in the midst of storm, did she want it to be? It seemed to her that she could not open the door until she knew. A great ball of thunder followed her out of the room she had left, hurtled down the hall and broke beside her, and in the midst of it the terrified bell rang repeatedly, in small staccato notes, shrilling through the depth of the thunder, prodding . . .

She did not know. She knew only, as she closed her eyes and slowly turned the handle of the door, and drew it in toward herself, that she wished that one of them, Gerald or her mother, were dead.

Hisaye Yamamoto

Seventeen Syllables
1949

*The second of eight stories by Hisaye Yamamoto published between 1948 and
1961, "Seventeen Syllables" first appeared in* Partisan Review *in November
1949. A 1951 story, "Yoneko's Earthquake," which also has a mother-daughter
theme, was included in Martha Foley's* Best American Short Stories *of
1952. Since 1969, five of Yamamoto's stories have been reprinted at least
twenty times in one or more of twelve anthologies specializing either in Asian-
American, United States minority, regional, or women writers. For more than
twenty-five years, Yamamoto has contributed poetry, book reviews, essays, and
reminiscences to a variety of Japanese-American publications. Herself a Nisei
(second generation Japanese American), she has written with tenderness and
humor about the relationships between Japanese immigrants and their American-
born children and grandchildren. She has also written about the experience of
Japanese Americans incarcerated in U.S. prison camps during World War II.*

*Hisaye Yamamoto was born in Redondo Beach, California in 1921 and grew
up in various small southern California towns. Her parents had emigrated from
Kumamoto, Japan. She studied at Excelsior Union High School and Compton
Junior College, majoring in foreign languages. She received encouragement
from an English teacher, Lela May Garver, and became friendly with several
other young Asian-American women interested in writing. Then came World
War II and she, along with 110,000 other Japanese Americans, was subjected
to relocation and imprisonment mandated by the Japanese Relocation Act of
1942.*

*During the war, she moved to Massachusetts for a summer, but returned to
camp, and then to California in 1945, where she was employed by the* Los
Angeles Tribune, *a black weekly newspaper. Her brother Jemo helped support*

her for a few months when she left the Tribune *to try writing full time. An insurance bequest from her brother Johnny, killed at the age of nineteen fighting with the American army in Italy, added more time to that struggle. In 1950 she was awarded a John Hay Whitney Foundation Opportunity Fellowship. She was already raising an adopted son and, although the support included funds for nearby babysitting, she remembers in "Writing," an autobiographical essay, that " . . . he used to pound on the door, demanding to be let in, or he would wedge himself between the typewriter and me and, spreading out his arms, say, 'Don't type!' " In her thirties, she married Anthony De Soto and became the mother of four more children. She is now also a grandmother.*

Frank Chin and Shawn Wong, co-editors of Yardbird Reader, No. 3, *a 1974 collection of Asian-American writing, have called her "Asian America's most accomplished living fiction writer." However, in "Writing," she states, "But, alas, when I have occasion to fill out a questionnaire, I must in all honesty list my occupation as housewife."*

"Seventeen Syllables" weaves together several of the mother-daughter categories, for it is an occasional story commemorating two life-cycle events: a daughter's menarche and a mother's death. It is a "disgraceful mother" story, and a story about multiple confrontations with the patriarchy, a story speaking to the experiences of multiple oppressions—racism and classism as well as sexism. Commenting on the story in a letter (March 12, 1984), Yamamoto writes,

> . . . it is so painful, when I think of how [my mother] could have used a more understanding daughter at the time—but, of course, I was wrapped up in myself at that age. Even though none of the details are true, "Seventeen Syllables" is [my mother's] story. It is the most reprinted of all the stories. Maybe she, wherever she is, guided the writing of it, and, even now, the propagation of it—in textbooks yet, from junior high to community college level—so her story would be known. Or is this too far-fetched to contemplate?

"Seventeen Syllables," like so many of the stories in this collection, is a testimony of a daughter's powerful love and respect for her mother. The existence of such stories is strong evidence of the history of love and alliance between mothers and daughters.

The first Rosie knew that her mother had taken to writing poems was one evening when she finished one and read it aloud for her daughter's approval. It was about cats, and Rosie pretended to understand it thoroughly and appreciate it no end, partly because she hesitated to disillusion her mother about the quantity and quality of Japanese she had learned in all the years now that she had been going to Japanese school every Saturday (and Wednesday, too, in the Summer). Even so, her mother must have been skeptical about the depth of Rosie's understanding, because she explained afterwards about the kind of poem she was trying to write.

See, Rosie, she said, it was a *haiku*, a poem in which she must pack all her meaning into seventeen syllables only, which were divided into three lines of five, seven, and five syllables. In the one she had just read, she had tried to capture the charm of a kitten, as well as comment on the superstition that owning a cat of three colors meant good luck.

"Yes, yes, I understand. How utterly lovely," Rosie said, and her mother, either satisfied or seeing through the deception and resigned, went back to composing.

The truth was that Rosie was lazy; English lay ready on the tongue but Japanese had to be searched for and examined, and even then put forth tentatively (probably to meet with laughter). It was so much easier to say yes, yes, even when one meant no, no. Besides, this was what was in her mind to say: I was looking through one of your magazines from Japan last night, Mother, and towards the back I found some *haiku* in English that delighted me. There was one that made me giggle off and on until I fell asleep—

> It is morning, and lo!
> I lie awake, comme il faut,
> sighing for some dough.

Now, how to reach her mother, how to communicate the melancholy song? Rosie knew formal Japanese by fits and starts, her mother had even less English, no French. It was much more possible to say yes, yes.

It developed that her mother was writing the *haiku* for a daily newspaper, the *Mainichi Shinbun*, that was published in San Francisco. Los Angeles, to be sure, was closer to the farming community in which the Hayashi family lived and several

Japanese vernaculars were printed there, but Rosie's parents said they preferred the tone of the northern paper. Once a week, the *Mainichi* would have a section devoted to *haiku,* and her mother became an extravagant contributor, taking for herself the blossoming pen name, Ume Hanazono.

So Rosie and her father lived for awhile with two women, her mother and Ume Hanazono. Her mother (Tome Hayashi by name) kept house, cooked, washed, and, along with her husband and the Carrascos, the Mexican family hired for the harvest, did her ample share of picking tomatoes out in the sweltering fields and boxing them in tidy strata in the cool packing shed. Ume Hanazono, who came to life after the dinner dishes were done, was an earnest, muttering stranger who often neglected speaking when spoken to and stayed busy at the parlor table as late as midnight scribbling with pencil on scratch paper or carefully copying characters on good paper with her fat, pale green Parker.

The new interest had some repercussions on the household routine. Before, Rosie had been accustomed to her parents and herself taking their hot baths early and going to bed almost immediately afterwards, unless her parents challenged each other to a game of flower cards or unless company dropped in. Now, if her father wanted to play cards, he had to resort to solitaire (at which he always cheated fearlessly), and if a group of friends came over, it was bound to contain someone who was also writing *haiku,* and the small assemblage would be split in two, her father entertaining the nonliterary members and her mother comparing ecstatic notes with the visiting poet.

If they went out, it was more of the same thing. But Ume Hanazono's life span, even for a poet's, was very brief—perhaps three months at most.

One night they went over to see the Hayano family in the neighboring town to the west, an adventure both painful and attractive to Rosie. It was attractive because there were four Hayano girls, all lovely and each one named after a season of the year (Haru, Natsu, Aki, Fuyu), painful because something had been wrong with Mrs. Hayano ever since the birth of her first child. Rosie would sometimes watch Mrs. Hayano, reputed to have been the belle of her native village, making her way about a room, stooped, slowly shuffling, violently trembling (*always* tembling), and she would be reminded that this woman, in this same condition, had carried and given issue to three babies. She would look wonderingly at Mr. Hayano, handsome, tall, and strong, and she would look at her four pretty friends. But it was not a matter she could come to any decision about.

On this visit, however, Mrs. Hayano sat all evening in the rocker, as motionless and unobtrusive as it was possible for her to be, and Rosie found the greater part of the evening practically anaesthetic. Too, Rosie spent most of it in the girls' room, because Haru, the garrulous one, said almost as soon as the bows and other greetings were over, "Oh, you must see my new coat!"

It was a pale plaid of grey, sand, and blue, with an enormous collar, and Rosie, seeing nothing special in it, said, "Gee, how nice."

"Nice?" said Haru, indignantly. "Is that all you can say about it? It's gorgeous! And so cheap, too. Only seventeen-ninety-eight, because it was a sale. The saleslady said it was twenty-five dollars regular."

"Gee," said Rosie. Natsu, who never said much and when she said anything said it shyly, fingered the coat covetously and Haru pulled it away.

"Mine," she said, putting it on. She minced in the aisle between two large beds and smiled happily. "Let's see how your mother likes it."

She broke into the front room and the adult conversation, and went to stand in front of Rosie's mother, while the rest watched from the door. Rosie's mother was properly envious. "May I inherit it when you're through with it?"

Haru, pleased, giggled and said yes, she could, but Natsu reminded gravely from the door, "You promised me, Haru."

Everyone laughed but Natsu, who shamefacedly retreated into the bedroom. Haru came in laughing, taking off the coat. "We were only kidding, Natsu," she said. "Here, you try it on now."

After Natsu buttoned herself into the coat, inspected herself solemnly in the bureau mirror, and reluctantly shed it, Rosie, Aki, and Fuyu got their turns, and Fuyu, who was eight, drowned in it while her sisters and Rosie doubled up in amusement. They all went into the front room later, because Haru's mother quaveringly called to her to fix the tea and rice cakes and open a can of sliced peaches for everybody. Rosie noticed that her mother and Mr. Hayano were talking together at the little table— they were discussing a *haiku* that Mr. Hayano was planning to send to the *Mainichi,* while her father was sitting at one end of the sofa looking through a copy of *Life,* the new picture magazine. Occasionally, her father would comment on a photograph, holding it toward Mrs. Hayano and speaking to her as he always did—loudly, as though he thought someone such as she must surely be at least a trifle deaf also.

The five girls had their refreshments at the kitchen table, and it was while Rosie was showing the sisters her trick of swallowing peach slices without chewing (she chased each slippery crescent down with a swig of tea) that her father brought his empty teacup and untouched saucer to the sink and said, "Come on, Rosie, we're going home now."

"Already?" asked Rosie.

"Work tomorrow," he said.

He sounded irritated, and Rosie, puzzled, gulped one last yellow slice and stood up to go, while the sisters began protesting, as was their wont.

"We have to get up at five-thirty," he told them, going into the front room quickly, so that they did not have their usual chance to hang onto his hands and plead for an extension of time.

Rosie, following, saw that her mother and Mr. Hayano were sipping tea and still talking together, while Mrs. Hayano concentrated, quivering, on raising the handleless Japanese cup to her lips with both her hands and lowering it back to her lap. Her father, saying nothing, went out the door, onto the bright porch, and down the steps. Her mother looked up and asked, "Where is he going?"

"Where is he going?" Rosie said. "He said we were going home now."

"Going home?" Her mother looked with embarrassment at

Mr. Hayano and his absorbed wife and then forced a smile. "He must be tired," she said.

Haru was not giving up yet. "May Rosie stay overnight?" she asked, and Natsu, Aki, and Fuyu came to reinforce their sister's plea by helping her make a circle around Rosie's mother. Rosie, for once, having no desire to stay, was relieved when her mother, apologizing to the perturbed Mr. and Mrs. Hayano for her father's abruptness at the same time, managed to shake her head no at the quartet, kindly but adamant, so that they broke their circle to let her go.

Rosie's father looked ahead into the windshield as the two joined him. "I'm sorry," her mother said. "You must be tired." Her father, stepping on the starter, said nothing. "You know how I get when it's *haiku*," she continued, "I forget what time it is." He only grunted.

As they rode homeward, silently, Rosie sitting between, felt a rush of hate for both, for her mother for begging, for her father for denying her mother. I wish this old Ford would crash, right now, she thought, then immediately, no, no, I wish my father would laugh, but it was too late: already the vision had passed through her mind of the green pick-up crumpled in the dark against one of the mighty eucalyptus trees they were just riding past, of the three contorted, bleeding bodies, one of them hers.

Rosie ran between two patches of tomatoes, her heart working more rambunctiously than she had ever known it to. How lucky it was that Aunt Taka and Uncle Gimpachi had come tonight, though, how very lucky. Otherwise, she might not have really kept her half-promise to meet Jesus Carrasco. Jesus, who was going to be a senior in September at the same school she went to, and his parents were the ones helping with the tomatoes this year. She and Jesus, who hardly remembered seeing each other at Cleveland High, where there were so many other people and two whole grades between them, had become great friends this Summer—he always had a joke for her when he periodically drove the loaded pick-up up from the fields to the shed where she was usually sorting while her mother and father did the packing, and they laughed a great deal together over infinitesimal repartee during the afternoon break for chilled watermelon or ice cream in the shade of the shed.

What she enjoyed most was racing him to see which could finish picking a double row first. He, who could work faster, would tease her by slowing down until she thought she would surely pass him this time, then speeding up furiously to leave her several sprawling vines behind. Once he had made her screech hideously by crossing over, while her back was turned, to place atop the tomatoes in her green-stained bucket a truly monstrous, pale green worm (it had looked more like an infant snake). And it was when they had finished a contest this morning, after she had pantingly pointed a green finger at the immature tomatoes evident in the lugs at the end of his row and he had returned the accusation (with justice), that he had startlingly brought up the matter of their possible meeting outside the range of both their parents' dubious eyes.

"What for?" she had asked.

"I've got a secret I want to tell you," he said.

"Tell me now," she demanded.

"It won't be ready till tonight," he said.

She laughed. "Tell me tomorrow then."

"It'll be gone tomorrow," he threatened.

"Well, for seven hakes, what is it?" she had asked, more than twice, and when he had suggested that the packing shed would be an appropriate place to find out, she had cautiously answered maybe. She had not been certain she was going to keep the appointment until the arrival of her mother's sister and her husband. Their coming seemed a sort of signal of permission, of grace, and she had definitely made up her mind to lie and leave as she was bowing them welcome.

So, as soon as everyone appeared settled back for the evening, she announced loudly that she was going to the privy outside. "I'm going to the *benjo!*" and slipped out the door. And now that she was actually on her way, her heart pumped in such an undisciplined way that she could hear it with her ears. It's because I'm running, she told herself, slowing to a walk. The shed was up ahead, one more patch away, in the middle of the fields. Its bulk, looming in the dimness, took on a sinisterness that was funny when Rosie reminded herself that it was only a wooden frame with a canvas roof and three canvas walls that made a slapping noise on breezy days.

Jesus was sitting on the narrow plank that was the sorting platform and she went around to the other side and jumped backwards to seat herself on the rim of a packing stand. "Well, tell me," she said, without greeting, thinking her voice sounded reassuringly familiar.

"I saw you coming out the door," Jesus said. "I heard you running part of the way, too."

"Uh-huh," Rosie said, "Now tell me the secret."

"I was afraid you wouldn't come," he said.

Rosie delved around on the chicken-wire bottom of the stall for number two tomatoes, ripe, which she was sitting beside, and came up with a left-over that felt edible. She bit into it and began sucking out the pulp and seeds. "I'm here," she pointed out.

"Rosie, are you sorry you came?"

"Sorry? What for?" she said. "You said you were going to tell me something."

"I will, I will," Jesus said, but his voice contained disappointment, and Rosie, fleetingly, felt the older of the two, realizing a brand-new power which vanished without category under her recognition.

"I have to go back in a minute," she said. "My aunt and uncle are here from Wintersburg. I told them I was going to the privy."

Jesus laughed. "You funny thing," he said. "You slay me!"

"Just because you have a bathroom *inside*," Rosie said. "Come on, tell me."

Chuckling, Jesus came around to lean on the stand facing her. They still could not see each other very clearly, but Rosie noticed that Jesus became very sober again as he took the hollow tomato from her hand and dropped it back into the stall. When he took hold of her empty hand, she could find no words to protest; her vocabulary had become distressingly constricted and she thought desperately that all that remained intact now was yes and no and oh, and even these few sounds would not easily out.

Thus, kissed by Jesus, Rosie fell, for the first time, entirely victim to a helplessness delectable beyond speech. But the terrible, beautiful sensation lasted no more than a second, and the reality of Jesus' lips and tongue and teeth and hands made her pull away with such strength that she nearly tumbled.

Rosie stopped running as she approached the lights from the windows of home. How long since she had left? She could not guess, but gasping yet, she went to the privy in back and locked herself in. Her own breathing deafened her in the dark, close space, and she sat and waited until she could hear at last the nightly calling of the frogs and crickets. Even then, all she could think to say was oh, my, and the pressure of Jesus' face against her face would not leave.

No one had missed her in the parlor, however, and Rosie walked in and through quickly, announcing that she was next going to take a bath. "Your father's in the bathhouse," her mother said, and Rosie, in her room, recalled that she had not seen him when she entered. There had been only Aunt Taka and Uncle Gimpachi with her mother at the table, drinking tea. She got her robe and straw sandals and crossed the parlor again to go outside. Her mother was telling them about the *haiku* competition in the *Mainichi* and the poem she had entered.

Rosie met her father coming out of the bathhouse. "Are you through, Father?" she asked. "I was going to ask you to scrub my back."

"Scrub your own back," he said shortly, going toward the main house.

"What have I done now?" she yelled after him. She suddenly felt like doing a lot of yelling. But he did not answer, and she went into the bathhouse. Turning on the dangling light, she removed her denims and T-shirt and threw them in the big carton for dirty clothes standing next to the washing machine. Her other things she took with her into the bath compartment to wash after her bath. After she had scooped a basin of hot water from the square wooden tub, she sat on the grey cement of the floor and soaped herself at exaggerated leisure, singing "Red Sails in the Sunset" at the top of her voice and using da-da-da where she suspected her words. Then, standing, still singing, for she was possessed by the notion that any attempt now to analyze would result in spoilage and she believed that the larger her volume the less she would be able to hear herself think, she obtained more hot water and poured it on until she was free of lather. Only then did she allow herself to step into the steaming vat, one leg first, then the remainder of her body inch by inch until the water no longer stung and she could move around at will.

She took a long time soaking, afterwards remembering to go around outside to stoke the embers of the tin-lined fireplace beneath the tub and to throw on a few more sticks so that the water might keep its heat for her mother, and when she finally returned to the parlor, she found her mother still talking *haiku* with her aunt and uncle, the three of them on another round of tea. Her father was nowhere in sight.

At Japanese school the next day (Wednesday, it was), Rosie was grave and giddy by turns. Preoccupied at her desk in the row for students on Book Eight, she made up for it at recess by performing wild mimicry for the benefit of her friend Chizuko. She held her nose and whined a witticism or two in what she considered was the manner of Fred Allen; she assumed intoxication and a British accent to go over the climax of the Rudy Vallee recording of the pub conversation about William Ewart Gladstone; she was the child Shirley Temple piping "On the Good Ship Lollipop"; she was the gentleman soprano of the Four Inkspots trilling "If I Didn't Care." And she felt reasonably satisfied when Chizuko wept and gasped, "Oh, Rosie, you ought to be in the movies!"

Her father came after her at noon, bringing her sandwiches of minced ham and two nectarines to eat while she rode, so that she could pitch right into the sorting when they got home. The lugs were piling up, he said, and the ripe tomatoes in them would probably have to be taken to the cannery tomorrow if they were not ready for the produce haulers tonight. "This heat's not doing them any good. And we've got no time for a break today."

It *was* hot, probably the hottest day of the year, and Rosie's blouse stuck damply to her back even under the protection of the canvas. But she worked as efficiently as a flawless machine and kept the stalls heaped, with one part of her mind listening in to the parental murmuring about the heat and the tomatoes and with another part planning the exact words she would say to Jesus when he drove up with the first load of the afternoon. But when at last she saw that the pick-up was coming, her hands went berserk and the tomatoes started falling in the wrong stalls, and her father said, "Hey, hey! Rosie, watch what you're doing!"

"Well, I have to go to the *benjo*," she said, hiding panic.

"Go in the weeds over there," he said, only half-joking.

"Oh, Father!" she protested.

"Oh, go on home," her mother said. "We'll make out for awhile."

In the privy, Rosie peered through a knothole toward the fields, watching as much as she could of Jesus. Happily she thought she saw him look in the direction of the house from time to time before he finished unloading and went back toward the patch where his mother and father worked. As she was heading for the shed, a very presentable black car purred up the dirt driveway to the house and its driver motioned to her. Was this the Hayashi home, he wanted to know. She nodded. Was she a Hayashi? Yes, she said, thinking that he was a good-looking man. He got out of the car with a huge, flat package and she saw that he warmly wore a business suit. "I have something here for your mother then," he said, in a more elegant Japanese than she was used to.

She told him where her mother was and he came along with her, patting his face with an immaculate white handkerchief and saying something about the coolness of San Francisco. To her surprised mother and father, he bowed and introduced himself as, among other things, the *haiku* editor of the *Mainichi Shinbun*, saying that since he had been coming as far as Los Angeles anyway, he had decided to bring her the first prize she had won in the recent contest.

"First prize?" her mother echoed, believing and not believing, pleased and overwhelmed. Handed the package with a bow, she bobbed her head up and down numerous times to express her utter gratitude.

"It is nothing much," he added, "but I hope it will serve as a token of our great appreciation for your contributions and our great admiration of your considerable talent."

"I am not worthy," she said, falling easily into his style. "It is I who should make some sign of my humble thanks for being permitted to contribute."

"No, no, to the contrary," he said, bowing again.

But Rosie's mother insisted, and then saying that she knew she was being unorthodox, she asked if she might open the package because her curiosity was so great. Certainly she might. In fact, he would like her reaction to it, for personally, it was one of his favorite *Hiroshiges*.*

Rosie thought it was a pleasant picture, which looked to have been sketched with delicate quickness. There were pink clouds, containing some graceful calligraphy, and a sea that was a pale blue except at the edges, containing four sampans with indications of people in them. Pines edged the water and on the far-off beach there was a cluster of thatched huts towered over by pine-dotted mountains of grey and blue. The frame was scalloped and gilt.

After Rosie's mother pronounced it without peer and somewhat prodded her father into nodding agreement, she said Mr. Kuroda must at least have a cup of tea, after coming all this way, and although Mr. Kuroda did not want to impose, he soon agreed that a cup of tea would be refreshing and went along with her to the house, carrying the picture for her.

"Ha, your mother's crazy!" Rosie's father said, and Rosie laughed uneasily as she resumed judgment on the tomatoes. She had emptied six lugs when he broke into an imaginary conversation with Jesus to tell her to go and remind her mother of the tomatoes, and she went slowly.

Mr. Kuroda was in his shirtsleeves expounding some *haiku* theory as he munched a rice cake, and her mother was rapt. Abashed in the great man's presence, Rosie stood next to her mother's chair until her mother looked up inquiringly, and then she started to whisper the message, but her mother pushed her gently away and reproached, "You are not being very polite to our guest."

---

* Japanese artist (1797–1858).

"Father says the tomatoes . . ." Rosie said aloud, smiling foolishly.

"Tell him I shall only be a minute," her mother said, speaking the language of Mr. Kuroda.

When Rosie carried the reply to her father, he did not seem to hear and she said again, "Mother says she'll be back in a minute."

"All right, all right," he nodded, and they worked again in silence. But suddenly, her father uttered an incredible noise, exactly like the cork of a bottle popping, and the next Rosie knew, he was stalking angrily toward the house, almost running, in fact, and she chased after him crying, "Father! Father! What are you going to do?"

He stopped long enough to order her back to the shed. "Never mind!" he shouted. "Get on with the sorting!"

And from the place in the fields where she stood, frightened and vacillating, Rosie saw her father enter the house. Soon Mr. Kuroda came out alone, putting on his coat. Mr. Kuroda got into his car and backed out down the driveway, onto the highway. Next her father emerged, also alone, something in his arms (it was the picture, she realized), and going over to the bathhouse woodpile, he threw the picture on the ground and picked up the axe. Smashing the picture, glass and all (she heard the explosion faintly), he reached over the kerosene that was used to encourage the bath fire and poured it over the wreckage. I am dreaming, Rosie said to herself, I am dreaming, but her father, having made sure that his act of cremation was irrevocable, was even then returning to the fields.

Rosie ran past him and toward the house. What had become of her mother? She burst into the parlor and found her mother at the back window, watching the dying fire. They watched together until there remained only a feeble smoke under the blazing sun. Her mother was very calm.

"Do you know why I married your father?" she said, without turning.

"No," said Rosie. It was the most frightening question she had ever been called upon to answer. Don't tell me now, she wanted to say, tell me tomorrow, tell me next week, don't tell me today. But she knew she would be told now, that the telling would combine with the other violence of the hot afternoon to level her life, her world (so various, so beautiful, so new?) to the very ground.

It was like a story out of the magazines, illustrated in sepia, which she had consumed so greedily for a period until the information had somehow reached her that those wretchedly unhappy autobiographies, offered to her as the testimonials of living men and women, were largely inventions: Her mother, at nineteen, had come to America and married her father as an alternative to suicide.

At eighteen, she had been in love with the first son of one of the well-to-do families in her village. The two had met whenever and wherever they could, secretly, because it would not have done for his family to see him favor her—her father had no money; he was a drunkard and a gambler besides. She had learned she was with child; an excellent match had already been arranged for her lover. Despised by her family, she had given premature birth to a stillborn son, who would be seventeen now. Her family did not turn her out, but she could no longer project herself in any direction without refreshing in them the memory of her indiscretion. She wrote to Aunt Taka, her favorite sister, in America, threatening to kill herself if Aunt Taka would not send for her. Aunt Taka hastily arranged a marriage with a young man, but lately arrived from Japan, of whom she knew, a young man of simple mind, it was said, but of kindly heart. The young man was never told why his unseen betrothed was so eager to hasten the day of meeting.

The story was told perfectly, with neither groping for words nor untoward passion. It was as though her mother had memorized it by heart, reciting it to herself so many times over that its nagging vileness had long since gone.

"I had a brother then?" Rosie asked, for this was what seemed to matter now; she would think about the other later, she assured herself, pushing back the illumination which threatened all that darkness that had hitherto been merely mysterious or even glamorous. "A half-brother?"

"Yes."

"I would have liked a brother," she said.

Suddenly, her mother knelt on the floor and took her by the

wrists. "Rosie," she said urgently, "promise me you will never marry!" Shocked more by the request than the revelation, Rosie stared at her mother's face. Jesus, Jesus, she called silently, not certain whether she was invoking the help of the son of the Carrascos or of God, until there returned sweetly the memory of Jesus' hand, how it had touched her and where. Still her mother waited for an answer, holding her wrists so tightly that her hands were going numb. She tried to pull free. "Promise," her mother whispered fiercely, "promise." "Yes, yes, I promise," Rosie said. But for an instant she turned away, and her mother, hearing the familiar glib agreement, released her, Oh, you, you, you, her eyes and twisted mouth said, you fool. Rosie, covering her face, began at last to cry, and the embrace and consoling hand came much later than she expected.

Tillie Olsen

I Stand Here Ironing
1956

Tillie Olsen was born in Nebraska in 1913 (or perhaps 1912), and has lived in San Francisco most of her life. Coming of age during the Depression, she points out that she fared better than most of her generation: She got almost all the way through high school. Public libraries were her college. Her origin, most of her life, and identification are primarily working class. She became early on a member of the world of "everyday" jobs. She wrote and published while young, but the necessity of rearing and supporting four children silenced her for twenty years. She was in her mid-forties when she began to write again.

Tell Me a Riddle, *a collection of four short stories including "I Stand Here Ironing," was first published in 1962. The title story won the O. Henry Memorial Prize Award as the best story of 1961. In 1974, forty years after its opening chapter appeared in an early* Partisan Review, *her "lost" novel,* Yonnondio: From the Thirties, *was published.* Silences, *a collection of essays on the relationship between circumstances and human creativity, was published in 1978.*

In recent years, Olsen has spoken on various topics on many university campuses. She has taught at Amherst, the Massachusetts Institute of Technology, Stanford, and the University of Massachusetts. She is the recipient of Ford Foundation and National Endowment for the Arts grants, a Guggenheim Fellowship, various other literary honors, and three honorary degrees, including Doctor of Arts and Letters from the University of Nebraska, her home state. In 1980, the Unitarian Women's Federation conferred on her their annual "Ministry to Women Award." Also in 1980, in conjunction with their issuance of stamps commemorating Emily Bronte, Charlotte Bronte, George Eliot, and Elizabeth Gaskell, the British Post Office (and Business and Professional Women) selected Olsen for a special award. May 18, 1981 was proclaimed "Tillie Olsen Day" in San Francisco by the Mayor and Board of Supervisors of that city.

"I Stand Here Ironing" originally appeared in 1956 in Pacific Spectator, *a publication of the Pacific Coast Committee for the Humanities of the American Council of Learned Societies. Along with the three other stories in* Tell Me a Riddle, *it has been anthologized in dozens of places, performed on numerous college campuses and in stage productions, and adapted into films and an opera. It is one of the very few stories, and perhaps the first, written about the mother-daughter relationship from the perspective of a mother.*

The late Elizabeth Fisher, feminist, novelist, anthropologist, essayist, and founder and editor of Aphra: The Feminist Literary Magazine, *wrote in a 1972 review in* The Nation:

> "I Stand Here Ironing" is the story told by a mother of how, wanting to do the best for her daughter, she was so often forced to do the worst, and it is one that every parent can recognize. In tight, economical prose she tears us with the parental experience, how we listen, wrongly, to other people, or are just imprisoned by events we could not foresee—desertion, poverty, expanding families; it is also a hopeful story of how children survive, sometimes even making strength, or talent, out of the deprivations they've endured. Tillie Olsen's is an unsparing but tender vision in which love is a need that is rarely answered, a vision of communication on strange, imperfect, levels, and, above all, of resilience, a belief that human beings are not passive, that there is more in them "than this dress on the ironing board, helpless before the iron."

As we see in this story, mothers are given responsibilities for the rearing and well-being of their children that are too heavy to bear successfully under the best of circumstances—and rarely do the best of circumstances exist. Mothers must learn to look at the lives of children, to see and understand how they have been damaged, how their potential to love and work, to trust and create, has been diminished because as mothers we have been unable to accomplish on their behalf all that mothers are charged to accomplish. We must learn to see and understand their losses while simultaneously we learn to refuse the blame. Maternal guilt muddies our ability to analyze the causes and understand the sources of children's and women's pain and deprivations. Mothers and daughters must absolve each other of guilt and learn to share a vision of a world in which the responsibilities are shared and the potentials can be fulfilled.

Toward the end of "A Dream-Vision," a reminiscence of her mother as she lay dying, Olsen writes about such a shared mother-daughter vision:

I had seen my mother but three times in my adult life, separated as we were by the continent between, by lack of means, by jobs I had to keep and by the needs of my four children. She could scarcely write English—her only education in this country, a few months of night school. When at last I flew to her, it was in the last days she had language at all. Too late to talk with her of what was in our hearts; or of harms and crucifyings and strengths as she had known and experienced them; or of whys and knowledge, of wisdom. She died a few weeks later.

She, who had no worldly goods to leave, yet left to me an inexhaustible legacy. Inherent in it, this heritage of summoning resources to make out of song, food, warmth, expressions of human love—courage, hope, resistance, belief; this vision of universality and illimitability born with each human infant, before the lessenings, harms, divisions of the world are visited upon it.

As she sheltered and carried us and others, she sheltered and carried that belief, that wisdom throughout a lifetime lived in a world whose season was, as still it is, a time of winter.

I stand here ironing, and what you asked me moves tormented back and forth with the iron.

"I wish you would manage the time to come in and talk with me about your daughter. I'm sure you can help me understand her. She's a youngster who needs help and whom I'm deeply interested in helping."

"Who needs help. . . ." Even if I came, what good would it do? You think because I am her mother I have a key, or that in some way you could use me as a key? She has lived for nineteen years. There is all that life that has happened outside of me, beyond me.

And when is there time to remember, to sift, to weigh, to estimate, to total? I will start and there will be an interruption and I will have to gather it all together again. Or I will become engulfed with all I did or did not do, with what should have been and what cannot be helped.

She was a beautiful baby. The first and only one of our five that was beautiful at birth. You do not guess how new and uneasy her tenancy in her now-loveliness. You did not know her all those years she was thought homely, or see her poring over her baby pictures, making me tell her over and over how beautiful she had been—and would be, I would tell her—and was now, to the seeing eye. But the seeing eyes were few or non-existent. Including mine.

I nursed her. They feel that's important nowadays. I nursed all the children, but with her, with all the fierce rigidity of first motherhood, I did like the books then said. Though her cries battered me to trembling and my breasts ached with swollenness, I waited till the clock decreed.

Why do I put that first? I do not even know if it matters, or if it explains anything.

She was a beautiful baby. She blew shining bubbles of sound. She loved motion, loved light, loved color and music and textures. She would lie on the floor in her blue overalls patting the surface so hard in ecstasy her hands and feet would blur. She was a miracle to me, but when she was eight months old I had to leave her daytimes with the woman downstairs to whom she was no miracle at all, for I worked or looked for work and for Emily's father, who "could no longer endure" (he wrote in his good-bye note) "sharing want with us."

I was nineteen. It was the pre-relief, pre-WPA world of the depression. I would start running as soon as I got off the streetcar, running up the stairs, the place smelling sour, and awake or asleep to startle awake, when she saw me she would break into a clogged weeping that could not be comforted, a weeping I can hear yet.

After a while I found a job hashing at night so I could be with her days, and it was better. But it came to where I had to bring her to his family and leave her.

It took a long time to raise the money for her fare back. Then she got chicken pox and I had to wait longer. When she finally came, I hardly knew her, walking quick and nervous like her father, looking like her father, thin, and dressed in a shoddy red that yellowed her skin and glared at the pockmarks. All the baby loveliness gone.

She was two. Old enough for nursery school they said, and I

did not know then what I know now—the fatigue of the long day, and the lacerations of group life in the kinds of nurseries that are only parking places for children.

Except that it would have made no difference if I had known. It was the only place there was. It was the only way we could be together, the only way I could hold a job.

And even without knowing, I knew. I knew the teacher that was evil because all these years it has curdled into my memory, the little boy hunched in the corner, her rasp, "why aren't you outside, because Alvin hits you? that's no reason, go out, scaredy." I knew Emily hated it even if she did not clutch and implore "don't go Mommy" like the other children, mornings.

She always had a reason why we should stay home. Momma, you look sick. Momma, I feel sick. Momma, the teachers aren't there today, they're sick. Momma, we can't go, there was a fire there last night. Momma, it's a holiday today, no school, they told me.

But never a direct protest, never rebellion. I think of our others in their three-, four-year-oldness—the explosions, the tempers, the denunciations, the demands—and I feel suddenly ill. I put the iron down. What in me demanded that goodness in her? And what was the cost, the cost to her of such goodness?

The old man living in the back once said in his gentle way: "You should smile at Emily more when you look at her." What *was* in my face when I looked at her? I loved her. There were all the acts of love.

It was only with the others I remembered what he said, and it was the face of joy, and not of care or tightness or worry I turned to them—too late for Emily. She does not smile easily, let alone almost always as her brothers and sisters do. Her face is closed and sombre, but when she wants, how fluid. You must have seen it in her pantomimes, you spoke of her rare gift for comedy on the stage that rouses a laughter out of the audience so dear they applaud and applaud and do not want to let her go.

Where does it come from, that comedy? There was none of it in her when she came back to me that second time, after I had had to send her away again. She had a new daddy now to learn to love, and I think perhaps it was a better time.

Except when we left her alone nights, telling ourselves she was old enough.

"Can't you go some other time, Mommy, like tomorrow?" she would ask. "Will it be just a little while you'll be gone? Do you promise?"

The time we came back, the front door open, the clock on the floor in the hall. She rigid awake. "It wasn't just a little while. I didn't cry. Three times I called you, just three times, and then I ran downstairs to open the door so you could come faster. The clock talked loud. I threw it away, it scared me what it talked."

She said the clock talked loud again that night I went to the hospital to have Susan. She was delirious with the fever that comes before red measles, but she was fully conscious all the week I was gone and the week after we were home when she could not come near the new baby or me.

She did not get well. She stayed skeleton thin, not wanting to eat, and night after night she had nightmares. She would call for me, and I would rouse from exhaustion to sleepily call back: "You're all right, darling, go to sleep, it's just a dream," and if she still called, in a sterner voice, "now go to sleep, Emily, there's nothing to hurt you." Twice, only twice, when I had to get up for Susan anyhow, I went in to sit with her.

Now when it is too late (as if she would let me hold and comfort her like I do the others) I get up and go to her at once at her moan or restless stirring. "Are you awake, Emily? Can I get you something?" And the answer is always the same: "No, I'm all right, go back to sleep, Mother."

They persuaded me at the clinic to send her away to a convalescent home in the country where "she can have the kind of food and care you can't manage for her, and you'll be free to concentrate on the new baby." They still send children to that place. I see pictures on the society page of sleek young women planning affairs to raise money for it, or dancing at the affairs, or decorating Easter eggs or filling Christmas stockings for the children.

They never have a picture of the children so I do not know if the girls still wear those gigantic red bows and the ravaged looks on the every other Sunday when parents can come to visit "unless otherwise notified"—as we were notified the first six weeks.

Oh it is a handsome place, green lawns and tall trees and fluted flower beds. High up on the balconies of each cottage the children stand, the girls in their red bows and white dresses, the boys in white suits and giant red ties. The parents stand below shrieking up to be heard and the children shriek down to be heard, and between them the invisible wall "Not To Be Contaminated by Parental Germs or Physical Affection."

There was a tiny girl who always stood hand in hand with Emily. Her parents never came. One visit she was gone. "They moved her to Rose Cottage" Emily shouted in explanation. "They don't like you to love anybody here."

She wrote once a week, the labored writing of a seven-year-old. "I am fine. How is the baby. If I write my leter nicly I will have a star. Love." There never was a star. We wrote every other day, letters she could never hold or keep but only hear read—once. "We simply do not have room for children to keep any personal possessions," they patiently explained when we pieced one Sunday's shrieking together to plead how much it would mean to Emily, who loved so to keep things, to be allowed to keep her letters and cards.

Each visit she looked frailer. "She isn't eating," they told us.

(They had runny eggs for breakfast or mush with lumps, Emily said later, I'd hold it in my mouth and not swallow. Nothing ever tasted good, just when they had chicken.)

It took us eight months to get her released home, and only the fact that she gained back so little of her seven lost pounds convinced the social worker.

I used to try to hold and love her after she came back, but her body would stay stiff, and after a while she'd push away. She ate little. Food sickened her, and I think much of life too. Oh she had physical lightness and brightness, twinkling by on skates, bouncing like a ball up and down up and down over the jump rope, skimming over the hill; but these were momentary.

She fretted about her appearance, thin and dark and foreign-looking at a time when every little girl was supposed to look or thought she should look a chubby blonde replica of Shirley Temple. The doorbell sometimes rang for her, but no one seemed to come and play in the house or be a best friend. Maybe because we moved so much.

There was a boy she loved painfully through two school semesters. Months later she told me how she had taken pennies from my purse to buy him candy. "Licorice was his favorite and I brought him some every day, but he still liked Jennifer better'n me. Why, Mommy?" The kind of question for which there is no answer.

School was a worry to her. She was not glib or quick in a world where glibness and quickness were easily confused with ability to learn. To her overworked and exasperated teachers she was an overconscientious "slow learner" who kept trying to catch up and was absent entirely too often.

I let her be absent, though sometimes the illness was imaginary. (How different from my now-strictness about attendance with the others.) I wasn't working. We had a new baby, I was home anyhow. Sometimes, after Susan grew old enough, I would keep her home from school, too, to have them all together.

Mostly Emily had asthma, and her breathing, harsh and labored, would fill the house with a curiously tranquil sound. I would bring the two old dresser mirrors and her boxes of collections to her bed. She would select beads and single earrings, bottle tops and shells, dried flowers and pebbles, old postcards and scraps, all sorts of oddments; then she and Susan would play Kingdom, setting up landscapes and furniture, peopling them with action.

Those were the only times of peaceful companionship between her and Susan. I have edged away from it, that poisonous feeling between them, that terrible balancing of hurts and needs I had to do between the two, and did so badly, those earlier years.

Oh there are conflicts between the others too, each one human, needing, demanding, hurting, taking—but only between Emily and Susan, no Emily toward Susan that corroding resentment. It seems so obvious on the surface, yet it is not obvious. Susan, the second child, Susan, golden- and curly-haired and chubby, quick and articulate and assured, everything in appearance and manner Emily was not; Susan, not able to resist Emily's precious things, losing or sometimes clumsily breaking them; Susan telling jokes and riddles to company for applause while Emily sat silent (to say to me later: that was *my* riddle, Mother, I told it to Susan); Susan, who for all the five years' difference in age was just a year behind Emily in developing physically.

I am glad for that slow physical development that widened the difference between her and her contemporaries, though she suffered over it. She was too vulnerable for that terrible world of youthful competition, of preening and parading, of constant measuring of yourself against every other, of envy, "If I had that copper hair," "If I had that skin. . . ." She tormented herself enough about not looking like the others, there was enough of the unsureness, the having to be conscious of words before you speak, the constant caring—what are they thinking of me? without having it all magnified by the merciless physical drives.

Ronnie is calling. He is wet and I change him. It is rare there is such a cry now. That time of motherhood is almost behind me when the ear is not one's own but must always be racked and listening for the child cry, the child call. We sit for a while and I hold him, looking out over the city spread in charcoal with its soft aisles of light. *"Shoogily,"* he breathes and curls closer. I carry him back to bed, asleep. *Shoogily.* A funny word, a family word, inherited from Emily, invented by her to say: *comfort.*

In this and other ways she leaves her seal, I say aloud. And startle at my saying it. What do I mean? What did I start to gather together, to try and make coherent? I was at the terrible, growing years. War years. I do not remember them well. I was working, there were four smaller ones now, there was not time for her. She had to help be a mother, and housekeeper, and shopper. She had to set her seal. Mornings of crisis and near hysteria trying to get lunches packed, hair combed, coats and shoes found, everyone to school or Child Care on time, the baby ready for transportation. And always the paper scribbled on by a smaller one, the book looked at by Susan then mislaid, the homework not done. Running out to that huge school where she was one, she was lost, she was a drop; suffering over her unpreparedness, stammering and unsure in her classes.

There was so little time left at night after the kids were bedded down. She would struggle over books, always eating (it was in those years she developed her enormous appetite that is legend-

ary in our family) and I would be ironing, or preparing food
for the next day, or writing V-mail to Bill, or tending the baby.
Sometimes, to make me laugh, or out of her despair, she would
imitate happenings or types at school.

I think I said once: "Why don't you do something like this in
the school amateur show?" One morning she phoned me at
work, hardly understandable through the weeping: "Mother, I
did it. I won, I won; they gave me first prize; they clapped and
clapped and wouldn't let me go."

Now suddenly she was Somebody, and as imprisoned in her
difference as she had been in her anonymity.

She began to be asked to perform at other high schools, even
in colleges, then at city and state-wide affairs. The first one we
went to, I only recognized her that first moment when thin, shy,
she almost drowned herself into the curtains. Then: Was this
Emily? The control, the command, the convulsing and deadly
clowning, the spell, then the roaring, stamping audience, unwilling to let this rare and precious laughter out of their lives.

Afterwards: You ought to do something about her with a gift
like that—but without money or knowing how, what does one
do? We have left it all to her, and the gift has as often eddied
inside, clogged and clotted, as been used and growing.

She is coming. She runs up the stairs two at a time with her
light graceful step, and I know she is happy tonight. Whatever
it was that occasioned your call did not happen today.

"Aren't you ever going to finish the ironing, Mother? Whistler
painted his mother in a rocker. I'd have to paint mine standing
over an ironing board." This is one of her communicative nights
and she tells me everything and nothing as she fixes herself a
plate of food out of the icebox.

She is so lovely. Why did you want me to come in at all? Why
were you concerned? She will find her way.

She starts up the stairs to bed. "Don't get *me* up with the rest
in the morning." "But I thought you were having midterms."
"Oh, those," she comes back in, kisses me, and says quite lightly,
"in a couple of years when we'll all be atom-dead they won't
matter a bit."

She has said it before. She *believes* it. But because I have been dredging the past, and all that compounds a human being is so heavy and meaningful in me, I cannot endure it tonight.

I will never total it all. I will never come in to say: She was a child seldom smiled at. Her father left me before she was a year old. I had to work her first six years when there was work, or I sent her home and to his relatives. There were years she had care she hated. She was dark and thin and foreign-looking in a world where the prestige went to blondeness and curly hair and dimples, she was slow where glibness was prized. She was a child of anxious, not proud, love. We were poor and could not afford for her the soil of easy growth. I was a young mother, I was a distracted mother. There were the other children pushing up, demanding. Her younger sister seemed all that she was not. There were years she did not let me touch her. She kept too much in herself, her life was such she had to keep too much in herself. My wisdom came too late. She has much to her and probably little will come of it. She is a child of her age, of depression, of war, of fear.

Let her be. So all that is in her will not bloom—but in how many does it? There is still enough left to live by. Only help her to know—help make it so there is cause for her to know—that she is more than this dress on the ironing board, helpless before the iron.

Guadalupe Valdes

Recuerdo
1963

In her commentary on the origins of this story, its place in her life, and the course of her life since the writing of the story, Guadalupe Valdes attributes to her mother the intellectual encouragement and creative support that made it possible for her to write. But, at the same time, like so many women, the disappointments Valdes experienced as a young married mother of two small children seemed to her to be her mother's fault.

My story "Recuerdo" might well be entitled "Mother's Advice." It is a bitter story, written at a time in which I was angry about my own life and about having followed my own mother's counsel. I was trying to make sense of the world, trying to understand why one could follow all the rules and yet end up unhappy. I felt betrayed, trapped, and all alone.

Until recently, it had not occurred to me that my mother has also been betrayed and trapped. . . . like so many women, she had also tried to follow rules; to make sense of so many things that seemed unfair; and to hope that somehow, for her daughters, things would be different.

Clearly, my anger was misdirected. My mother gave me what she could. She said, "Marry a man who doesn't drink." Amazing that, like the mother in "Recuerdo," her formula for happiness was so simple. She focused on the one thing that had made her life unhappy, and she wanted more for *me*. It seems sad now, that I blamed her for so many years, blamed her because I believed her,

blamed her because the formula was not complete and
did not bring happiness.

*Like many women writers, among them in this collection Elizabeth Stuart
Phelps, Hisaye Yamamoto, Alice Walker, and Joanna Russ, Valdes testifies to
her mother's strong influence on her own ability to imagine herself as a writer.
The artist's mother as artist manqué is a figure revealed more and more frequently
as scholars have begun to look at the maternal influence on writers. Valdes
writes:*

My mother had a lot to do with my writing. I can
remember bringing her the first poems I ever wrote. She
found them brilliant, of course, and praised me warmly.
Recently in looking through old papers, I found them.
She had kept them all these years.

I began to write in the fourth grade. I wrote in English,
the language that I learned at school, the language of the
country that I spent eight hours in every day, before
recrossing the border back to my Mexican world. I wrote
in English, and took the poems home and showed them
to my mother. It didn't seem strange to me.

She always read them carefully. For she liked poetry
too; and had thick scrapbooks of poems she'd typed out,
or copied, or cut out from books and magazines. And it's
only now that I'm aware that those poems were all in
English too.

"Recuerdo" (meaning "Remembrance") was first published in De Colores
Journal *in 1976, thirteen years after its original composition. "At the time I
sent the story everywhere, and of course, it was rejected," comments Valdes.
"Minority themes only recently became popular." She continues:*

. . . one day, looking in an old file, I found "Recuerdo."
Having become an expert at sending things out, I sent it
off to a new "minority" little magazine; and it was published. I was pleased and yet saddened. I remembered the
young woman (myself at 20) who had written it; and
wondered how different her life would have been if only
it had been published then.

*In this story, as in "A Marriage of Persuasion," the mother is portrayed as a
woman who fails her daughter—who, indeed, cannot do other than fail her
daughter. But because the stories are written by artists who transcend their
personal feelings about and understandings of their own mothers, these fictional
mothers are portrayed as vulnerable and victimized women without power. The
reader can see, however, that the mother is not to blame for anything.*

It was noon. It was dusty. And the sun, blinding in its brightness, shone unmercifully on the narrow dirty street.

It was empty. And to Rosa, walking slowly past the bars and the shops and the curios stands, it seemed as if they all were peering out at her, curiously watching what she did.

She walked on . . . toward the river, toward the narrow, muddy strip of land that was the dry Rio Grande; and she wished suddenly that it were night and that the tourists had come across, making the street noisy and gay and full of life.

But it was noon. And there were no happy or laughing Americanos; no eager girls painted and perfumed and waiting for customers; no blaring horns or booming bongos . . . only here and there a hungry dog, a crippled beggar, or a drunk thirsty and broke from the night before.

She was almost there. She could see the narrow door and the splintered wooden steps. And instinctively she stopped. Afraid suddenly, feeling the hollow emptiness again, and the tightness when she swallowed.

And yet, it was not as if she did not know why he had wanted her to come, why he had sent for her. It was not as though she were a child. Her reflection in a smudged and dirty window told her that she was no longer even a girl.

And still, it was not as if she were old, she told herself, it was only that her body was rounded and full, and her eyes in the dark smooth face were hard and knowing, mirroring the pain and the disappointment and the tears of thirty-five years . . .

She walked to the narrow door slowly, and up the stairs . . . thumping softly on the creaking swollen wood. At the top, across a dingy hallway, she knocked softly at a door. It was ajar, and Rosa could see the worn chairs and the torn linoleum and the paper-littered desk. But she did not go in. Not until the man came to the door and looked out at her impatiently.

He saw her feet first and the tattered sandals. Then her dress clean but faded, a best dress obviously, because it was not patched. Finally, after what seemed to Rosa an eternity, he looked at her face, at her dark black hair knotted neatly on top of her head; and at last, into her eyes.

"Come in, Rosa," he said slowly, "I am glad that you could come."

"Buenas tardes Don Lorenzo," Rosa said meekly, looking up uneasily at the bulky smelly man. "I am sorry I am late."

"Yes," he said mockingly; and turning, he walked back into the small and dirty room.

Rosa followed him, studying him, while he could not see her, seeing the wrinkled trousers, the sweat stained shirt, and the overgrown greasy hair on the back of his pudgy neck.

He turned suddenly, his beady eyes surveying his domain smugly; then deliberately, he walked to the window and straightened the sign that said:

DIVORCES
LORENZO PEREZ SAUZA
ATTORNEY AT LAW

It was not as important as the neon blinking sign, of course, but sometimes people came from the side street, and it was good to be prepared.

"Well, Rosa," he said, looking at her again, "and where is Maruca?"

"She is sick, señor."

"Sick?"

"Yes, she has had headaches and she is not well ... she ..."

"Has she seen a doctor, Rosa?" The question was mocking again.

"No ... she ... it will pass, señor ... It's only that now ... I do not think that she should come to work."

"Oh?" He was looking out of the window distractedly, ignoring her.

"I am sorry, I should have come before," she continued meekly ...

"Maruca is very pretty, Rosa," Don Lorenzo said suddenly.

"Thank you, señor, you are very kind." She was calmer now ...

"She will make a man very happy, someday," he continued.

"Yes."

"Do you think she will marry soon then?" he asked her, watching her closely.

"No," she hesitated, "that is, I don't know, she ... there isn't anyone yet."

"Ah!" It was said quietly but somehow triumphantly . . .
And Rosa waited, wondering what he wanted, sensing something
and suddenly suspicious.

"Do you think she likes me, Rosa," he asked her deliberately,
baiting her.

And she remembered Maruca's face, tear-stained, embarrassed
telling her: "I can't go back, mama. He does not want me to
help in his work. He touches me, mother . . . and smiles. And
today, he put his large sweaty hand on my breast, and held it,
smiling, like a cow. Ugly!"

"Why, yes, Don Lorenzo," she lied quickly. "She thinks you
are very nice." Her heart was racing now, hoping and yet not
daring to—

"I am much of a man, Rosa," he went on slowly, "and the girl
is pretty . . . I would take care of her . . . if she let me."

"Take care of her?" Rosa was praying now, her fingers crossed
behind her back.

"Yes, take care of her," he repeated. "I would be good to her,
you would have money. And then, perhaps, if there is a child
. . . she would need a house . . ."

"A house." Rosa repeated dully. A house for Maruca. That it
might be. That it might be, really, was unbelievable. To think
of the security, of the happy future frightened her suddenly,
and she could only stare at the fat man, her eyes round and
very black.

"Think about it, Rosita," he said smiling benevolently . . . "You
know me . . ." And Rosa looked at him angrily, remembering,
and suddenly feeling very much like being sick.

The walk home was long; and in the heat Rosa grew tired.
She wished that she might come to a tree, so that she could sit
in the shade and think. But the hills were bare and dry, and
there were no trees. There were only shacks surrounded by
hungry crying children.

And Rosa thought about her own, about the little ones. The
ones that still depended on her even for something to eat. And
she felt it again, the strange despair of wanting to cry out:
"Don't, don't depend on me! I can hardly depend on myself."

But they had no one else; and until they could beg or steal a
piece of bread and a bowl of beans, they would turn to her, only
to her, not ever to Pablo.

And it wasn't because he was drunk and lazy, or even because
only the last two children belonged to him. He was kind enough
to all of them. It was, though, as if they sensed that he was only
temporary.

And still it was not that Pablo was bad. He was better actually
than the others. He did not beat her when he drank, or steal
food from the children. He was not even too demanding. And
it gave them a man, after all, a man to protect them . . . It was
enough, really.

True, he had begun to look at Maruca, and it had bothered
Rosa. But perhaps it *was* really time for Maruca to leave. For
the little ones, particularly. Because men are men, she said to
herself, and if there is a temptation. . . .

But she was not fooling anyone, and when at last she saw the
tin and cardboard shack against the side of the hill, with its
cluttered front and screaming children, she wanted to turn back.

Maruca saw her first.

"There's mama," she told the others triumphantly, and at
once they took up the shout: "mama! mama! mama!"

The other girl, standing with Maruca, turned to leave as Rosa
came closer.

"Buenas tardes," she said uncomfortably, sensing the dislike
and wanting to hurry away.

"What did Petra want?" Rosa asked Maruca angrily, even
before Petra was out of earshot.

"Mama, *por favor*, she'll hear you."

"I told you I did not want her in this house."

"We were only talking, mama. She was telling me about her
friends."

"Her friends!" Rosa cut in sharply, "as if we did not know
that she goes with the first American that looks at her. Always
by the river that one, with one soldier and another, her friends
indeed!"

"But she says she has fun, mama, and they take her to dance
and buy her pretty things."

"Yes, yes, and tomorrow, they will give her a baby . . . And
where is the fun then . . . eh? She is in the streets . . . no?" Rosa
was shaking with anger. "Is that what you want? Do you?"

"No, mama," Maruca said meekly, "I was just listening to her talk."

"Well, remember it," Rosa snapped furiously, but then seeing Maruca's face, she stopped suddenly. "There, there, it's alright," she said softly. "We will talk about it later."

And Rosa watched her, then, herding the children into the house gently, gracefully; slim and small, angular still, with something perhaps a little doltish in the way she held herself, impatient, and yet distrusting, not quite daring to go forward.

And she thought of Don Lorenzo, and for a moment, she wished that he were not so fat, or so ugly, and especially, so sweaty.

But it was an irrecoverable chance! Old men with money did not often come into their world, and never to stay.

To Rosa, they had been merely far away gods at whose houses she had worked as a maid or as a cook; faultless beings who were to be obeyed without question; powerful creatures who had commanded her to come when they needed variety or adventure . . .

But only that.

She had never been clever enough, or even pretty enough to make it be more.

But Maruca! Maruca could have the world.

No need for her to marry a poor young bum who could not even get a job. No need for her to have ten children all hungry and crying. No need for her to dread, even, that the bum might leave her. No need at all.

"Maruca," Rosa said decidedly, turning to where she sat playing with the baby, "I went to see Don Lorenzo."

"Oh?" There was fear in the bright brown eyes.

"And he wants to take care of you," Rosa continued softly. "He thinks you're pretty, and he likes you."

"Take care of me?" It was more of a statement than a question.

"He wants to make an arrangement with you, Maruca." Rosa too was afraid now. "He would come to see you . . . and . . . well . . . if there is a baby, there might very well be a house."

"A baby?" The face was pale now, the eyes surprised and angry. "You want me to go to bed with Don Lorenzo? You want

me to let him put his greasy hands all over me, and make love
to me? You want that? Is that how much better I can do than
Petra?"

"Don't you see, I want you to be happy, to be safe. I want you
to have pretty things and not to be afraid. I want you to love
your babies when you have them, to hear them laugh with full
fat stomachs . . . I want you to love life, to be glad that you were
born."

"To be happy?" Maruca repeated slowly, as if it had never
occurred to her that she was not.

"Yes, to be happy."

"And sleeping with Don Lorenzo," Maruca asked uncertainly,
"will that make me glad that I was born?"

And Rosa looked at her, saw her waiting for an answer,
depending on it . . .

And she wanted to scream out. "No, no! You will hate it
probably, and you will dread his touch on you and his breath
smelling of garlic. But it isn't *he,* that will make you happy. It's
the rest of it. Don't you see, can't you understand how important
he is?"

But the brown eyes stared at her pleadingly, filling with tears,
like a child's, and Rosa said quietly: "Yes, Maruca, it will make
you happy."

But then suddenly, unexpectedly, she felt alone and very, very
tired.

"Go on to church now," she said slowly, "it's time for bene-
diction and you have the novena to complete." And Rosa watched
her go, prayer book clutched tightly in one hand, hopeful still,
trusting still, and so very, very young still. And she wondered if
she would change much, really, after Don Lorenzo, and the
baby and the house. She wondered if she would still be gay and
proud and impatient.

But then suddenly Maruca was out of sight, and Rosa turned
to the others, kissing one, patting another's head, and hurrying
to have the beans hot and the house tidy for the time that Pablo
would come home.

┌── James Tiptree, Jr. ──┐

The Women Men Don't See
1973

The Science Fiction Writers of America annually vote to determine who among them shall be honored by their colleagues with the Nebula Award for the best work in a variety of genres. James Tiptree, Jr. (b. 1915) was awarded the Nebula for best short story in 1973, for "Love is the Plan, the Plan is Death"; for best novella in 1976, for "Houston, Houston, Do You Read?"; and for the best novelette in 1977, for "The Screwfly Solution," published under the pseudonym Racoona Sheldon. Science fiction fans, who also vote on annual literary prizes, awarded the 1974 Hugo for the best novella to "The Girl Who Was Plugged In" (included in The Other Woman, *ed.* Susan Koppelman, The Feminist Press, 1984).

Tiptree has published four volumes of short stories: Ten Thousand Light-Years From Home, *(1973),* Warm Worlds and Otherwise *(1975),* Star-Songs of an Old Primate *(1978), and* Out of the Everywhere and Other Extraordinary Visions *(1981), and one novel,* Up the Walls of the World *(1978).*

Tiptree's biography includes an exotic childhood (as the only one of ten siblings to survive beyond birth) spent largely in Africa and India on exploratory expeditions with extraordinarily talented, accomplished, adventuresome, and achievement-oriented parents; an early career as a graphic artist and painter; a stint in the United States air force during World War II as a photo-intelligence officer; involvement in the creation of the Central Intelligence Agency; a midlife career change leading to the successful pursuit of a Ph.D. in experimental psychology; and a brief teaching career. Tiptree has written that the early exposure to "dozens of cultures and sub-cultures whose values, taboos, imperatives,

religions, languages, and mores conflicted with each other" resulted in "profound
alienation from any nominal peers, and an enduring cultural relativism."

Among Tiptree's experiences as a youngster was that of being given "one of
the most expensive debutante parties ever seen, in the middle of the Depression."
Like the nineteenth-century writers George Eliot, George Sand, and Ellis, Acton,
and Currer Bell (Emily, Anne, and Charlotte Bronte), James Tiptree, Jr. is a
woman. (Tiptree is not the only writer in this collection to use a male pseudonym.
Alice Brown's story, "The Way of Peace," was published under the name of
Martin Redfield.) Tiptree, whose real name is Alice Sheldon, explains her choice
of a male nom de plume on the grounds that "it seemed like a good camouflage.
I had the feeling that a man would slip by less observed. . . . Men have so pre-
empted the area of human experience that when you write about universal
motives, you are assumed to be writing like a man." That male name gives the
writer the privilege of assuming that her perspective is normative. That which
makes the work distinctive is not gender, but other, chosen and personal matters.

One of the aspects of Tiptree's distinctiveness is the authorial assumption that
her reader is leisured, well-educated, and well-travelled. Her stories are filled
with geographical and cultural details reflecting her own wide experience. When
a woman writer is presumptuous about her audience in this way, she is often
criticized as an elitist, while a man making similar use of his life experience is
honored as erudite and sophisticated. The reader has to work hard when reading
Tiptree's stories, but as her colleagues and fans have indicated by the awards
they have voted her work, the effort is well worth it.

"The Women Men Don't See" was first published in The Magazine of
Fantasy and Science Fiction *in December 1973 and collected in* Warm
Worlds and Otherwise *two years later. In his introduction to the book, Robert
Silverberg, who didn't know the secret of Tiptree's identity (Joanna Russ has
called Alice Sheldon's masquerade the most successful and the most sustained in
literary history), pays special attention to this story, labelling it a "masterpiece
of short-story writing," and observing:*

> The thematic solution is an ancient s-f cliche . . . re-
> deemed and wholly transformed by its sudden shattering
> vision of women, stolid and enduring, calmly trading one
> set of alien masters for another that may be more tolera-
> ble. It is a profoundly feminist story told in entirely mas-
> culine manner, and deserves close attention by those in
> the front lines of the wars of sexual liberation, male and
> female.

I see her first while the Mexicana 727 is barreling down to
Cozumel Island. I come out of the can and lurch into her seat,

saying "Sorry," at a double female blur. The near blur nods quietly. The younger one in the window seat goes on looking out. I continue down the aisle, registering nothing. Zero. I never would have looked at them or thought of them again.

Cozumel airport is the usual mix of panicky Yanks dressed for the sand pile and calm Mexicans dressed for lunch at the Presidente. I am a used-up Yank dressed for serious fishing; I extract my rods and duffel from the riot and hike across the field to find my charter pilot. One Captain Estéban has contracted to deliver me to the bonefish flats of Belize three hundred kilometers down the coast.

Captain Estéban turns out to be four feet nine of mahogany Mayan *puro*. He is also in a somber Maya snit. He tells me my Cessna is grounded somewhere and his Bonanza is booked to take a party to Chetumal.

Well, Chetumal is south; can he take me along and go on to Belize after he drops them? Gloomily he concedes the possibility—*if* the other party permits, and *if* there are not too many *equipajes*.

The Chetumal party approaches. It's the woman and her young companion—daughter?—neatly picking their way across the gravel and yucca apron. Their Ventura two-suiters, like themselves, are small, plain and neutral-colored. No problem. When the captain asks if I may ride along, the mother says mildly "Of course," without looking at me.

I think that's when my inner tilt-detector sends up its first faint click. How come this woman has already looked me over carefully enough to accept on her plane? I disregard it. Paranoia hasn't been useful in my business for years, but the habit is hard to break.

As we clamber into the Bonanza, I see the girl has what could be an attractive body if there was any spark at all. There isn't. Captain Estéban folds a serape to sit on so he can see over the cowling and runs a meticulous check-down. And then we're up and trundling over the turquoise Jello of the Caribbean into a stiff south wind.

The coast on our right is the territory of Quintana Roo. If you haven't seen Yucatán, imagine the world's biggest absolutely flat green-gray rug. An empty-looking land. We pass the white ruin of Tulum and the gash of the road to Chichén Itzá, a half-dozen coconut plantations, and then nothing but reef and low scrub jungle all the way to the horizon, just about the way the conquistadors saw it four centuries back.

Long strings of cumulus are racing at us, shadowing the coast. I have gathered that part of our pilot's gloom concerns the weather. A cold front is dying on the henequen fields of Mérida to the west, and the south wind has piled up a string of coastal storms: what they call *llovisnos*. Estéban detours methodically around a couple of small thunderheads. The Bonanza jinks, and I look back with a vague notion of reassuring the women. They are calmly intent on what can be seen of Yucatán. Well, they were offered the copilot's view, but they turned it down. Too shy?

Another *llovisno* puffs up ahead. Estéban takes the Bonanza upstairs, rising in his seat to sight his course. I relax for the first time in too long, savoring the latitudes between me and my desk, the week of fishing ahead. Our captain's classic Maya profile attracts my gaze: forehead sloping back from his predatory nose, lips and jaw stepping back below it. If his slant eyes had been any more crossed, he couldn't have made his license. That's a handsome combination, believe it or not. On the little Maya chicks in their minishifts with iridescent gloop on those cockeyes, it's also highly erotic. Nothing like the oriental doll thing; these people have stone bones. Captain Estéban's old grandmother could probably tow the Bonanza . . .

I'm snapped awake by the cabin hitting my ear. Estéban is barking into his headset over a drumming racket of hail; the windows are dark gray.

One important noise is missing—the motor. I realize Estéban is fighting a dead plane. Thirty-six hundred; we've lost two thousand feet!

He slaps tank switches as the storm throws us around; I catch something about *gasolina* in a snarl that shows his big teeth. The Bonanza reels down. As he reaches for an overhead toggle, I see the fuel gauges are high. Maybe a clogged gravity feed line; I've heard of dirty gas down here. He drops the set; it's a million to one nobody can read us through the storm at this range anyway. Twenty-five hundred—going down.

His electric feed pump seems to have cut in: the motor explodes—quits—explodes—and quits again for good. We are suddenly out of the bottom of the clouds. Below us is a long white line almost hidden by rain: the reef. But there isn't any beach behind it, only a big meandering bay with a few mangrove flats—and it's coming up at us fast.

This is going to be bad, I tell myself with great unoriginality. The women behind me haven't made a sound. I look back and see they've braced down with their coats by their heads. With a stalling speed around eighty, all this isn't much use, but I wedge myself in.

Estéban yells some more into his set, flying a falling plane. He is doing one jesus job, too—as the water rushes up at us he dives into a hair-raising turn and hangs us into the wind—with a long pale ridge of sandbar in front of our nose.

Where in hell he found it I never know. The Bonanza mushes down, and we belly-hit with a tremendous tearing crash—bounce—hit again—and everything slews wildly as we flat-spin into the mangroves at the end of the bar. Crash! Clang! The plane is wrapping itself into a mound of strangler fig with one wing up. The crashing quits with us all in one piece. And no fire. Fantastic.

Captain Estéban pries open his door, which is now in the roof. Behind me a woman is repeating quietly, "Mother. Mother." I climb up the floor and find the girl trying to free herself from her mother's embrace. The woman's eyes are closed. Then she opens them and suddenly lets go, sane as soap. Estéban starts hauling them out. I grab the Bonanza's aid kit and scramble out after them into brilliant sun and wind. The storm that hit us is already vanishing up the coast.

"Great landing, Captain."

"Oh, yes! It was beautiful." The women are shaky, but no hysteria. Estéban is surveying the scenery with the expression his ancestors used on the Spaniards.

If you've been in one of these things, you know the slow-motion inanity that goes on. Euphoria, first. We straggle down the fig tree and out onto the sandbar in the roaring hot wind, noting without alarm that there's nothing but miles of crystalline water on all sides. It's only a foot or so deep, and the bottom is the olive color of silt. The distant shore around us is all flat mangrove swamp, totally uninhabitable.

"Bahía Espiritu Santo." Estéban confirms my guess that we're down in that huge water wilderness. I always wanted to fish it.

"What's all that smoke?" The girl is pointing at the plumes blowing around the horizon.

"Alligator hunters," says Estéban. Maya poachers have left burn-offs in the swamps. It occurs to me that any signal fires we make aren't going to be too conspicuous. And I now note that our plane is well-buried in the mound of fig. Hard to see it from the air.

Just as the question of how the hell we get out of here surfaces in my mind, the older woman asks composedly, "If they didn't hear you, Captain, when will they start looking for us? Tomorrow?"

"Correct," Estéban agrees dourly. I recall that air-sea rescue is fairly informal here. Like, keep an eye open for Mario, his mother says he hasn't been home all week.

It dawns on me we may be here quite some while.

Furthermore, the diesel-truck noise on our left is the Caribbean piling back into the mouth of the bay. The wind is pushing it at us, and the bare bottoms on the mangroves show that our bar is covered at high tide. I recall seeing a full moon this morning in—believe it, St. Louis—which means maximal tides. Well, we can climb up in the plane. But what about drinking water?

There's a small splat! behind me. The older woman has sampled the bay. She shakes her head, smiling ruefully. It's the first real expression on either of them; I take it as the signal for introductions. When I say I'm Don Fenton from St. Louis, she tells me their name is Parsons, from Bethesda, Maryland. She says it so nicely I don't at first notice we aren't being given first names. We all compliment Captain Estéban again.

His left eye is swelled shut, an inconvenience beneath his attention as a Maya, but Mrs. Parsons spots the way he's bracing his elbow in his ribs.

"You're hurt, Captain."

"*Roto*—I think is broken." He's embarrassed at being in pain.

We get him to peel off his Jaime shirt, revealing a nasty bruise in his superb dark-bay torso.

"Is there tape in that kit, Mr. Fenton? I've had a little first-aid training."

She begins to deal competently and very impersonally with the tape. Miss Parsons and I wander to the end of the bar and have a conversation which I am later to recall acutely.

"Roseate spoonbills," I tell her as three pink birds flap away.

"They're beautiful," she says in her tiny voice. They both have tiny voices. "He's a Mayan Indian, isn't he? The pilot, I mean."

"Right. The real thing, straight out of the Bonampak murals. Have you seen Chichén and Uxmal?"

"Yes. We were in Mérida. We're going to Tikal in Guatemala . . . I mean, we were."

"You'll get there." It occurs to me the girl needs cheering up. "Have they told you that Maya mothers used to tie a board on the infant's forehead to get that slant? They also hung a ball of tallow over its nose to make the eyes cross. It was considered aristocratic."

She smiles and takes another peek at Estéban. "People seem different in Yucatán," she says thoughtfully. "Not like the Indians around Mexico City. More, I don't know, independent."

"Comes from never having been conquered. Mayas got massacred and chased a lot, but nobody ever really flattened them. I bet you didn't know that the last Mexican-Maya war ended with a negotiated truce in nineteen thirty-five?"

"No!" Then she says seriously, "I like that."

"So do I."

"The water is really rising very fast," says Mrs. Parsons gently from behind us.

It is, and so is another *llovisno*. We climb back into the Bonanza. I try to rig my parka for a rain catcher, which blows loose as the storm hits fast and furious. We sort a couple of malt bars and my bottle of Jack Daniels out of the jumble in the cabin and make ourselves reasonably comfortable. The Parsons take a sip of whiskey each, Estéban and I considerably more. The Bonanza begins to bump soggily. Estéban makes an ancient one-eyed Mayan face at the water seeping into his cabin and goes to sleep. We all nap.

When the water goes down, the euphoria has gone with it, and we're very, very thirsty. It's also damn near sunset. I get to work with a bait-casting rod and some treble hooks and manage to foul-hook four small mullets. Estéban and the women tie the Bonanza's midget life raft out in the mangroves to catch rain. The wind is parching hot. No planes go by.

Finally another shower comes over and yields us six ounces of water apiece. When the sunset envelops the world in golden smoke, we squat on the sandbar to eat wet raw mullet and Instant Breakfast crumbs. The women are now in shorts, neat but definitely not sexy.

"I never realized how refreshing raw fish is," Mrs. Parsons says pleasantly. Her daughter chuckles, also pleasantly. She's on Mamma's far side away from Estéban and me. I have Mrs. Parsons figured now; Mother Hen protecting only chick from male predators. That's all right with me. I came here to fish.

But something is irritating me. The damn women haven't complained once, you understand. Not a peep, not a quaver, no personal manifestations whatever. They're like something out of a manual.

"You really seem at home in the wilderness, Mrs. Parsons. You do much camping?"

"Oh goodness no." Diffident laugh. "Not since my girl scout days. Oh, look—are those man-of-war birds?"

Answer a question with a question. I wait while the frigate birds sail nobly into the sunset.

"Bethesda . . . Would I be wrong in guessing you work for Uncle Sam?"

"Why yes. You must be very familiar with Washington, Mr. Fenton. Does your work bring you there often?"

Anywhere but on our sandbar the little ploy would have worked. My hunter's gene twitches.

"Which agency are you with?"

She gives up gracefully. "Oh, just GSA records. I'm a librarian."

Of course. I know her now, all the Mrs. Parsonses in records divisions, accounting sections, research branches, personnel and administration offices. Tell Mrs. Parsons we need a recap on the external service contracts for fiscal '73. So Yucatán is on the tours now? Pity . . . I offer her the tired little joke. "You know where the bodies are buried."

She smiles deprecatingly and stands up. "It does get dark quickly, doesn't it?"

Time to get back into the plane.

A flock of ibis are circling us, evidently accustomed to roosting in our fig tree. Estéban produces a machete and a Mayan string hammock. He proceeds to sling it between tree and plane, refusing help. His machete stroke is noticeably tentative.

The Parsons are taking a pee behind the tail vane. I hear one of them slip and squeal faintly. When they come back over the hull, Mrs. Parsons asks, "Might we sleep in the hammock, Captain?"

Estéban splits an unbelieving grin. I protest about rain and mosquitoes.

"Oh, we have insect repellent and we do enjoy fresh air."

The air is rushing by about force five and colder by the minute.

"We have our raincoats," the girl adds cheerfully.

Well, okay, ladies. We dangerous males retire inside the damp cabin. Through the wind I hear the women laugh softly now and then, apparently cosy in their chilly ibis roost. A private insanity, I decide. I know myself for the least threatening of men; my non-charisma has been in fact an asset jobwise, over the years. Are they having fantasies about Estéban? Or maybe they really are fresh-air nuts . . . Sleep comes for me in invisible diesels roaring by on the reef outside.

We emerge dry-mouthed into a vast windy salmon sunrise. A diamond chip of sun breaks out of the sea and promptly submerges in cloud. I go to work with the rod and some mullet bait while two showers detour around us. Breakfast is a strip of wet barracuda apiece.

The Parsons continue stoic and helpful. Under Estéban's direction they set up a section of cowling for a gasoline flare in case we hear a plane, but nothing goes over except one unseen jet droning toward Panama. The wind howls, hot and dry and full of coral dust. So are we.

"They look first in the sea." Estéban remarks. His aristocratic frontal slope is beaded with sweat; Mrs. Parsons watches him concernedly. I watch the cloud blanket tearing by above, getting higher and dryer and thicker. While that lasts nobody is going to find us, and the water business is now unfunny.

Finally I borrow Estéban's machete and hack a long light pole. "There's a stream coming in back there, I saw it from the plane. Can't be more than two, three miles."

"I'm afraid the raft's torn." Mrs. Parsons shows me the cracks in the orange plastic; irritatingly, it's a Delaware label.

"All right," I hear myself announce. "The tide's going down. If we cut the good end of that air tube, I can haul water back in it. I've waded flats before."

Even to me it sounds crazy.

"Stay by plane," Estéban says. He's right, of course. He's also clearly running a fever. I look at the overcast and taste grit and old barracuda. The hell with the manual.

When I start cutting up the raft, Estéban tells me to take the serape. "You stay one night." He's right about that, too; I'll have to wait out the tide.

"I'll come with you," says Mrs. Parsons calmly.

I simply stare at her. What new madness has got into Mother Hen? Does she imagine Estéban is too battered to be functional? While I'm being astounded, my eyes take in the fact that Mrs. Parsons is now quite rosy around the knees, with her hair loose and a sunburn starting on her nose. A trim, in fact a very neat shading-forty.

"Look, that stuff is horrible going. Mud up to your ears and water over your head."

"I'm really quite fit and I swim a great deal. I'll try to keep up. Two would be much safer, Mr. Fenton, and we can bring more water."

She's serious. Well, I'm about as fit as a marshmallow at this time of winter, and I can't pretend I'm depressed by the idea of company. So be it.

"Let me show Miss Parsons how to work this rod."

Miss Parsons is even rosier and more windblown, and she's not clumsy with my tackle. A good girl, Miss Parsons, in her nothing way. We cut another staff and get some gear together. At the last minute Estéban shows how sick he feels: he offers me the machete. I thank him, but, no; I'm used to my Wirkkala knife. We tie some air into the plastic tube for a float and set out along the sandiest looking line.

Estéban raises one dark palm. *"Buen viaje."* Miss Parsons has hugged her mother and gone to cast from the mangrove. She waves. We wave.

An hour later we're barely out of waving distance. The going is surely god-awful. The sand keeps dissolving into silt you can't walk on or swim through, and the bottom is spiked with dead mangrove spears. We flounder from one pothole to the next, scaring up rays and turtles and hoping to god we don't kick a moray eel. Where we're not soaked in slime, we're desiccated, and we smell like the Old Cretaceous.

Mrs. Parsons keeps up doggedly. I only have to pull her out once. When I do so, I notice the sandbar is now out of sight.

Finally we reach the gap in the mangrove line I thought was the creek. It turns out to open into another arm of the bay, with more mangroves ahead. And the tide is coming in.

"I've had the world's lousiest idea."

Mrs. Parsons only says mildly, "It's so different from the view from the plane."

I revise my opinion of the girl scouts, and we plow on past the mangroves toward the smoky haze that has to be shore. The sun is setting in our faces, making it hard to see. Ibis and herons fly up around us, and once a big permit spooks ahead, his fin cutting a rooster tail. We fall into more potholes. The flashlights get soaked. I am having fantasies of the mangrove as universal obstacle; it's hard to recall I ever walked down a street, for instance, without stumbling over or under or through mangrove roots. And the sun is dropping down, down.

Suddenly we hit a ledge and fall over it into a cold flow.

"The stream! It's fresh water!"

We guzzle and garble and douse our heads; it's the best drink I remember. "Oh my, oh my—!" Mrs. Parsons is laughing right out loud.

"That dark place over to the right looks like real land."

We flounder across the flow and follow a hard shelf, which turns into solid bank and rises over our heads. Shortly there's a break beside a clump of spiny bromels, and we scramble up and flop down at the top, dripping and stinking. Out of sheer reflex my arm goes around my companion's shoulder—but Mrs. Parsons isn't there; she's up on her knees peering at the burnt-over plain around us.

"It's so good to see land one can walk on!" The tone is too innocent. *Noli me tangere.*

"Don't try it." I'm exasperated; the muddy little woman, what does she think? "That ground out there is a crush of ashes over muck, and it's full of stubs. You can go in over your knees."

"It seems firm here."

"We're in an alligator nursery. That was the slide we came up. Don't worry, by now the old lady's doubtless on her way to be made into handbags."

"What a shame."

"I better set a line down in the stream while I can still see."

I slide back down and rig a string of hooks that may get us breakfast. When I get back Mrs. Parsons is wringing muck out of the serape.

"I'm glad you warned me, Mr. Fenton. It *is* treacherous."

"Yeah." I'm over my irritation; god knows I don't want to *tangere* Mrs. Parsons, even if I weren't beat down to mush. "In its quiet way, Yucatán is a tough place to get around in. You can see why the Mayas built roads. Speaking of which—look!"

The last of the sunset is silhouetting a small square shape a couple of kilometers inland; a Maya *ruina* with a fig tree growing out of it.

"Lot of those around. People think they were guard towers."

"What a deserted-feeling land."

"Let's hope it's deserted by mosquitoes."

We slump down in the 'gator nursery and share the last malt bar, watching the stars slide in and out of the blowing clouds. The bugs aren't too bad; maybe the burn did them in. And it isn't hot any more, either—in fact, it's not even warm, wet as we are. Mrs. Parsons continues tranquilly interested in Yucatán and unmistakably uninterested in togetherness.

Just as I'm beginning to get aggressive notions about how we're going to spend the night if she expects me to give her the serape, she stands up, scuffs at a couple of hummocks and says, "I expect this is as good a place as any, isn't it, Mr. Fenton?"

With which she spreads out the raft bag for a pillow and lies down on her side in the dirt with exactly half the serape over her and the other corner folded neatly open. Her small back is toward me.

The demonstration is so convincing that I'm halfway under my share of serape before the preposterousness of it stops me.

"By the way. My name is Don."

"Oh, of course." Her voice is graciousness itself, "I'm Ruth."

I get in not quite touching her, and we lie there like two fish on a plate, exposed to the stars and smelling the smoke in the wind and feeling things underneath us. It is absolutely the most intimately awkward moment I've had in years.

The woman doesn't mean one thing to me, but the obtrusive recessiveness of her, the defiance of her little rump eight inches from my fly—for two pesos I'd have those shorts down and introduce myself. If I were twenty years younger. If I wasn't so bushed . . . But the twenty years and the exhaustion are there, and it comes to me wryly that Mrs. Ruth Parsons has judged things to a nicety. If I *were* twenty years younger, she wouldn't be here. Like the butterfish that float around a sated barracuda, only to vanish away the instant his intent changes, Mrs. Parsons knows her little shorts are safe. Those firmly filled little shorts, so close . . .

A warm nerve stirs in my groin—and just as it does I become aware of a silent emptiness beside me. Mrs. Parsons is imperceptibly inching away. Did my breathing change? Whatever, I'm perfectly sure that if my hand reached, she'd be elsewhere—probably announcing her intention to take a dip. The twenty years bring a chuckle to my throat, and I relax.

"Good night, Ruth."

"Good night, Don."

And believe it or not, we sleep, while the armadas of the wind roar overhead.

Light wakes me—a cold white glare.

My first thought is 'gator hunters. Best to manifest ourselves as *turistas* as fast as possible. I scramble up, noting that Ruth has dived under the bromel clump.

"*Quién estás? A secorro!* Help, *señores!*"

No answer except the light goes out, leaving me blind.

I yell some more in a couple of languages. It stays dark. There's a vague scrabbling, whistling sound somewhere in the burn-off. Liking everything less by the minute, I try a speech about our plane having crashed and we need help.

A very narrow pencil of light flicks over us and snaps off.

"Eh-ep," says a blurry voice and something metallic twitters. They for sure aren't locals. I'm getting unpleasant ideas.

"Yes, help!"

Something goes *crackle-crackle whish-whish,* and all sounds fade away.

"What the holy hell!" I stumble toward where they were.

"Look." Ruth whispers behind me. "Over by the ruin."

I look and catch a multiple flicker which winks out fast.

"A camp?"

And I take two more blind strides. My leg goes down through the crust, and a spike spears me just where you stick the knife in to unjoint a drumstick. By the pain that goes through my bladder I recognize that my trick kneecap has caught it.

For instant basket-case you can't beat kneecaps. First you discover your knee doesn't bend any more, so you try putting some weight on it, and a bayonet goes up your spine and unhinges your jaw. Little grains of gristle have got into the sensitive bearing surface. The knee tries to buckle and can't, and mercifully you fall down.

Ruth helps me back to the serape.

"What a fool, what a god-forgotten imbecile—"

"Not at all, Don. It was perfectly natural." We strike matches; her fingers push mine aside, exploring. "I think it's in place, but it's swelling fast. I'll lay a wet handkerchief on it. We'll have to wait for morning to check the cut. Were they poachers, do you think?"

"Probably," I lie. What I think they were is smugglers.

She comes back with a soaked bandanna and drapes it on. "We must have frightened them. That light . . . it seemed so bright."

"Some hunting party. People do crazy things around here."

"Perhaps they'll come back in the morning."

"Could be."

Ruth pulls up the wet serape, and we say goodnight again. Neither of us are mentioning how we're going to get back to the plane without help.

I lie staring south where Alpha Centauri is blinking in and out of the overcast and cursing myself for the sweet mess I've made. My first idea is giving way to an even less pleasing one.

Smuggling, around here, is a couple of guys in an outboard

meeting a shrimp boat by the reef. They don't light up the sky or have some kind of swamp buggy that goes whoosh. Plus a big camp . . . paramilitary-type equipment?

I've seen a report of Guevarista infiltrators operating on the British Honduran border, which is about a hundred kilometers—sixty miles—south of here. Right under those clouds. If that's what looked us over, I'll be more than happy if they don't come back . . .

I wake up in pelting rain, alone. My first move confirms that my leg is as expected—a giant misplaced erection bulging out of my shorts. I raise up painfully to see Ruth standing by the bromels, looking over the bay. Solid wet nimbus is pouring out of the south.

"No planes today."

"Oh, good morning, Don. Should we look at that cut now?"

"It's minimal." In fact the skin is hardly broken, and no deep puncture. Totally out of proportion to the havoc inside.

"Well, they have water to drink," Ruth says tranquilly. "Maybe those hunters will come back. I'll go see if we have a fish—that is, can I help you in any way, Don?"

Very tactful. I emit an ungracious negative, and she goes off about her private concerns.

They certainly are private, too; when I recover from my own sanitary efforts, she's still away. Finally I hear splashing.

"It's a big fish!" More splashing. Then she climbs up the bank with a three-pound mangrove snapper—and something else.

It isn't until after the messy work of filleting the fish that I begin to notice.

She's making a smudge of chaff and twigs to singe the fillets, small hands very quick, tension in that female upper lip. The rain has eased off for the moment; we're sluicing wet but warm enough. Ruth brings me my fish on a mangrove skewer and sits back on her heels with an odd breathy sigh.

"Aren't you joining me?"

"Oh, of course." She gets a strip and picks at it, saying quickly, "We either have too much salt or too little, don't we? I should fetch some brine." Her eyes are roving from nothing to noplace.

"Good thought." I hear another sigh and decide the girl scouts need an assist. "Your daughter mentioned you've come from Mérida. Have you seen much of Mexico?"

"Not really. Last year we went to Mazatlán and Cuerna-vaca . . . " She puts the fish down, frowning.

"And you're going to see Tikal. Going to Bonampak too?"

"No." Suddenly she jumps up brushing rain off her face. "I'll bring you some water, Don."

She ducks down the slide, and after a fair while comes back with a full bromel stalk.

"Thanks." She's standing above me, staring restlessly round the horizon.

"Ruth, I hate to say it, but those guys are not coming back and it's probably just as well. Whatever they were up to, we looked like trouble. The most they'll do is tell someone we're here. That'll take a day or two to get around, we'll be back at the plane by then."

"I'm sure you're right, Don." She wanders over to the smudge fire.

"And quit fretting about your daughter. She's a big girl."

"Oh, I'm sure Althea's all right . . . They have plenty of water now." Her fingers drum on her thigh. It's raining again.

"Come on, Ruth. Sit down. Tell me about Althea. Is she still in college?"

She gives that sighing little laugh and sits. "Althea got her degree last year. She's in computer programming."

"Good for her. And what about you, what do you do in GSA records?"

"I'm in Foreign Procurement Archives." She smiles mechanically, but her breathing is shallow. "It's very interesting."

"I know a Jack Wittig in Contracts, maybe you know him?"

It sounds pretty absurd, there in the 'gator slide.

"Oh, I've met Mr. Wittig. I'm sure he wouldn't remember me."

"Why not?"

"I'm not very memorable."

Her voice is factual. She's perfectly right, of course. Who was that woman, Mrs. Jannings, Janny, who coped with my per diem for years? Competent, agreeable, impersonal. She had a sick father or something. But dammit, Ruth is a lot younger and better-looking. Comparatively speaking.

"Maybe Mrs. Parsons doesn't want to be memorable."

She makes a vague sound, and I suddenly realize Ruth isn't listening to me at all. Her hands are clenched around her knees, she's staring inland at the ruin.

"Ruth. I tell you our friends with the light are in the next county by now. Forget it, we don't need them."

Her eyes come back to me as if she'd forgotten I was there, and she nods slowly. It seems to be too much effort to speak. Suddenly she cocks her head and jumps up again.

"I'll go look at the line, Don. I thought I heard something—" She's gone like a rabbit.

While she's away I try getting up onto my good leg and the staff. The pain is sickening; knees seem to have some kind of hot line to the stomach. I take a couple of hops to test whether the Demerol I have in my belt would get me walking. As I do so, Ruth comes up the bank with a fish flapping in her hands.

"Oh, no, Don! *No!*" She actually clasps the snapper to her breast.

"The water will take some of my weight. I'd like to give it a try."

"You mustn't!" Ruth says quite violently and instantly modulates down. "Look at the bay, Don. One can't see a thing."

I teeter there, tasting bile and looking at the mingled curtains of sun and rain driving across the water. She's right, thank god. Even with two good legs we could get into trouble out there.

"I guess one more night won't kill us."

I let her collapse me back onto the gritty plastic, and she positively bustles around, finding me a chunk to lean on, stretching the serape on both staffs to keep rain off me, bringing another drink, grubbing for dry tinder.

"I'll make us a real bonfire as soon as it lets up, Don. They'll see our smoke, they'll know we're all right. We just have to wait." Cheery smile. "Is there any way we can make you more comfortable?"

Holy Saint Sterculius: playing house in a mud puddle. For a fatuous moment I wonder if Mrs. Parsons has designs on me. And then she lets out another sigh and sinks back onto her heels with that listening look. Unconsciously her rump wiggles a little. My ear picks up the operative word: *wait.*

Ruth Parsons is waiting. In fact, she acts as if she's waiting so hard it's killing her. For what? For someone to get us out of here, what else? . . . But why was she so horrified when I got up to try to leave? Why all this tension?

My paranoia stirs. I grab it by the collar and start idly checking back. Up to when whoever it was showed up last night, Mrs. Parsons was, I guess, normal. Calm and sensible, anyway. Now she's humming like a high wire. And she seems to want to stay here and wait. Just as an intellectual pastime, why?

Could she have intended to come here? No way. Where she planned to be was Chetumal, which is on the border. Come to think, Chetumal is an odd way round to Tikal. Let's say the scenario was that she's meeting somebody in Chetumal. Some-body who's part of an organization. So now her contact in Chetumal knows she's overdue. And when those types appeared last night, something suggests to her that they're part of the same organization. And she hopes they'll put one and one together and come back for her?

"May I have the knife, Don? I'll clean the fish."

Rather slowly I pass the knife, kicking my subconscious. Such a decent ordinary little woman, a good girl scout. My trouble is that I've bumped into too many professional agilities under the careful stereotypes. *I'm not very memorable* . . .

What's in Foreign Procurement Archives? Wittig handles classified contracts. Lots of money stuff; foreign currency ne-gotiations, commodity price schedules, some industrial technol-ogy. Or—just as a hypothesis—it could be as simple as a wad of bills back in that modest beige Ventura, to be exchanged for a packet from say, Costa Rica. If she were a courier, they'd want to get at the plane. And then what about me and maybe Estéban? Even hypothetically, not good.

I watch her hacking at the fish, forehead knotted with effort, teeth in her lip. Mrs. Ruth Parsons of Bethesda, this thrumming, private woman. How crazy can I get? *They'll see our smoke* . . .

"Here's your knife, Don. I washed it. Does the leg hurt very badly?"

I blink away the fantasies and see a scared little woman in a mangrove swamp.

"Sit down, rest. You've been going all out."

She sits obediently, like a kid in a dentist chair.

"You're stewing about Althea. And she's probably worried about you. We'll get back tomorrow under our own steam, Ruth."

"Honestly I'm not worried at all, Don." The smile fades; she nibbles her lip, frowning out at the bay.

"You know, Ruth, you surprised me when you offered to come along. Not that I don't appreciate it. But I rather thought you'd be concerned about leaving Althea alone with our good pilot. Or was it only me?"

This gets her attention at last.

"I believe Captain Estéban is a very fine type of man."

The words surprise me a little. Isn't the correct line more like "I trust Althea," or even, indignantly, "Althea is a good girl?"

"He's a man. Althea seemed to think he was interesting."

She goes on staring at the bay. And then I notice her tongue flick out and lick that prehensile upper lip. There's a flush that isn't sunburn around her ears and throat too, and one hand is gently rubbing her thigh. What's she seeing, out there in the flats?

Oho.

Captain Estéban's mahogany arms clasping Miss Althea Parsons' pearly body. Captain Estéban's archaic nostrils snuffling in Miss Parsons' tender neck. Captain Estéban's copper buttocks pumping into Althea's creamy upturned bottom . . . The hammock, very bouncy. Mayas know all about it.

Well, well. So Mother Hen has her little quirks.

I feel fairly silly and more than a little irritated. *Now* I find out . . . But even vicarious lust has much to recommend it, here in the mud and rain. I settle back, recalling that Miss Althea the computer programmer had waved good-bye very composedly. Was she sending her mother to flounder across the bay with me so she can get programmed in Maya? The memory of Honduran mahogany logs drifting in and out of the opalescent sand comes to me. Just as I am about to suggest that Mrs. Parsons might care to share my rain shelter, she remarks serenely, "The Mayas seem to be a very fine type of people. I believe you said so to Althea."

The implications fall on me with the rain. *Type.* As in breeding, bloodline, sire. Am I supposed to have certified Estéban not only as a stud but as a genetic donor?

"Ruth, are you telling me you're prepared to accept a half-Indian grandchild?"

"Why, Don, that's up to Althea, you know."

Looking at the mother, I guess it is. Oh, for mahogany gonads.

Ruth has gone back to listening to the wind, but I'm not about to let her off that easy. Not after all that *noli me tangere* jazz.

"What will Althea's father think?"

Her face snaps around at me, genuinely startled.

"Althea's father?" Complicated semismile. "He won't mind."

"He'll accept it too, eh?" I see her shake her head as if a fly were bothering her, and add with a cripple's malice: "Your husband must be a very fine type of a man."

Ruth looks at me, pushing her wet hair back abruptly. I have the impression that mousy Mrs. Parsons is roaring out of control, but her voice is quiet.

"There isn't any Mr. Parsons, Don. There never was. Althea's father was a Danish medical student . . . I believe he has gained considerable prominence."

"Oh." Something warns me not to say I'm sorry. "You mean he doesn't know about Althea?"

"No." She smiles, her eyes bright and cuckoo.

"Seems like rather a rough deal for her."

"I grew up quite happily under the same circumstances."

Bang, I'm dead. Well, well, well. A mad image blooms in my mind: generations of solitary Parsons women selecting sires, making impregnation trips. Well, I hear the world is moving their way.

"I better look at the fish line."

She leaves. The glow fades. *No.* Just no, no contact. Goodbye, Captain Estéban. My leg is very uncomfortable. The hell with Mrs. Parsons' long-distance orgasm.

We don't talk much after that, which seems to suit Ruth. The odd day drags by. Squall after squall blows over us. Ruth singes up some more fillets, but the rain drowns her smudge; it seems to pour hardest just as the sun's about to show.

Finally she comes to sit under my sagging serape, but there's no warmth there. I doze, aware of her getting up now and then to look around. My subconscious notes that she's still twitchy. I tell my subconscious to knock it off.

Presently I wake up to find her penciling on the water-soaked pages of a little notepad.

"What's that, a shopping list for alligators?"

Automatic polite laugh. "Oh, just an address. In case we—I'm being silly, Don."

"Hey," I sit up, wincing, "Ruth, quit fretting. I mean it. We'll all be out of this soon. You'll have a great story to tell."

She doesn't look up. "Yes . . . I guess we will."

"Come on, we're doing fine. There isn't any real danger here, you know. Unless you're allergic to fish?"

Another good-little-girl laugh, but there's a shiver in it.

"Sometimes I think I'd like to go . . . really far away."

To keep her talking I say the first thing in my head.

"Tell me, Ruth. I'm curious why you would settle for that kind of lonely life, there in Washington? I mean, a woman like you—"

"Should get married?" She gives a shaky sigh, pushing the notebook back in her wet pocket.

"Why not? It's the normal source of companionship. Don't tell me you're trying to be some kind of professional man-hater."

"Lesbian, you mean?" Her laugh sounds better. "With my security rating? No, I'm not."

"Well, then. Whatever trauma you went through, these things don't last forever. You can't hate all men."

The smile is back. "Oh, there wasn't any trauma, Don, and I *don't* hate men. That would be as silly as—as hating the weather." She glances wryly at the blowing rain.

"I think you have a grudge. You're even spooky of me."

Smooth as a mouse bite she says, "I'd love to hear about your family, Don?"

Touché. I give her the edited version of how I don't have one any more, and she says she's sorry, how sad. And we chat about what a good life a single person really has, and how she and her friends enjoy plays and concerts and travel, and one of them is head cashier for Ringling Brothers, how about that?

But it's coming out jerkier and jerkier like a bad tape, with her eyes going round the horizon in the pauses and her face listening for something that isn't my voice. What's wrong with her? Well, what's wrong with any furtively unconventional middle-aged woman with an empty bed. And a security clearance. An old habit of mind remarks unkindly that Mrs. Parsons represents what is known as the classic penetration target.

"—so much more opportunity now." Her voice trails off.

"Hurrah for women's lib, eh?"

"The lib?" Impatiently she leans forward and tugs the serape straight. "Oh, that's doomed."

The apocalyptic word jars my attention.

"What do you mean, doomed?"

She glances at me as if I weren't hanging straight either and says vaguely, "Oh . . . "

"Come on, why doomed? Didn't they get that equal rights bill?"

Long hesitation. When she speaks again her voice is different.

"Women have no rights, Don, except what men allow us. Men are more aggressive and powerful, and they run the world. When the next real crisis upsets them, our so-called rights will vanish like—like that smoke. We'll be back where we always were: property. And whatever has gone wrong will be blamed on our freedom, like the fall of Rome was. You'll see."

Now all this is delivered in a gray tone of total conviction. The last time I heard that tone, the speaker was explaining why he had to keep his file drawers full of dead pigeons.

"Oh, come on. You and your friends are the backbone of the system; if you quit, the country would come to a screeching halt before lunch."

No answering smile.

"That's fantasy." Her voice is still quiet. "Women don't work that way. We're a—a toothless world." She looks around as if she wanted to stop talking. "What women do is survive. We live by ones and twos in the chinks of your world-machine."

"Sounds like a guerrilla operation." I'm not really joking, here in the 'gator den. In fact, I'm wondering if I spent too much thought on mahogany logs.

"Guerrillas have something to hope for." Suddenly she switches on a jolly smile. "Think of us as opossums, Don. Did you know there are opossums living all over? Even in New York City."

I smile back with my neck prickling. I thought I was the paranoid one.

"Men and women aren't different species, Ruth. Women do everything men do."

"Do they?" Our eyes meet, but she seems to be seeing ghosts between us in the rain. She mutters something that could be "My Lai" and looks away. "All the endless wars . . . " Her voice is a whisper. "All the huge authoritarian organizations for doing unreal things. Men live to struggle against each other; we're just part of the battlefields. It'll never change unless you change the whole world. I dream sometimes of—of going away—" She checks and abruptly changes voice. "Forgive me, Don, it's so stupid saying all this."

"Men hate wars too, Ruth," I say as gently as I can.

"I know." She shrugs and climbs to her feet. "But that's your problem, isn't it?"

End of communication. Mrs. Ruth Parsons isn't even living in the same world with me.

I watch her move around restlessly, head turning toward the ruins. Alienation like that can add up to dead pigeons, which would be GSA's problem. It could also lead to believing some joker who's promising to change the whole world. Which could just probably be my problem if one of them was over in that camp last night, where she keeps looking. *Guerrillas have something to hope for . . . ?*

Nonsense. I try another position and see that the sky seems to be clearing as the sun sets. The wind is quieting down at last too. Insane to think this little woman is acting out some fantasy in this swamp. But that equipment last night was no fantasy; if those lads have some connection with her, I'll be in the way. You couldn't find a handier spot to dispose of the body . . . Maybe some Guevarista is a fine type of man?

Absurd. Sure . . . The only thing more absurd would be to come through the wars and get myself terminated by a mad librarian's boyfriend on a fishing trip.

A fish flops in the stream below us. Ruth spins around so fast she hits the serape. "I better start the fire," she says, her eyes still on the plain and her head cocked, listening.

All right, let's test.

"Expecting company?"

It rocks her. She freezes, and her eyes come swiveling around at me like a film take captioned Fright. I can see her decide to smile.

"Oh, one never can tell!" She laughs weirdly, the eyes not changed. "I'll get the—the kindling." She fairly scuttles into the brush.

Nobody, paranoid or not, could call *that* a normal reaction.

Ruth Parsons is either psycho or she's expecting something to happen—and it has nothing to do with me; I scared her pissless.

Well, she could be nuts. And I could be wrong, but there are some mistakes you only make once.

Reluctantly I unzip my body belt, telling myself that if I think what I think, my only course is to take something for my leg and get as far as possible from Mrs. Ruth Parsons before whoever she's waiting for arrives.

In my belt also is a .32 caliber asset Ruth doesn't know about— and it's going to stay there. My longevity program leaves the shoot-outs to TV and stresses being somewhere else when the roof falls in. I can spend a perfectly safe and also perfectly horrible night out in one of those mangrove flats . . . Am I insane?

At this moment Ruth stands up and stares blatantly inland with her hand shading her eyes. Then she tucks something into her pocket, buttons up and tightens her belt.

That does it.

I dry-swallow two 100 mg tabs, which should get me ambulatory and still leave me wits to hide. Give it a few minutes. I make sure my compass and some hooks are in my own pocket and sit waiting while Ruth fusses with her smudge fire, sneaking looks away when she thinks I'm not watching.

The flat world around us is turning into an unearthly amber and violet light show as the first numbness sweeps into my leg. Ruth has crawled under the bromels for more dry stuff; I can see her foot. Okay. I reach for my staff.

Suddenly the foot jerks, and Ruth yells—or rather, her throat makes that *Uh-uh-hhh* that means pure horror. The foot disappears in a rattle of bromel stalks.

I lunge upright on the crutch and look over the bank at a frozen scene.

Ruth is crouching sideways on the ledge, clutching her stomach. They are about a yard below, floating on the river in a skiff. While I was making up my stupid mind, her friends have glided right under my ass. There are three of them.

They are tall and white. I try to see them as men in some kind of white jumpsuits. The one nearest the bank is stretching out a long white arm toward Ruth. She jerks and scuttles further away.

The arm stretches after her. It stretches and stretches. It stretches two yards and stays hanging in the air. Small black things are wiggling from its tip.

I look where their faces should be and see black hollow dishes with vertical stripes. The stripes move slowly . . .

There is no more possibility of their being human—or anything else I've ever seen. What has Ruth conjured up?

The scene is totally silent. I blink, blink—this cannot be real. The two in the far end of the skiff are writhing those arms around an apparatus on a tripod. A weapon? Suddenly I hear the same blurry voice I heard in the night.

"Guh-give," it groans. "G-give . . ."

Dear god, it's real, whatever it is. I'm terrified. My mind is trying not to form a word.

And Ruth—Jesus, of course—Ruth is terrified too; she's edging along the bank away from them, gaping at the monsters in the skiff, who are obviously nobody's friends. She's hugging something to her body. Why doesn't she get over the bank and circle back behind me?

"G-g-give." That wheeze is coming from the tripod. "Pee-eeze give." The skiff is moving upstream below Ruth, following her. The arm undulates out at her again, its black digits looping. Ruth scrambles to the top of the bank.

"Ruth!" My voice cracks. "Ruth, get over here behind me!"

She doesn't look at me, only keeps sidling farther away. My terror detonates into anger.

"Come back here!" With my free hand I'm working the .32 out of my belt. The sun has gone down.

She doesn't turn but straightens up warily, still hugging the thing. I see her mouth working. Is she actually trying to *talk* to them?

"Please . . ." She swallows. "Please speak to me. I need your help."

"RUTH!!"

At this moment the nearest white monster whips into a great S-curve and sails right onto the bank at her, eight feet of snowy rippling horror.

And I shoot Ruth.

I don't know that for a minute—I've yanked the gun up so fast that my staff slips and dumps me as I fire. I stagger up, hearing Ruth scream "No! No! No!"

The creature is back down by his boat, and Ruth is still farther away, clutching herself. Blood is running down her elbow.

"Stop it, Don! They aren't attacking you!"

"For god's sake! Don't be a fool, I can't help you if you won't get away from them!"

No reply. Nobody moves. No sound except the drone of a jet passing far above. In the darkening stream below me the three white figures shift uneasily; I get the impression of radar dishes focusing. The word spells itself in my head: *Aliens.*

Extraterrestrials.

What do I do, call the President? Capture them single-handed with my peashooter? . . . I'm alone in the arse end of nowhere with one leg and my brain cuddled in meperidine hydrochloride.

"Prrr-eese," their machine blurs again. "Wa-wat hep . . ."

"Our plane fell down," Ruth says in a very distinct, eerie voice. She points up at the jet, out towards the bay. "My—my child is there. Please take us *there* in your boat."

Dear god. While she's gesturing, I get a look at the thing she's hugging in her wounded arm. It's metallic, like a big glimmering distributor head. What—?

Wait a minute. This morning: when she was gone so long, she could have found that thing. Something they left behind. Or dropped. And she hid it, not telling me. That's why she kept going under that bromel clump—she was peeking at it. Waiting. And the owners came back and caught her. They want it. She's trying to bargain, by god.

"—Water," Ruth is pointing again. "Take us. Me. And him."

The black faces turn toward me, blind and horrible. Later on I may be grateful for that "us." Not now.

"Throw your gun away, Don. They'll take us back." Her voice is weak.

"Like hell I will. You—who are you? What are you doing here?"

"Oh god, does it matter? He's frightened," she cries to them. "Can you understand?"

She's as alien as they, there in the twilight. The beings in the skiff are twittering among themselves. Their box starts to moan. "Ss-stu-dens," I make out. "S-stu-ding . . . not—huh-arm-ing . . . w-we . . . buh . . . " It fades into garble and then says "G-give . . . we . . . g-go . . ."

Peace-loving cultural-exchange students—on the interstellar level now. Oh, no.

"Bring that thing here, Ruth—right now!"

But she's starting down the bank toward them saying, "Take me."

"Wait! You need a tourniquet on that arm."

"I know. Please put the gun down, Don."

She's actually at the skiff, right by them. They aren't moving.

"Jesus Christ." Slowly, reluctantly, I drop the .32. When I start down the slide, I find I'm floating; adrenaline and Demerol are a bad mix.

The skiff comes gliding toward me, Ruth in the bow clutching the thing and her arm. The aliens stay in the stern behind their tripod, away from me. I note the skiff is camouflaged tan and green. The world around us is deep shadowy blue.

"Don, bring the water bag!"

As I'm dragging down the plastic bag, it occurs to me that Ruth really is cracking up, the water isn't needed now. But my own brain seems to have gone into overload. All I can focus on is a long white rubbery arm with black worms clutching the far end of the orange tube, helping me fill it. This isn't happening.

"Can you get in, Don?" As I hoist my numb legs up, two long white pipes reach for me. *No you don't.* I kick and tumble in beside Ruth. She moves away.

A creaky hum starts up, it's coming from a wedge in the center of the skiff. And we're in motion, sliding toward dark mangrove files.

I stare mindlessly at the wedge. Alien technological secrets? I can't see any, the power source is under that triangular cover, about two feet long. The gadgets on the tripod are equally cryptic, except that one has a big lens. Their light?

As we hit the open bay, the hum rises and we start planing faster and faster still. Thirty knots? Hard to judge in the dark. Their hull seems to be a modified trihedral much like ours, with a remarkable absence of slap. Say twenty-two feet. Schemes of capturing it swirl in my mind. I'll need Estéban.

Suddenly a huge flood of white light fans out over us from the tripod, blotting out the aliens in the stern. I see Ruth pulling at a belt around her arm still hugging the gizmo.

"I'll tie that for you."

"It's all right."

The alien device is twinkling or phosphorescing slightly. I lean over to look, whispering, "Give that to me, I'll pass it to Estéban."

"No!" She scoots away, almost over the side. "It's theirs, they need it!"

"What? Are you crazy?" I'm so taken aback by this idiocy I literally stammer. "We have to, we—"

"They haven't hurt us. I'm sure they could." Her eyes are watching me with feral intensity; in the light her face has a lunatic look. Numb as I am, I realize that the wretched woman is poised to throw herself over the side if I move. With the alien thing.

"I think they're gentle," she mutters.

"For Christ's sake, Ruth, they're *aliens!*"

"I'm used to it," she says absently. "There's the island! Stop! Stop here!"

The skiff slows, turning. A mound of foliage is tiny in the light. Metal glints—the plane.

"Althea! Althea! Are you all right?"

Yells, movement on the plane. The water is high, we're floating over the bar. The aliens are keeping us in the lead with the light hiding them. I see one pale figure splashing toward us and a dark one behind, coming more slowly. Estéban must be puzzled by that light.

"Mr. Fenton is hurt, Althea. These people brought us back with the water. Are you all right?"

"A-okay." Althea flounders up, peering excitedly. "You all right? Whew, that light!" Automatically I start handing her the idiotic water bag.

"Leave that for the captain," Ruth says sharply. "Althea, can you climb in the boat? Quickly, it's important."

"Coming."

"No, no!" I protest, but the skiff tilts as Althea swarms in. The aliens twitter, and their voice box starts groaning. "Gu-give . . . now . . . give . . . "

"*Que llega?*" Estéban's face appears beside me, squinting fiercely into the light.

"Grab it, get it from her—that thing she has—" but Ruth's voice rides over mine. "Captain, lift Mr. Fenton out of the boat. He's hurt his leg. Hurry, please."

"Goddamn it, wait!" I shout, but an arm has grabbed my middle. When a Maya boosts you, you go. I hear Althea saying, "Mother, your arm!" and fall onto Estéban. We stagger around in water up to my waist; I can't feel my feet at all.

When I get steady, the boat is yards away. The two women are head-to-head, murmuring.

"Get them!" I tug loose from Estéban and flounder forward. Ruth stands up in the boat facing the invisible aliens.

"Take us with you. Please. We want to go with you, away from here."

"Ruth! Estéban, get that boat!" I lunge and lose my feet again. The aliens are chirruping madly behind their light.

"Please take us. We don't mind what your planet is like; we'll learn—we'll do anything! We won't cause any trouble. Please. Oh *please.*" The skiff is drifting farther away.

"Ruth! Althea! Are you crazy? Wait—" But I can only shuffle nightmarelike in the ooze, hearing that damn voice box wheeze, "N-not come . . . more . . . not come . . . " Althea's face turns to it, open-mouthed grin.

"Yes, we understand," Ruth cries. "We don't want to come back. Please take us with you!"

I shout and Estéban splashes past me shouting too, something about radio.

"Yes-s-s" groans the voice.

Ruth sits down suddenly, clutching Althea. At that moment
Estéban grabs the edge of the skiff beside her.

"Hold them, Estéban! Don't let her go."

He gives me one slit-eyed glance over his shoulder, and I
recognize his total uninvolvement. He's had a good look at that
camouflage paint and the absence of fishing gear. I make a
desperate rush and slip again. When I come up Ruth is saying,
"We're going with these people, Captain. Please take your money
out of my purse, it's in the plane. And give this to Mr. Fenton."

She passes him something small; the notebook. He takes it
slowly.

"Estéban! No!"

He has released the skiff.

"Thank you so much," Ruth says as they float apart. Her voice
is shaky; she raises it. "There won't be any trouble, Don. Please
send this cable. It's to a friend of mine, she'll take care of
everything." Then she adds the craziest touch of the entire
night. "She's a grand person; she's director of nursing training
at N.I.H."

As the skiff drifts, I hear Althea add something that sounds
like "Right on."

Sweet Jesus . . . Next minute the humming has started; the
light is receding fast. The last I see of Mrs. Ruth Parsons and
Miss Althea Parsons is two small shadows against that light, like
two opossums. The light snaps off, the hum deepens—and
they're going, going, gone away.

In the dark water beside me Estéban is instructing everybody
in general to *chingarse* themselves.

"Friends, or something," I tell him lamely. "She seemed to
want to go with them."

He is pointedly silent, hauling me back to the plane. He knows
what could be around here better than I do, and Mayas have
their own longevity program. His condition seems improved. As
we get in I notice the hammock has been repositioned.

In the night—of which I remember little—the wind changes.
And at seven thirty next morning a Cessna buzzes the sandbar
under cloudless skies.

By noon we're back in Cozumel, Captain Estéban accepts his
fees and departs laconically for his insurance wars. I leave the

Parsons' bags with the Caribe agent, who couldn't care less. The cable goes to a Mrs. Priscilla Hayes Smith, also of Bethesda. I take myself to a medico and by three PM I'm sitting on the Cabañas terrace with a fat leg and a double margharita, trying to believe the whole thing.

The cable said, *Althea and I taking extraordinary opportunity for travel. Gone several years. Please take charge our affairs. Love, Ruth.*

She'd written it that afternoon, you understand.

I order another double, wishing to hell I'd gotten a good look at that gizmo. Did it have a label. Made by Betelgeusians? No matter how weird it was, *how* could a person be crazy enough to imagine—?

Not only that but to hope, to plan? *If I could only go away . . .* That's what she was doing, all day. Waiting, hoping, figuring how to get Althea. To go sight unseen to an alien world . . .

With the third margharita I try a joke about alienated women, but my heart's not in it. And I'm certain there won't be any bother, any trouble at all. Two human women, one of them possibly pregnant, have departed for, I guess, the stars; and the fabric of society will never show a ripple. I brood: do all Mrs. Parsons' friends hold themselves in readiness for any eventuality, including leaving Earth? And will Mrs. Parsons somehow one day contrive to send for Mrs. Priscilla Hayes Smith, that grand person?

I can only send for another cold one, musing on Althea. What suns will Captain Estéban's sloe-eyed offspring, if any, look upon? "Get in, Althea, we're taking off for Orion." "A-okay, Mother." Is that some system of upbringing? *We survive by ones and twos in the chinks of your world-machine . . . I'm used to aliens . . .* She'd meant every word. Insane. How could a woman choose to live among unknown monsters, to say good-bye to her home, her world?

As the margharitas take hold, the whole mad scenario melts down to the image of those two small shapes sitting side by side in the receding alien glare.

Two of our opossums are missing.

Sherley Anne Williams

The Lawd Don't Like Ugly
1974

*Writer, teacher, and critic Sherley Anne Williams (b. 1944) has published three books.
Her first,* Give Birth to Brightness *(1972), a volume of literary analysis, includes her
definition of the black aesthetic and explores the notion of the hero in the work of Amiri
Baraka, James Baldwin, and Ernest Gaines. Her two volumes of poetry are* The
Peacock Poems *(1976), a National Book Award nominee, and* Someone Sweet Angel
Chile *(1982). She has also published essays on black poetry and black music, including "The Blues Roots of Contemporary Afro-American Poetry" (*Massachusetts Review,
*Autumn 1977), in which she defines her own literary goal as "the re-creation of a new
tradition built on a synthesis of black oral traditions and Western literate forms." It is
precisely that goal—the synthesis between oral and written traditions—that is one of the
vitalizing stylistic characteristics of most of the best short stories written by women. In
particular, this characteristic has distinguished the work of ethnic writers, such as
Williams in the black tradition, and, earlier, Fannie Hurst in the Yiddish tradition.*

"The Lawd Don't Like Ugly" was first published in New Letters, *in December
1974. Two other stories by Williams have appeared: "Tell Martha Not to Moan," first
published in* Massachusetts Review *in 1968 has been reprinted in* The Black
Woman: An Anthology, *edited and with an introduction by Toni Cade (Bambara)
(1970); and "Meditation on History" in* Midnight Birds *is preceded by a short but
moving and informative autobiographical essay. A lengthy interview of Williams is
included in Claudia Tate's 1983 volume,* Black Women Writers at Work *(New York:
Crossroads Press).*

*Williams was born in Bakersfield, California, into a family of agricultural workers
who settled out of the migrant stream in Fresno. Only fifteen when her mother died,
Williams came under the charge of her older, divorced sister, who struggled to care for
her own child as well, while finishing high school and working as a maid and cook for*

a white family. Ill health finally forced the family onto welfare. Under the guidance and urging of her sister and other women in their community, Williams prepared for a career as a teacher, completing a B.A. at California State University at Fresno in 1966 and an M.A. in 1972 at Brown University. Realizing that she preferred creating literature to analyzing the literature of others, she left her Ph.D. program to teach and write. She is now a professor of literature and department head at the University of California, San Diego. She is the mother of one son.

Many of William's poems testify to her love and respect for the community of black women, struggling with racism, sexism, classism, poverty, and the welfare system, struggling to bring up their children to survive not just materially, but emotionally and spiritually. In "you were never miss brown to me" from Someone Sweet Angel Chile, *she offers tribute*

> to the women of that time,
> the mothers of friends, the friends,
> of my mother, mamma
> herself . . .
> who taught what it is to be grown.

"The Lawd Don't Like Ugly," a surrogate-mother story, presents a version of the mother-daughter alliance in which the mother's lesson to her daughter about the conditions for survival of women in the patriarchy reveals the same pessimism that characterizes Tiptree's vision in "The Women Men Don't See." In both stories, we see the absolute necessity for women to achieve economic and emotional independence. The irony of Williams's story lies in the apparent brutality resulting from Miss Ead's tender regard for the girl becoming a woman. But perhaps by making clear to Queenie the essential connection between economics and sex, Queenie's own innocence and budding self-love are protected.

That *must* be Vista Park—and it actually looked good. Q.T. almost choked on her excitement as she leaned over the side of the old pick-up truck and watched the group of buildings that seemed to cover the city block grow larger, more distinct as the truck neared them. She had been waiting for this first glimpse ever since they turned off the highway back by the park. "There it is," she said and poked Sudy Mae. Sudy Mae lay in the bottom of the truck, her head resting against a bundle of clothes, a true confession magazine held close to her face; she didn't look up. Candy and Ryce were seated with their backs to the truck cab. Ryce looked over at Q.T. and smiled.

"Well," Ryce said, turning to Candy, "whatever it is, it couldn't be no worse than Salinas."

Candy laughed. "Salinas wa'n't that bad—once you got out them damn fields."

Ryce was laughing harder. "Girl—"

But Q.T. stopped listening. Bryant swung the truck past the front row of buildings and pulled up on the side street beside the third row of buildings. Bryant and Mo-dear got out and stood a moment before going up the walk toward the door at the near end of the building.

Ryce stood up. "Let's go see what this mess looks like."

Candy didn't move. "Girl, ain't nothing in that house interest me. I want to see what's happenin back there on that road we come down."

"Well, it sho don't look like nothing ever go on here."

"That's wh—"

"Yo'all come on, start unloadin," Bryant called as he came down the walk.

From her perch on a bundle of bedding, Q.T. looked at the buildings, ignoring Bryant's impatient call to get a move on herself. This was Vista Park.

The night before, in Salinas, she had lain on the pallet she shared with Sudy Mae trying to picture the housing project in her mind. But she had never imagined anything like this, not the way the housing project sprawled over the city block in regulation ugliness. The buildings stood in lackluster formation, row after row of them all alike, like barracks or a fort. Each long building had four sets of steps leading up to four separate doors; two screened windows flanked each door and each window, each door looked across a small plot of grass, a sidewalk, to a repetition of the plot of grass and the windows and doors that faced them. Front to front and back to back, the long buildings seemed to march before her eyes.

There were trees, just as Bryant had told them, a sycamore down toward the middle of this row of buildings and a couple of smaller grey green olive trees and grass, some of it thick and green. And even though Bryant hadn't said a thing about the flaked and peeling green paint that trimmed the cream colored houses—which were scarred and dirty—Q.T. lived there a long time before she noticed that for herself. She had never seen so many buildings alike. Front to front and back to back like the game the kids played around the school grounds. Front to front, they would hold hands and go around in pairs, chanting "front to front and back to back" or "hey, hey, get out of my way; I just got back and I'm here to stay," and she always wanted to play, to have someone hold her hand—which was really like saying they were friends—and skip around the grounds swinging arms and turning bodies to show everyone that she could be with someone, too. Back to back and front to front. That's what the buildings reminded her of.

Look like, Q.T. thought, look like every row telling the one behind it, 'kiss my ass, kiss my natural ass.' But it wasn't so much that Vista Park didn't look as good as it had in her mind ever since Bryant had told them about the government housing project—and Q.T. had hung on his every word. And it would take a lot to be worse than the tents and one-room shacks of the labor camps they had lived in—It was, well, if the houses were telling each other to kiss ass, what would they tell her?

Where were the kids Bryant had told them about, the ones who were supposed to be her friends? It took so much time to make friends, so much time. And there had never been time before, following the crops the way they had when Daddy was alive or the time they had spent in Lanare after Daddy died. It had been a new experience for her living in one place for longer than it took to harvest a crop. And in some ways it had been good, living on what Mo-dear called that ol wore out piece-a ground (to which Mamma had always replied that it had been good enough to feed her and ten other peoples in its time and Mo-dear didn't seem to find it too 'wore out' to come back to every time she needed something), feeding the chickens and slopping the two hogs that they would slaughter come fall, and helping Great-Uncle Jason with the other chores around the small truck farm. And if Q.T. hated school, well, she managed to miss the bus often enough and slip back into the fields to help Uncle. He didn't ask questions and he didn't tell Mamma—who would have taken a switch at her for playing truant—just showed her what to do and explained that she had been helping when Mamma asked why her clothes were so dirty. And Sudy Mae never seemed to care one way or another about whether Q.T. was with her on the bus.

Q.T. never told Uncle about the black kids who called her boy and shorthair. She didn't know what to tell him about that. It had never happened before—the black kids in the labor camps always stuck together, especially in any school, sometimes banding together to fight the Mexicans or banding together with the Mexicans to fight the white kids. But people really lived in Lanare. They didn't just stay there until the work gave out, then move on to another place where there was more work. She thought it had to be that, that staying in one place that made the kids in Lanare so different from the ones she'd known before. But knowing there was a difference, even being able to say to herself, this is the reason for the difference, didn't provide her with the key that would make her one of them. She was the girl with the funny name and short hair, the "boy." They had made up things about her, saying she stank—and how could that be true when Mamma took down the big zinc wash tub every Saturday night, heated water on the new, yellow and green gas stove and made her and Sudy Mae (and Ryce and Candy too, if they were around) strip and bathe. She watched you as you lathered up the large cake of yellow laundry soap muttering about how Mo-dear wasn't teaching these kids a thing that would ever be worth knowing. Then, for good measure, Mamma herself would scrub your back and wash your ears, and, she made you wash between your legs each morning. They made fun of her because she wore levis with patches and Mamma made her stuff her dress tails in the pants because she didn't think blouses provided sufficient protection against the cold; they laughed at her name, saying "what is a Q.T.?," "who ever heard of a Q.T.?" "you must be a boy cause only boys ain't no first name." A couple of times she started to ask Sudy Mae if the kids talked about her, too, but she was too embarrassed; she wanted at least to ask what she should do about it. Sudy Mae was already twelve and twelve must make you know *some*thing, not as much as Candy and Ryce (but they were always laughing and talking between themselves, shutting everybody else out), but something. She could never ask, though; she was always afraid that Sudy Mae would laugh at her, too.

They stayed in Lanare until late March when Bryant had come along with all his promises and seemingly endless money and Mo-dear had packed up Q.T. and the other girls and followed Bryant to Salinas. Q.T. had wanted to stay with Mamma—Mamma worked you hard but she never got evil the way Mo-dear could—but Mo-dear had said they needed her help in the fields. And when she asked Mamma if she could stay on in Lanare, Mamma had sighed, "I'm yo grandmother, true enough, but Ryce Ann yo mother and you got to do what she say do."

"Q.T." That was Mo-dear, and Q.T. moved, scrambling over the heaped up bundles and boxes. Vista Park was home.

Shoulda knowed, she told herself as she carried a load of bedding up the rickety wooden steps, I shoulda knowed Bryant wa'n't doin nothing but lyin bout this town. He ain't done nothin but lie since the first day Mo-dear brung him home. Tellin us what a good time we have in Salinas. 'Pickin strawberries ain't nothin like cutting grapes.' Well, he wa'n't lyin bout that, she thought grimly. At least when you cut grapes, you were on your knees, not all bent over and stooped down as you had to be to pick strawberries. Fun, humph, and likin to eat strawberries ain't got nothing to do with likin to pick em. And after he talk all his talk, he want come tickle you and play with you, knowin all the time he ain't gon be doin nothin. Just be layin up drinking his wine while Mo-dear and us be workin.

The unloading was finished quickly—there really wasn't much to unload, clothes, bedding, Ryce's and Candy's cots, the big iron bedstead that supported Mo-dear's mattress and took up most of the space in the small bedroom, the faded sway back sofa couch that Bryant had picked up in Salinas for ten dollars which Q.T. and Sudy Mae would let down at night and make into a bed, and the dinette table that Mamma had given them. A stove and refrigerator came with the apartment and Mo-dear had promised to buy them chests of drawers as soon as grape-cutting started in another month or so. Q.T. went into the older girls' bedroom; they had already left but Sudy Mae lay on one of the cots reading her magazine. Q.T. went to the closet, a recess in the wall with a road across the front of it for hanging a curtain, and began to paw through the bundles on the floor.

"What you lookin for?" Sudy Mae asked.

"My clothes."

"Was they wrapped in that blue print?"

"Yeah."

"Over there beside that other cot. On the other side," she added when Q.T. hesitated. "And you betta put the community pile back in that closet fo Ryce see it and have a fit."

Q.T. began piling the clothes back in the closet. The pile contained some of everything, blouses, skirts, slips, even rags, all of it given to them by various people in various places, most of which they all wore at one time or another as night gowns or slop-around clothes but did not care to claim as their own; some of which none of them would ever wear but which they carted around with them on the chance that they might or that they might be able to pass an item on to someone else who could use it. Q.T. had her own personal bundle of clothing—all of them did—culled from the community pile but also a few items, like the pair of white panties with 'Sunday' embroidered across the front in red thread that Mamma had given her for Christmas, that had never belonged to anyone but her.

Q.T. opened the bundle and pulled out a yellow flowered dress with short puffed sleeves edged with small ruffles. The dress skirt was full and would flare out around her legs. Long thick sashes tied in the back and nipped the fitted bodice in at the waistline. The dress had been too large in the top, the waist dropping below her own waist line and the sleeve ruffles down to her elbows when Mamma give it to her on her last birthday. One of the white women she sometimes worked for had given it to Mamma. Mamma had been reluctant to alter it because she was afraid that when it was let out again, the alterations would show in the fine cotton material. Q.T. had agreed that it was best to wait until she grew into it. It was the prettiest dress she had ever owned and she wanted nothing to mar it.

She took the dress and the panties into the bathroom and closed the door. She had seen flush toilets in schools and big department stores but never in a house and she stared at it a moment. She had bragged to the other kids at the camp in Salinas about the house where Bryant was taking them. They had listened in envy and some disbelief to talk about the trees and swings and hot and cold running water. She'd only half believed the part about the inside flush toilet herself. She turned on both faucets on the sink and passed her hand under the streams of water, drawing it back quickly from the one on the left. It was hot. She looked at the open stall with a faucet hung overhead. The big zinc wash tub was set in the bottom of the stall. Well, least we ain't got to be totin water from the faucet to the tub, she thought. Then she grinned. This was the best they'd ever had it. She shimmied out of her baggy pedal pushers and over large tee shirt. No one could laugh at her, laugh at her name—not and they were doing this good. And she would just tell them her name, say it was Quotha. Quotha, after her daddy's second cousin. The name always seemed to stick in her throat when she tried to tell people that it was hers. But it wasn't exactly a lie. Daddy had had a second cousin named Quotha. Q.T. had seen a picture of her, a bright-skinned woman with long wavy hair, that was good, not straightened. And wasn't Candy, Candence after Daddy's Mamma, Ryce named after Mo-dear and Sudy Mae, Susan after Mamma. Maybe they had meant to name her Quotha and Mo-dear had been mad or something and decided not to do it out of spite. Mo-dear was always talking about Daddy's family, calling them shit-colored niggas who thought they were better than anybody else. And maybe they were; Q.T. had never seen any of them. But it was really hard not to wish that some of that long wavy hair and shit-color had rubbed off on her along with the name Quotha.

"Quotha," she whispered to herself. "Quotha. My name Quotha."

She brushed her hair with a little water and grease, trying to water-wave it, and stood on tip tow so that she could see herself in the small mirror that hung over the sink. She really did not know if her face were pretty, but she wanted it to be. The cute girls were the ones with the friends. She had almost given up hoping that her hair would grow, or that it would somehow turn out to be good and had settled for wanting to be cute. And it was not so much to look a certain way, cute could be anything, look at Alice Cunning ham and Fay: one no lighter than she herself was, the other almost as black as the ace of spades and people called them cute, always wanted to play with them. And Alice sweated on her nose which meant she was mean. So, if people just *thought* she was cute, then she would be. They would treat her the same way they treated cute girls—like she was somebody, like she belonged to someone.

She pulled off the dirty underpants—almost bloomers, really; they were probably big enough for Mo-dear—all pulled on the white ones. They fitted nicely and she wagged her butt a little so that she could feel the cool rayon slide against her skin. She was Quotha Jean and Quotha Jean was pretty. She smiled at the mirror, a large grin showing her pinky brown gums and even white teeth. Quotha Jean was pretty.

She looked down at herself, smiling, posing, a favorite game she played when she could get by herself in front of the long mirror on Mamma's dresser. She could see the mound of her breasts, the dark brown rosette around the nipple seemed huge and she paused, remembering Miss Margarite in Salinas who'd told Mo-dear laughingly that she'd better get a bra for Q.T. Mamma had laughed, "This girl only ten years old, won't be eleven til way off in November—knowin I ain't never gon fo'git 19 and forty-four—but I put a bra on her and next thing you know I got mo little pissy tail boys hangin round her, jes like they be round Ryce and Candy. She betta be studying at how Sudy Mae go on, steadda worryin bout some bra round her chest."

It was a frightening conversation. When your breasts hung down, you had babies and she didn't even have a boyfriend to tease her or try to kiss her. The boys did pat her on the behind; she felt their touches were somehow connected with her growing breasts. They didn't do it around the teachers or other grownups and she knew the behind touching was on the way to doing something nasty, going in the bushes. But she knew that if having big breasts meant that she was included in a game the other kids played then she would take the touching, not go on in the bushes because if you did that people talked bad about you, but still brag about someone's wanting her to go.

She was reaching for the yellow dress when the door opened and Bryant came in. "Oh, 'cuse m— What you doin in here?" He came toward her slowly. "Getting to be a regular little lady, ain't you?" and he touched her breast lightly with one finger.

"I-I-I- was just lookin at my tooth, it loose." She grabbed her dress and ran around him and out the door.

After dressing, she stood on the back stoop, tugging at the skirt of her dress; it was too short. The lines of her body were still lost in baby fat. This and her budding bust line made the bodice of her dress too tight. She ignored this fact for a moment as she surveyed the narrow space between the two rows of apartment units. A few patches of scorched grass dotted the ground. Farther down to the left, there were some swings and a slide. Several children were playing down there and Q.T. could plainly hear their shouts and laughter.

She fidgeted, trying to gather enough courage to join the children. She touched the dress, thinking how pretty it was. They would think it pretty. "Pretty dress," they'd say. Then, "What yo name?" "Quotha Jean? That's a pretty name." And it wouldn't be long before they'd say, "Let's play on the swings; I push you." The yellow dress would billow as she swung high in the air and her laughter would mingle with that of the other children. Yeah, it was all there; it was all true. She tugged once more at the dress and was rewarded with a dull plopping sound as two buttons came off. "Shoot, shoot, shoot. Ain't nothing going right." But the vision of herself in the yellow dress beckoned to her and she plunged off the porch and ran down to where the other children were playing.

"Hi." There were three girls, all of them about her own age, and two boys who seemed a little older. The girls whore shorts and thin cotton tops. She felt suddenly uncomfortable in her torn dress that was already becoming stained with sweat.

"What yo name?" demanded the bigger of the three girls.

The bright-skinned girl with long thick hair giggled behind her hands. "I know what her name. Her name, 'Boy.'"

She could feel the prickly sweat in her armpits. It was always, always like this. Boy or—

"It ain't. It Q.T." And she had said it herself. Oh, shoot, shoot, shoot, *shoot.*

"Q.T.? That ain't no girl's name."

"That's cause she a boy."

They were talking so fast that she couldn't tell who was saying what, but she answered them all.

"I ain't. I ain't."

"Yes you is."

"Then what them letters stand for?"

"They stand for Queer Kinks."

"You can't even spell, Hattie Lee." But the girl was laughing. "How bout, Tiny Queers, cause she gots tiny hair."

Q.T. wanted to cry. "It's Quotha. Quotha Jean."

"Quotha," The little bright one was laughing so hard she could barely stand up. "Quotha Jean? You mean Quotha Boy."

Q.T. looked at them. They had formed a semi-circle around her, the boys standing a little to one side. They were grinning at her. They ain't gon never be my friends, she thought. "Go to hell, you ole black niggas," she screamed, "you ol shit-ass, you ol—"

"You bet'not be callin no black niggas," the bigger girl charged.

"Fight. Fight." Q.T. heard the boy's words dimly. She was lost in an effort first to keep her footing and then, after she had been knocked down, to keep the arms and legs out of her stomach. She had a hold on someone's hair while someone else pounded her on the back. The yellow dress was coming apart at the waistline.

"What goin on here? I declare, you chi'ren just gets worse and worse. Always fightin. Ain't yo mamma done told you the lawd don't like ugly?" Q.T. felt the weight being lifted from her and she rolled over, pulling her dress down.

"She started it, Miss Ead." The bright girl pointed a trembling finger at Q.T. and began to cry. "She called us niggas and we didn't even do nothin to her and then she started fightin all of us."

"You just be quiet, now, Hattie Lee. I knows what been goin on here. Now yo'all betta git on home fo I tells yo Mammas." The three girls scrambled up; the boys had already gone. As soon as she saw them disappear around the corner, Q.T. began to cry.

"Well, baby. Don't cry. Miss Ead knows all bout it." She hugged Q.T. to a bosom that smelled of Lifebuoy and Cashmere Bouquet.

"You just moved in, huh? Yeah, I thought that truck I saw stopped round here somewheres. Well, you sho got a fine welcome to the neighborhood, didn't you?"

"They always makin fun of my hair, my name—"

"And what's that, baby?"

"Ain't nothin but Q.T., just only Q.T. and it don't stand for nothin." It was almost like being with Mamma again, to have this woman hold her, except that she would never have fun crying to Mamma. Mamma said you

had to be strong and if all it took to make you cry was some little old nothing words, and spoken by kids at that, then she would spend many a day
boo-hooing. There would always be someone who would try to bring you
down or put you low, but they couldn't put you as low as you put yourself
by listening to them. Mamma just didn't seem to believe that what people
said could hurt you so bad, could put you so low you couldn't get up by
yourself. The only way for it not to hurt, not to put you low was for them
not to say it; but Q.T. hadn't learned how to stop them.

"Well, now you know, 'Q' stand for Queen." The woman held Q.T.
away from her. "You a big girl," she said forcing Q.T. to look at her, "big
enough to know that. So it ain't nothin wrong with having a 'Q' in yo
name." She held her close once more. "And 'T' is fo tall and fo true and fo
a lotta good thangs. So I wouldn't even let that worry me. And," she said,
passing a hand over Q.T.'s nubby head, "you come on over my house
tomorrow and I help you with this. I gots a growin hand; done growed
lottsa people hair—man and woman, child and grownup. I uses a special
brush and comb. You come on over tomorrow evening, bout seven." Q.T.
settled herself against the big golden woman as her voice crooned on and
on and Miss Ead's hair brushed softly against her tear-stained cheek.

Q.T. skipped along, her neatly braided head bobbing in time to the
tune she heard in her mind. "Goin down to Miss Ead's, going down to
Miss Ead's. Gon get some hair on this head, when I goes down to Miss
Ead's." She laughed and skipped higher.

"Hey. Hey, Q.T."

Q.T. turned to see Melissa and Hattie Lee sitting in the shadows of
Hattie Lee's front porch. "What you want?" she asked edging away from
them. They were funny sometimes. Sometimes they'd let her play with
them, but almost always they ended by making fun of her.

"You know how to ride a bike?" Melissa asked.

"Yeah."

Melissa smiled now. "Well, Hattie Lee just got a bike and she don't even
know how to ride it." Q.T. laughed with her a little uncertainly. "We going
to the playground and I gon hike Linda on mine. If you wanna go, you can
hike Hattie Lee on her'n."

Q.T. hesitated.

"Teach you to do the Texas Hop, if you go." Hattie Lee said smiling.

"I can do that," Q.T. told her. She wanted to go, but it felt nice to have
them asking her instead of having to tag along the way she usually did.

"Can you do the chicken?"

"Naw." Q.T. had seen some of the older kids doing that dance the last time they went to the playground, but she hadn't caught on enough to do it yet.

"Well, we teach you that if you want to go. Can you go?"

"Yeah."

Melissa and Hattie Lee stood up. "Come on."

"Oh, I can't go now. I gotta go down to Miss Ead's so she can do my hair."

There was a pause as Melissa considered. "How long you gon be?"

"Not long. It only takes a few minutes," she said eagerly.

"Well, you don't be too long and we wait. We gotta wait for Linda, anyway," she said turning to Hattie Lee.

"I'll be right back." Q.T. ran on, the tune growing louder in her head. She knocked softly on Miss Ead's door and said a stilted "hello" when Miss Ead opened it. Even after two weeks she was still rather shy around her.

"Well, here's my little Queenie." Miss Ead called her that all the time now and Q.T. smiled self-consciously, each time. But she really liked the name. "You kinda late tonight. I done already started cleanin up." This cleaning up was part of their routine. Q.T. would help Miss Ead tidy the house, then they would eat. After dinner and the washing up, Miss Ead would start on Q.T.'s hair.

"Miss Ead, I can't stay long tonight; I'm gon go to the playground with some friends." She could say that now. They had asked her; not the other way around and she wouldn't be just tagging along; she would be with them, with Hattie Lee, in fact, the cutest one. "They gon be leaving in a few minutes."

"Which kids is these?"

"Hattie Lee 'nem."

"Humph. They done finally asked you to play wid em, huh?"

"Yes."

"Well seem like, evil as they been to you, you wouldn't want to play wid em. It's otha kids round here."

Q.T. looked down. She would die before she'd tell Miss Ead that the other kids were just like Hattie Lee and Melissa, that she was the same with the other kids as she was with Hattie Lee and Melissa. It wasn't that they laughed at her or even about her. It was that she felt they were going to. Sometimes she could really *feel* that they were going to and she would tense up and get quiet and even after the moment passed and the taunt didn't come, she would be nervous. It was really easier to play with her stick doll or draw paper dolls or take one of Sudy Mae's love books and read, than it was to be with any of the kids. But they had asked her this time and it would be different.

"I want to go, Miss Ead," she said looking up.

"Well, come on," Miss Ead said turning away, "I be finished soon as I can."

It was always nice and cool in Miss Ead's house, and clean. Q.T. loved to feel the slick cleanness of the linoleum under her hot, dusty feet. This the way my house gon be, she thought as she wiggled her toes on the floor. Miss Ead pulled over a bar stool and settled her comfortable bottom on it. Q.T. sat in a kitchen chair.

"What yo'all gon do at the playground?"

"Play, I guess. And some nights they dance."

"Huh?" Miss Ead bent down. "Honey, you talk so low, sometimes I can't understand you." Q.T. repeated herself. "Well, I guess it good you getting to be friends with these kids."

Miss Ead had been drinking; Q.T. smelled the liquor on her breath. Usually by the time she had finished with Q.T.'s hair, her trips to the bedroom—she never drank in front of Q.T.—would have made her high. "I happy drunk," she would say then; "I tipshe."

"Too bad you can't stay for supper. Miss Carr had two steaks left over from they supper. That white woman got so much, she ain't gon miss two steaks. I ever tell you bout Fred? That one man sho liked his steaks. He could pay for em too. Owned some 'partments. He tell everybody was movin in, 'Don't come runnin to be 'plainin bout nobody else and they won't come 'plaining bout you. If they gives a loud party one night, you just give one the next night. Then can't nobody say nothin. They be happy; you be happy; I be happy.' That what he tell em."

"Ain't nobody ever complain?"

Miss Ead laughed. "Nobody cept *his* neighbors. That nigga gave a party every night. He ain't never give his neighbors no chance to git back at him." They both laughed.

"You most finished, Miss Ead?" Q.T. asked a little impatiently.

"Yeah," Miss Ead said mimicking Q.T.'s tone. "I most finished."

She parted off another section of hair, then got up and went into the bedroom. When she came back the smell of liquor was stronger. She sat down again.

They listened to the drone of the swamp cooler. Q.T. could tell that

Miss Ead was angry and she chewed her lip wondering if Miss Ead were angry with her. The silence was too much. "Me and Sudy Mae went to church Sunday." It was something to say.

"Well, that's nice." Miss Ead didn't sound too interested but at least she was talking.

"Sudy Mae had some of that grape juice and crackers, but that's not supposed to be fo kids, is it?"

"If you been baptized—least that's what the ol folks say."

"Well, Sudy Mae ain't been baptized."

"Oh, she still a sinner, huh?"

"I'on't know if she be *sinnin*," Q.T. said seriously, "but I know she ain't been baptized."

Miss Ead was laughing. "Baby, I'm only teasin. The ones what is, do as much dirt as the ones what ain't. There, that's the last one." Miss Ead got up and went over to the phonograph. "I sho like the way this man sing," she said as she put on a record. "*Mister* Ray Charles."

The record sounded almost like church music and Q.T. sat listening, wanting to hear it all but conscious also of the time. She moved uneasily and finally stood up. "Thank you."

"This the way they used to do it when I was young," Miss Ead said swinging around. She was light on her feet and her heavy body moved easily. "And I thought I would party jes till I had a chile. So I balled with this un and that un—even got married once. But I never did have me no baby. And it make me feel bad, cause I ain't got no one, no one so's I can pass on to them what I learned in my life. And I'm not sayin I know all there is to know."

She stopped and Q.T. was frightened. Miss Ead's face was shiny, the skin gathered in a knot between her eyes. The fullness of her bottom lip was flattened against her teeth. She ran her hands through the graying waves of her hair and shook her head. "Go'n go, chile; go'n go. Can't no one stop you from yo pain."

"Miss Ead—" Q.T. was breathing fast. She hadn't meant to hurt Miss Ead, didn't know how or when she had hurt Miss Ead; but she could see that Miss Ead was hurting.

Miss Ead smiled, "Hey I'm drunk, you know." She reached out and hugged Q.T. "But I am sober nough to tell you this: you treat people like they treat you in this world—at least treat em that way in yo heart if you can't treat em that way in yo action."

Q.T. looked down. Miss Ead didn't want her to go to the playground with Melissa and them. She was saying that they wouldn't all of a sudden become her friends.

Miss Ead patted her shoulder and walked with her to the door. "You have a good time at this playground, now. And be careful. I be here." She smiled.

Q.T. looked up at her. Miss Ead knew she was going. And Miss Ead would still go on, go on combing her hair in the evening. "I be careful," she said, and shyly hugged the woman around the waist.

They began cutting grapes in July, everybody except Candy who had gotten into an argument with Mo-dear about working in the fields again. "I thought that was why you had Bryant. What the use of havin a nigga if he ain't brangin in nothin?" she asked, adding, "at least my daddy did work." Mo-dear had slapped her for talking back; as she had said then, fifteen which Candy was, wasn't grown. Candy had slammed out of the house, shouting back over her shoulder that she didn't have to work her fingers to the bones for a four dollar pair of shoes. Ryce had followed her but had come back late that same night. Candy didn't return for three days; when she did she had on a new, tight black skirt with a long split up the back, a thin nylon blouse with long puffed sleeves, red fox stockings, two inch spike heels and a new fuschia lipstick. Her hair was curled in a poodle style and it was obvious that she had gotten it done at the beauty shop. Mo-dear called her a little whore ("Which," Q.T. heard Candy tell Ryce, "isa lie; I ain't gave *nothin* away."), but didn't say anything, not even when they got ready to go to the fields the next morning and Candy refused to get up. And Q.T. wondered about that; Candy, and Ryce, too, just seemed to not be the way they used to be when daddy was alive or even the way they had been in Lanare. Every time they said something to Mo-dear, they always seemed to be on the verge of talking back and quite a bit of the time actually doing it. And cutting raisin grapes was easier than picking strawberries; Mo-dear had even said that they could keep half of all the money they made—something they'd never been allowed before. Ryce and Sudy Mae were talking about burying purple quilted skirts and black sweaters and capizio shoes. All Q.T. wanted was a pair of penny loafers and Bonnie Donne socks and, since she was spreading trays for Sudy Mae, that was about all she would make enough to buy.

The days settled into a patter, up early to be in the field by six o'clock where they worked until five or six in the afternoon. They would get home about seven and then everybody would wash up. Q.T. was last because she was the youngest. And when she was through, she would walk through the courts to Miss Eads. She liked that time of day best. It would be dusk then or just about and walking through the courts, Q.T. would think them almost beautiful. This not a bad place when you got some—when you know people, she thought. It was late August, almost September now and even though she got along with Melissa and the other children, she never, even in her thoughts, called them her friends any more. They still gon play wid me when school start, when—she touched her hair. It hadn't grown much in the two, almost three months she had been going to Miss Ead's. She'd finally accepted the fact that Miss Ead could not perform a miracle and make her hair long. But maybe, if I had some clothes, they would be my friends. Mo-dear and her ol boyfriend! But, she thought hopefully, Miss Ead know what to do.

"Good evenin, Mamma Hattie."

"Hattie Lee not home, Q.T. She gon over her cousin's house to spend the night." Hattie Lee's grandmother sat in a rocking chair on the front stoop, her hands folded underneath her droopy stomach.

"Oh." Q.T. pushed a pebble with her toe. Mamma Hattie always managed to start talking about things and after saying 'hello' Q.T. never knew what else to say. She looked down, knowing she must say something. Mamma Hattie continued to rock placidly. "You know if Miss Ead home?"

"She just come in not five minutes ago. She really got yo hair to growin. Pretty soon, yo hair be as long as Hattie Lee's. Ead sho got a growing hand."

"Yes she do and she be waitin for me now." And throwing a polite smile in the general direction of the porch, Q.T. went down to Miss Ead's.

Tonight, the first part of the routine was quickly over. Miss Ead stacked the dishes in the sink and pulled over the big bar stool. "Yo mamma got a new boyfriend, I see." She settled on the stool.

Q.T. sat in her usual chair, feeling a little surprised at how much Miss Ead knew about what went on in the projects. Sometimes in the evenings she would sit out on the lawn with Melissa and Hattie Lee, Linda and some of the other kids and listen to the grown-ups talk as they played whist or dominoes under the big sycamore tree. Sometimes Miss Ead would join them, catching up, as she called it, on the happenings. But even though Miss Ead didn't go down to the tree that often, she could give you an almost day by day account of what went on (and sometimes why) in the courts. Mo-dear had been down to the tree no more than once or twice. She called the women a bunch of biddies worried about keeping their lame-ass men (just like she'd want something like that) and trying to get into everybody's business. "Don't you say nothin bout what go on in this house, Q.T. I pays the rent here and ain't nobody got no business knowin what I do." Miss Ead was an exception, though; Q.T. knew she could tell Miss Ead anything and it wouldn't go any further.

"Yeah," she said now, "Mo-dear put Bryant out so we could get on the welfare. Mo-dear say he wa'n't doin enough fo us no way. Sides that, she think he got another woman."

"Well, I can see which one you think is most important, tween that woman and his takin care of yo all."

"But Miss Ead, you said if a man can't do nothin fo a woman than a woman don't need him."

"That right, chile. You learn that early, you won't have nothin to worry bout."

Q.T. grinned, then sobered. "Miss Ead, I think the new one, George come round and lookin the window when Candy and Ryce be undressin."

"Tell yo mamma."

"I did."

"Have em pull the shades down."

There was a pause and Q.T. squirmed in her chair, wanting to talk about the school clothes, but feeling reluctant to do so. She didn't want Miss Ead to think badly about Mo-dear but if she didn't tell Miss Ead about the clothes, if Miss Ead couldn't think up something, then she would have to go to school raggedty just like always.

"Yeah," Miss Ead said, "Yo mamma got that straight, at least. Don't care how many womens a nigga got, long as he putting that money in the right pocket. Which is *mines*." She laughed. "Aw, yeah you can be a hypocrite bout it, talk bout how you don't want to be 'sharin yo stuff with nobody,' like I hear soma these ol foolish womens talkin. But only stuff that belongst to you is what's between you l—is you," she finished with a laugh. "Yeah, people sho will try to be hypocrites with they dirt. And if it one thing I can't stand it a hypocrite. I drinks my liquor but you don't see me sitting up in church on Sunday, makin like I ain't never touched a drop. But just cause I don't go to church, don't mean you shouldn't go. Yeah," she said tapping Q.T.'s shoulder with the comb, "I saw you out there last Sunday, playin wid them kids. It ugly when chi'ren don't go to church or Sunday School and the Lawd don't like ugly. But some people just be so hypocritical when they goes to church—"

It was one of Miss Ead's favorite subjects and Q.T. knew she'd never get a chance to say anything if Miss Ead really got wound up. "Miss Ead," she said swinging around to face her, "Mo-dear gived the money for our school clothes to George." Her lip quivered a moment as she struggled with her tears. "She say half that money gon be ours, for whatever we want to buy. That's all our grape cutting money, what we worked for all summer and just cause George say he need just that little mo fo the down payment on that ol piece-a car, Mo-dear gived it to him. And now I ain't gon never get no penny loafers and Bonnie Donne socks." Q.T. buried her head in Miss Ead's lap.

Miss Ead rocked Q.T. for a moment. "Queenie. Queenie, I can probably squeeze out enough to get you that pair of shoes."

Q.T. felt better for a moment and then the words, 'probably squeeze out enough,' sank in. That's what Mamma always said when she really didn't have enough money to get what you'd asked for, but would scrimp on something else so you could have what you wanted, or else it was something she felt you really shouldn't have, didn't need and she might have second thoughts about getting it for you. She shook her head. She didn't want Miss Ead scrimping for her and if Miss Ead couldn't understand how badly she needed those loafers—everybody would have loafers, loafers or white saddle shoes.

"Chile sweet as you shouldn't have to rake and scrap fo nothin." Miss Ead held her tightly and rocked for a long time. Q.T. lay quiet and drowsy; the rhythm of Miss Ead's body keeping thought away. "Well, you come stay the night wid me tomorrow and I see what I can do. Okay?" Q.T. nodded. "Now you turn around so I can finish yo hair."

"Miss Ead, Mo-dear say fo me to come back quick, case the L.B. Price man come collectin fo his bill, so I can answer the door." Q.T. grinned, feeling better now, knowing that somehow Miss Ead had made things right. "She say she ain't gon let no bill collector dun her to death."

"And thy sho will if you don't watch em close. But you ask if you can spend tomorrow night wid me. Be sho, now." She patted Q.T.'s shoulder and started on the last braid.

Q.T. could hear Miss Ead and Miss Ead's friend, Duncan, in the kitchen. They were drinking and every now and then Q.T. heard Duncan laugh or Miss Ead giggle. Miss Ead had sent Q.T. to bed when Duncan brought out the bottle. "Now you know, the lawd don't like ugly, Queenie; you go on to bed," She'd said when Q.T. seemed about to protest. Q.T. had gone with a falling sensation in her stomach, wondering how this could have anything to do with school clothes. Duncan her boyfriend, she thought now as she lay in the darkened room; she must be gon talk him out the money. She strained to understand the low voices that came from the kitchen, then sighed in frustration and turned over. Her eyes caught the outline of a dress hanging on the closet door. It was her dress, a present from Duncan. "Ead done told me what a good girl you been so I brung you a present," he said as he kissed her forehead. Q.T. accepted the kiss, trying to conceal her impatience. When she was finally allowed to open the package, the dress wavered before her eyes and seemed for a moment to be one of her dreams come true. The dress, green with white stripes and a large, lace edged collar, felt good and looked good on her. "Now that's the way you should always look. Don't she look cute, Duncan?" Q.T. had bounced up and down in her excitement, and imagined herself in the dress on the first day of school. The picture danced before her eyes. First, everyone would gather around her to admire her dress. "You look good, girl." "That a pretty dress." Then they would ask her to play. "Queenie, that yo name?" And she would say, well, that's what some people call me. Maybe if she said it that way, the name would come out okay. She would be Queenie and not Q.T. Queenie was cute and then the kids would say, "Queenie, come on." "Queenie, the swings." "The—" The voices faded but their echo gave her 'thank you' an added fervency and her smile an added brilliance.

If Duncan wa'n't her friend, I bet Miss Ead'd call him a slick nigga, Q.T. thought. 'Black as tar, can't git to heaven on electric wire.' And he ain't even that big. She snapped her fingers. His ol boney knees look like they gon tear a hole through that suit every time he sit down. But that sho musta been a pretty suit when it was new. Wonder if it silk? I gon git me a silk suit one of these days, but I gon keep it good. It ain't never gon git ol and raggedty-looking like that one. Do women wear silk suits? I don't care. I is. She rolled over, squirming against the slickness of the new sheets. He sho keep his hair nice though. She felt funny about Duncan's hair. His beautifully processed hair was longer than hers and lay in smooth waves against his skinny head. Yeah, Q.T. nodded solemnly in the dark, he sho a slick nigga. But since he done come on in wid this dress, I tell the world he the best nigga ever was. She laughed at this last thought, thinking how much she sounded like Miss Ead.

She hadn't heard the door open and the squeaking of its hinges startled her. "Miss Ead?"

"No. It Duncan." He stood silhouetted in the door way, shoes in hand. "What you want?"

"I comin to bed." He closed the door and moved toward the bed, unbuttoning his shirt.

"You supposed to sleep on the couch, ain't you?"

"No, I suppose to sleep right here."

By this time Duncan had pulled off his clothes and was slipping into the bed. As Q.T. felt his weight depressing the bed, she began to scream. "Miss Ead. Miss Ead, Duncan tryin' to get in bed wid me. Miss Ead. Miss—" Duncan put his hand over her mouth, whispering "Shut up." Q.T. wiggled away from him and stood up in the bed, dragging the cover with her. She kicked out at him, screaming all the while. Duncan grabbed for the covers. Q.T. jumped back and jerked the covers out of his reach. "Stop it Duncan. You ain't even supposed to be here. Miss Ead." Duncan reached for her legs and fell flat when she moved out of his reach.

"Be still, girl. I ain't gon hurt you." He struggled to his knees and grabbed again for Q.T.'s legs. Q.T. dropped the covers on his head and leaped from the bed just in time. She picked up the bedside lamp and held it over her head, watching as Duncan struggled out of the tangled bed clothes. "You move Duncan and I throws it. Duncan. Dun—" Duncan moved. Q.T. threw the lamp and Miss Ead opened the door, turning on the light as the lamp caught Duncan in his chest and knocked him flat in the bed. He lay there panting.

Q.T. moved back against the wall. "Miss Ead," she stopped for breath. "Miss—"

"God damn it Ead," Duncan gasped. "Damn it, I thought you said she know what goin on. Damn it Ead, you too ol to be fumblin the way you do."

"Me? Fumblin?" Miss Ead's bosom heaved. "Me fumblin. Shit, you ol enough to know you ain't supposed to go round crawlin in peoples bed when it dark. Least you coulda done was turn on the lights. Fumblin! Shit. You git on outta here and let me talk to her."

Duncan picked up his clothes and started out. "Woman say, I got everythin un'er control. I know what goin down; I handle it. Ead, you can't handle shit."

"I ain't supposed to be handlin shit; I handlin this. Now go on Duncan, fo you mouth git yo ass in a world of hurt." Miss Ead waited until he closed the door, then came and sat down on the bed. She held out her arms, and, after a moment's hesitation, Q.T. scrambled across the bed to her and lay panting on her breast. Miss Ead rocked her silently. Then, she held her away and looked her in the eyes. "Queenie you member I always sayin if a nigga can't do nothing for you, then that a nigga you best be leavin alone? Well, Duncan do lots for you—that is, if you let him. But it a give and git world, and if he do for you, you gotta do for him too. You ain't really losin that much when you let him sleep in here, no way."

"That all he gon do is sleep?"

"Sometime, I think that all Duncan can do is sleep; he so silly," she said with a laugh. "But I wouldn't let him do nothin to hurt you."

There was a pause. Q.T. picked at the bedspread, her eyes downcast. "The lady at church say it wrong for a boy and girl to do that," she said in a low voice.

"That right, it is wrong for a boy and a girl. But," Miss Ead said, "Duncan a man. Now I gon tell him to come back, okay?" Q.T. said nothing. Her fingers still plucked at the bedspread. Finally Miss Ead rose to go. She stopped at the door. "Q.T." she spoke sharply and the use of her name made Q.T. look up. "Lawd don't like ugly. Now you be a pretty girl."

"Queenie?" Duncan's voice was hoarse. He stood in the doorway, his clothes clutched in front of him. His thin legs seemed to hang suspended from the too large legs of his boxer shorts. He grinned at her hesitantly showing the gap where a front tooth should have been.

Q.T. lowered her head and from the back of her mind, coming closer to the front, marched a vision of all the pretty dresses she could have. She could see herself on the first day of school, dressed in Duncan's present, hair pressed and curled. The admiring crowd, the voices joining together: "Come on, Queenie, let's play . . . Queenie let's swing . . . Come on . . ." You be a pretty girl.

She turned her back to him. "Turn out the light, Duncan."

Joanna Russ

Autobiography of My Mother
1975

Born in 1937 to second generation American Jewish school teacher parents, Joanna Russ, an only child, grew up in the Bronx. She was one of the top ten Westinghouse Science Talent Search winners in her senior year in high school. While an undergraduate at Cornell University, she studied with Vladimir Nabokov. Next, at the Yale Drama School, she completed an MFA in playwriting and dramatic literature. She had known from her pre-teen years that she wanted to write and in her last year at Yale she began writing science fiction while continuing to write plays. Her first published science fiction story, "Nor Custom Stale," appeared in The Magazine of Fantasy and Science Fiction *in 1959.*

While teaching full time (she is now a professor at the University of Washington in Seattle), she has managed to publish an impressive quantity of work, ranging from short stories to novels to literary criticism to a volume of literary theory and history. Russ's 1972 story, "When It Changed," literally changed—expanded—what readers and writers thought possible in the field of science fiction. It was chosen by the members of the Science Fiction Writers of America to receive the Nebula Award as the best short story of the year. Her feminist academic colleagues bestowed the Florence Howe Literary Criticism Award on her essay, "What Can a Heroine Do? Or, Why Women Can't Write," in 1974. [This essay opens the collection Images of Women in Fiction: Feminist Perspectives, *ed. Susan Koppelman Cornillon, 1972.] "Autobiography of My Mother," first published in* Epoch *at Cornell in1975, was one of the 1977 O. Henry Memorial Prize Stories. In 1983, science fiction readers voted "Souls" the Hugo Award for best novella of the year.*

In his introduction to the 1976 Gregg Press reprinting of Alyx, *Russ's collection of four long stories and one short novel, Samual Delany called* Picnic on Paradise, *her first novel, "an incredibly liberating work for the s-f genre," adding that "it was a book which, after reading and rereading, has left me unable to think of writing quite so complacently as I had. And that is the highest compliment any writer can pay another."*

Her other books include the novels And Chaos Died *(1970),* The Female Man *(1975),* We Who are About To . . . *(1975),* The Two Of Them *(1978),* and On Strike Against God *(1980); the children's book* Kittatinny: A Tale of Magic *(1978); the short story collection* The Zanzibar Cat *(1983); and* How to Suppress Women's Writing *(1983), an analysis of the ways in which women have been discouraged from writing.*

"Autobiography of My Mother" is a classical, yet unique, mother-daughter story. The daughter is portrayed encountering her mother at different periods in her mother's life, including a time before the daughter was born. These encounters enable the daughter to recognize her mother as a woman with needs, imperatives, and a history of her own. The daughter must also come to terms with what her birth and the responsibility for her care meant in her mother's life. The daughter is reconciled to her mother as a sister-woman and emerges as a woman who can look at her mother as a person in her own right and not solely as a mother. The daughter achieves a sense of continuity that will allow her to move into her own future as a woman with roots, strength, and love-roots in a woman's history, strength from understanding a woman's life, and love for and a sense of sisterhood with the woman who gave her life.

This story is classical in that it adheres to the pattern of a daughter questing for her origins and place in the history of women's lives. It is unique among quest stories, however, in that the mother in the story is not dead. In other stories of this type the quest is precipitated by, or becomes psychologically possible only after the mother's death. "Autobiography of My Mother" represents a juncture among the genre of fantasy, women's history, and feminist utopianism (a theme that Russ developed further in The Female Man*). This type of imagining seems to have been unavailable until now. So while this story is firmly rooted in women's literary tradition, it is also a major breakthrough to something new.*

I'm an I.
Sometimes I'm a she.
Sometimes I'm even a he.
Sometimes I'm vervvery I.
Sometimes I'm my mother.

I WAS VISITING FRIENDS in Woodstock; you may find it surprising that I met my mother there for the first time. I certainly do. She was two years old. My mother and I live on different ends of a balance; thus it's not surprising to find that when I'm thirty-five she's just a little tot. She sat on the living room rug and started at me, with her legs bent under her in a position impossible to anyone but a baby. Babies might be lobsters or some other strange form of life, considering what positions they take up. A little light tug at the ornamental tassel of my shoe—not apologetic or tentative, she feels both modest and confident, but she has small hands. "What's that?" she says.

"That's a tassel." She decamped and settled her attention on the other shoe. "And what's *that*?"

"Another tassel." This baby has flossy black hair, a pinched little chin, and round pale-green eyes. Even at the age of two her upper lip is distinctive: long, obstinate, almost a chimp's. I think she thinks that every object has its own proper name and so—without intending to—I made her commit her first error. She said: "That's *a tassel*. That's *another tassel*." I nodded, bored. She's of the age at which they always take off their clothes; patiently, with her own understanding of what she likes and what's necessary to her, she took off all of hers: her little sailor dress, her patent leather shoes, her draggy black cotton stockings. It's only history that gave her these instead of a ruff and stomacher. She practiced talking in the corner of the living room for half an hour; then she came over to me, nude, without her underwear and remarked:

"That's a tassel. That's another tassel."

"Uh-huh," I said. Pleased at having learned something, she pondered for a moment and then switched them around, declaring:

"That's *another tassel* and that's *a tassel*."

"No, no," I said. "They're both tassels. This is a tassel and that's a tassel."

She backed away from me. I don't think she likes me now. Later that night I saw her scream with excitement when her father came home; he held the tail of her night shirt in one hand and her brother's in the other; they both played the great game of trying to scramble away from him on all fours. My mother shrieked and laughed. Even at the age of two she's addicted to pleasure.

It'll ruin her.

YOU GET STUCK IN TIME, not when you're born exactly, but when you "sit up and take notice," as they say, when you become aware that you have an individuality and there's something out there that either likes you or doesn't like you. This happens at about eighteen months. It isn't that you really prefer some other time, you don't know anything about that; you just back off (still crawling, perhaps), not shaking your head (for you don't know about that, either) just wary and knowing you don't like *that staircase* or *those visitors* or *this parent*. But what can be done about it? You're stuck. It would be the same if you could travel through time but not through space.

Like this story.

AT A CHINESE RESTAURANT: that is, a big room with a high ceiling and dun walls, like a converted gymnasium. Sepia-colored screens in front of the Men's and Ladies'. There is a fan of crimson coral over my mother's head and the chairs are high backed and plain, the ultimate in chic for 1925. My mother is nineteen. When I was that age I discovered her diary and some poems she had written; they didn't mention the restaurant but here she is anyway, having dinner with her best friend. I've looked everywhere in them to find any evidence that she was abnormal, but there's none. Nobody hugs anybody or says anything they shouldn't, and if there's any morbidity, that's gone too. My mother's written remains are perfect. At that time I wasn't born yet. I'm not even a ghost in her thought because she's not going to get married or even have children; she's going to be a famous poet. It was known then that you had to have children. It was a fact, like the Empire State Building I saw every morning out of the corner of my eye at breakfast (through the kitchen window). When you looked at childlessness in those days you didn't even realize that you had made a judgment, an inference from one set of conditions to another, you just *knew*.

I sat down imprudently at my mother's table.

Now I'm not as pretty as she is (I don't look a bit like her with my big behind and my buck teeth) but I'm much better dressed, and having been able to arrange my entry to suit myself, I can turn on to the full that bullying, leering, ironical boldness I adopt so easily with women; I place my well-cut suede coat, my smart gloves, my modernique pearl earrings and Dior scarf directly in the track of my mother's green, beautiful, puzzled, nearsighted eyes. My mother didn't want me to sit next to her—she wanted her friend to come back. Strangers alarm her. When my mother is not with a good friend her spirits flag, she becomes vague, she loses control of herself and stares around the room, not because she wants to look at things but because she's diffused and anxious; it's a way of not meeting anyone's eye. She ducks her head and mutters (mannerisms that won't look so cute at fifty-nine). I want to protect her. Years later I'll hold her elbow when she crosses the street, suffer with her when she can't breathe in a crowd, but this is before she's perfected any suck tricks, so I can only bare my teeth at her in a way that makes her uncomfortable. She essays a smile.

"Do you come here often?" I say and she draws on her gloves; that is, she wanted to draw on her gloves, began to move her hands as if she would do so, then didn't. She looked guilty. Mother has been taught to be nice to everybody but she doesn't want to be nice to me. Last week she wrote a romantic love story about a girl whose mouth was like a slow flame. When I'm eleven I will get felt up on my rear end in a crowd and will be too ashamed to run away. It may occur to you that the context between us is sexual. I think it is parental.

"Would you care to step outside?" I said politely. Mother demurred. Sitting there—I mean us sitting there—well, you might have taken us for cousins. I picked up the check and she suffered because she didn't know what to do. Her friend, who will never get here in time, forms in my mother's memory a little bright door. I dropped two anachronistic quarters on the tablecloth and then put my French purse back in my navy-blue suede bag, an easy forty-five dollars which she has never seen, no, not even in dreams.

"Do you mind if we chat?" I said; "Shall we have coffee?" and went on to explain: that I was a stranger in town, that I was new here, that I was going to catch a train in a few hours, I told her that I was her daughter, that she was going to marry eventually and after two spontaneous abortions bear me, that I didn't usually ask for favors but this was different.

"Consider what you gain by not marrying," I said. We walked out onto Columbus Avenue. "All this can be yours." (Be the first one on your block; astonish your friends.) I told her that the most sacred female function was motherhood, that by her expression I knew that she knew it too, that nobody would dream of interfering with an already-accomplished pregnancy (and that she knew that) and that life was the greatest gift anybody could give, although only a woman could understand that or believe it. I said:

"And I want you to take it back."

WE WERE BOTH ELEVEN, on roller skates, skating towards Bronx Park with our braids flying behind us, but my mother was a little younger and a little slower, like my younger sister. I called her "Stupid."

IN THE FIRST PLACE I never borrowed it, in the second place it hasn't got a hole in it now, and in the third place it already had a hole in it when I borrowed it. I was going to show her all the kingdoms of the world. I wanted to protect my mother. Walking down Columbus Avenue in this expansive and generous mood—well, my mother didn't know what to make of me; like so many people she's puzzled by a woman who isn't beautiful, who doesn't make any pretense of being beautiful, and who yet flaunts herself. That's me. I asked my mother to tell me her daydreams, daydreams of meeting The Right Man, of being kept by an Older Woman, of inheriting money. Money means blood in dreams and blood means money. The autumn foliage in the park, for example, because the sun hadn't quite set. My mother was wearing a shapeless brown cloth coat that concealed her figure. It's very odd to think that this is 1921. Overheard: I thought it would be different.

I told my mother that when women first meet they dislike each other (because it's expected of them) but that's all right; that soon gives way to a feeling of mutual weakness and worthlessness and the feeling of being one species leads in turn to plotting, scheming, and shared conspiracies. I said that if we were going to be mother and daughter we ought to get to know each other. As we walked on the stone-flagged park paths my mother's soul flew out from under my fingers at every turn, to every man who passed, a terrible yearning, an awful lack, a down-on-your-knees appeal to anybody in the passing scene. She didn't like my company at all.

"Do you know what I want you to do?" I said. "Well, do you?"

"Well, do you?" my mother echoed earnestly, looking up at me with her nymph's green eyes.

"Look here—" I said.

("Look here—")

I suppose you expect me to say that I listened to her artlessly simple chatter, that I confided in her, or that next she will be a big girl and I the little one, but if you expect me to risk her being older than me, you're crazy. I remember what that was like from last time. I told her all of it— the blood, the sweat, the nastiness, the invasion of personality, the utter indecency (except in middle age, except with money) and she only looked up at me as if she knew things, that girl. She didn't like me. The palisade looking out over the river. The mild October air. We stood arm in arm, like chums, watching the wakes of the boats in the water. She said I couldn't understand. She said with complete conviction:

"You were never young."

MY MOTHER, a matron of fifty but for some reason shrunk to the size of an infant and wrapped in baby clothes, is lying in her cradle. Swaddled, her arms at her sides, furious. Frowning—this is no way to treat a grown woman! She is about to bawl. I could leave her there and she'd die—dirty herself, starve, become mute and apathetic—she's just a baby. Maternally I take into my arms my fifty-year-old mother because you can't leave a baby, can you? and cradling her tenderly to my breast I start dancing around the room. She hates it. Screaming and red-faced. Maybe she wants a different dance. I change into a waltz, rocking her softly, and right away, my goodness, the little baby is rocked into quiet, she's straightening her corrugated little brows, unwrapping the snaky moist curls that come finely from under her cap, smoothing her sulky little mouth. I guess she likes waltzing. If I didn't take care of her, how would she ever grow up to be my mother? It would be infanti-suicide, to say the least (if not something worse). When she stops crying I'll put her back into the cradle and sneak off, but there is command in that steely little face, those snapping little eyes, she stares up at me like a snapping turtle making plans, telling me with her expression all the terrible things she's going to do to me when I'm the baby and she's the mother and I know she did them because I was there. *You keep on rocking me!* she says.

So we keep on waltzing around the room.

WHEN I was a child-
   a child-
  When I was a chidden child-

I came into my right mind at a certain age, I think I inherited it, so it speak, although they didn't allow me to use it until I was already fairly cracked. Coming home from the dentist at sixteen on winter evenings with the sky hot-pink and amber in the west and the wind going right through your coat; it's discouraging to find automata in the living room. Cars shooting by to cheery dinners, homey lights from the windows above the stoop. Mirages. Inside, a steamy kitchen, something horrible like an abstract sort of Frankenstein's monster made up of old furniture, plates, window misted over. My mother, who is with us tonight, is also sixteen, and going this time under the name of Harriet (I think) which is a false name and no kin to the beautiful, imaginary playmate I had when I was four, who could fly and would write me letters with hand-painted stamps on them (canceled). After coming all the way in the cold, to be in a room with no living persons in it. To be distressed. To feel superior. To hold myself in good and hard, to know what's possible and what's good for me. Little Harriet Shelley watches wide-eyed the intercourse of a real human family.

AUNT LUCY: No one would tell you the truth about yourself, Harriet, unless they loved you very much. I love you and that's why you can trust me when I tell you the truth about yourself. The truth is that you are bad all through. There isn't a thing about you that's good. You are thoroughly unlovable. And only a person who loves you very much could tell you this.

UNCLE GEORGE: Tell me all your troubles, but don't say a word against your aunt. Your aunt is a saint.

MY MOTHER SITS listening to the radio, learning how to sew. She's making a patchwork quilt. Does she dislike her family? She denies it. She's not really going to grow up to be a poet. My mother has a mind like a bog; contraries meet in it and everything becomes instantly rotted away. Or her mind is a peat bog that preserves whole corpses. The truth is that I haven't the right to say what's going on in her mind because I know nothing about it.

She goes on sewing, gentle, placid, and serene, everything she should be. I told her that she could have any color car she wanted as long as it was black but even this failed to shake my soundless mother; One's Personal History Is Bunk, she might have answered me but didn't; she didn't even move away down the couch because my mother is not even mildly stubborn. Perhaps if she were not so polite she would say, "I don't know what you're talking about," but no, she's perfect, and when she raises her great, wondering, credulous, tear-filled gaze, it's not for me but on account of bad Mr. X in the kitchen, who is telling stories to Uncle George about the women who have jobs with him, for example, that their asses stick out:

Mr. X: _ _ _ _ _ ass.

UNCLE GEORGE: Mr. X is only joking, dear.

MR. X: That's right don't be so sensitive. How can you go out and get a job someday if you're so sensitive? I don't have anything against the ladies who work with me. I think they're fine. I think you're fine, even though you're so sensitive.

AUNT LUCY: See? Mr. X thinks you're fine.

MR. X: I think your aunt is fine, too.

UNCLE GEORGE: He thinks your aunt is fine, too, because he *likes* ladies.

AUNT LUCY: See? Mr. X is generous.

UNCLE GEORGE: Even though your aunt Lucy is a fool.

To cut out those noises people emit from time to time. To be hard and old. To retreat finally. To be free.

"My parents love each other," says my mother, shaking out her work, malignancy in its every fold. She's a wonder. She really believes. I used to think I knew the form of the ultimate relation between my mother and myself but now I'm not so sure; there's that unbreakable steel spring in her accepting head, no longer can I come clattering up the King's highway on my centaur/centurion's hindquarters (half Irish hunter, half plough horse, gray, fat, lazy, name: Mr. Ed) and I no longer look down from my wild, crazy, hero-assassin's eminence at the innkeeper's little daughter in her chaste yet svelte gingham (with its décolletage) and her beautiful, spiritual, dumb eyes and her crumby soul.

"Do you," I said, "Do you-tell me!-oh do you-believe me!-*do you*-DO YOU-BELIEVE ALL THAT?"

"Yes," she says.

Oh if you only knew! says her face. Her hands, resting on their sewing, change their import: Life is so hard, hard, hard. An unspoken rule between us has been that I can hate her but she can't hate me; this breaks. (A day in the longed-for life: for once when my mother is carried across the crumbling battlements on the screen the audience laughs, they hoot when she wrings her hands, when she obeys her father's prohibition they howl, when she is seduced they screech, when it starts to snow and the hero walks on her face with his lovely black boots it's all over, and by the time she commits suicide, *there is nobody there*.)

"I think," says my mother thoughtfully, biting a thread, "that I'm going to get married." She looks at me, shrewdly and with considerable hatred.

"That way," she says in a low, controlled voice, *"I will be able to get away from you!"*

(When she was little my mother used to scare her relatives by asking them if they were happy; they would always answer, *"Of course* I'm happy." When I was little I once asked her if she was happy and she said "Of course I'm happy.")

SOMETHING that will never happen: my mother and I, chums, sharing secrets, giggling at the dinner table, writing in each other's slambooks, going to the movies together. Doing up each other's hair. It's not dreadful that she doesn't want me, just embarrassing, considering that I made the proposal first. She would beam, saying sentimental things about her motherhood, anxiously reaching for my hand across the table. She was not wicked, ever, or cruel, or unkind. We'll never go skating together, never make cocoa in the kitchen at midnight, snurfing in our cups and whooping it up behind the stove. I was never eight. I was never eleven. I was never thirteen. The mind I am in now came to me some time after puberty, not the initiation into sex (which is supposed to be the important thing) but the understanding that everything I had suffered from as a child, all my queerness, all my neuroses, the awful stiffnesses, the things people scorned in me, that all these would be all right when I was an adult because when I was an adult I would have power.

And I do. I do.

Power gave me life. I like it. Here's something else I like: when I was twenty-nine and my mother—flustered and ingenuous—told me that she'd had an embarrassing dream about me. Did she expect to be hit? It was embarrassing (she said) because it was incestuous. She dreamed we had eloped and were making love.

Don't laugh. I told it for years against her. I said all sorts of awful things. But what matters still matters, i.e. my mother's kicking a wastebasket the length of the living room in a rage (as she once bragged to me she did) or striking her breast, crying melodramatically, "Me Martian! Me good! You Jupiterian! You bad!" (as she also did). Bless you! do you think she married to get away from me, the Lesbian love-object? I wasn't born yet.

It's immensely sweet of her to offer to marry me, but what I want to know is: do you think we're suited?

DON JOSÉ, the Brazilian heiress—wait a minute, I'm getting them muddled up, that was the other one where I was the Brazilian heiress, this one's Don José and he's *Argentinian* and an *Heir*—anyway, his cruel smile undressed her with his eyes, I don't think I can go on writing like this, she said. Are you not woman enough to know? And the unfortunate sadist tossed his typewriter out the window. That is what they called working girls in those days. My mother will never forgive me. For what? cried the incautious maid with the almond-blue eyes. Thank you, sir, I shall make the bed, she sobbed. Only do not lay me in it; that will crease the counterpane and I will be fired. And your children, his mustache twitching, I have sworn to have them, have me first, no, have a shashlik; there is blood on my dress.

Blood!

I have murdered the butler.

(A lively game of bed-to-bed trash filled the evening air as the charming little summer-campmaedchen disemboweled the myth and passed it gigglingly from hand to hand. Salugi! Gesundheit. Thank you very much.)

What Every Woman Knows.

IT IS QUITE POSSIBLE that none of this happened or has value; still

I wish life could have been different for my mother. But we're all Tiamat's lap, so there's no use complaining. In the daytime we stand on Her knees, looking up at Her face, and at night She hides Her face so we get uneasy. Our Father Witch (in whom I used to believe) is very jealous of his name or it's a secret or it's too ugly (or maybe he hasn't got any) but you can call Her Nyame and Tanit, call her 'Anat, Atea, Tabiti, Tibirra. over the place and She doesn't mind kiddies pulling at her skirt; call her Nyame and Tanit, call Her 'Anat, Atea, Tabiti Tibirra. This is what comes of re-meeting one's mother when she was only two—how willful she was! how charming, and how strong. I wish she had not grown up to be a door-mat, but all the same what a blessing it is not to have been made by somebody's hands like a piece of clay, and then he breathed a spirit in you, etc. so you are clay and not-clay, your ingredients fighting each other like the irritable vitamin pill in the ad—what a joy and a pleasure to have been born, just ordinary born, you know, out of dirt and flesh, all of one piece and of the same stuff She is. To be my mother's child. (Your pleasures and pains are your belly-button-cord to the Great Mother; they prove you were once part of Her.)

I asked, Why couldn't my mother have been more like You? But She didn't answer. I felt something coming from Her. Time She doesn't like me—I don't always like myself—but we're still the same stuff.

Change my life! I said.

Sorry, won't. Her fog veiled Her face (that is one of Her moods) and Her towns (which are the rings on Her fingers) grew ugly. Tiamat is talking. She spoke through me as in the Bible, that is I spoke, knowing the answer:

Am I my mother's mother?

ON WINTER NIGHTS, when my mother and I were twelve, we would go out together with chocolate cigarettes and pose under street lights like little prostitutes, pretending that we were smoking. It was very glamorous. Now we do it in our cheap dresses, our tight shoes; my mother has waited for The Man all her life, that's why she had no time for me. In the beauty parlor, on the street, in the nursing home, waiting for The Man. We lean on each other, very tired, in our make-up, a sad friendship between us. We even hold hands.

Will you be my best friend? she says.

I say yes.

Will you live with me?

I say yes.
Will you sleep with me and wake with me?
I say yes.
Will you marry me?
I say yes.

ALL YOU NEED IS LOVE.

Nicholasa Mohr

Tell The Truth
1975

"From the moment my mother handed me some scrap paper, a pencil, and a few crayons, I decided that by making pictures and writing letters I could create my own world—like magic. In the small crowded apartment I shared with my large family, 'making magic' permitted me all the space and freedom my imagination could handle.

"El cuento puertorriqueno, storytelling, has always been an intrinsic part of Puerto Rican culture. When our family faced difficulties, an adult would say, 'Don't lose hope, sit back and relax, and I'll tell you a story.' Our family would gather around the storyteller, fascinated by the ancient folk tale or modern adventure. Our problems and burdens began to seem lighter, and life appeared promising."

—*www.scholastic.com/teachers/authorsandbooks*

Nicholasa Mohr was born on November 1, 1935 in New York City after her parents moved from the Commonwealth of Puerto Rico during the first poverty-driven mass Puerto Rican migration of the 1930s, following the devastating hurricanes of the first half of the decade. Nicholasa Mohr and her family came to the United States before the "Migracion," the great influx of Puerto Ricans in the 1950s following the collapse of the sugar industry. But the poverty and inventiveness of the Puerto Rican people, whether on the island or the mainland, continued to be a feature of the Mohr family life. Tragically, her father died when she was eight years old, leaving her mother with seven children, and her mother died when she was fourteen.

In order to escape the poverty that surrounded her, Mohr used her fantastic imagination to express her feelings. Her artistic talents helped earn her much praise in school and gave her the confidence which led to her success as an author. She has become one of the most cherished writers of not only her Puerto Rican ethnicity, but of poor and working class women. In her work, we find those characteristics of poor and working class women that Michelle Tea writes about in the introduction to her 2003 book Without a Net: The Female Experience of Growing up Working Class (Seal Press):

> I knew that these stories were out there, and the image they'd present of the working-class experience in the U.S. would be deeper and more complicated than the tragic view the middle class always takes on our lives. There's tragedy, for sure there's tragedy, but there are also kick-ass survival skills to be proud of, so many ingenious approaches to surviving poverty—everything from the focused, determined march out from under it via college and hard work to a gleeful, defiant, dumpster-diving exultation that can accompany living at the bottom. There is joy in poor people's lives, and humor and camaraderie. Girls who grow up working class grow up tough and clever. There is hope in our lives. . . . We are all survivors, and have no use for the pity and condescension that often accompany discussions about our lives. (p.xiv)

After graduating from high school in 1953 she went to the Arts Student's League in New York. Here she discovered the works of Diego Rivera and Jose Clemente Orozco which inspired her to study Hispanic art and travel to Mexico City. After a year she returned to the United States and attended the New School for Social Research. Then in 1959 she went to the Brooklyn Museum of Art School. Throughout her studies Mohr was drawn to artwork with powerful messages about social change.

Mohr used bold letters and symbols in her paintings. She attempted to tell stories through these works. Eventually she switched from painting to short stories. It took a few tries for a publisher to offer her a contract, but when he did, she started writing her first book, Nilda. *Many of Mohr's books are about characters growing up in Hispanic neighborhoods in New York City, much like herself.*

Her second book, El Bronx Remembered, *1975, in which 'Tell the Truth. . . .' first appeared, was awarded The New York Times' Outstanding Book Award in teenage fiction and received the Best Book award from the School Library Journal. Since that time, Mohr has been a full-time writer. The title of the story refers to Emily Dickinson's poem "Tell all the truth but tell it slant" and a reading of that poem enhances the reading of this story. On the other hand, this story will stand just fine on its own, without enhancement of any kind. Vickie's courage, tenacity, and trust in the words of her mother in the face of the power, blandishments, promises, and other interrogatory tactics of the Man are exemplary.*

Mohr speaks positively of her transition from visual to written art. "The visual art world is very exclusive and expensive. You have to have a lot of money to buy a work of art, because the artist has to make a living from selling single works. But when an artist writes a book, it becomes accessible to a wider audience. You can go to the library and read the book or buy it as an inexpensive paperback. I feel better about working in that world."

American women writers have been Mohr's greatest influence. *"Shirley Jackson, Carson McCullers, and Katherine Anne Porter were the ones I learned in school and came to love. (It wasn't until later in life that I read the great Latin American writers like Julia de Burgos and Gabriel Garcia Marquez),"* she explains.

"From the American women writers I appreciated that the more specific you are in your writing, the more universal your appeal. So I write about what I know best—the woman's experience and the Puerto Rican community in New York City. I have to write from my own experiences, but I always hope readers can share these experiences and become more aware of other peoples' struggles, and thereby make connections with each other through my writing. I want my readers to see that we're all connected as members of the human family and have this common ground, no matter what our ancestry."

Her 1985 book, Rituals of Survival: A Woman's Portfolio *is used in many training programs against sexual violence and is in the library of many battered women shelters. In 1981 she received the American Book Award for* Felita. *In 1989 she received an Honorary Doctor of Letters degree from The State University of New York. She was a 1997 honoree by the Hispanic Heritage Award Foundation. In her acceptance speech, she said: "Because of who I am, I feel blessed by the work I do, for it permits me to use my talents and continue to 'make magic.' I can recreate those deepest of personal memories as well as validate and celebrate my heritage and my future."*

Like many of the women writers represented in this collection, Nicholasa Mohr is a multi-generic virtuoso, writing fiction of various lengths for children, young adults, and adults; drama; screenplays; and teleplays. Her work in all genres is intensely visual and dynamic. When her characters are forced to sit still, you can almost feel them trembling with energy and straining against the constraints.

Vickie had been waiting in the reception room for almost one hour. Except for the thin lady who sat typing behind the desk opposite her, no one else was present. Once more, Vickie reread the name on the large dark wood door. THEODORE M. CRANE, ESQ., ATTORNEY-AT-LAW was printed in gold with a black outline. The man inside that room behind the large door was her mother's lawyer. He had been retained by the people her mother worked for. Mr. Crane was supposed to tell her when she could see her mother again.

The telephone rang and the thin lady spoke softly. "She's right here. . . . Certainly, Mr. Crane." She put down the receiver and continued to type.

The door opened and Vickie saw Mr. Crane standing in the doorway. He beckoned to her and she followed him into a large room furnished with a black leather couch, two matching armchairs, and a large dark mahogany desk. The walls had wood paneling and bookshelves lined with law books. Many framed diplomas and certificates bearing his name and title were displayed on the wall.

He pointed to one of the armchairs in front of the desk and Vickie quickly and obediently sat down.

She sat on the edge of the chair so that her feet could touch the floor. Vickie felt the soft carpeting under her shoes. Being able to touch the floor made her feel more secure. She was quite small for her age. She was thirteen, but people often thought she was younger.

Mr. Crane came over and bent down, patting Vickie on the shoulder a few times. He sighed deeply and then sat on the edge of his desk, facing her. She became aware of a dryness in her throat, and of the saliva that was quickly gathering in her mouth. Suddenly, it seemed she could not swallow. In panic, she looked all around the large office wondering where she could spit.

Mr. Crane looked down at her and smiled. With tremendous effort, Vickie swallowed, gulping down the saliva, and felt a sense of calm returning. Good, she thought, now if I can just hold down the spit, I'll be all right.

"Well," Mr. Crane said, and picked up a folder from his desk. He looked over the contents, then put it back. "You want to help your mother, don't you?" he asked. Vickie nodded. "Good. That's what this is about, to help your mother." He smiled again.

Vickie wanted to ask him when she could see her mother, but she didn't dare to interrupt, so she waited to hear what Mr. Crane would say.

"You know, Victoria . . . Now that's a beautiful name. Victoria! And a famous one. You know, Queen Victoria. She was queen of the entire British Empire. And Victoria Falls. That's a famous waterfall in Africa. Did you know that? Well, then, Victoria, we are relying on you for the truth. For your mother's sake, you must tell us what was going on, what really happened. Now . . . I'm going to ask you sincerely and honestly . . . so that you may help your mother. . . ." Mr. Crane hesitated. "Listen to me. Your mother deals in the numbers. Isn't that the truth? What you people call 'The Bolita'?" Mr. Crane stopped speaking and waited for her to respond.

". . . Not a word, Vickie, not a word . . . no matter what they ask, or who may talk to you. You don't know nothing! We don't know nothing. Remember!" Vickie could still hear her mother's voice speaking out to her in Spanish. She had returned from the movies on an afternoon three days

ago to find her mother handcuffed, surrounded by detectives, and her little sisters and brother waiting in the kitchen. ". . .Not a word. This is a
frame-up! The people I work for . . . they want to use me. It's serious. Don't
say anything." Her mother's voice, loud and clear, still echoed in her head.
Even as the detective led her out of the apartment, her mother called out,
". . . Nothing! Not one word to anyone. God bless you and . . ."

"Well?" Mr. Crane asked, looking at Vickie. She could feel her face
flush in embarrassment as she shrugged her shoulders. "Victoria, you must
tell the truth," he continued. "Doesn't your mother work for some bad
people? Who make her sell drugs? Now, we know she's not the bad one. It's
the others who are bad. Look here. . . . I don't mean the numbers; we know
all about that. In fact"—his voice softened to a whisper—"these are the
nice people who want to help your mother. They are the ones who want to
take care of her." He paused, sighing, and spoke in a loud tone. "Everyone
knows what your mother does, and that's not important. . . . But if you tell
me the truth about the drugs and let me know who some of these bad people are, it will help your mother. Make it easier on her. Understand?"

Vickie looked down at the floor, not speaking or moving.

"Answer me, please. Your mother is the one who is going to get into
serious trouble unless we know the absolute truth about the drugs, so we
can help her. Now, I have been retained as the family lawyer, and it is my
responsibility . . ." Mr. Crane kept his voice low and intimate. In a friendly
manner, he continued to speak. "You know, after all, Vickie, I have kids of
my own. I wouldn't ask you to do anything wrong. You must believe that."

The saliva gathered in her mouth once more, and she tried hard to swallow. It won't go down, she said to herself, frightened that the watery mess
would begin to drip out of the sides of her mouth. Again, with great effort
and concentration, she pushed hard. For a split second Vickie felt that she
might choke, but instead managed to swallow and breathe. A close call! she
thought.

". . . for instance, cómo estás?" Mr. Crane laughed softly. "See, how's
that? I love Spanish, and I love your country. My family and I were in San
Juan last winter. What an Island of Paradise! You should be proud of your
country, Victoria. I know many, many Puerto Ricans. They visit us and we
visit them. . . ."

Vickie and her younger sisters and brother were born in New York and
had seldom left the Bronx. Every morning in school they pledged allegiance "to the flag of the United States of America, and to the Republic for
which it stands." She had never thought of Puerto Rico as her country. As

Mr. Crane spoke, she remembered all the pictures of Puerto Rico she had seen in the Spanish magazines that her mother and Aunt Josefina read. "When I make a killing on the bolita—a big hit—" her mother had promised them, "I am taking you all on a trip to Santurce to meet your cousins, aunts and uncles." Although this had been the second arrest since her mother had been a numbers runner, things had been much better for them in the past two years. They were no longer on welfare and always had plenty of food and clothes. Except for the pressure not to open the door to anyone or discuss what their mother did with anybody, everyday living seemed easier. Only Titi Josefina and her husband Paco could come and go as they pleased in the apartment. They lived in the next building and were close to Vickie and her little sisters and brother. No one else was allowed in the apartment. Not even school friends. A vague memory of her father remained. He had gone back to Puerto Rico.

". . . We want to help you, and your sisters and little brother. Believe me, I am your friend!" As Mr. Crane spoke, his voice became louder and held a note of irritation. "Victoria, please look at me when I speak to you. Don't look away! I'm trying to tell you something for your own good. Now please listen to me. Those people are trying to . . ."

Vickie had always been taught that children never looked directly at adults when they spoke, but rather lowered their eyes as a sign of respect. Now she was afraid not to look at Mr. Crane, so she observed him carefully. He had a full head of grey hair, neatly trimmed and combed. His face was clean-shaven, almost looking benevolent. Like Santa Claus with no beard, Vickie said to herself. Except for his eyes; when she looked at his eyes, behind the thick lenses of his rimless glasses, they appeared distorted and strange.

He was dressed in a light-grey suit and a crisp white shirt and wore highly polished shoes. She concentrated on a tiny red-blue-and-green geometric design that covered his dark-blue socks. It looked like a tiny maze, and Vickie played a game, as he spoke, finding several ways in and out of the zigzag pattern.

"It's no longer a question of numbers, you know that? Drugs are involved now. That's right, drugs! Your mother will be involved unless she comes clean." Mr. Crane was almost shouting by now. His face had become a deep pink, and he waved his hands. They were a whitish-grey, and the nails had a coat of clear polish. Just as shiny as his shoes, Vickie said to herself. "Come on, Victoria. There are witnesses that can say your mother had drugs in the apartment. Don't try to deny this." He stopped shouting and lowered his voice. "Why don't you make it easier for your mother? I'll tell you what: Just admit that you saw that package in the house. The one containing that white powder . . . wrapped up in a plastic bag. . . . That's all you have to do, nothing else. Just so we get that cleared up, and everything will be easier for her." Mr. Crane folded his hands and waited. After a moment of silence, he asked, "Well?"

Vickie felt the saliva once more. Her mouth was so full she could hardly move her tongue. Opening her mouth, she took a breath and swallowed. "I don't know," she said.

Mr. Crane stood up and walked slowly around the room, coming back once more to where she was. "You must tell the truth and save your mother!" he shouted. Vickie looked at the floor and quietly shrugged her shoulders; she felt herself trembling, unable to speak.

"You don't want to be the one responsible for your mother's trouble, do you? You will send her to jail for twenty years! Do you want that? Do you? Answer!"

"No," she said. Vickie could still hear her mother's warnings in Spanish. "Remember, they put that package here themselves to harm me. You must not say a word about anything! No matter who asks you. These people will frame me. Talk to no one, Vickie!"

"Well, then. Speak up. I want to hear you. Right now! Let me hear what you have to say."

"I don't know nothing. I can't tell you nothing. I don't know nothing about no numbers or drugs or nothing like that. At all." Vickie's voice was shaking, but she spoke clearly and deliberately. "Me and my kid sisters and little brother, we don't know nothing. There's nothing I can tell you about anything. I don't know nothing . . ."

"Stand up!" Mr. Crane interrupted. She stood up, wondering if she would be arrested. "How old are you?" he asked.

"Thirteen."

"You ought to be ashamed. Ashamed! You call yourself a young lady? I wouldn't be proud to call you my—" The telephone rang and Mr. Crane stopped speaking and picked up the receiver.

"Hello, Crane here." He waited a moment and then spoke in a very low voice. "No, not a thing either. She won't cooperate. The kid is tight-lipped. . . . You know how these people are. . . . She's not about to say anything. . . .The package is insufficient. . . . Not without help. . . . Couldn't get anything here. There's not enough to hold her. No . . . no, that's right. They'll have to let her go. No. Under the circumstances I can't plea bargain.

This will have to go as a misdemeanor. . . . Look, there's nothing I can do. We'll have to look for someone else. . . . All right then. All right, bring her here. Good-bye." Without looking at Vickie, he said, "Wait outside."

Vickie was not sure that he was speaking to her, so she didn't dare move. "I said wait outside. Now, go on!" Vickie looked at Mr. Crane; he had his back to her. She wanted to ask him when she could see her mother. But when she opened her mouth, she heard herself say, "Thank you."

Mr. Crane did not respond. Quietly and swiftly, Vickie opened the door and stepped into the reception room.

"All right," she heard the thin lady say. "Your mother will be here very soon." Vickie's heart jumped. "My mother?" she asked.

The thin lady nodded, and without looking up said, "Just stay seated and be patient. Read a magazine. She'll be right here, shortly."

Vickie felt herself shaking with joy. Her mother would be here very soon. After a short while, she realized with great relief that she could swallow again. Taking a deep breath, she picked up a magazine and began to read and look at the pictures.

Before she could finish the article, the outside door opened, and Vickie saw her mother enter. She went toward Vickie with her arms outstretched. They embraced, and her mother asked her how she and the other children were.

The thin lady called in to Mr. Crane, and he came out to greet them. He smiled and shook hands with her mother.

"You have a fine girl there, Mrs. Vargas," he said.

"I know that," said Mrs. Vargas, hugging Vickie.

Without looking in Vickie's direction, Mr. Crane disappeared as he shut the door to his office.

The thin lady continued her typing and raised her arm in a gesture of good-bye.

Outside, in the street, Vickie said, "Mami, I didn't say one word. Not one word, just like you told me." Her mother stopped walking and with a big smile looked at her daughter.

"I know. . . . I know," she said happily. And they walked along with their arms around each other, heading for the subway and the long ride home to the Bronx.

Arny Christine Straayer

High Heels
1980

Arny Christine Straayer, a Chicago-based writer and film-maker, is co-editor of Black Maria *magazine and co-founder of Metis Press, a feminist publishing company. With an M.A. in creative writing and publishing from the Goddard Feminist Studies Program, she has published stories in such periodicals as* Sinister Wisdom, Womanspirit, Sojourner, Albatross, Moving Out, *and* Black Maria. *She co-authored* A Book of One's Own: Guide to Self-Publishing, *with Christine Leslie Johnson, has written a children's book,* The Rock and Me Immediately, *and collected her short stories, of which "High Heels" is one, in* Hurtin & Healin and Talkin It Over. *In 1980, Straayer received a Literary Arts Award from the Illinois Arts Council. She has been employed by the Artists-in-Residence Program of the Chicago Council on Fine Arts.*

Many of Straayer's stories examine relationships between women with biological links, particularly adult sisters and mothers and daughters. She writes, "There are so many clichés about mother-daughter relationships. Most of them work against us, replacing our real or potential experiences with acted-out scripts that serve patriarchal society."

All forms of interaction can become clichéd, but for many people, prescribed language and the stranglehold it has on our thinking is the most difficult form of stereotypical behavior from which to free ourselves. In this story, the girl and her mother work to refrain their original, authentic love and trust by using language as a pointer toward memories of other kinds of communication, earlier sharing of sensory experience.

Perhaps the final difference between stereotypes and archetypes is that the former are attributed to us by others and serve to diminish our sense of self while the latter are recognized by us and expand our sense of connection with those who have lived before us and that which lives on in us. "High Heels," an occasional story celebrating the reunion of a working-class mother and daughter, portrays two women struggling with themselves and each other for freedom from those "acted-out scripts," that is, from stereotypical behavior that has estranged them from each other. In their struggle, they reinvent "the pause" (discussed in the introduction), the archetypal ritual form of women's interactions with each other.

The thorazine girl and her mother sit on adjacent stools at a counter, facing the same direction. They have just walked here from Youtown Psychiatric Hospital. The short fat mother walked a few steps ahead, scouting out a narrow path between the dirty piles of snow and the sidewalk puddles. Her arms flapped at each side of her body for balance while only the pointed toes of her rubber boots touched the wet concrete. Her daughter followed, taller but slouchy, tennis shoes splashing through the muddy puddles, arms hugging a brown paper sack full of clothing.

Both women have cups of light coffee in front of them. They are not talking. The thorazine girl wears a lavender nylon jacket zipped up to her chin. Anchoring the pocket with one hand, she pushes the other inside for cigarettes. Her fingers do not bend well, making it difficult to flick the lighter. She holds the cigarette at the tips of her straight fingers like tweezers, touching it to the middle of her puckered lips, wetting the paper. It is a long thin menthol.

Her mother smokes a Camel, non-filter, and grips it between her teeth. She wears a turquoise plaid suit: a jacket that can no longer be buttoned, and a skirt that makes sitting on this stool difficult. Her legs want to spread under the counter but the skirt binds them. Feeling them stick to the plastic seat, she scooches her thighs to one side. The stool twirls. She pulls at the bottom ribbing of an orange shell, straightening it over her larger breasts and stomach, rattling several strings of heavy green beads. A column of ashes is beginning to droop from her Camel. Cupping her whole hand over her mouth, she clasps the cigarette deep in the web of her fingers. Nonetheless, the ashes fall, in a stack to her lap. She tries to whisk them away, but they crumble and smear on her skirt.

The mother is nervous. She wants to stare at her daughter, to brush the shaggy blonde hair back behind her ears, to look into her mouth for the color of her tongue. Her daughter's skin is transparent. She needs sunshine. The blue veins along her temples make her look like a fetus. In the middle of her forehead is a scab. The mother wants to spread ointment on the scab and cradle the pale head. If she were not afraid, she would ask about the scab, how it happened, but perhaps her girl would get angry.

It is disheartening to be afraid of one's own daughter, to fear her rejection. Yes, the hospital had been a mistake. But hadn't she suffered enough during these long months of longing, not being allowed to visit. The love is throbbing inside her. How long can her body hold still?

She slides the palm of her hand across the top of her head. Her hand is red and tough like leather. Her hair is dyed pitch black, is tangled and dry. She has not combed it today and the set is nearly out. Neither has she washed her face. Last night's lipstick has been rubbed into her thin lips, leaving them orange, but dull. She stretches them back and forth and bites at them, trying to contain the emotions inside her.

Yesterday, the daughter had finally accepted her phone call. She did not say hello. She said, "Get me out of here." Her voice was hostile. The mother answered, "Yes, yes, my darling," and the daughter said, "Don't call me darling."

It was a second chance for the mother. She pressed a hand to her chest as she hung up the phone. Her breathing was fast. Tomorrow she would see her girl. They would be together again. She would not make another bad mistake. At work that night, she dropped a customer's roast beef dinner on the floor. She was clumsy and giddy. She laughed about it. Later she had cried, not sleeping at all, making her eyes puffy and red for this morning.

The daughter's head is hanging over her coffee. She cannot bear the thought of looking into her mother's eyes. At the hospital, they were red and puffy. She had walked behind her mother down the sidewalk so as not to see them again. Maybe, under the redness, there is still a yellow bruise from where she hit her mother. Maybe there is a scar still fresh red.

The doctors thought she'd forgotten about hitting her mother, that the drugs had erased it from her brain. They said it was not wrong anyway but just the normal reaction of a girl who needed to break away from her mother and grow up. But that was not why she had hit her mother. It was because her mother betrayed her and called them to come after her. She hit her mother's eye with the telephone handle and saw it turn black while they rode to the hospital.

Her mother must not turn to face her. If she does, the daughter will close her eyes or stand up and walk out, rather than see the redness. She is guilty. She is the worst. She clubbed her own mother. She is not a darling.

For months in the hospital, she had dreamed of the old days when she sat in a booth waiting for her mother to get off work. Every evening seemed so long before they could walk home holding hands, she carrying her mother's high heels in summer, sometimes resting on some doorstep to rub her mother's sore feet. She wants to do that now. Her mother doesn't wear high heels anymore, but her feet are calloused from all the hard years. They need lotion. She wants to kiss them with her full lips, wet them with her tears. She wants to lie with her mother's feet tickling her belly again, with her mother laughing too, her loud shrill laughter. But she does not deserve it.

When those eyes are not red anymore, the daughter will be able to apologize. For now, she must not look, but keep busy instead with her cigarette and coffee. She moves her hand to the ashtray and pecks at the long thin menthol. The thorazine makes her hand far away. The cigarette rolls in to the bowl of the ashtray. She reaches for her coffee cup with both hands. It is cold. When did it get cold? The thorazine makes her head sluggish. She raises the cup in slow motion. Then bracing her elbows on the counter, she bends forward until her mouth touches the edge, and drinks down all the cold coffee, so she can ask the waitress for more. She tries to wave to the waitress but cannot control her hand.

What have I done to her, the mother is thinking as the daughter uses one hand to lift the other. Her mouth opens to shriek for the waitress before she remembers the doctors' instructions to stay quiet for her daughter's sake. She is too loud and coarse for her big girl. Her shoulders hunch up around the chin. But the daughter hasn't noticed. She is staring into space again, her eyes glazed, far away.

The mother's blunt fingers thump against the counter. She cannot stand this separation. She'd been wrong. Wrong. Why had she thought her girl needed a hospital? It had only forced them apart, her daughter helpless, herself excluded. Her daughter didn't need treatment. Everyone was just trying to separate them. One way or another, those doctors were determined to force them apart. They were just jealous. What did they know? So what if she'd driven two hundred miles to the university, and her daughter wouldn't get out of the car. It was not wrong. It didn't mean she needed a hospital. Oh, what had happened to her girl in there while she was out here abandoned?

The waitress refills their cups. The coffee is too hot, and the daughter spills it on her chin. It dribbles down into the dimple below her mouth. Oh, my poor damaged baby, thinks the mother, turning towards her. My poor broken baby. She looks at her daughter's fragile lips and thin eyelids closed. The dimple looks sad on her face now, as if she were crying. That cute little dimple that used to make her look so happy.

The mother is seeing her daughter at five, playing dress-up lady in mamma's high heels; at eight, sitting in the restaurant booth, her dimple filled with mamma's pink powder; at eleven, sticking out that sensitive chin and saying, "It's you and me, partner;" at sixteen, filling the pockets of mother's red blouse with candy kisses.

"Hey, remember the candy kisses you gave me?" she blurts out unintentionally. Her daughter's head is lowered towards the counter. But from the side, the mother sees a delicate eyelash twitch, a corner of the mouth curl. "Remember the matching red blouses?"

The daughter's chin is moving tentatively. The lips begin to open. Words are coming out slowly, one by one, in a whisper. "Remember the picture of me in your high heels?"

The voice is barely her daughter's. The mother knows without looking that the tongue is too thick. "Yes . . . I do." She stubs out her Camel, tipping the ashtray and flipping ashes onto the counter. Tears are welling in her eyes. Her thin lips are stretching and jerking into a smile.

The daughter's head is lifting. She is holding one hand at the back of her neck as if to support it. Her eyelids flutter. "There was a woman in the hospital who still wore high heels." She stops for a moment to rest. "Whenever the halls were mopped and slippery, she wobbled, like I used to do, in yours." The daughter glances timidly at the dimple in her mother's fat chin. "I told her, I sure wished my mom could see that."

Ann Allen Shockley

A Birthday Remembered 1980

In "Towards a Black Feminist Criticism," Barbara Smith names Ann Allen Shockley (b. 1927) as one of "a handful of Black women who have risked everything for truth" having "broken ground in the vast wilderness of works that do not exist." A librarian and professor of library science at Fisk University, Shockley has written a number of important works in the field of black librarianship, as well as the novels Loving Her (1974) *and* Say Jesus and Come to Me (1982), *and the short story collection* The Black and White of It (1980), *from which "A Birthday Remembered" is reprinted. In addition, she has published several dozen stories in such periodicals as* Negro Digest, Freedomways, Black World, Feminary, Umbra, *and* Sinister Wisdom. *She writes about herself,*

[I] was born in Louisville, Kentucky, where an eighth
grade English teacher helped to give birth to my thoughts
of becoming a writer. I have been writing since that time.
I was a newspaper reporter, free-lance writer and substitute teacher before entering the field of librarianship. . . . Working as an academic librarian, I write on
weekends, holidays, and summer months, with my dogs,
Tiffany and Bianca, watching the birthing pains. I wish it
could be different.

She is divorced and has two grown children.

Most of Shockley's short fiction deals with how the lives of individual and coupled black heterosexuals—mostly middle class—and black and racially unidentified lesbians are short-circuited by racism, sexism, and homophobia. There is a constant interface between intracouple tensions—those that exist between the partners in every relationship who choose each other and yet need to define personal boundaries—and the tensions of shared victimization.

Shockley's work illuminates how shared oppression and, in the case of lesbians, social invisibility, make the partners in a relationship more dependent on and desperate for each other in comparison to couples for whom external validations exist. Such partners are often pushed closer together than autonomous adults can stand to be. At the same time, the shared oppression gives greater priority to their shared persecution and to those attributes for which they are victimized than to the unique personal qualities that make or break relationships undertaken in greater freedom and with social reinforcement. Shockley documents the erosions of hope, the challenges to loyalty presented by threats to survival, the insecurities of those trapped in socially devalued categories, and the poisoning of love and intimacy by invasions of bigotry. She writes poignantly of the personal and illuminates by implication the political.

"A Birthday Remembered," while it touches on all the pain and cruelty delineated in her other stories, is one of the few that ends with an affirmation, testifying that mothering is something more than a biological accident, that the spirit and the activities of nurturance equal or transcend the claims of blood. With this message, Shockley reaffirms the points made in Helen Hull's story, "The Fire," in Fannie Hurst's story, "Oats for the Woman," and in Sherley Anne Williams's story, "The Lawd Don't Like Ugly": Women give the gift of mothering to women across the generations not only as mothers, but as teachers, as step-mothers, as mentors, and as friends.

"Hello—Aunt El—?"

The familiar voice came over the telephone, young, vivacious, excited—a girlish echo reminding her of the past. "Tobie—"

"Happy birthday!"

"Thank you—" Ellen felt a rush of warmth, pleased that Tobie had remembered. But hadn't Tobie always. Besides, her birthday wasn't difficult to remember, falling on Valentine's Day. *A heart born especially for me,* Jackie used to tease.

"May I come over?"

Now Tobie's voice sounded a little strained. Ellen could visualize the puckers of thin lines forming between her wide-spaced eyes. The tightness in her throat delayed an answer. Why shouldn't she? Then again, why *should* she really want to? Tobie no longer belonged to her—*them.* When Jackie died a year ago, Tobie had to go back to her father. A splintering separation, after all their years of living together, *belonging* together—Tobie, Jackie and herself.

The three of them had survived through the tumultuous stress of trying to make it, ever since Jackie walked out on Roger and came to live with her. Tobie was just five years old—too small and pale for her age, too nervous from the parental arguments.

Roger had been furious, appalled and angry at his wife's leaving him for a woman. Ellen knew it was more an affront to his male ego than losing Jackie. Particularly when it belonged to one who was striving ruthlessly to become a top business executive, amassing along the way all the exterior garnishments that were supposed to go along with it. He had purchased a large, two-story brick colonial house in the suburbs, replete with swimming pool and a paneled country squire station wagon for Jackie to do her errands. When she left him, he had tried to declare her temporarily insane.

Ellen thought that perhaps Jackie *had* been crazy to leave all of that and come to live with her in a cramped apartment on her salary. She wasn't making that much at the time as a staff writer for *Women's Homemaking* magazine's food section. But, somehow, they had made out, until Jackie got a job teaching in an elementary school. Jackie loved children, and had a way with them.

"Hey—Aunt El. You still with me?"

Tobie was waiting for an answer. One could get so involved in the past. "Of course, dear. Please *do* come over," she invited, thinking it wasn't until later she was to have dinner with Harriet. All she had to do was change from her jumpsuit to a dress.

"I'm bringing a friend who I want you to meet. Ok?"

Tobie never had an abundance of friends, only special ones who were close, for that was her way. At first, she and Jackie had mistakenly thought Tobie was ashamed of their first relationship—what they were to each other. They knew Tobie was aware of it. How could she not have been? Real love can't be hidden. It inevitably is transmitted through a glance, affectionate touch, strong feelings that show.

Then there was the rainy, cold night in November, one month after Jackie had left him, when Roger came to the apartment, hurling threats, shouting obscenities. He was going to take them to court, declare them perverts, unfit to raise a child. Tobie must have heard the words flung out at them through the paper-thin walls.

"Wonderful, darling. I'll look forward to meeting your—friend."

The phone clicked and Tobie wasn't there anymore. Ellen remained seated on the couch, motionless, as if the remembrance of all that had gone by in ten years had risen like a mist to cover her in sadness. There had not been a divorce because of his man-stubbornness and Jackie's woman-fear for Tobie. When she died, he buried her. She hadn't been allowed to do this one last thing for Jackie. To *be* with her during the last rituals, to hold a fourteen-year-old who was all but flesh, her daughter too. The next morning after the funeral, Tobie came by to be with her, to cry her tears, sustain her grief. The sorrow shared as one was their solitary entombment for her. Through the passing days, the biting cruelty of it all slowly healed, leaving only the scar tissue. Jackie had been laid to rest in her heart.

Ellen's eyes fell on the array of birthday cards on the coffee table and the vase of red roses that Harriet had sent. Meeting Harriet had helped her to get over the travail of death's cruel separation. Incurable illnesses are like earthquakes—they swallow quickly. It wasn't too bad now. She could look back and recall without too much pain. All it takes is someone to help, someone who cares, and the eraser of time.

The living room was beginning to become shaded with dark-fingered lances of shadows. She reached over and turned on a table lamp. The day was quickly vanishing into the grayness of night. What she should do was get a drink. A good, stiff celebrating birthday martini. After all, she was forty-four years old. Six more years, if still alive, she would reach the half-century mark.

She got up and went to the kitchen. There she turned on the light which brought into sharp, garish focus the ultra-modern bright chrome and copper, resembling the spacious kitchens featured in her magazine articles where various culinary talents were exhibited. Thankfully, through her writing skills, she had been able to help make their living better before Jackie passed. She had become editor of the food section and had written a cookbook. Her publisher had assured her that cookbooks always sell, and hers had.

A martini called for gin, vermouth, lemon, and an olive. She got out a glass pitcher and stirrer. Jackie preferred sunrises. She made them for her in the evenings, after the lengthy daily struggles of climbing the ladder together. Jackie had become principal of the school, a model for those beneath her, and an in-school parent for the students. Ellen marveled at how she had blossomed, learning to become independent after being a college-trained housewife to Roger. *There's so much to living that I did not know before*, Jackie had told her happily. Yes, indeed, there was a lot to living that neither had known before.

She mixed the drink in the shaker, stirred it slowly and poured some in a glass, topping it with a round green olive with a small red eye-circle. *Here's to you, Ellen Simms, on your birthday!* She lifted the glass in a toast and the drink went down smoothly. Then the doorbell rang. Tobie must have been just around the corner. As soon as she responded, Tobie sang out cheerfully: "Happy birthday to you—happy birthday to you!"

Tobie hugged her and Ellen found her nose pressed into the cold leather of her jacket. Tobie seemed taller. *They do grow*, she mockingly reminded herself, comparing her own short stockiness to Tobie's height.

"A present for you, Aunt El—"

When Tobie thrust the gift into her arms, Ellen protested: "You shouldn't have." The package was neatly store wrapped and tied with a pink ribbon holding a card.

"You know I never forget your birthday, Aunt El—"

At that moment, she saw the boy standing awkwardly behind her. He had a round, friendly face and a mass of dark brown hair parted on the side.

"Hello—" she spoke to him.

"Aunt El—this is Warrick."

"Come in and take off your coats. Would you like some hot cocoa to warm you up? I know it's cold outside." Tobie used to love hot cocoa with a marshmallow floating like a full-grown moon on top. This was her favorite on Sunday mornings when they had a leisurely breakfast together.

"Cocoa—you *know* what I like!" Tobie exclaimed, throwing off her coat and curling up on the sofa.

Ellen watched her, noting the girlishness hadn't gone yet in the transitional adolescent stage. She looked older. Her blonde hair was cut short and bangs covered her forehead. Physically, she looked more like her father with the sharp, angular face, but there was her mother where it counted most, in her warmth and quickness of smile. Did her father know that she was here—with her? Like visiting a widowed parent—eight years of child-rearing, child-caring, child-loving.

"Open your present, Aunt El—"

"All right." First she read the heart shaped card with the fringed edges about Valentine birthdays, and then the scribbled message: *To my one and only Aunt El, with love, always.* She blinked back the tears and made a fanfare out of unwrapping the gift. It was a big, glossy, illustrated, expensive cookbook of ancient Eastern recipes.

"Thank you, my dear." She leaned over to kiss Tobie's cheek. "It's lovely."

"Tobie saved up a week's salary to buy it—" Warrick announced proudly, settling in the rocker opposite the sofa. His voice was changing, and there was an inflamed red pimple beside his nose. On the front of his red and white pullover sweater were the words *Terrence Academy*. The right sleeve had a large white T.

"Warrick! Shame on you giving my secrets away," Tobie laughed, playfully chastising him.

"Where are you working?" Ellen asked, hanging their coats in the closet. She couldn't imagine Roger Ewing permitting his teen-aged daughter to work.

"I'm a library page after school at the branch near home. I like to have my *own* money—" she added reflectively.

Ellen hesitated, wondering if she should ask. Don't forget the social amenities. Isn't that what they had taught Tobie throughout the years. "How is your—father?" she asked, the words sounding like cracked dry ice.

"Oh, Dad's ok," she shrugged, kicking off the high wooden wedge platforms with interlacing straps. "His main object in life seems to be to prove how much money he can make and *keep.*"

Roger's a miser at heart: he wants every cent I spend accounted for, yet he'll go out and buy something outlandishly showy to prove he's got money, Jackie had commented about him.

Why was it that people happen to be in certain places at the right or wrong time? Like the dinner party she had been assigned to write up for the magazine to describe the elegance of the food, drinks and table setting. There seated next to her was Jackie, looking small, frail and lost among the spirited laughter and inane chitchat of the moneyed. Roger was on her other side, appearing to be thoroughly enjoying himself talking to the big-bosomed woman with the glittering necklace and frosted white hair. There was the interest at first sight, hidden hormones clashing while a subtle intuitive knowingness flashed hidden messages above the clamor of the room. *If only we could decide our own fates, what would life then be?*

"I'll make the cocoa—" she said, retreating to the kitchen.

The martini pitcher was on the counter where she had left it. Immediately she poured another drink. She had been ruminating too much. Stop the past. Drink and be merry. Chase the haunting memories away.

"Aunt El—need any help?"

Tobie came in. She had put her shoes back on and they made a hard noise against the linoleum. The wedges looked like ancient ships, causing her to wonder if they were comfortable. The bell-bottom blue jeans billowed over them like sails. "No—nothing to making cocoa. After all the times of doing it for you—" The reminder slipped out. She wished it hadn't.

Tobie laughed, and the sound made everything all right again. "What do you think of Warrick?" she asked, reaching into the closet for cups and saucers. Everything was known to her in a place that had once been home.

"He seems like a nice—boy." Suppose it had been a girl? People choose who they want. This they had tried to instill in her in their unobtrusive way. "How does your father like him?"

"Dad hasn't met him yet," Tobie said quietly. "I wanted to get *your* opinion *first*. Anyway, Dad stays busy and away so much that we don't have much time to talk. The housekeeper takes care of the house—and me— who, I suppose, goes with the house." She gazed down at the floor, biting her lip, face clouded. "I miss Mom—don't you?"

"Yes—" she replied softly. "But we have to get used to living without loved ones. That time must inevitably come, sooner or later, for some-body."

She turned away, pretending to search the refrigerator so Tobie couldn't see her face. Do something else while waiting for the milk to warm. Prepare sandwiches. Young people were always hungry—feeding growth. She had cold chicken and potato salad left over from last night.

"I thought if *you* liked Warrick, Mom would too. He plays on the bas-ketball team," Tobie continued, watching her slice the chicken and take out the jars of pickles and mustard from the refrigerator.

"Are you—serious, about him?" Ellen asked, praying that she wasn't. Not at this stage of youth—almost fifteen.

"Of course not! We're just friends. He's someone to go places and do things with."

"Good!" Ellen exclaimed, feeling an impending burden lifted. "There's plenty of time for the other. You have to go to college and—" she went on hurriedly about those things which normally fall in place for young lives.

Tobie smiled. "I *knew* you were going to say that, Aunt El." Then she looked directly at her, blue eyes locking Ellen's in a vise. "Anyway, some-day, if I ever *do* get serious about someone, I hope it will be as wonderful and beautiful as what you and Mom had together."

God, for the first time, it was out in the open! She felt the shock of the words, unexpected, frank—a blessing. "I do too, dear. Like we had." Her hands trembled from the weight of the moment between them. A bridge had transformed Tobie from girl to woman now to her.

"Aunt El, the milk's boiling over!"

"I've lost my cocoa-making expertise," Ellen laughed, snatching the pan off the burner. The milk had boiled into a bubbling white-coated cascade of foam.

When the tray of food was ready, they went back to the living room where Warrick was watching TV. While they ate hungrily, Ellen finished her drink, feeling light, warm and happy.

When the telephone rang, it was like a rude interruption into a special cradle of time. Harriet wanted to know if she would be ready around seven-thirty for dinner. She glanced at her watch. It was just six o'clock. Besides, what was more important to her than this?

Later, Tobie said: "We'd better be going. Warrick's taking me to the movies. Thanks for the treat, Aunt El."

"And, thank *you* for the present. I'm glad you came by to make my birthday a happy one. *Both* of you."

"Nice meeting you, Miss Simms," Warrick said, extending his hand. "Tobie talks about you all the time. Now I can see why!"

She liked him. "Come back—anytime."

Tobie kissed her goodbye at the door. When they left, the tears were finally freed—in sadness and happiness too. Tobie was going to make it all right. Jackie would have been proud. They had made good parents.

Alma Luz Villanueva

Her Choice
1981

Making the decision to terminate a pregnancy or to bring a fetus to term is by far the most wrenching experience I've ever had. The right to choose is not a luxury; it is a responsibility that demands intense introspection and awareness."
S. Boyd, " Give us liberty: The approval of RU-486 isn't about morals, it's about options," Salon.com at: http://www.salon.com/

Abortion Has Always Been With Us

"In 1955, the anthropologist George Devereux demonstrated that abortion has been practiced in almost all human communities from the earliest times. The patterns of abortion use, in hundreds of societies around the world since before recorded history, have been strikingly similar. Women faced with unwanted pregnancies have turned to abortion, regardless of religious or legal sanction and often at considerable risk. Used to deal with upheavals in personal, family, and community life, abortion has been called 'a fundamental aspect of human behavior.'"
From *Abortion in Law, History, and Religion.* Published by: Childbirth by Choice Trust 344 Bloor Street West, Suite 306, Toronto, Canada M5S 3A7 (416) 961-1507 Revised, 1995.

We can never know how many stories have been written about a particular subject or theme. We can only know, and then perhaps only approximately, how many of such stories have been published. Many of us have been faced with the issue of abortion in our personal lives, when we or a woman, a grandmother, mother, sister, daughter, friend, etc., whom we love, faces an unplanned, unhealthy, or unwanted pregnancy. Many women have written that private story, often coded, in journals that have been as hidden as the reality it recounts. Abortion continues to be a reality that breaks hearts, binds or separates people forever, stirs public passions, and brings versions of peace or hell into private lives.

However, I have found very few published stories by U.S. women writers about abortion— the desperation attaching to the desire and need for an abortion, the obtaining of abortions, the pain and terror of illegal abortions, the unavailability of abortions, and the subsequent horror of self-induced abortions and/or the relationship between an unwilling or unable mother and the child whom she would have aborted, the experience of having an abortion, the memory of an abortion, the entire range of abortion stories. It is a subject so wrapped in secrecy and so circumscribed by taboo that its absence as a central story issue is not surprising. And yet the sometimes unwelcome consequences of our fertility is so looming a reality in the lives of women that it cannot be entirely absent from our imaginative literature.

Among the very few published stories about abortion, Alma Luz Villanueva's 1993 story "Her Choice" is, in its very few words, perhaps the most complex in terms of the issues it raises for readers. Would the mother have had an abortion if it had been available? Does she regret her daughter's life? If the unavailable abortion which resulted in the daughter's birth is no longer regretted because the daughter is cherished and the mother/daughter relationship is the highlight of the mother's life, then how can the mother participate in the obtaining of an abortion of the pregnancy that would culminate, if not terminate, in the birth of her first grandchild? If the mother participates in the obtaining of her daughter's abortion will her daughter retroactively feel unwanted? Which child's life is more important—the daughter's which will be inevitably altered by her pregnancy or the child who would be born if the pregnancy continued? Does the daughter suffer emotionally at the thought that her mother might have aborted the pregnancy that culminated in her birth if abortion had been available? Does the daughter undertake a new kind or level of obligation to her mother if her mother participates in the obtaining of the daughter's abortion? How might the mutually sought abortion transform the relationship of the mother and daughter?

This story is also about a mother relinquishing her adult control over her child's life in recognition that her daughter is no longer a child. At the same time that the mother has to negotiate both the reality of her daughter's maturing sexuality and the imminence of a potential grandchild as well, as its loss, she must negotiate the loss of her own child. Not only is something new gained in transformations, but something old is lost: when the child becomes a woman, she is lost to the mother.

Alma Luz Villanueva was born in Santa Barbara, California in 1944 and raised in San Francisco's Mission District by her grandmother, a Yaqui Indian from Sonora, Mexico. She is of Yaqui, Spanish, and German ancestry. Her grandmother died when Villanueva was twelve and it's no coincidence that Villanueva then began writing poetry. She dropped out of high school in the tenth grade, having her first child at age fifteen and her second at age seventeen. She lived on welfare in a brutal public housing project in San Francisco married to a violent man. While living in the projects, she made ends meet by modeling for a local agency, and the proceeds helped to finance her education. She stopped modeling after she declined a European contract offered to her by the agency that required her to be separated from her children for one year. She later finished college and earned her M.F.A. She now has four grown children, all of whom are involved in one sort of healing profession or another—physical, emotional, and social—following in the curandera tradition of Villanueva's grandmother. She also has three grandchildren.

"So that period of my life was an early drama, quite a challenge to survive. So I didn't write anything from age 13 to 26 because I was struggling for survival," she said. "My first marriage lasted for 10 years, then my best friend died of breast cancer at age 27," she said. *Later, her late friend's husband and Villanueva bought a farm in Sebastopol and moved there with five kids, three of hers and two of his.*

"It was a beautiful farm, a beautiful spot," she said. "There on the farm all the poetry, all the words, all the crying, all the laughter just erupted. Poetry for me is the source, the mother tongue . . . the sun, moon and stars. Almost daily I will sit down to my poetry first and see what it has to tell me."

After living on the farm for some time, then moving to a cabin in the Plumas National Forest, and after having her fourth child at age thirty-six, Villanueva moved to Santa Cruz where she lived for the next fourteen years. Villanueva, who holds a M.F.A. in Writing from Vermont College at Norwich University, teaches in the low-residency M.F.A. creative writing program at Antioch University, Los Angeles. Currently she is living in Santa Fe, New Mexico, and writing.

Her first book of poetry, Bloodroot (1977), *attracted considerable critical attention. That same year, her manuscript simply entitled* Poems *won the Third Annual Chicano Literary Prize at the University of California at Irvine. Villanueva's autobiographical poem,* Mother, May I? *(1978), long her best-known work, fictionalizes through personalized myth the cyclic changes in a woman's life and the joyous emergence into wholeness. Her first novel,* The Ultraviolet Sky (1988), *received the American Book Award of the Before Columbus Foundation and was reissued by Anchor/Doubleday. Her second novel,* Naked Ladies (1994), *received the PEN Oakland Josephine Miles Award. Villanueva's later novels include* Luna's California Poppies (2001). *Other poetry collections include* La Chingada (1985), *an epic poem published in English and Spanish,* Life Span (1984), *and* Planet (1993). Planet, *which won the Latin American Writers Institute Award in poetry (1994, New York), spotlights such issues as racism, sexual abuse, and poverty. Prior to* Vida, *Villanueva's last collection of poetry was* Desire (1998). *Her poetry has been chosen for inclusion in "The Best American Poetry 1996" and has been published in many magazines and anthologies.*

She is the author of a collection of short fiction, Weeping Woman: La Llorona and Other Stories (1994) *and has published short stories in various anthologies and periodicals that have not yet been collected. "Her Choice" was first published in* Infinite Divisions: An Anthology of Chicana Literature *edited by Tey Diana*

Rebolledo & Eliana S. Rivero (The University of Arizona Press, 1993). Stories from Weeping Woman *have been republished in* Under the Fifth Sun (Heydey Books), Latina, Women's Voices from the Borderland (Simon and Schuster), *Ms. Magazine, and some textbooks for junior and high schools as well as college. Her newest novel is entitled* The Infrared Earth.

The way her whole body moves, the way she sits: the mood of sulky expectancy. The longing. She's barely sixteen, about the same age her mother was when she had her. The coincidence was too obvious.

I always wanted you to make love from your own choice the first time—not to be raped or forced in any way. I always wanted you to enjoy your own body, the mother thinks. She knows her daughter longs to be pregnant—she feels it like a magnet. She feels pulled by her daughter's longing, and her own—the body's strange urge to fill up warm and full and sexual. Only, her daughter's urge is to the boy, her first lover, and her own to the knowledge of baby weight. The smell, the feel, the urgent suckle, the silent language of mother-lust.

Tania heard her mother and friends talking, always, about the most intimate things. She loved to listen. It made her tremble. And when she heard her mother's voice lower, she felt cheated. There's *more*, she thought.

Tania had sat on her mother's lap until her legs dangled quite comfortably on the floor. They had a game. When Tania would come home after school, she'd open the front door and shout, "I'm home!" Her mother, wherever she was, would sit down, and Tania would leap on her. They'd talk and smell each other, then Tania's mother would spank her on the panties and tell her to change and go play.

Little by little, as Tania grew older, she'd loiter by the older women. Then, once she sat down and they all looked at her, exchanged looks, and let her stay.

Tania liked her mother's friends better than her own. They really liked each other. She loved to go to the different women's houses and spend the night, being everyone's daughter. That's about when she stopped needing her mother to come during the night and lie next to her, talking, till the fear went away. That's about when she began to keep a secret or two from her mother.

"How are you feeling?" Vida asked.

"Okay, I guess, Mom—kind of sad," Tania replied.

"Do you want some coffee? I'm going to make some." That meant a talk. Tania slowly sipped the coffee. It didn't even smell good, though she knew the coffee must be delicious. She and her mother had talked over pots of it, talking at faster pitches, till they realized they'd had enough—the ritual over. They'd go out to the bridge and sit and let the sun cook their faces, their tongues resting in their wet hollows. Or sometimes they'd separate in a burst—not one more word—to a task, to a separateness that each respected. Though, sometimes, Tania would shout, "Mom, can I have a ride to the bookstore?" where she worked. Vida replied with studied irritation in her voice, implying she was late because they'd been talking, "Okay, but I don't want to pick you up tonight—so get a ride. If you really can't get a ride, call." You to your world, me to mine—I'm not a flunky, Vida thought. Balancing, always balancing, this growth—mother to daughter, daughter to mother.

There was no exchange, no flow between them today. Vida looked at her daughter and realized that to pry, would mean to pry a fury from Tania. She wasn't interested in doing that. It felt so heavy, sullen like clotted blood. A dam of blood needing to be released, Vida thought: a dam of dark anger where her child once was. There, she had been able to mirror herself once, quite clearly, in the pools of her daughter's eyes. Now, Tania locked her out with churned mud from a bottom that left her dazed.

They lived side by side like two women, some sympathy taking the place of words. Vida, herself, was planning to leave her second husband. *Planning* was the word: again? how? why? I must. She could think of having a child entirely separate from a man, except for the short tenderness of lovemaking. It was as though a man considered it a victory to make a woman pregnant. Then the victory lost its flavor, its appeal altogether; after all, the prize was won. It took her three children to realize this; three offerings to the male. Now she could envision having one for herself, if she chose. After all, these children *were* for herself—she hadn't blundered that far. They gave her a joy that seemed, at times, inexhaustible.

Tania's boyfriend stopped dropping by the house and waved quickly, looking away, in the street.

"How's Scott?" Vida would ask neutrally.

"He's all right," Tania would answer just as neutrally.

Oh, she's learned very well, Vida thought, letting it go. If she pressed, Tania looked trapped and the water would rise to her eyes. So Vida waited, the blood clotting thicker, it seemed. Something. A flesh, a membrane, a growth wouldn't let them reach or touch.

Tania remembered her father as charming and handsome and fun, when he wanted to be. Then, she remembered him gone for long periods (with terrible relief); then home, drunk (she remembered flying into the room, toward the end, just before her father left, when a fight seemed worse than the others—her mother yelling, "Don't you touch me!"). She remembered screaming, "You leave *my* mother alone!" He'd grabbed Tania by the arm, leading her back to bed, trying to say things like, "This is between your mother and I." Tania was struggling, still crying hysterically, and Vida ran in, pulling her daughter from him, shouting, "Leave us alone, goddamn you!" It was a moment of murder; they all knew it. He could kill her; it in was his power—but Vida was so angry, so desperate she'd kill her husband if he touched either of them now. He left, Tania remembered.

Tania loved her mother's strength and worried about her mother's weakness. But, then, she knew her mother—a cup of coffee, a braided cinnamon roll, a special omelet, and there was her mother, full, again. At the center of her mother was a power she had never seen crushed.

Tania had been cutting school. They'd called with a list of days that were inexcusable. A day too beautiful to go to school, a day to stay home and hide: this Vida had condoned, always. But this new creature wanted to flaunt old trusts.

Tania walked in an hour late, with an off-hand apology and no offer to help with dinner.

"*Where* are you late from, Tania?" Vida spit.

Tania felt her mother open and close the door in an instant. She was in, whether she answered or not, and Tania knew it.

"Can I talk to you about it later?"

"I'll give you till tonight, and no later." And Tania knew she meant it. She'd heard everything in her mother's voice: anger, hurt, disappointment in a trust so long extended. The weapons of the gentle are harsher than the weapons of the cruel, Tania thought. The first seems inside of you and so hard to distinguish. The other can be fought like an outside pain.

Well, I can lie and be punished like everyone else, Tania comforted herself, and went to help with dinner in the guise of a sulky child.

Later, after dinner, the dishes were washed, the last log of the night in the fire toward morning—she came into her mother's room to lie:

"I'm pregnant. Tomorrow I'm going for an abortion. That's where I was all those days, trying to get an abortion." Her eyes were clear, the dam burst and nearly drowned Vida.

Vida choked, "My grandchild!" It slapped Tania's face. No anger, no shame—that would come later, Tania thought. She ran to her room and heard her mother begin to cry in a horrible hoarse voice, like something ancient being pulled from her belly. She'd never heard her mother cry like that before, and she was instantly frightened and sorry. She heard Vida slam and lock her door, and every time Tania passed the room that night, she knew a candle was burning, which made her feel a little better. She knew her mother was thinking and taking comfort from that thin flame.

The fire was dying in the fireplace. Tania poured herself a glass of wine, taking it to her room. In the dark she drank it, lay on her stomach and cried her own tears. She didn't want this child: she knew that. She fell into her own sleep.

Tania woke up to the smell of coffee and remembered, instantly, the bus schedule. She ran to the bathroom, got dressed, ran to the kitchen trying not to look at Vida.

"How are you getting there?"

"By bus," Tania whispered.

Vida's eyes were huge in her head, "I'll take you."

Tania stumbled to her mother's arms, bending her head just a little, heaving her sorrow on the small shoulder. She had outgrown her mother this year, only in height.

Now they were both women.

Beth Brant
(Degonwadonti)

A Long Story
1985

I figure by now most readers know me as "that Mohawk lesbian" or "that nice Indian Granny who lives in the States." Both statements are true. And I know who I am—something I couldn't have said years ago when I was a battered woman, a self-hating half-breed, a woman who self-destructed at every turning, before I acknowledged my lesbianism and before I began to write. Anyway, most of my stories are about lesbians and gay men; all are about Indians.

From "To Be or Not To Be Has Never Been the Question,"
in Writing as Witness: Essay and Talk, Women's Press, *1995.*

Indian people remember, as Jews remember, children roughly removed by men in uniform, sent away on trains to attend government schools to be robbed not only of their family but of their heritage. So Beth Brant recalls in tears that dampen the page the loss of her own daughter to her white father's family because Beth is not only Indian but a lesbian. In "A Long Story" she juxtaposes her own terrible loss with the story of the wholesale removal of Indian children a century ago:

I would have killed him if I'd had the chance. He took her hand and pulled her to the car. The look in his eyes of triumph. I know he will teach her to hate us. He will! I see her dear face. Her face looking out the back window of his car. Her mouth forming the words over and over . . . Mommy Mama.

Awakened Woman e-magazine, goddessaltar.com
http://www.awakenedwoman.com/gathering_of_spirit.htm

Beth Brant is a citizen of the Borderlands defined by Gloria Anzaldua as follows:

She is an American in the sense of the word that her roots are in the lands of the American continent; she is not quite an American in the sense that American has come to mean an inhabitant of the United States because she is equally an inhabitant of Canada. She was born in 1941 in Detroit—because her American roots predate the separation of those two political entities and because she is both a Mohawk and Irish-Scots.

It may seem that there are two stories being told in this story by Beth Brant. One is the story from 1891 about an Indian woman who loses her daughter to government agents who want to "civilize" her. The other is a story from 1979 about a lesbian Indian who loses her son to his father's white family when the courts, i.e., government agents, decide that she is an unfit mother. Two separate stories? But the title is "A Long Story." Is Brant saying with her title that these are not separate stories?

Like Lydia Maria Child's 1842 abolitionist story "The Quadroons" about two generations, mother and child, of enslaved light-skinned African-American women (to read this story see my collection The Other Woman: Stories of Two Women and a Man, *(The Feminist Press, 1984), Brant's "A Long Story" violates the expected architecture of a short story. Most readers expect a beginning, middle, and end; we expect a single cast of characters; we expect a story that ends and then stops. And yet these stories violate our expectations; each of these stories contains the recounting of two atrocities, neither one of them remedied, revenged, or resolved. In both stories we see the utter inability of members of oppressed communities unable to protect themselves or those for whom they are expected to be responsible. African-American, Native American, lesbians, and women of all kinds—all are vulnerable to the patriarchal theft of what is most precious to them—their children. Anguish, helplessness, weariness, rage, an aching need for the return of the lost, the stolen, the missing. And then the pain is finally tamed enough to speak of, to squeeze into words. Episodes of the long story begin to appear in print.*

"A Long Story" by Beth Brant has been and continues to be cherished by many literary and identity communities. Evidence of its ability to speak to and touch multiple audiences resides in the many reprintings of this story. It was first published in the 1983 special double issue of Sinister Wisdom: A Journal for the Lesbian Imagination in Arts and Politics *that Brant edited under the title* A Gathering of Spirit: Writing and Art by North American Indian Women. *Demand for the special issue was so great that it was released as a book the following year by Sinister Wisdom Books (Montpelier, Vermont, 1984) and reissued in 1989 by Firebrand Books. Next it appeared in Brant's collection of short stories,* Mohawk Trail (Firebrand Books, Ithaca, New York, 1985). *Since then, it has been reprinted in many collections, including* Politics of the Heart: A Lesbian Parenting Anthology (Firebrand Books, 1987), The Adoption Reader: Birth Mothers, Adoptive Mothers, and

Adopted Daughters Tell Their Stories *edited by Susan Wadia-Ells* (Seal Press, 1995), An Anthology of Canadian Native Literature in English, Second Edition *edited by Daniel David Moses and Terry Goldie* (York University, 1997), Oxford Book of Stories by Canadian Women in English *edited by Rosemary Sullivan* (Oxford University Press 1999), Longman Anthology of Women's Literature *edited by Mary K. DeShazer* (Longman, 2000), *and in* Women: Images and Reality, A Multicultural Anthology *edited by Amy Kesselman, Lily D. McNair, and Nancy Schniedewind* (McGraw-Hill, 2003). *Its inclusion in this 2004 expanded edition of* Between Mothers and Daughters: Stories Across a Generation *means that this story has been in print nonstop for twenty-two years.*

In addition to the book quoted at the top of this headnote and the two other books mentioned above, one edited and one written by Brant, she published a second collection of her short stories with Firebrand in 1991, Food and Spirits, *which was reprinted in 1997 by Press Gang Publishers. In 1996, McGilligan Books published her* I'll Sing 'Til the Day I Die: Conversations With Tyendinaga Elders.

> " . . . a heart-stopping, lawful terror makes a common wound of all wounds. . ."
> > *"Not Comedy, Not Farce" from Eva-Mary by Linda McCarriston,*
> > *A TriQuarterly Book/Northwestern University published by Another*
> > *Chicago Press, 1991, p. 32.*

Dedicated to my Great-Grandmothers Eliza Powless and Catherine Brant

> "About 40 Indian children took the train at this depot for the Philadelphia Indian School last Friday. They were accompanied by the government agent, and seemed a bright looking lot."
> > *The Northern Observer*
> > (Massena, New York, July 20, 1892)

> "I am only beginning to understand what it means for a mother to lose a child."
> > Anna Demeter, *Legal Kidnapping*
> > (Beacon Press, Boston, 1977)

1890

It has been two days since they came and took the children away. My body is greatly chilled. All our blankets have been used to bring me warmth. The women keep the fire blazing. The men sit. They talk among themselves. We are frightened by this sudden child-stealing. We signed papers, the agent said. This gave them rights to take our babies. It is good for them, the agent said. I do not know *civilized*.

I hold myself tight in fear of flying apart in the air. The others try to feed me. Can they feed a dead woman? I have stopped talking. When my mouth opens, only air escapes. I have used up my sound screaming their names—She Sees Deer! He Catches The Leaves! My eyes stare at the room, the walls of scrubbed wood, the floor of dirt. I know there are people here, but I cannot see them. I see a darkness, like the lake at New Moon. Black, unmoving. In the center, a picture of my son and daughter being lifted onto the train. My daughter wearing the dark blue, heavy dress. All of the girls dressed alike. Never have I seen such eyes! They burn into my head even now. My son. His hair cut. Dressed as the white men, his arms and legs covered by cloth that made him sweat. His face, streaked with tears. So many children crying, screaming. The sun on our bodies, our heads. The train screeching like a crow, sounding like laughter. Smoke and dirt pumping out the insides of the train. So many people. So many children. The women, standing as if in prayer, our hands lifted, reaching. The dust sifting down on our palms. Our palms making motions at the sky. Our fingers closing like the claws of the bear.

I see this now. The hair of my son held in my hands. I rub the strands, the heavy braids coming alive as the fire flares and casts a bright light on the black hair. They slip from my fingers and lie coiled on the ground. I see this. My husband picks up the braids, wraps them in cloth; he takes the pieces of our son away. He walks outside, the eyes of the people on him. I see this. He will find a bottle and drink with the men. Some of the women will join him. They will end the night by singing or crying. It is all the same. I see this. No sounds of children playing games and laughing. Even the dogs have ceased their noise. They lay outside each doorway, waiting. I hear this. The voices of the children. They cry. They pray. They call me. *Nisten ha.* I hear this. *Nisten ha.* [1]

1978

I am awakened by the dream. In the dream my daughter is dead. Her father is returning her body to me in pieces. He keeps her heart. I thought I screamed . . . *Patricia!* I sit up in bed, swallowing air as if for nourishment. The dream remains in the air. I rise to go to her room. Ellen tries to lead me back to bed, but I have to see once again. I open her door. She is gone. The room is empty, lonely. They said it was in her best interests. How can that be? She is only six, a baby who needs her mothers. She loves us. This has not happened. I will not believe this. Oh god, I think I have died.

Night after night, Ellen holds me as I shake. Our sobs stifling the air in our room. We lie in our bed and try to give comfort. My mind can't think beyond last week when she left. I would have killed him if I'd had the chance! He took her hand and pulled her to the car. The look in his eyes of triumph. It was a contest to him, Patricia the prize. He will teach her to hate us. He will! I see her dear face. That face looking out the back window of his car. Her mouth forming the words *Mommy, Mama*. Her dark braids tied with red yarn. Her front teeth missing. Her overalls with the yellow flower on the pocket, embroidered by Ellen's hands. So lovingly she sewed the yellow wool. Patricia waiting quietly until she was finished. Ellen promising to teach her designs—chain stitch, french knot, split stitch. How Patricia told everyone that Ellen made the flower just for her. So proud of her overalls.

I open the closet door. Almost everything is gone. A few things hang there limp, abandoned. I pull a blue dress from the hanger and take it back to my room. Ellen tries to take it from me, but I hold on, the soft blue cotton smelling of my daughter. How is it possible to feel such pain and live? "Ellen?!" She croons my name. "Mary, Mary, I love you." She sings me to sleep.

1890

The agent was here to deliver a letter. I screamed at him and sent curses his way. I threw dirt in his face as he mounted his horse. He thinks I'm a crazy woman and warns me, "You better settle down Annie." What can they do to me? I am a crazy woman. This letter hurts my hand. It is written in their hateful language. It is evil, but there is a message for me.

I start the walk up the road to my other brother. He works for the whites and understands their meanings. I think about my brother as I pull the shawl closer to my body. It is cold now. Soon there will be snow. The corn has been dried and hangs from our cabin, waiting to be used. The corn never changes. My brother is changed. He says that *I* have changed and bring shame to our clan. He says I should accept the fate. But I do not believe in the fate of child-stealing. There is evil here. There is much wrong in our village. My brother says I am a crazy woman because I howl at the sky every evening. He is a fool. I am calling the children. He says the people are becoming afraid of me because I talk to the air and laugh like the raven overhead. But I am talking to the children. They need to hear the sound of me. I laugh to cheer them. They cry for us.

This letter burns my hands. I hurry to my brother. He has taken the sign of the wolf from over the doorway. He pretends to be like those who hate us. He gets more and more like the child-stealers. His eyes move away from mine. He takes the letter from me and begins the reading of it. I am confused. This letter is from two strangers with the names Martha and Daniel. They say they are learning civilized ways. Daniel works in the fields, growing food for the school. Martha cooks and is being taught to sew aprons. She will be going to live with the schoolmaster's wife. She will be a live-in girl. What is a *live-in girl?* I shake my head. The words sound the same to me. I am afraid of Martha and Daniel, these strangers who know my name. My hands and arms are becoming numb.

I tear the letter from my brother's fingers. He stares at me, his eyes traitors in his face. He calls after me, "Annie! Annie!" That is not my name! I run to the road. That is not my name! There is no Martha! There is no Daniel! This is witch work. The paper burns and burns. At my cabin, I quickly dig a hole in the field. The earth is hard and cold, but I dig with my nails. I dig, my hands feeling weaker. I tear the paper and bury the scraps. As the earth drifts and settles, the names Martha and Daniel are covered. I look to the sky and find nothing but endless blue. My eyes are blinded by the color. I begin the howling.

1978

When I get home from work, there is a letter from Patricia. I make coffee and wait for Ellen, pacing the rooms of our apartment. My back is sore from the line, bending over and down, screwing the handles on the doors of the flashy cars moving by. My work protects me from questions, the guys making jokes at my expense. But some of them touch my shoulder lightly and briefly as a sign of understanding. The few women, eyes averted or smiling in sympathy. No one talks. There is no time to talk. No room to talk, the noise taking up all space and breath.

I carry the letter with me as I move from room to room. Finally I sit at the kitchen table, turning the paper around in my hands. Patricia's printing is large and uneven. The stamp has been glued on halfheartedly and is coming loose. Each time a letter arrives, I dread it, even as I long to hear from my child. I hear Ellen's key in the door. She walks into the kitchen, bringing the smell of the hospital with her. She comes toward me, her face set in new lines, her uniform crumpled and stained, her brown hair pulled back in an imitation of a french twist. She knows there is a letter. I kiss her and bring mugs of coffee to the table. We look at each other. She reaches for my hand, bringing it to her lips. Her hazel eyes are steady in her round face.

I open the letter. *Dear Mommy, I am fine. Daddy got me a new bike. My big teeth are coming in. We are going to see Grandma for my birthday. Daddy got me new shoes. Love, Patricia.* She doesn't ask about Ellen. I imagine her father standing over her, coaxing her, coaching her. The letter becomes ugly. I tear it in bits and scatter them out the window. The wind scoops the pieces into a tight fist before strewing them into the street. A car drives over the paper, shredding it to garbage and mud.

Ellen makes a garbled sound. "I'll leave. If it will make it better, I'll leave." I quickly hold her as the dusk moves into the room and covers us. "Don't leave. Don't leave." I feel her sturdy back shiver against my hands. She kisses my throat, and her arms tighten as we move closer. "Ah Mary, I love you so much." As the tears threaten our eyes, the taste of salt is on our lips and tongues. We stare into ourselves, touching the place of pain, reaching past the fear, the guilt, the anger, the loneliness.

We go to our room. It is beautiful again. I am seeing it anew. The sun is barely there. The colors of cream, brown, green mixing with the wood floor. The rug with its design of wild birds. The black ash basket glowing on the dresser, holding a bouquet of dried flowers bought at a vendor's stand. I remember the old woman, laughing and speaking rapidly in Polish as she wrapped the blossoms in newspaper. Ellen undresses me as I cry. My desire for her breaking through the heartbreak as we share. She pulls the covers back, smoothing the white sheets, her hands repeating the gestures done at work. She guides me onto the cool material. I watch her remove the uniform of work. An aide to nurses. A healer of spirit.

She comes to me full in flesh. My hands are taken with the curves and soft roundness of her. She covers me with the beating of her heart. The rhythm steadies me. Her heat is centering me. I am grounded by the peace between us. I smile at her face above me, round like a moon, her long hair loose and touching my breasts. I take her breast in my hand, bring it to my mouth, suck her as a woman—in desire, in faith. Our bodies join. Our hair braids together on the pillow. Brown, black, silver, catching the last light of the sun. We kiss, touch, move to our place of power. Her mouth, moving over my body, stopping at curves and swells of skin, kissing, removing pain. Closer, close, together, woven, my legs are heat, the center of my soul is speaking to her, I am sliding into her, her mouth is medicine, her heart is the earth, we are dancing with flying arms, I shout, I sing, I weep salty liquid, sweet and warm it coats her throat. This is my life. I love you Ellen, I love you Mary, I love, we love.

1891

The moon is full. The air is cold. This cold strikes at my flesh as I remove my clothes and set them on fire in the withered cornfield. I cut my hair, the knife sawing through the heavy mass. I bring the sharp blade to my arms, legs and breasts. The blood trickles like small red rivers down my body. I feel nothing. I throw the tangled webs of my hair into the flames. The smell, like a burning animal, fills my nostrils. As the fire stretches to touch the stars, the people come out to watch me—the crazy woman. The ice in the air touches me.

They caught me as I tried to board the train and search for my babies. The white men tell my husband to watch me. I am dangerous. I laugh and laugh. My husband is good only for tipping bottles and swallowing anger. He wanders from the cabin and looks out on the corn. He whispers our names. He calls after the children. He is a dead man.

Where have they taken the children? I ask the question of each one who travels the road past our door. The women come and we talk. We ask and ask. They say there is nothing we can do. The white man is like a ghost. He slips in and out where we cannot see. Even in our dreams he comes to take away our questions. He works magic that resists our medicine. This magic has made us weak. What is the secret about them? Why do they want our children? They sent the Blackrobes many years ago to teach us new magic. It was evil! They lied and tricked us. They spoke of gods who would forgive us if we believed as they do. They brought the rum with the cross. This god is ugly! He killed our masks. He killed our men. He sends the women screaming at the moon in terror. They want our power. They take our children to remove the inside of them. Our power. They steal our food, our sacred rattle, the stories, our names. What is left?

I am a crazy woman. I look to the fire that consumes my hair and see their faces. My daughter. My son. They still cry for me, though the sound grows fainter. The wind picks up their keening and brings it to me. The sound has bored into my brain. I begin howling. At night I dare not sleep. I fear the dreams. It is too terrible, the things that happen there. In my dream there is wind and blood moving as a stream. Red, dark blood in my dream. Rushing for our village. The blood moves faster. There are screams of wounded people. Animals are dead, thrown in the blood stream. There is nothing left. Only the air echoing nothing. Only the earth soaking up blood, spreading it in the four directions, becoming a thing there is no name for. I stand in the field watching the fire, The People watching me. We are waiting, but the answer is not clear yet. A crazy woman. That is what they call me.

1979

After taking a morning off work to see my lawyer, I come home, not caring if I call in. Not caring, for once, at the loss in pay. Not caring. My lawyer says there is nothing more we can do. I must wait. As if there has been something other than waiting. He has custody and calls the shots. We must wait and see how long it takes for him to get tired of being a mommy and a daddy. So, I wait.

I open the door to Patricia's room. Ellen and I keep it dusted and cleaned in case my baby will be allowed to visit us. The yellow and blue walls feel like a mockery. I walk to the windows, begin to systematically tear down the curtains. I slowly start to rip the cloth apart. I enjoy hearing the sounds of destruction. Faster, I tear the material into strips. What won't come apart with my hands, I pull at with my teeth. Looking for more to destroy, I gather the sheets and bedspread in my arms and wildly shred them to pieces. Grunting and sweating, I am pushed by rage and the searing wound in my soul. Like a wolf, caught in a trap, gnawing at her own leg to set herself free, I begin to beat my breasts to deaden the pain inside. A noise gathers in my throat and finds the way out. I begin a scream that turns to howling, then becomes hoarse choking. I want to take my fists, my strong fists, my brown fists, and smash the world until it bleeds. Bleeds! And all the judges in their flapping robes, and the fathers who look for revenge, are ground, ground into dust and disappear with the wind.

The word *lesbian*. Lesbian. The word that makes them panic, makes them afraid, makes them destroy children. The word that dares them. Lesbian. I am one. Even for Patricia, even for her, *I will not cease to be!* As I kneel amidst the colorful scraps, Raggedy Anns smiling up at me, my chest gives a sigh. My heart slows to its normal speech. I feel the blood pumping outward to my veins, carrying nourishment and life. I strip the room naked. I close the door.

---

[1] mother

Jane Bradley

Noises
1985

"Young women who see their mother abused are far more likely to be abused as adults: As many as 80 percent of battered women who have fled to shelters remember seeing their own mother being assaulted by their father when they were growing up."

–KidsGrowth.com. KidsGrowth.com is a unique Web site that was developed and created by well-respected medical leaders in the field of pediatrics and adolescent medicine. Members of the Medical Advisory Board oversee all KidsGrowth content, thereby guaranteeing its medical accuracy.
http://www.kidsgrowth.com/resources/articledetail.cfm?id=120

"'Noises' isn't autobiographical precisely. It was inspired as I half-slept through the night, always attending to the slightest cough, stir, cry from my own infant daughter. Knowing that for the rest of my life I would be in love with this fine and wondrous creature and would be desperately worried about her well-being always, I then wondered how things might have been for my mother who watched her own beloved eldest daughter grow up to be a woman who drank hard and loved harder the men who routinely beat her. The story is my imagining of the sorrow it must be to watch a child grow to hate her own life and the struggle it must be sometimes to save a child from self-destruction. To this day my sister is still on that dark and dangerous path, and my daughter happily thrives."

—Email communication to editor from Jane Bradley, May 21, 2004.

Associate Professor of English at the University of Toledo, Jane Bradley (b. August 8, 1955) was born and reared in Chattanooga, Tennessee. She teaches creative writing, fiction workshops and screenwriting. She received her B.A. from UT-Chattanooga with highest honors, her M.A. from Syracuse University, and her M.F.A from Vermont College. Her 1989 short story collection, Power Lines, *from which "Noises" is taken, was listed as an editor's choice for a Notable Book in The New York Times Book Review. The collection was widely and well reviewed.*

Her 1995 novel Living Doll *is used in many graduate education and psychiatric intern programs at mental hospitals as a text on psychological fragmentation and reintegration. It was made available as an e-book in 2001 by Fictionwise and an excerpt can be accessed at http://www.fictionwise.com/ebooks/eBook670.htm, where the book is described as follows: "Little Shirley lives in a bewildering home inhabited by her mother, her sister, a younger brother, relatives, a number of "Daddies" and an assortment of people who pass through her house. Retreating from this world of exploitation and pain, she pretends that she is a living doll, a perfect Shirley Temple. She carefully constructs an inner life of Barbie dolls, pet cemeteries, and a constant winning smile. But as the years progress, Shirley yearns for a better and different world, and with courage and determination begins to take the first unsettling and painful steps that lead to a re-invention of herself."*

Bradley, also an award-winning playwright, is working on various writing projects. She travels whenever she has the chance. Originally from the hills of Tennessee, Jane Bradley is still working to adapt to those funny Ohio accents and trying to make sense of all the pavement and parking lots around her.

"Noises" was first published in Sou'wester, *13: 58-66, in Spring, 1985. An exigent story, it will be a painful encounter for many readers of this collection of mother/daughter stories. But its theme must not be ignored, as it is one of the major thematic sub-genres of mother/daughter stories by U.S. women writers. Stories of domestic violence belong among the sacred stories of women. This intricate and evocative story contains multiple overlapping triangular relationships—the mother, her husband, their daughter; the daughter, her husband, the mother; the mother, her husband, her son-in-law—but the central relationship is a dyad, a pair: a battered woman and her adult daughter who has grown up to be a battered woman herself after having witnessed the abuse of her mother during her girlhood. Structurally, the story resembles a Double Wedding Ring pieced quilt—a type of quilt pattern with overlapping rings creating a composite knot at the points of overlap.*

The mother's complex emotional responses to her daughter's situation are powerfully and painfully portrayed in "Noises." With its theme of domestic violence, and its complex intergenerational dynamics, this story represents a large category of mother/daughter stories. Six of the thirty stories in Women in the Trees: U.S. Women's Short Stories about Battering and Resistance, 1839-1994, *my collection of stories about domestic violence, are mother/daughter (or surrogate daughter) stories. I include this story from that book here to encourage readers to consider it in both contexts, and to lead readers from one book to the other in order to explore the interlocking dynamics of the themes. It is common for the first episode of domestic violence in a marriage to occur during the wife's first pregnancy or shortly after the birth of the first child. Once begun, it rarely stops; the pattern of abuse is predictable and the incidence of abuse predictably escalates. The impulse of the child of an abused mother to protect her, to intervene to stop the abuse, is strong, and, often, as it does in "Noises," leads to the child her (or him) self being abused. The sight of her child being abused, as she has been abused, is frequently the trigger, as it was for Connie, the mother in "Noises," to leave the abusive husband/father. But separation from an abuser is incredibly difficult, as Bradley makes clear in her portrayal of Trisha. Additionally, "domestic violence is the primary cause of alcoholism in women, accounting for more than half of all women alcoholics." (Peterson, J. (1999). Literature review. Dept. of Human and Community Development, University of Illinois at Urbana-Champaign.)*

In this story of a mother and her daughter "up against the patriarchy" we see the competing attractions and repulsions inherent in the cycle of violence, a pattern named and first described by Dr. Lenore Walker and now detailed in most educational materials about family violence, but never so well illustrated as it is in this story. We see the three stages: the honeymoon phase in which everything between the couple is idyllic, the building of tension, the explosion into violence, and the return to the honeymoon phase expedited by apologies, expressions of remorse, and contrition. Connie and Trisha both know that Jimbo will explode again. He doesn't deny it. But Connie has begun to fight fiercely for her daughter's salvation from the hell her marriage has become and her struggle to rescue her daughter from hell is a modern retelling of the myth of Demeter and Persephone. Bradley's story ends, but we can only speculate about the conclusion.

Connie remembered how for months after Trisha was born, she would wake in a panic suddenly in the night. She would swear she had heard something: a gasp, a cough, or even too much silence, but something screamed "Danger!" and Connie would bolt from her bed and run to her daughter's room. She would touch the baby's face, lift an arm, jostle a shoulder, do something that would make the baby stir and let her mother know that yes, of course, she was still alive and safe.

Looking at her grown daughter's face Connie remembered that old panic, but now there was a reason. At twenty-six, Trisha was filthy and so drunk that her words slurred and spit flew when she talked. Her bottom lip was cracked, caked with dried blood, and her eye was bruised, her cheek swollen, her nose smeared with blood and dirt. Connie reached for her.

"That's it!" Trisha said. "He's done it this time, by god." She leaned back on the couch and slowly exhaled smoke from her cigarette.

"I hope you mean it," Connie said, knowing the old line repeated, "I'm leaving," then the loneliness of leaving, the running back, the constant running back again.

"Of course I mean it," Trisha said. "I've had enough. I told him. I said,

'You hit me one more time, Jimbo Jones, and I'm leaving, I swear.' Then he hit me again! See?"

"I see it," Connie said. She reached for her daughter, pulled her close to her chest, smelled the oil in her hair, thought, "How did my little girl get so dirty?"

Trisha jerked away. "It hurts my neck when you do that." She started to cry. "I've been hurt enough already. Just leave me alone."

Connie sat back on the couch. "You don't have to live with him. You've got a home right here if you want."

Trisha shook her head. "Don't you have any cold beer or nothing?"

Connie got up and made Trisha a Coke. She wanted to kill this Jimbo Jones who used to love her daughter. He did love her until she got drunk, then he got drunk, and they started circling each other like two dogs finally released from their chains. Connie put the tall cool glass on the table in front of Trisha. "He'll kill you one day," she said.

Trisha stared at the floor, took a sharp breath. Connie watched her hand clench into a fist, saw the fist beat softly one, two, three into the cushion of the couch. "He won't kill me," she said. "He loves me. He's just crazy sometimes."

Connie went to the door to make sure it was locked. Nobody ever doubted that he loved Trisha. Anybody could see it in the way his face went soft and warm when he watched her do something as simple as scramble an egg. Connie remembered watching him watch Trisha make potato salad for the Fourth of July picnic. It was supposed to have been a good day, a day when they both promised not to drink, not to fight. They had promised. And it had started to be a good day, in Connie's kitchen with Connie frying chicken, Trisha making the salad, and Jimbo sitting at the table, drinking coffee, smiling, peaceful as a prince. "He's a prince," Trisha had said. "I finally got me a prince, Mom." And that day he did seem like a prince, so calm, so happy, so soft and warm when he watched Trisha move across the floor, looking so sweet Connie couldn't help saying, "You really love my girl, don't you, Jimbo?"

He nodded once and looked at his coffee. Connie said, "He couldn't live without me, Momma. He told me. Couldn't get up in the morning if he didn't have me."

"Shit," he said. But he was grinning, that strange grin, the way Larry used to grin when he looked at a poker hand, knew he was losing, knew he couldn't let that loser's hand show. But Trisha was peeling potatoes and didn't see it. So Trisha said, "It's true, Jimbo, you said it. You couldn't live without me."

"Like hell." He looked at Connie. "She's good in the mornings, but you get her out drinking and she's nothing but a goddamned whore."

Trisha had stared at the potatoes. She wouldn't cry, but Connie could see that she could break any second from the way she held her mouth set tight and closed, while her hands moved like there was nothing else in the whole world but peeling potatoes.

Connie knew that game. It was an old game that Trisha's Daddy had played. Connie had called it "the black turn game." She had seen it a hundred times before, and now she saw it in Jimbo: that soft look of a boy in love turn in a second to something mean. The man could be happy as a prince until you said the wrong word, made the wrong sound that could make a man in love swoop like a hawk ready to grab anything that dared to move across the ground.

Connie could hear the old words screaming, "You asked for it!" Larry had always said that just after the hit. Now Jimbo said the words. Now even Connie said the words when she was shaking Trisha by the shoulders, yelling, knowing that Jimbo wouldn't hit Trisha if she would just behave. "You asked for it!" Connie has said to her own daughter who stood there bleeding, saying, "Momma, he did it again."

Now she looked at Trisha, wondered, "Did anybody really ask for that?" She reached for her daughter's hand. "He's gonna come for you," Connie said. He would come crying and want to talk, make up, then he'd buy her flowers, a new sweater, buy something as a promise, the old promise: "If you be good, I'll be good," then they would start all over. That was the only promise. They would go round and around and around, mad dogs circling again.

Now Trisha was laughing, holding her hand to her mouth to sooth the torn lip. "Damn right he'll come for me," she said. "As soon as he finds I'm gone. He thinks I'm locked in the bathroom. Guess he forgot about windows." She smiled and tapped her head with her finger. "He might be good-looking, but he ain't too smart. I climbed out of that window like a ten-year-old boy. Good thing I'm tough. I'm too tough for him, right Momma?"

"Right," Connie said, thinking, "Wrong," feeling in her chest that old panic at the wrong sound in the night. Trisha would never say the right thing, and as long as Trisha said the wrong thing, took the wrong step, Larry would be there to swoop down and grab her and squeeze until she bled in his hands.

"Why don't you get some sleep," Connie said. "I got to clean the kitchen."

"I hurt too bad to sleep. Don't you have a cold beer?"

"No." Connie stood and turned off the lamp. Trisha sighed and lay down. From the door of the kitchen, Connie watched as Trisha groaned and shifted her body on the couch. "At least she's here," Connie thought. She stood and listened to Trisha's breath rise and fall. The living room was dark except for the new streetlight that shone through the curtains. All around the house stretched silence and darkness except for the one light that made Connie happy because it meant that the city was growing toward her house where there was nothing but woods, rabbits, birds, and a blacktop road that was hardly used.

From where Connie stood, Trisha looked like a child who had fallen asleep in front of the TV. There was her baby girl, the girl who once left wild flowers in a vase at the front door and a card to Connie signed "Love, Elvis." Trisha who was once always trying to find a way to get her Momma laughing. They both had loved Elvis, spent afternoons together in the front-porch swing, rocking, singing "Love Me Tender," the only song they both knew well enough to sing all the words. Connie took a blanket from the closet to cover Trisha, and as she leaned she smelled the stale cigarettes, sour whiskey, and a faint musky body odor that made her wonder when Trisha had last had a bath. Trisha snored softly, and Connie wanted to kill Jimbo Jones who once broke her daughter's nose.

She went to the kitchen, ran the water hot, and filled the sink to wash a few dishes. She thought she should mop the floor or clean the shelves. She wanted the smell of bleach, ammonia, lemon, pine. She wanted to be strong enough to throw Trisha in the shower and lock her in with the soap and steam until Trisha could stand straight, smell sweet, and smile.

Connie remembered how Trisha used to be so pretty with those brown eyes and dark skin like her Daddy, her Daddy's girl all right with those eyes flashing and the sad way of getting wild after just one beer, that one beer that could make most people happy, but made Trisha, like her Daddy, throw her head to the side a little and say something loud and mean.

Yes, Connie believed it when Jimbo said Trisha would start on other men when they were out drinking. Yes, Connie believed Trisha would grin at other men, say Jimbo didn't make enough money, Jimbo snored at night, say Jimbo couldn't get it up, say anything to let Jimbo know that he didn't own the words that could fly from her mouth. Sometimes even Connie thought Trisha deserved getting smacked. Who could blame him? But when she had seen Trisha's face, the lip torn, eye swelling, the purple, yellow welt spreading across her skin, she had thought, "Nobody asks for that."

Connie could hear the voice again, someone's voice, rushing, rumbling, cracking like a summer storm, "You asked for it!" Larry screaming, her own voice screaming, "Larry, please," then Trisha, crying "Please, Jimbo, stop hitting me." Connie heard it, the sad wailing scream, "Please."

"Jimbo could be polite. He's a prince," Trisha had said. And even Connie thought he might be that day she first met him in the hospital room. They had thought she was dying then, and everybody was polite when they thought you were dying. Jimbo was sweet as a puppy that day Trisha brought him to the hospital. "This is Jimbo, Momma," she had said. And he stood at the foot of the bed smiling, wrapped his long arms around her daughter, said, "Don't you worry, Mrs. Jenkins, I'll take care of your little girl."

And with the way he smiled back then, anybody would believe him. He took good care of them both for a while, sneaking fried catfish dinners and hot fudge sundaes up to the hospital room. Sometimes she thought she would have given up if it hadn't been for Jimbo. There he was smiling, saying he'd take care of her girl. And he had kept them laughing with his stories of how he could walk into Penney's and walk out carrying a television, a rug, a bicycle if he wanted, right under the cashier's nose. Connie couldn't help laughing, couldn't help sitting back in her bed, couldn't help asking, "How do you do it, Jimbo?"

And he grinned, said, "You just have to look like you know what you're doing. You just look like that little color TV in your hand belongs in your hand and you walk out that door, and that big-eyed little check-out girl just watches, while you say, 'Have a nice day ma'am.' And she says, 'Thank you.'" He had laughed, nudged Trisha's shoulder just a little too hard. Connie didn't like that laugh. He brought flowers and catfish and hot fudge sundaes, but she had heard that laugh before, knew the sound of danger, so she fought to keep on living to take care of her girl.

Connie finished the dishes and went back to the living room. Trisha lay flat on her back with the blanket pulled up and tangled around her neck. Connie carefully straightened the covers and pulled off Trisha's new shoes and took them to the closet so if Trisha wanted to leave, she would have to ask for her shoes. Connie picked up the leather jacket to hang, and thought of Trisha all dressed up the way Jimbo dressed her like something out of a magazine: silk shirts, good leather, wool sweaters, and designer jeans. Whenever Connie complained about Jimbo, Trisha always said, "But Momma, look at all my pretty things." Now she heard Trisha snore, then mumble the slurred tangled words of a little girl dreaming. "Just sleep,"

Connie thought. She had always loved her baby most when she was sleeping.

Connie unplugged the phone and went to the kitchen. She decided to clean out what she called the junk drawer. Everything in the house that had no place to go found its way there: coupons, pencils, nails, string. She emptied the drawer on the table and sat with a fresh cup of coffee.

She wondered how so many odd things could wind up in the drawer, as if they had sneaked in there of their own will: the imitation pearl earring she thought she had lost months ago, a piece of dried-up macaroni that must have slid off the counter, toothpicks, a perfume bottle, a hickory nut, the sample of fabric softener she got who knows when in the mail. She never remembered putting things in there, but somehow they piled up till one day she opened the drawer, looked in, thought, "How in the world have I been living around such a mess?"

She had always prided herself on keeping a good house. Even back when Larry kept her so scared she couldn't see straight, she had always found a way to keep the floor waxed and the windows clean. But a mess in a drawer always grew somehow, like a spider's web in a corner you couldn't reach. She leaned back from the table, closed her eyes, felt that old tangle of voices rise up in her head. She could hear him screaming, "Shut up, god damn you!" She could hear her own crying, "Stop, please, Larry!" She could see her little girl running in circles, shaking her hands like she was flinging something hot. She could hear that scream.

Connie sat up in the chair and tried to think of something else to clean. The house was still, quiet as a well, but all those voices kept screaming. She thought, "It's all right. It's all right. Your girl is sleeping, and the only real sound you hear is the refrigerator." She forced her mind to listen to that easy hum.

She heard Trisha moan. "Momma, Momma, I'm sick." Connie hurried to help Trisha to the bathroom. She sat by the toilet and soothed Trisha's head with a cold cloth while she vomited and cried.

Connie washed Trisha's face, helped her into a flannel nightgown, and led her back to the couch. "Water," Trisha said. Connie made a tall glass of ice water, placed it carefully between Trisha's hands, then sat in a chair and watched Trisha drink.

"You don't have to live like this," Connie said. She wanted to shake her, wanted to throw her against the wall and scream, "Why do you do this?"

"You think I'm happy?" Trisha said. "I know he'll do it again." She was crying. "He says he won't. He don't mean to hurt me, Momma. He loves me. He kisses me, Momma. When he kisses me sometimes, it's like sinking my mouth into a bowl of whipped cream." She covered her face with her hands. "You'll never know what I mean."

Connie reached for her, tried to rock her like a baby. Oh yes, she remembered those kisses before the black turn, kisses that spread across your mouth like cream. Connie gave her a tissue to wipe the lip that was bleeding again. "We aren't giving him another chance," she said. "You're leaving for good, this time. Remember?"

Trisha dabbed at her lip. "I guess I'll have to see him sometime." She looked at the floor. "He's got all my stuff. My clothes. My boots. My plants."

Connie stood to take the empty glass to the kitchen. "I'm coming with you this time," she said. "We'll walk in there together, get everything that's yours, right down to the knives and forks."

She held Trisha tightly, but Trisha shrugged her shoulders and pulled away. "He loves me, Momma. We have a real good time, sometimes. Like the other night he went out for pizza just because I was hungry. So we sat up in bed and ate pizza. See, Momma, he loves me." Trisha shook her head and stared at the floor. "He'd die for me, Momma. He said that once, he said, 'I'd die for you, girl. Would you die for me?' And he tickled me till I said yes. Oh Momma, you don't know how he can get me laughing. He tickled and tickled till I couldn't breathe, till I said, 'Yes, oh yes, Jimbo, I'd die for you.' And I would, Momma, 'cause I know he'd die for me."

"He's lying," Connie said.

Trisha sat back on the couch and pulled the blanket up around her. "It's your fault," she said. "If you weren't so sick, I wouldn't need Jimbo. I wouldn't need somebody to take care of me."

"I'm not sick!" Connie said.

"But you will be," Trisha said. "We all know it. You'll get sick again. And you'll die one day."

Connie reached for her, held her again, thinking she could hang on. She would hang on forever for Trisha. She owed her life to Trisha. It was Trisha who saved her that night when Larry had beaten her so badly she was passing out on the floor, and he started kicking, aiming for her head. Trisha had screamed and grabbed his leg, and he had tried to shake her off, but she held on until he grabbed her and threw her across the room.

That night Connie had taken Trisha and left, thinking, "You can hit me, Larry, but not my girl." She had hoped that by leaving the man she could leave it all like a bad dream, but he put his mark on Trisha. Trisha was still wearing the mark of a fist like a brand. A voice hissed in her head, "It's you, Larry. You're the reason my girl is sitting on my couch bleeding." Connie stroked Trisha's hair. "I did all I could," she thought. "It was him that did this. I just loved a man who could hurt me." She took Trisha's hand and pulled it as if they were walking and Connie could pull her to the right way. "Don't love anybody that can hurt you, honey," she said, thinking, "The only safe love is a mother love." But she wouldn't say that because she knew better. Any kind of love was a danger.

She looked up and saw a face peering in the window, and she pulled Trisha close. She heard a rustle outside, then a step on the front porch.

Trisha sat up. "It's Jimbo," she whispered.

"Hush!" Connie said. She covered Trisha's shoulders with the blanket, then left the room to get the .38 out of her top drawer. She was ready. She would not let him win now. She wasn't sick and wouldn't die for a long time.

"Trisha!" Jimbo said. "I didn't mean to hurt you so bad, honey."

Trisha ran to the door, leaned against it and yelled, "You get away from me!"

Connie pulled Trisha from the door and turned on the porch light. "Leave her alone, Jimbo."

"This ain't your business," he said.

"I got my .38 pointed at the door," she said. "I can use it."

"No!" Trisha screamed.

"Don't fight her, Trisha," Jimbo said. "The gun might go off. She won't shoot."

Connie took a breath and stared at the gun in her hand, suddenly wondering if she really held a weapon. She thought, "How can he talk like that, so easy, like she was saying, 'Don't bump her arm, she might spill her coffee.' Like being careful had nothing to do with staying alive." She yelled through the door. "You don't know me!" She waved her empty hand at Trisha, said, "Get over there and sit down."

"Now, Connie," Jimbo said. "You know I love Trisha. You know I don't want to hurt your girl."

She wouldn't listen to his words. She yelled, "Get away, Jimbo!" She thought, "Careful, don't let him get started on love." She forced her words over his deep, heavy voice. "Stay away from my girl!"

Trisha was pulling Connie's arm. "He just wants to talk." She leaned next to the window. "I'm listening, Jimbo. Just tell me you love me, Jimbo. Just say you love me, please."

Connie tried to pull Trisha's hand from the curtain, but Trisha wouldn't move. She and Jimbo stared at one another through the glass. Trisha's mouth was bleeding again, and Jimbo just stood there, his handsome face calm, his dark eyes just a little bit worried, just sad enough to make you think he was sorry, just gentle enough to make you think he was safe. He was too good-looking, Connie thought, to get so mean.

She saw blood smeared on his green shirt with the alligator stitched on the front. He always wore those shirts and designer jeans. He liked to brag about those shirts he stole. She looked at his face, thought he looked like a sad little boy trying to be brave, the back straight, standing tall, but the mouth tight, the eyes looking down at some scary thing just there in the air between them. She forced her eyes to look at the blood on his shirt, not at the face of a sad boy. She stared hard at the dark stain of Trisha's blood on his shirt.

Trisha cried, "Go on, Jimbo. Tomorrow I'll come back and we can talk."

"I want you now!" he yelled. "I drove all the way out here!" He slapped his hand against he window. "God damn it, Trisha you know I've been good to you."

Connie stepped back from the window, moved back toward the center of the living room to get away from the sight of that stain on his shirt, knowing if she looked long enough she would kill him. The gun was heavy in her hand, so heavy it pulled her arm, her shoulder, her whole body to a deep heavy place in the center of the room. Even if the house were burning down in that instant, she wouldn't be able to move. She saw Trisha reach, open the door, and heard the word "No!" jump from her mouth like a quick hard breath. The gun was so heavy. She tried to pull it up, hold it steady with both hands.

Jimbo stepped back from the open door. "Easy now, Connie. I'm not coming in." Trisha stood there holding the doorknob, half leaning out toward Jimbo, but holding back to be safe from where his hand could reach. "Look at my face, Jimbo. Look what you did to me."

"I know what I did," he said in the quiet voice Connie hated. It made her shiver to hear a man talk as if he had the power to do anything, as if he were something more than a man that walked the earth on two legs and lived and died like everything else. But he did have the power with that voice. She had heard it in Larry, that deep man's voice that could make you put down the telephone when you were calling for help, that voice that wrapped around you like a rope, pulled you down, yanked at your chest while your feet carried you across the floor. Connie looked at Trisha, saw the voice work as her baby girl leaned against the door and cried.

Connie grabbed her under both arms and pulled her to the center of the living room. She felt strong, stronger than his voice as she turned and looked Jimbo in the face and said, "You leave her alone. I swear I'll blow your head off and tell the cops I thought you were a thief."

He looked down, shook his head. "I don't have to come in," he said. "Ask Trisha." He looked straight at Connie. "Ask Trisha if she wants to go."

Trisha was crying, crawling across the floor, looking for her shoes. Connie put the gun down in the corner of the room and gripped Trisha's arm and sat down beside her on the floor. She held her swollen blotchy face that wasn't Trisha but some strange girl that stank with sweat and blood. "You don't have to go," Connie said. "In a few minutes he'll be gone, and I'll buy you all new stuff. I promise I'm gonna live a long time. I can do it, honey. I can live. Even the doctor said it's a matter of will."

Trisha shook her head and fought to get to the door. Connie looked up and saw Jimbo's face staring down at them. He looked peaceful. Even with the blood on his shirt, he looked happy as a man sitting on a bench and just watching the clouds change. He would wait all night if he had to because he knew he had the power. Connie cried, "Trisha, please!" She cringed at that old word, "Please," the sound that tore from her throat just before Larry had slammed her head against the wall. Trisha yanked her hands free, ran to the door and was gone.

Connie sat on the floor and stared at the open door. Trisha had run off barefoot, with her nightgown flapping around her jeans. Connie saw the gun lying in the corner where she had put it down, out of the way, where it would do no harm. She had never even pushed back the safety catch.

She looked up at the door thrown open wide to the dark night. The house was still now. She couldn't remember when her head had felt so empty of human sound, those talking voices tangled and rushing, the old constant noise. She was empty now. Still. She heard tires screech somewhere in the distance. She heard crickets chirping loud and strong, the sound mixing with the pulse beating in her head, and she wondered if they had been singing like that while she and Trisha were screaming and Jimbo was talking so easy and winning just as he knew he would. The sound of the crickets filled the air, the house, her head, growing stronger, then fading, then stronger again, and she wondered how long their song filled the night and how long would they sing. Connie strained to hear a human voice. Connie heard her heartbeat. She heard an owl scream in the trees.

Andrea Benton Rushing

Hair-Raising
1988

Born in Manhattan and the oldest of three children, Andrea Benton Rushing was reared in New York but spent summers with her maternal family in Jacksonville, Florida with side trips to rural Dothan, Alabama. Like Nicholasa Mohr's parents' participation in the Puerto Rican migration, Rushing's parents moved from the South to New York during the African-American Great Migration that began in earnest in 1913 when the cotton crops were devastated by boll weevils while simultaneously cotton prices crashed worldwide and picked up speed after the Mississippi Valley floods of 1915 wiped out the already impoverished sharecroppers and tenant farmers. "Epic in scale, monumental in its long-term social and cultural impact, the Great Migration stands as the largest internal movement of people in the history of the United States. Between the years 1900 and 1960, over 4,809,000 African-Americans fled the South's oppressive conditions." (http://northbysouth.kenyon.edu/) Jim Crow laws were increasingly oppressive and World War I brought the promise of employment in the urban industrial cities of the north. "By 1960, 40 percent of all blacks lived outside the South, while 75 percent of all blacks lived in cities. By transforming their rural southern backgrounds to fit their new urban homes, African-Americans created a new black culture." (http://www.factmonster.com/spot/bhmcities1.html) Andrea Benton Rushing has been both a participant in the creation of the new culture and a beneficiary of it.

She received her B.A. from Queens College, her M.A. from Simmons College and her Ph.D. in English from University of Massachusetts-Amherst. She has taught at Amherst College since 1975 where she is Professor of English and Black Studies and has also chaired the Black Studies Department. Sonia Sanchez preceded her as the first and she is the second woman hired to teach at Amherst. Rushing has "been teaching ever since I had younger siblings: Sunday School, Freedom Schools, Model Cities, Simmons College, University of Massachusetts in Boston, Colby College, and Harvard." She

worked for a living, in both the civil rights and the Black Power movements.
She first left the U.S. in 1969 for a honeymoon in Jamaica (her husband's mother
was Jamaican). That trip sparked her desire to travel to Africa, but it took her fourteen
more years to get there. In the meantime she went back to Jamaica and to the Bahamas,
Trinidad, Antigua, Guadeloupe, St. Croix, and Barbados. Recently she finally visited
Salvador da Bahia, inspired by Black Orpheus, *the first movie she, like many African-*
American intellectuals of her generation, had ever seen.

From 1983-84 Rushing went to southwestern Nigeria on a Fulbright lectureship
where she taught African literature. Research trips in 1986, 1987, and 1988 took her
back to Nigeria. She also went to Freetown, Sierra Leone to help establish a women's lit-
eracy program.

The daughter and niece of hairdressers, she is the mother of a daughter born in 1970
and the grandmother of a granddaughter born in April 2004. She learned storytelling
from family; in beauty parlors and barbershops; in the movement; and, of course, in the
Black Church—which she calls the most African of African-American institutions.

She started keeping a journal in 1970. Fragments from her journals were included
in her essay "On Becoming a Feminist: Learning from Africa, Part Two" included in
Go Girl: The Black Woman's Book of Travel & Adventure, *edited by Elaine Lee, the*
first travel book of autobiographical essays by women of African descent. (Portland,
Oregon: The Eighth Mountain Press, 1997). With Rosalyn Terborg-Penn she edited
Women in Africa and the African Diaspora: A Reader, second edition.
(Washington, DC: Howard University, 1996).

Andrea Benton Rushing participated in the creation of Black Women's Studies,
bonding with her peers in discovering their literary past and, through the strength of
those bonds, in creating a place for that past to become part of the mainstream. While
an instructor in the Afro-American Studies Department at Harvard, she remembers
reading Zora Neale Hurston's Their Eyes Were Watching God *in a women's study*
group with Nellie McKay, Barbara Smith, and Gail Pemberton. "Hair-Raising" grows
out of a conversation with a group of African-American women, including friend and
first reader Toni Cade Bambara, about a rite of passage: going from straightened to
unstraightened hair. "Such conversations are almost canonical among women of my
generation. They inevitably include memories of getting our hair done. Each story is
more hilarious than the next. I said something like 'You think you had problems! My
mother and two of her aunties were beauticians!!!'

'Then you write the story,' Toni said. And I did." (Email, May 24, 2004) (The cen-
trality of hair in African-American culture has since become the subject of academic dis-
course and there's an anthology entitled Hair Raising.*)*

Among those Americans who have (and know about and acknowledge) African
ancestry, there are at the very least dual and contradictory heritages and traditions to
negotiate and to select among. For an African American who can trace ancestry back to
multiple African nations/communities/tribes/ethnicities, the choices are compounded.
Which set of ancestral traditions and artifacts are to be honored by being incorporated

into one's everyday life? What ways of being a woman, of presenting her body to the world, does a mother pass on to her daughters? Andrea Benton Rushing deals with these issues in "Hair-Raising," her first published short story (first published in Feminist Studies, Vol.14, no. 2, Summer 1988) in a way that is memorable because the story is so suffused with love—for the daughters, for the mother's immediate forebears, for her political alliances, and for the new land she has come to, knowing it is the Old Country. There is no angst about "bad hair," no anger against the women who reared her, no desire for revenge in the form of rejection to ease or excuse whatever choices she makes; there is just love—which love shall she honor and pass on to her daughters? A story in which there is none of the traditional conflict defined in terms of the central character has proved so unusual that most readers believe this story to be an autobiographical memoir rather than fiction. But Rushing assures us that the story is fiction, triggered by that challenge from Bambara, her beloved friend.

Andrea Benton Rushing describes herself as a "liminal" person, a cultural translator. She is less interested in race than in culture. As a scholar and critic, Rushing's work has often focused on the role, the power, and the portrayals of mothers in African and African American culture. She became a Pan-Africanist during the Black Power movement and she looks at Black Studies through the lens of the Diaspora. "If you don't know anything about Africa, you believe Africans "lost" their culture during the Middle Passage and chattel slavery. Once you do, you see Africa everywhere. Everywhere!" (Andrea Benton Rushing, 2004)

Wherever my three daughters and I go—to the islands, Africa, down-South to Memphis and New Orleans to visit with Harold's people, or up-South to Chicago and Detroit—people stare at us. No matter what colors we have on, what jewelry we're wearing (usually silver, brass, and copper because my politics won't let me buy gold), or whether my makeup is on straight, women and men, elders and adolescents point at us. Sporting Jeri curls and relaxers, brothers and sisters ask if we have extensions braided in (we don't), admire the patterns our parts make, and study the thin neatness of each plait. Senegalese men are surprised that cornrows survived the middle passage. College-educated Liberian women marvel at our ability to sit still for hours to get our braids done and rush to say they've relaxed theirs (as though that takes less time) because it was so thick that they couldn't do anything with it. White people want to touch our braids, invoke Bo Derek's name, wonder (more often than you'd expect) if they can get their lank hair in styles like ours, and ask how much our do's cost. The attention used to be unnerving. Now that we're accustomed to it, we've worked out a routine. Because Amina inherited her father's perfect teeth, she smiles sweetly. Adeola and Adjoa answer the factual questions. I say, "The hard part is undoing it . . . I wish they'd invent a machine that would just whoosh the braids out" or "It's a wash-and-wear thing. I don't have to comb it every day, and I can swim, shower and get caught in the rain without worrying about it. Talk about liberation!"

Naïve New World Africans, we landed in Accra sporting J-5 Afros and entirely too tired to kiss the ground. Our halos of hair were, first of all, hot. (One-third of your body's heat escapes through the scalp's pores. While it struggles to fight its way through six inches of hair, you just plain suffer.) Then you notice that little girls have close-cropped hair, adolescents and adults who haven't succumbed to Western ways wear complicated braids, and married women sport the added status of gelées. While Harold settled into his engineering gig, I went looking for a braider.

My initiation was in a sort of salon where Mrs. Akwei did my cornrows while her purple-uniformed, barefoot apprentices whose chipped nail polish was at war with their careful black eyeliner sectioned my hair into its initial eight parts, adjusted the clattering table to fan to blow on my sticky face, and watched her fast fingers weave each three-part braid from its thick beginning at my scalp to its thin end. (Blunt-cut ends make the neat braids unravel quickly, so I regretted ever having had a beautifully contoured Afro.) I got charged by the braid and marveled at the three Ghanaians (two Akan-speaking government workers and one Ewe microbiologist) who were having their chemically-straightened hair washed, set, combed out, and sprayed into place. After years under an over-spreading bush, I looked kind of strange to myself with my hair close to my head and my scalp showing, but cornrows were cooler, and the few Ghanaians I knew complimented me.

I forget who told me it was cheaper to go down to the harbor where they did authentic traditional styles, maybe one of the clerks in Harold's office, where the slow ceiling fan took you back to a grade-B movie about Africa, or someone at the shiny U.S. embassy with its air-conditioning and Crane plumbing. Anyhow, when I had the girls' hair plaited, I took them under a baobab tree, spoke pidgin, used hand motions to describe what we wanted, and hoped Mama Kofi and Mama Kwaku understood me. They nodded and smiled, but they didn't. Not really. We were, with our reddish-brown skin and nose freckles, too different. One of Mama Kofi's senior daughters advised Adeola to eat less protein so she'd have less hair to trouble her. Amina walked away with a style that might have looked stunning on a thirty-year-old at a wedding, naming ceremony, or festival but was much too elaborate for a ten-year-old to sleep on. We learned fast. Harold photographed signboards with styles we liked, and we pulled them out of pockets and purses whenever we put ourselves under the experts' hands.

When Harold's orientation ended, we left Accra for Kumasi and became regulars at the harbor market. We'd arrive around 8 A.M. before the heat became an assailant. Small, dusty children in patched school uniforms gathered as soon as we sat down on empty beer crates. They offered to sell us lukewarm soft drinks, kelewele plantain chips, groundnuts, and the deep-fried black-eyed pea fritters they call akara. Smelling of sweat, talcum, and red palm oil, Mama Kwaku and Mama Kofi gossiped in Fanti. Every now and then they'd punctuate their seamless movements to stir the palava sauce or put their teak breasts in their silk-skinned children's crying mouths. Just about the time my neck began to ache from being bent forward so long, fishermen started calling their wares. Money belts under their faded wrappas, market women took their okra, yam, garden eggs, and peppers from the baskets on their heads and knelt to arrange their goods in irresistible pyramids. In husky morning voices they complained about supply, demand, government interference, and profit. By the time all four of us had our hair done, the market was a sun-stabbed hive. Our stomachs had forgotten the tea, toasted bread, and pawpaw we'd had for breakfast and were growling for jollof rice or foofoo and fish stew. And ripples of sweat were sliding along the paths in my hair into my blinking eyes.

In the States, Tiny comes to our apartment and usually does two heads in one night. Because she and I go way back before movement days and had our first children around the same time, our sessions are a little like parties. The wizened stereo plays Aretha or Otis, Koko Taylor or Bobby Blue Bland, Johnny Hartman or Sweet Honey in the Rock. Weather determines the menu. Summers we nibble peaches, bite honeydew melon off of toothpicks, and drink seltzer or Chablis. Winters it's oxtails, or kale and ham hocks, and we alternate between Earl Grey tea and hot rum punch. We talk trash and laugh at the punch lines of jokes that make my daughters groan. The folk who drop by thread in and out of our talk about what could possibly have made so-and-so decide to run for office *again*, who's running with (or from) whom, and what passes for U.S. foreign policy in Africa.

Until about six years ago the girls and I wore naturals. Back then we'd make a two-hour Subaru drive to the Apple to get our Afros shaped up and soak up our culture after three-week stints in the land of the blue eyes. At Talk of the Town, Khalid and his team of five supplied manicures, facials, shampoos, and dark hair for the disconsolately gray. They kept up a steady stream of rap about Harlem politics—pro-Percy, and anti-Koch; announced job openings, boat rides, marriages, and funerals—and let customers know when friends had been in looking for them. Mostly men in the shop, brothers between say, twenty-five and fifty. Big tippers came in on Saturday: professional athletes—local and visiting—strode in, sure of instant recognition. Brothers from the life started seeping in later in the day—flashing gold Rolexes, diamond pinky rings, and women who faithfully put quarters in the parking meters near their pimps' Jaguars. Customers (who didn't see how they acted up at home) talked about what wonderful old-fashioned manners my three A's had, how nicely they were growing, and how their looks combined Harold's this and my that.

Sitting there after my own graying hair had been shaped, I'd watch the girls getting their naturals trimmed and feel satisfied. Long before they were born, back in the glory days of black being beautiful, I'd vowed that no daughter of mine would have her hair straightened as long as she lived with me. Keeping that promise has been harder than I imagined. My caul didn't let me see that relaxing hair (*Who* invented that term? I mean what's tense hair?) would come back in style or that Classy Curl would be concocted. I didn't foresee all the places where I'd be the only sister in the room whose hair wasn't fried, dyed, and laid to the side or, as Adjoa puts it, flipped, dipped, and whipped. When gelées became as scarce as hen's teeth and movement friends told me that what mattered was in their heads, not how they wore their hair, I put my hands on my hips and cut my eyes. *Essence* hair-care talked the flexibility of straightened hairdos, and I sucked my teeth. But I had no comeback at all when sisters said their patent-leather coiffures were required on their dress-for-success jobs. On the home front, Amina, who stays on the verge of tears, was crying herself to sleep because "everyone in the world but us had straight hair." Adjoa convinced Harold's mother and my mother—two women who never agree about anything—to casually suggest putting just a little Vigorol or Lustrasilk in her hair to make it easier to comb, but I was as immovable as that tree planted by the water. I have kept faith with the nappy pride of black as beautiful. And yet, I've betrayed my heritage after all. I am, you see, a beautician's daughter.

Before *Vogue* ran its column on our tresses, before downtown New York City salons had Revlon's Realistic Conditioning Crème Relaxer on hand to help manage our waves and kinks, we had our mops washed and straightened every two weeks, by a sister with a beautician's license. Women on both sides of my family were in that guild, but I don't own

their tools and wouldn't know how to use them if I did. Along with the
separate but memory-melded flavors of neckbones, mustard greens, dusty
sewing rooms, and kerosene; the feel of textures of quilts, cornbread, okra,
and washboards; and the sounds of Louis Jordan, Ruth Brown, Roberta
Martin, and Brother Joe May, my stash of childhood memories includes
hours in womanhood institutes my own daughters don't know a thing
about. Busy being true to the African part of my ancestry, I've been false
to all this other. But it's not entirely my fault.

By the time she finally had me, Mama had had two or three miscar-
riages and given up hope, so although Daddy named me Thelma (for his
side of the family) Nadine (for Mama's), my whole family called me
Precious. And all my godparents called me Jewel. While my father sky-
capped at JFK, my mother did hair in her sister-in-law's second-story
Harlem shop and, later on, in the L-shaped kitchen of our Brooklyn
brownstone. They wanted the best for me, and, once our minister's wife
told them about me and music, I became their Phillipa Schuyler. Fingers
that spent hours on scales, chords, and arpeggios, learned to combine subway speed and the precision that gave each note its distinct sound, had no
business scratching up dandruff, applying hot olive oil treatments and
henna rinses, or tinting yellowing gray hair a purple toned silver. My God-
given gifts were double-mittened in winter. The hands that won a Henry
Street music scholarship at six and would take me through music and art
and Julliard couldn't give egg shampoos and vinegar rinses, use a broad-
tooth hard rubber black comb to get through damp knotted hair, section
it into twisted balls to air dry, or manipulate a metal comb heated on a gas
burner. They were too precious to use negotiating the difficult spots
around folded ears, going over the short hairs in the customer's "kitchen"
until her tight coils disappeared, replaced (until her hair got wet or the two
weeks were up) by the required, the absolutely mandated, straight hair.
Besides, going to music and theory lessons three times a week; practicing
four hours a day; memorizing Scarlatti, Chopin, and Ravel; playing for
Calvary's junior choir; and auditioning and performing didn't leave me
time to learn how to blow on the smoking curling iron until it had cooled
off just enough or how to click-clack through a tender-headed customer's
hair. I picked up just enough of the craft to be able to touch up my own
edges without leaving the comb's tooth marks on my neck and forehead,
but I never even began to understand how the women in my family made
those careful rows of Vienna sausage curls and, after they had cooled,
cajoled them into glossy wavy hair styles that New York women sported to

the Apollo and Small's Paradise on Saturday nights and Mt. Olivet, St. Phillips, or Church of the Master, on Sunday mornings.

The South Carolina relatives I spent summers with did hair in their kitchens like Mama or in shops that faced out into backyards full of children, bantam hens, and pecans. And, like my New York family, they combined lathering heads and tugging through snarls with listening to troubles and triumphs with men; revealing what Deacon So-and-So had really meant when he told Stewardess board #1 something that adults, seeing me around, either whispered into each other's ears or translated into Pig Latin; and sympathizing about illnesses and the strange ways of white folks. None of them would have done the fancy styles New York customers wanted because no self-respecting, church-going family woman in Edgewood would wear those bold styles. I can hear Big Mama sucking her teeth, shaking her head, and wondering what kind of person would want to get herself gussied up like the women in *Ebony* and *Jet*.

If one of her customers had Choctaw blood and bushy hair that came down to her shoulders (like the woman whose three skinny sons thought they were so cute), people said she had a pretty head of hair, and Sister would run the comb through it with the same blue Apex pressing oil my mother, aunts, and cousins used in New York. Then my grandmother or one of my scrawny, freckled Yeldell cousins would pull it back in a bun and pin it in place at the back of her neck or part it down the middle and have the plaits cross on the top of her head. If the woman was like the meriney Miss Madison, the seamstress with the bad feet who was expecting to marry Uncle Charles and had her feelings all hurt when he started running on the railroad and spending all his free time in Savannah, and had short hair that seemed thin enough to read sheet music through, Big Mama's baby sister would put loose curls in it and fluff it out carefully with the end of her rat-tailed comb while she cooed about how the rainwater, coconut oil shampoo, and iodine applied to Miss Madison's scalp were making her hair grow in all nice and full.

Adeola has discovered the reference section of the local library and worn me out about Yoruba culture because the name Harold and I picked out of the book turns out to be Yoruban. Now I know about the orisha Oshun, a deity whose praise names include "owner of the beaded comb." Deola can go on and on about what this Yoruban hairdo is called—'Sukutu,' Mama, Yoruba's a tonal language and you have to get the inflection right," and what that one commemorates, "No, that's Eko bridge, not Akula, not Eju." And I've heard her telling her web of friends about how neatly braided hairdos are one Yoruban way of reflecting order and balance in the cosmos. I've kept her from Jeri curls, blow dryers, and styling rods. I've also let her, and her sisters, grow up ignorant about Sulphur-8 Hair and Scalp Conditioner, Posner's Bergamont, and Lustrasilk. She knows about Oshun rituals but she would give me her *most* bored look if I claimed all those hairdressers in our family were priestesses who could conjure. She'd laugh if I said that the rooms with combs and brushes soaking in sudsy ammonia and three-quarter mirrors framed with little cards advertising beauty supply wholesales and chicken and rib takeout joints were temples full of the paraphernalia for biweekly transformation rituals, gear used by the initiates who knew that you only had the ends of your hair trimmed when the moon was full and that you burned all your leftover hair—or flushed it down the toilet. I don't think it takes anything away from the claims Deola makes for her newfound "ancestry" to say that, like the styles Yoruban women create and wear, the ones my family did spoke, too; though what they said was about transformation, not about cosmic order. Sometimes the transformation didn't work out right, didn't say what customers wanted to hear.

. . . One Saturday afternoon when my mother had just come to New York City from South Carolina, hadn't even met my father (a New Orleans Wilson), she worked on a nurse's aide who wanted Shirley Temple curls. To hear Mama tell it, the woman's crinkly hair was much too short for the style and she tried to suggest something that *would* work, but the woman fussed and insisted. Mama spent an extra long time massaging the hot olive oil into the woman's ginger-colored scalp and sudsed her hair with the most sweet-smelling shampoo in the shop. She paid careful attention to the woman's talk about her job and her so she could respond with more than "uh-huh," "don't I know it!" and other staples in the beautician's working vocabulary. And she hoped the rib sandwich and the icy Pepsi or the talk about which figure was leading in the numbers and what folk were wearing to the Business and Professional Women's Scholarship Dinner would distract the woman. Miss Raymond was content until she put her tortoise shell glasses back on and looked in the mirror. Then she cried long tears and moaned so loudly that even customers in the front of the shop, heads buried in *Harper's Bazaar*, could hear her. "I asked for Shirley Temple curls and you gave me Orphan Annie curls!" Miss Raymond went to the place across the street after that, but Aunt Eva wasn't as put out as Mama had expected, because Miss Raymond had always been a stingy tipper and last-minute about making appointments.

The Wilson, Warren, Price, and Yeldell women usually satisfied the domestics, diet aides, and postal workers who came to see them. People loved to praise the work my father's baby sister did. Not only did she have a growing hand, her specialty was getting dead women's hair to look natural enough to please the family when it viewed the body, at the undertaker's before public visiting hours began. Harold thinks doing dead people's hair is ghoulish. That's probably because he didn't know Aunt Babe. Her work made the whole family proud. And, though she did at least one dead woman's hair a week, she wasn't morbid at all. She was the auntie who drove fast red cars; caught mullet, butterfish, and porgies on her day off; and had big crab feasts, where her choir members and missionary guild played Pokeno all night long in her small pear-shaped backyard.

And there was this short, soft fat woman who loved the way my grandmother's mother-in-law did her hair. Long after my great-grandmother had retired, she still worked on Miss Evelyn. When you saw her strutting down the aisle of Mr. Calvary A.M.E. late, as usual, with her purse tucked under her arm and her *fine* legs showing between her sling-back sandals and the hem of her pleated, polka-dot dress, you wouldn't have the slightest idea that she was bald, not completely bald, but bald the way men get bald. She looked so good when she slid into her third row pew and started fanning herself because Great-grandmama Patterson had worked on her the day before, combing her waved back hair up and forward so it blended in with the store-bought hair Miss Evelyn held on her scalp with a tiny black elastic. Cousin Lillie held the hairpiece in place while Great-grandmommy arranged all the hair in a stylish upsweep. Miss Evelyn's dimples showed when she smiled at herself in the hand mirror.

Oh, another time the transformation got messed up was when Daddy tried to help Mama by washing my hair while she was doing hair with Aunt Eva. His hair had waves in it, so he didn't know the danger of letting mine dry uncombed. I couldn't go to Sunday school because Mama had to soak my hair before she could get a comb through it. Talk about being sick of my father! I don't know if he understood what she was talking about. I'm a witness, though, that he never touched my hair again in life. And then, all these hair memories are coming back to me, there was the time I let my bangs get snow-covered while I walked home from a piano lesson. Must have been daydreaming or something. Anyhow, Mama decided to make me more careful by letting me go around with kinky bangs until it was time for me to get my hair done again. Every white person in the fifth grade wanted to know what had happened to me. I couldn't tell them about getting my hair straightened, and I couldn't think of a convincing lie either. Waiting for Mama to relent, I thought she was the meanest person in the world and cried to go live with one of my Yeldell cousins so I could get my hair done whenever I wanted in whatever style I wanted. Now that I've got three daughters who get on my very last nerve by only half-listening to what I'm telling them, I wonder if I shamed Mama by the way I looked. After all, my ribboned plaits were her advertisement.

Short hair, long hair, good hair, bad hair. Hair going back when you jumped into a pool or danced under a red light in a sweaty brownstone basement. Hair falling out when lovers and husbands get laid off or left, sons got drafted or hooked on drugs, daughters dropped out of high school to watch soap operas all day. Hair pomaded to shine like white people's, decorated with combs and pastel plastic barrettes. "Men like women with long hair." "Thank God the baby doesn't have that picky nappy hair her mother's daddy has." Hair today. Hair tomorrow.

Still remember the first time I ever saw a kinky-haired woman out in public. Autumn. The early sixties. Helmeted in my chemically straightened hair because hot comb pressing was out of style, I saw Odetta at the Village Gate. Watching her mahogany fingers kindle the twelve-string guitar, hearing her deep throbbing voice caress "All the Pretty Little Horses," mock "I Don't Want No Bald Headed Woman," and thunder "Ain't No Grave Can Hold My Body Down," I was mesmerized by her stunning face framed in its short kinky halo. She had a regal poise and power that I had never seen in a "Negro" (as we called ourselves back then) woman before— no matter how naturally "good" or diligently straightened her hair was. "But she's a famous entertainer with slanting cheekbones, and I'm a square student encased in braces and eyeglasses."

Almost ten years before, I dared to "come out." While our husbands watched an NBA playoff game, Tiny shampooed my hair and used a black plastic pick to fluff it into shape. I felt so self-conscious the next day—but brothers I didn't even know encouraged my heart, "Looking good, sister," "Watch out, African queen!" All my Price, Wilson, Warren, and Yeldell relatives thought I'd lost my mind and, of course, my teachers at Julliard stole sideways looks at me and talked about the importance of appearance in auditions and concerts. I talked about how the personal is political and how kinky hair was beautiful enough to jump out in public without a straightened disguise. Like an evangelist, I tried to convert shocked kin, bored friends, and folk on picket lines with me to the wonders of our natural hair.

The day Grandmama Price shook her head and mourned what I'd done to "all that pretty hair" was the same day I made the pledge that has kept Deola, Adjoa, and Amina with "virgin hair," as one Liberian hairdresser called it, while their age-mates on both sides of the Atlantic plait artificial hair into their own, wield electric curling irons with poise, and spray glycerine activator into their Jeri curls.

I don't expect Harold to back me up in here. Can't expect a civil engineer to understand me on this issue no matter how he tries. He never spent a second under a hairdryer or had a hot comb near his scalp. That author was right. You do have to go there to know there. He'd listen politely and even tell the girls to cooperate with me, but I'd know by the way he played with his beard that he thought I was making a big something out of a little nothing. It would take years to convince him that we've left important stuff out of his precious daughters' upbringing after all the time we've spent training them in the way they should go so that when they are old they will not depart from it. (You haven't seen a man go crazy over girl children until you've seen the dazed glow of pride this one sports when he's out with his.) Too late to do much with Deola. She's already in college and counting the days until she can go to Nigeria and learn more about Yoruban culture. Besides she always was a hard-headed one. More hope with Amina and Adjoa. Maybe I can persuade one of them to do a school report on Rose Morgan or Madame C.J. Walker. (Has anything been written about them?) Or, since Amina loves to collect things and has run through tea sets, unicorns, and bumper stickers, I may be able to get her to rummage around for her relatives' tools. And if I can't get the girls interested any other way, I'll just have to spend less time at the piano and weave hair stories into the hours we spend getting our hair done.

Preety Kalra

Home
1993

The internalization of abuse has a great effect on those who witness it. Seeing someone you love being emotionally and physically abused can strip you of feelings of security and hope. Can children who witness abuse free themselves from the cycle of hopelessness?

I survived by keeping faith in thebelief that individuals can have hope. Making choices and having a sense of control are privileged notions but can be attained. As a child I felt there wasn't much I could do to protect my mother. Being the eldest of her three children I become her confidante and shouldered much of her pain and abuse.

I remember sitting with my mom in our garage on a rainy day. My brother, sister and I sat on the floor while my mom stared out the side door looking at the grey sky and watching the rain fall. She told us all to sit quietly and to listen to the raindrops as they fell. The sound of raindrops was soothing and rhythmic. I looked up and saw my mother smiling. She was happy. This is a memory that has stayed with me for years because it was a time where I witnessed peace and security.

Children from abused homes *can* hope for security, trust, and meaningful relationships. I now live with my husband and daughter in our home—an environment that is safe and where nurturing, caring, and individual growth are highly valued.

Preety Kalra, email to editor, August 4, 2004.
In May of 1991, a group of South Asian-American women came together to organize

an editorial collective whose purpose was to create the first anthology ever published in which the voices of women of the South Asian Diaspora would tell their stories in many genres. These determined women engaged in outreach, trying to locate and involve as many women representing as many South Asian nations as they could. In January of 1992, when the group became an editorial collective, Preety Kalra joined the project. She stayed with the collective until publication of the pioneering anthology Our Feet Walk the Sky: Women of the South Asian Diaspora, *published by Aunt Lute Books in 1993. The collective grew out of a class on the history of South Asians taught at the University of California at Berkeley by Jane Singh, an important chronicler of the Sikh Diaspora in California. The final version of their work includes one hundred works by first- and second-generation women from India, Pakistan, Sri Lanka, Bangladesh, Nepal, Burma, and Afghanistan representing the range of classes, religions, and sexualities of South Asian-American women. The book has become a standard text in courses on the South Asian Diaspora in Asian Studies programs and has also been incorporated into courses on multiculturalism, ethnic studies, and women's studies. I have written elsewhere that the anthology, with its chorus of voices much like a consciousness raising group, is the penultimate feminist genre. A collectively edited anthology is the ultimate genre. How and by whom a book is made says much about the politics and perspective of the book itself.*

Preety Kalra was born in New Delhi, India on December 19, 1972 and came to the United States with her family, including her younger brother and sister, when she was five years old. Her parents immigrated to this country without any formal graduate level education or job skills, settling in the Bay Area in Northern California in 1976. Throughout her life both parents worked two jobs each and made only minimum wage. They both worked very hard and yet still struggled in their day-to-day lives. They were never in a position to have any financial security or benefits. However, her mother firmly believed in the value of an education and encouraged all of her three children to pursue professional careers. Kalra writes that "Coming from a low-income background has made my experiences in higher education more challenging but has also given me a greater understanding of the constraints that exist for people from low-income groups."

Preety has two pieces included in Our Feet Walk the Sky. *At the time of the publication of these works, she was a junior majoring in ethnic studies at UC-Berkeley who had already committed herself to a career in health care working with immigrant women. She finished at Berkeley and continued at Stanford University for an M.S. in epidemiology. She was trained at the Berkeley Free Clinic as a medic to address the primary care health concerns of the uninsured and homeless people. As a practicing epidemiologist she has worked with a range of populations in addition to the two already mentioned: immigrant women, individuals on MediCal, individuals in HMOs, South Asian community, Vietnamese community, Filipino community, and veterans. The combination of her work as a scientist with diverse populations and her work with the literary community associated with the anthology makes her bi-cultural in the sense that C. P. Snow referred to in his famous 1959 lecture and essay called "The Two Cultures" in which he proposed that the breakdown in communications between those in the sciences and those in the humanities made it impossible to understand, let alone, solve the world's problems. Kalra is one of those precious individuals who functions in both cultures.*

We learn from the contributor note about her in Our Feet Walk the Sky *that "Her writing is based on her experiences within the working class of the South Asian community. However, she does not want to project that physical and psychological abuse occur only within a particular class. She knows that it transcends these boundaries and hopes that more South Asians are open to giving support and understanding to one another." (p. 370)*

Kalra's second contribution to the anthology is clearly a poem, but a genre for "Home" is much more difficult to assign. It is a short-short story? Flash fiction? A prose poem? Its generic indeterminacy is irrelevant to its power to move us. And whatever genre it might be assigned, it is a powerful Cri de Coeur, what the fourth edition of the American Heritage Dictionary *defines as "An impassioned outcry, as of entreaty or protest." Kalra cautions her readers not to assume that domestic violence is class-related; I add to that caution that domestic violence is not limited to any race, nationality, religious community, or sexuality. However, for members of minority, oppressed, disenfranchised, and various religious communities, the potential danger of repercussions to the community that might result from bringing such problems to the authorities make getting help for the abused even more unlikely than otherwise. All the more reason to celebrate this courageous work and to cherish this broken-hearted, frightened, loving daughter.*

In my 1996 anthology by Beacon Press, Women in the Trees: U.S. Women's Short Stories about Battering and Resistance, 1839–1994, *I included thirty stories chosen from among the several hundred on this painful subject that I had gathered in my research. This is the only story I have ever found written from the perspective of the daughter of the abused woman. There have been stories written about a daughter's response to her mother's abuse. "The Jewelry Collection of Marta la Güera" by Mary Helen Ponce is included in the expanded, reissued edition of* Women in the Trees, *but that story is told in retrospect by a companion of the daughter. Jane Bradley's story "Noises" in this volume limns by indirection the consequences to a daughter of witnessing, of growing up with a mother who has been abused. But "Home" is the only time we hear the child herself, in pain.*

I stand pounding at the door. Staring at the door. Will you come out? I hear the water running and picture your tears sliding down the drain. Each time you go into the bathroom I don't think you'll ever come out. I fear the water is taking you away, allowing you that chance to be free. I hear the water and think that is the only place left you can go. I picture your blood running with the water, moving slowly down the drain. People in despair never come out of the bathroom; they die in there. I don't think you will come out. I don't think you want to come out.

Mumi, hold me and tell me you are okay behind that closed door; that door that separates us.

The screams fill my ears. No silence, no peace. Glass breaks. You are the one he blames. He burns a twenty dollar bill because we do not have money to pay the bills. He is drunk. I think he will fall and the house will burn. We all could burn.

He is the man. We must all see his power. See that he can hurt us. See that he can kill us. He wants us to live in fear. He hits you and you fall on the ground. Those hands do not caress; they only strike. Blood stains the walls. What can I do? I want to hide the knives. There's a pair of scissors on the table.

He hears my screams. He works in a factory all day and cannot come into a house that is screaming. He hates my screams. They mean I love you. His eyes look at me in disgust. His smells suffocate me and I want to vomit. Get away from your mother. He curses at me in Hindi; he wants to kill me. He shoves me onto the floor. I lay there dissolving. I cannot leave you Mumi. I will not leave you.

I feel as though I am still in you. I am your pain, exist as your sorrows. What you do to yourself, you do to me. What he does to you, he does to me. Tied up, in-between. I'll save you Mumi. I'll save you.

Merrill Joan Gerber

Anna's Archive
2002

". . . a writer's autobiography occurs regularly in his (sic) fiction. The facts, as we remember them, are not always as they were, and in many cases after we shape them to our artistic ends, we lose the "truth" entirely. I think the advantage is that we may emerge with a greater truth. I have used my own "facts of life" in my work in many ways and I have told many stories in many voices. Which story is the true story? Which voice is the true voice? I don't think the writer could begin to tell you the answer." *From "An Unfinished Autobiography: A Few Words" by Merrill Joan Gerber*

". . . Anna is not my mother at all. She didn't have that irony, that speed of retort. She is a combination of what I knew about her life, what I imagined a certain voice in her head would sound like—which is a combination of me and her—and my invention." *(From "Crossing Over," an interview with Merrill Joan Gerber by Judy Bart Kancigor, Detroit Jewish News, August 23, 2002.)*

It is entirely appropriate that this volume should draw to a close with a story by prize-winning novelist and short story writer Merrill Joan Gerber. She has been the most prolific chronicler of the mother/daughter relationship in twentieth century U.S. literature, publishing upwards of fifty stories that explore this primal connection. At the same time that she has been faithful to this task, she has been remarkably versatile in achieving mastery of multiple genres. She has published seven adult novels, six volumes of short stories, three volumes of memoirs and personal essays, and nine young adult novels.

Merrill Joan Gerber was born on March 15, 1938, the elder of two daughters of a *woman who was the elder of two daughters. Her parents, she, and her sister shared a two-family house in Brooklyn with her mother's sister, a beautician who lived upstairs with their mother. At fifteen, Gerber met Joe Spiro and seven years later they married. They moved from the Florida of their undergraduate years to Boston for graduate school, and then to California when Merrill was granted a Stegner Fellowship at Stanford. They settled in California and reared their three daughters. Eventually, Gerber's parents and aunt followed them to California. (For complete bibliographical information and more biographical information about Gerber, visit her website: <http://www.its.cal tech.edu/~mjgerber/>)*

Gerber found her vein of truth early and has mined it steadily for almost forty years. She has chronicled the developmental stages of mother/daughter relationships from her first published story in Mademoiselle in 1963, "The Cost Depends on What You Reckon It In," about an adult daughter visiting her dying mother in a nursing home, to her next published story, "A Daughter of My Own," published in Redbook, about a young mother's thoughts, feelings, and experience after the birth of a first child, a first daughter, to her 2002 collection Anna in the Afterlife *from which "Anna's Archive" is taken.*

On one level, "Anna's Archive" is simply a story about the disposal of the remnants of the life of someone who has died and who can no longer express preferences or explain the personal history of what remains, nor can she help determine what among the piles of detritus has value. Such rituals of removal and retention occur at the end of every human life—for we are, as a species, accumulators, collectors, hoarders, material memoirists, and, when we die, we leave "stuff" behind. The sorting and dispersing of such leavings from the lives of the famous and accomplished among us becomes the business of librarians, curators, and estate managers. But whose business is it to deal with the material remnants of the lives of the unknown, of those known only to their families?

"Anna's Archive" is a detective story: by sorting through what Anna has left behind, can her daughters unravel the mystery of who their mother was? Her daughters reclaim the personhood of their mother, freeing her from the limitations of the mother role. In the sense that the story imagines the daughters engaging with the mother as a woman separate from her relationship to them, a woman in relationship to the world of her own time, her peers, and her passions, it is similar to Joanna Russ' "Autobiography of My Mother." And in the connecting with the dead mother's personal history as a way of enlarging their knowledge of who she was just as they have lost her, "Anna's Archive" recalls the first story in this book, Caroline Healey Dall's "Annie Gray: A Tale" in which the mother, knowing she is on her deathbed, says to her daughter:

"Matty," said the invalid, with a faltering voice, "I have always told you, that, at the last hour, you should know your mother's entire history. I have no longer the right to keep it back."

Gerber's story is also about the power of those who survive to shape the memory of those who have died by what possessions of the dead person they choose to cherish and preserve and what they choose to ignore and dispose of. In a sense, it is a story about the final triumph, the ultimate assertion of power, of the daughter(s) over the mother in the power of whose gaze they have spent their lives.

There are many such stories among women's stories of mothers and daughters. In a very different mood and time, Alice Brown's "The Way of Peace" is one of these. One frequently anthologized in the mid-twentieth century is "The Middle Drawer" by Hortense Calisher (The New Yorker, 1949). But one crucial and mundane detail makes Gerber's story unique among stories dealing with the process of sorting, discerning, remembering, and taking power over the memory of a recently dead mother: the garbage bags, the undisguised disclosure of what happens to what is discarded. The middle-of-the-night rescue from the garbage of what has been discarded is evidence of Gerber's "life's instinct, to preserve and witness the lives of those close to me, and of my own" (Email, February 14, 2004).

In the driveway of Carol's house, conveniently situated catty-corner from Janet's, Anna watched her daughters disposing ruthlessly of her precious papers. Sitting in plastic garden chairs, they examined then flung these scraps of paper and notebooks and folders and flyers, her carefully collected medical bills, her filled calendars, lists of all the drugs she had ever taken, notes from all her classes, records of every phone call to people who had cheated her, a card file of all her customers from the antique store, her jury duty summonses, these and other precious notations they dumped—without ceremony—into a huge green plastic garbage can.

She felt it was premature for them to be doing this when their mother was not yet even warm in her grave. (Warmer, at least, than her remains were now in the mortuary refrigerator.) Not that Anna expected her children to lug her material leavings with them for the rest of their lives, but this seemed a precipitous rush to get rid of her, bag and baggage. Yet she understood her delayed burial presented many difficult hours for them to get through and this activity might be—in their view—an appropriate act of remembrance and devotion.

"Hold on a minute, my God, what *is* this?" Carol exclaimed, pulling out of a carton the moldy remains of Anna's brown corduroy jacket. Black pellets fell from it onto the cement of the driveway. "Rat droppings! Yuch!" Carol jumped up and flung the jacket away from her. "Now we'll probably catch the hanta virus. It lives forever in rat droppings—then the droppings dry into a powder and you breathe it in and you die."

"So I guess then we won't be separated from Mom too long," Janet said. "We can just follow her lead and join her in the afterlife."

"I'm not in such a hurry," Carol said. "Are you? Wait here a minute and don't touch anything. I'll be right back." She went into the garage. Anna noticed a breeze blowing, warm for January. In fact, it was like a picnic out in the driveway— tree branches sighing, birds chirping, the sky bright and blue overhead. Nature was not actually so bad. Anna couldn't understand why she had shunned it all her ninety years—never bothered to admire a sunrise, a lowering sky, the buds of spring, the chirp of baby birds. Probably because such matters were mindless. Anna had no patience for lack of thought, for slowness (what was slower than the growing of a tree from some kind of nut?), for repetition without purpose. Whereas in Chopin, in Mozart, if a theme were repeated and moved steadily through a sonata in varying patterns, it was there to bring the listener's heart to life, to bring someone musical (like herself) to her knees with its beauty and design.

Now Carol came back looking like an alien from outer space. She had a painter's mask over her mouth and nose and huge yellow rubber gloves on her hands. She handed a duplicate set to Janet. "Put these on. We're not breathing in hanta virus if we can help it. If I died and my sons inherited this house, they'd sell it and blow it all in two months."

So Anna's daughters went back to work shuffling through the miniscule record of their mother's life—her written remains, mere scraps of paper, lined notebook pages with meaningless lists, business cards of others, IRS tax returns, cancelled checks. Where were her great creative works? Her opus? Her poetry, her musical compositions, her art? What petty remains were left of her were going into a cracked garbage can—and those sending them there were the only substantial creations of her life: her children.

Not enough, not enough, Anna concluded. Thirty or forty years hence her girls would be in the grave as well and where would Anna be found? In the shape of the thumb of one of her grandchildren? In their inherited bunions? Even her renditions of White Christmas on the piano, performances that Abram recorded on plastic records back in Brooklyn in the '40s, were long crumbled and devoured by time. Maybe a few of her pieces were on those cassette tapes that Janet's husband, Danny, liked to make at family events. But it was little enough to show for a lifetime. Anna recalled how—as a little girl—she used to play make-believe piano on the edge of the wooden kitchen table in her parents' apartment in the Lower East Side of New York till one day her father gave in and bought her an old upright piano. Where did her longing come from? Her father's love of Caruso? Some distant rabbinical scribe, some cantor in the old country? She had never wasted time on these sorts of questions and wasn't going to now.

Music was Anna's passion and she knew she'd had it in her to be a great musician.

"Remember how Mom used to carry her music to the eye doctor's office? The way she would say, 'My glaucoma is so bad! I can't read my Mozart! I can't read my Chopin!'" Carol was looking with disgust at the pile of Anna's music notebooks in her lap.

"Of course I remember," Janet said.

"Weren't you embarrassed to death, the way she made such a fuss? As if, since she played music, she was more entitled not to go blind than the other old ladies who only watched soap operas?"

"She always needed to prove she was special," Janet said.

"Because she *wasn't* special," Carol said. "Look at this!"

She was holding, Anna could see, the *Bulletin* from the Hollywood Senior Multipurpose Center.

"Volunteer of the Month: Anna Goldman" Carol read aloud. "Listen to this information she gave them: *Anna Goldman was born in New York and lived there until her family moved to Florida and later to California. She has two daughters of whom she is justly proud. The elder daughter is a writer and teacher of international fame, and the younger is talented and celebrated in art and sculpture. Both are married and have families.*

"Notice she doesn't say that one of her daughter's husbands was a wife-batterer, and killed himself. Notice how she inflates your 'international fame' and my 'art genius'. She always used to say, when the three of us were together: 'Here we are, the musician, the writer and the artist.' We were three invisible nobodies, Janet, that's what we were."

"If it made her feel worthwhile to brag about us, why should you have minded so much? We didn't turn out so bad."

"Well, if you think you're that special, you have the same problem Mom had. She had to be in the limelight. She had to puff us up because we were really never good enough for her. I always minded! I was always so ashamed of her."

Anna felt a pang in whatever portion of her being was still extant. She had always believed her children thought as much of her as she did of herself. Maybe more, since she had the added power of being their mother.

"Throw it all out," Carol said. "Don't even read that stuff in her folders, her notebooks. Our mother was a hollow lady, Janet. I don't even know if she loved us. Maybe she only loved herself."

A hollow lady! Sharper than a serpent's tooth! But could it be true she loved no one but herself? Maybe not even herself?

There, in the balmy air of the driveway, Carol and Janet were having a tug of war. Carol was trying to pull a bunch of notebooks out of Janet's lap and toss them in the trash. "One second, don't do that!" Janet was pleading. "These are Mom's notes from her music class. I just want to look at them."

"Don't waste your time. Mom was just a parrot. Listen to this..." she said, leaning over Janet's shoulder and reading: 'Baroque Period, 1600–1750, Bach died in 1750 and Handel stopped writing in 1750—hit by blindness. Handel lived in England. Bach lived in Germany.' Her notes are totally mechanical. She never had an original thought."

"Where is all this anger coming from so suddenly?" Janet asked her sister. "I think you're just tired and stressed out. We've been stretched pretty thin these last few days. Maybe we need to take a break. Have a cup of tea. I just can't imagine what Mom could have done to you to make you this angry."

"It's what she didn't do! She never knew what I needed! I wanted nice clothes, and she bought me junk on sale that I looked awful in. I wanted to wear my hair long, and she made me cut it short with little bangs. She never knew who I was! She never thought of me as a person with needs. She wasn't sensitive to anything I needed."

"And would you say we did better with our children?" Janet asked. "Were we so sensitive?"

"We did better than Mom did. At least I tried to hear what my kids were saying. Mom didn't listen to anyone. I don't even know if she had any sense of the kind of man Daddy was. I don't even know if she loved him."

Anna felt unduly stirred by these accusations, unfairly attacked since she no longer could defend herself. Her girls glared at one another. She knew, from her own troubles with high blood pressure, that their systolic readings had to be up in the danger range. She hoped one of them wouldn't have a stroke and then they'd have to cancel Anna's funeral.

Janet had wrested one of the notebooks from Carol and was reading something in it, a big blue faded loose-leaf. Carol turned away and continued dumping papers into the garbage can, mumbling under her breath. "Why did she save all this junk? All her complaint letters, this one to Campbell's soup, 'There aren't enough noodles in your chicken noodle soup!' To Van De Kamp's bakery, 'I found a bran muffin in your box of chocolate cupcakes.' To the police department. 'I had gone out to do my civic duty and vote, and what did I get, but a parking ticket!' All that energy wasted. All that misplaced indignation. And these nonsense jingles she wrote to every stranger she met, to kiss up and curry favor. Listen to this one:

To Evelyn and Joe, (whoever on earth they were . . .):
Here's a heartfelt double tribute
That I'd fondly like to state
One-half goes to Evelyn
The other to Joe, her mate.
They're a very special couple
Who aim to please us all
They sing, they dance, they have a talent
It's almost ten feet tall...
When the news is grim and papers shout
Of recession, uneasy peace and fright
These two just turn the tide and say
'Everything's all right...'
And since this is their birthday month
Evelyn's the twelfth and Joe September three
We wish them forever good health and cheer
From you and you and ME!"

Carol put her finger down her throat. "Shall I throw up here or in the bushes?"

"Have a heart. She just did it for fun. It was almost a reflex of hers, to put everything into rhyme. But here's something different," Janet said, in a different tone of voice, looking down at a sheet in her lap. "Come here and look, Carol. Here's something that isn't a complaint letter or a non-sense jingle."

Carol came and leaned over Janet's back to see what it was. She squinted in the sun, shading her eyes.

"Read it to me, I can't focus out here . . . it's too bright."

"She wrote this among her notes from the music class at UCLA. It's dated November 1, 1967. That was Daddy's birthday, two years after he died. This page has notations from a lecture on Debussy and Chopin. But listen to what Mom wrote on the edge of the page:

"The cool damp earth the cake,
Each candle a star
Peaceful birthday my darling
Wherever you are."

Carol and Janet looked at one another.

"Mom wrote a real poem," Janet said. "She wrote Daddy a love poem."

"So you believe she really loved Daddy after all?"

"I think it *proves* we're children of a love match," Janet smiled. "You and I, we're love children."

"Alright, so we'll keep this one piece of paper, even the whole notebook," Carol conceded. "Maybe we could even make copies of this poem for our children."

"If you don't mind, I'd like to put the original in a frame and hang it on the wall."

"Good, you keep it. And I'll come every day to your house to visit it," Carol said.

Late that night, Janet came outside to her front yard to call her cat. It seemed to Anna that a moonbeam was illuminating the row of trash cans at the curb, across the street at Carol's house. The cracked green garbage can, the can without a cover, was filled to overflowing with Anna's papers, the edges of envelopes and the tips of folders like so many glistening points of a crown glowing in the strange, hushed light of the moon. Anna watched her daughter pause and stare at the can, take a few steps toward her own front door and turn and look again. Anna could see what her daughter saw, how the moon was a spotlight on her earthly remnants, the darkness like a stage from which actors were calling out all her written words.

Janet went quickly back into her house, and came out immediately holding a large yellow plastic bag. She rushed across the street to where Anna's trash heap shone in the moonlight. Working fast, she grabbed handfuls of her mother's papers and transferred them to the bag, stuffing them down till they were compressed, then adding others. She was bent halfway into the garbage can when a police car cruised by and slowed to a stop. Janet straightened up and waved at the officers: they waved back, no questions asked. Anna—because she had helped her daughters with the down payments on their homes—was glad to be responsible for the fact that they lived in one of the safest towns in America. An owl hooted and the chilling cry of a coyote spun upward from the distant hills while Anna's daughter, intent on her mission, went on rescuing from the garbage the treasures of Anna's archive.

Anna felt revived by the night wind. She could still know relief and its attendant pleasures. Now all her words would be preserved, and a good thing it was—for her descendents, her heirs, and for the nourishment of posterity.

PERMISSIONS

UPDATES AND CORRECTIONS
TO THE FIRST EDITION

1. Fannie Hurst's birth date was 1885, not 1889. She maintained the fiction of the 1889 date all her life and there are no dates on her gravestone. The 1885 date was discovered independently by me and by Brooke Kroeger, her biographer.

2. Although Tillie Olsen's "I Stand Here Ironing" is unusual for having been written in the mother's voice, it was certainly not the first story written from the point of view of the mother of a daughter. Among earlier stories are "The Unnatural Mother" by Charlotte Perkins Gilman from *The Forerunner* Nov., 1916, pp.281-285, "The Way of Life" by Lucy Huffaker from *Atlantic Narratives: Modern Short Stories* edited with an Introduction by Charles Swain Thomas, Second Series, 1918 and) "The Hossie-Frossie" by Fannie Hurst (First in *Cosmopolitan*, September, 1928. Collected in *Procession*, Harper & Bros., 1929: "More than in any other human relationship, overwhelmingly more, motherhood means being instantly interruptable, responsive, responsible, Children need one *now* (and remember, in our society, the family must often try to be the center for love and health the outside world is not). The very fact that these are real needs, that one feels them as one's own (love, not duty); *that there is no one else responsible for these needs*, gives them primacy. It is distraction, not meditation, that becomes habitual; interruption, not continuity; spasmodic, not constant toil....Work interrupted, deferred, relinquished, makes blockage—at best, lesser accomplishment. Unused capacities atrophy, cease to be." (*Silences* 18-19) Yet Olsen insists that the demands of mothering four children did not fracture her selfhood. Being female and an artist are complementary, not contradictory, she believes. Certainly a woman's experience is not antithetical to art, despite the view expressed by Le Sueur's editor at Scribner's who rejected "Annunciation" for its "ersatz" subject matter, and Olsen's

texts provide ample evidence that parenting richly fed her writing. However, since writing requires time and solitude, the practical question arises: Why did Olsen have as many as four children when she had the ambition and talent "to be a great writer" (Rosenfelt interview)? The answer lies partly in Olsen's firm belief that motherhood is not only the "core of women's oppression" but an extraordinary source of "transport" for women as well (*Silences* 202). Children and art "are different aspects of your being," she told me. "There is . . . no separation." A life combining meaningful work and motherhood "could and should be" possible for women (interview).

3. Sherley Ann Williams died of cancer at the age of 54 on July 8,1999. Her 1986 novel *Dessa Rose*, the story of two women, one black, one white, set in the 1830s in North Carolina, has come to be considered a classic. *The New York Times* praised the novel as "artistically brilliant, emotionally affecting and totally unforgettable." At the time of her death, she was working on a sequel to *Dessa Rose*. Her 1992 children's book "Working Cotton" received the American Library Association Caldecott Award. She also wrote a one-woman drama called "Letters From a New England Negro" that was performed at the National Black Theater Festival in 1991 and at the Chicago International Theater Festival in 1992.

4. On May 19, 1987 James Tiptree, Jr., Alice Sheldon, 72, ill with incurable and untreatable heart disease, took the life of her invalid husband, then 84, blind and bedridden and afflicted with Alzheimer's disease, and then shot herself in the head. They were found dead, hand in hand in bed, in their McLean, Virginia home, fulfilling a wish made in a letter (to Robert Silverberg) of 1976, to "take myself off the scene gracefully. . . while I am still me." (Davis A14)

5. In February of 1991 at WisCon (the world's only feminist-oriented science fiction convention), award-winning SF author Pat Murphy and Karen Joy Fowler announced the creation of the James Tiptree, Jr. Award, an annual literary prize for science fiction or fantasy that expands or explores our understanding of gender.

The Feminist Press at the City University of New York is a nonprofit literary and educational institution dedicated to publishing work by and about women. Our existence is grounded in the knowledge that women's writing has often been absent or underrepresented on bookstore and library shelves and in educational curricula—and that such absences contribute, in turn, to the exclusion of women from the literary canon, from the historical record, and from the public discourse.

The Feminist Press was founded in 1970. In its early decades, the Feminist Press launched the contemporary rediscovery of "lost" American women writers, and went on to diversify its list by publishing significant works by American women writers of color. More recently, the Press's publishing program has focused on international women writers, who remain far less likely to be translated than male writers, and on nonfiction works that explore issues affecting the lives of women around the world.

Founded in an activist spirit, the Feminist Press is currently undertaking initiatives that will bring its books and educational resources to underserved populations, including community colleges, public high schools and middle schools, literacy and ESL programs, and prison education programs. As we move forward into the twenty-first century, we continue to expand our work to respond to women's silences wherever they are found.

Many of our readers support the Press with their memberships, which are tax-deductible. Members receive numerous benefits, including complimentary publications, discounts on all purchases from our catalog or web site, pre-publication notification of new books and notice of special sales, invitations to special events, and a subscription to our email newsletter, *Women's Words: News from the Feminist Press.* For more information about membership and events, and for a complete catalog of the Press's 250 books, please refer to our web site: www.feministpress.org.